Ana Huang is a *USA Today*, international, and No.1 Amazon bestselling author. Best known for her *Twisted* series, she writes New Adult and contemporary romance with deliciously alpha heroes, strong heroines, and plenty of steam, angst, and swoon sprinkled in.

Her books have been sold to over two dozen foreign publishers for translation and featured in outlets such as NPR, *Cosmopolitan*, *Financial Times*, and *Glamour UK*.

A self-professed travel enthusiast, she loves incorporating beautiful destinations into her stories and will never say no to a good chai latte.

When she's not reading or writing, Ana is busy daydreaming and scouring Yelp for her next favourite restaurant.

By Ana Huang

KINGS OF SIN
A series of interconnected standalones

King of Wrath
King of Pride
King of Greed

TWISTED SERIES
A series of interconnected standalones

Twisted Love
Twisted Games
Twisted Hate
Twisted Lies

IF LOVE SERIES

If We Ever Meet Again (Duet Book 1)
If the Sun Never Sets (Duet Book 2)
If Love Had a Price (Standalone)
If We Were Perfect (Standalone)

KING
OF
PRIDE

ANA HUANG

PIATKUS

PIATKUS

First published in 2023 by Ana Huang
Published in Great Britain in 2023 by Piatkus
This paperback edition published in 2023

1 3 5 7 9 10 8 6 4 2

Editor: Becca Hensley Mysoor at the Fairy Plotmother,
Amy Briggs at Briggs Consulting LLC
Proofreader: Britt Tayler
Cover Designer: Cat Imb, TRC Designs

A CIP catalogue record for this book
is available from the British Library.

ISBN 978-0-349-43634-0

Printed and bound in Great Britain by Clays Ltd, Elcograf S.p.A.

Papers used by Piatkus are from well-managed forests
and other responsible sources.

Piatkus
An imprint of
Little, Brown Book Group
Carmelite House
50 Victoria Embankment
London EC4Y 0DZ

An Hachette UK Company

www.hachette.co.uk
www.littlebrown.co.uk

For all the girls who think smart is sexy.
(And who know the quiet ones are the freakiest).

Playlist

◄   ▶   ►|

I Knew You Were Trouble (Taylor's Version)
Taylor Swift

You Put a Spell on Me
Austin Giorgio

Love You Like a Love Song
Selena Gomez

Body Electric
Lana Del Rey

Collide
Justin Skye

Middle of the Night
Elley Duhé

Shameless
Camila Cabello

You Say
Lauren Daigle

Bleeding Love
Leona Lewis

Be Without You
Mary J. Blige

Content Notes

This story contains explicit sexual content, profanity, and topics that may be sensitive to some readers.

For a detailed list, please visit *anahuang.com/content-warnings*

KING

OF

PRIDE

CHAPTER 1
Isabella

"So you *didn't* use the glow-in-the-dark condoms I gave you?"

"Nope. Sorry." Tessa returned my crestfallen stare with an amused one of her own. "It was our first date. Where did you get those condoms anyway?"

"At last month's neon skate party." I'd attended the party in hopes it would free me from my creeping life rut. It hadn't, but it *had* supplied me with a bag of delightfully lurid party favors that I'd doled out to friends. Since I was suffering from a self-imposed man ban, I had to live vicariously through them, which was hard when said friends didn't cooperate.

Tessa's brow wrinkled. "Why were they handing out condoms at a skate party?"

"Because those parties always turn into giant orgies," I explained. "I saw someone use one of those condoms right there in the middle of the ice rink."

"You're kidding."

"Nope." I restocked the garnishes, then turned to straighten the various glasses and tumblers. "Wild, right? It was fun, even if some of the things I witnessed traumatized me for a good week after..."

I rambled on, only half paying attention to my movements. After a year of bartending at the Valhalla Club, an exclusive members-only society for the world's rich and powerful, most of my work was muscle memory.

It was six on a Monday evening—prime happy hour in other establishments but a dead zone at Valhalla. Tessa and I always used this time to gossip and catch each other up on our weekends.

I was only here for the paycheck until I finished my book and became a published author, but it was nice to work with someone I actually liked. A majority of my previous coworkers had been creeps.

"Did I tell you about the naked flag dude?" I said. "He was one of the ones who *always* participated in the orgies."

"Uh, Isa." My name squeaked out in a decidedly un-Tessa-like manner, but I was on too much of a roll to stop.

"Honestly, I never thought I'd see a glowing dick in—"

A polite cough interrupted my spiel.

A polite, *masculine* cough that very much did not belong to my favorite coworker.

My movements ground to a screeching halt. Tessa let out another distressed squeak, which confirmed what my gut already suspected: the newcomer was a club member, not our laid-back manager or one of the security guards dropping by on their break.

And they'd just overheard me talking about glowing dicks.

Fuck.

Flags of heat scorched my cheeks. Screw finishing my manuscript; what I wanted most now was for the earth to yawn and swallow me whole.

Sadly, not a single tremor quaked beneath my feet, so after a moment of wallowing in humiliation, I straightened my shoulders, pasted on my best customer service smile, and turned.

My mouth barely completed its upward curve before it froze. Just up and gave out, like a webpage that couldn't finish loading.

Because standing less than five feet away, looking bemused

and far more handsome than any man had the right to look, was Kai Young.

Esteemed member of the Valhalla Club's managing committee, heir to a multibillion-dollar media empire, and owner of an uncanny ability to show up in the middle of my most embarrassing conversations *every* time, Kai Young.

A fresh wave of mortification blazed across my face.

"Apologies for interrupting," he said, his neutral tone betraying no hint of his thoughts on our conversation. "But I'd like to order a drink, please."

Despite an all-consuming desire to hide under the bar until he left, I couldn't help but melt a little at the sound of his voice. Deep, smooth and velvety, wrapped in a British accent so posh it put the late Queen's to shame. It poured into my bloodstream like a half dozen shots of potent whiskey.

My body warmed.

Kai's brows lifted a fraction, and I realized I'd been so focused on his voice that I hadn't responded to his request yet. Meanwhile Tessa, the little traitor, had disappeared into the back room, leaving me to fend for myself. *She's never getting a condom out of me again.*

"Of course." I cleared my throat, attempting to lighten the cloud of thickening tension. "But I'm afraid we don't serve glow-in-the-dark gin and tonics." *Not without a black light to make the tonic glow, anyway.*

He gave me a blank look.

"Because of the last time you overheard me talking about con—er, protective products," I said. *Nothing.* I might as well be babbling about rush hour traffic patterns, for all the reaction he showed. "You ordered a strawberry gin and tonic because I was talking about strawberry-flavored..."

I was digging myself into a deeper and deeper hole. I didn't want to remind Kai about the time he overheard me discussing strawberry condoms at the club's fall gala, but I had to say *some-*

thing to divert his attention away from, well, my current condom predicament.

I should really stop talking about sex at work.

"Never mind," I said quickly. "Do you want your usual?"

His one-off strawberry gin and tonic aside, Kai ordered a scotch, neat every time. He was more predictable than a Mariah Carey song during the holidays.

"Not today," he said easily. "I'll have a Death in the Afternoon instead." He lifted his book so I could see the title scrawled across the worn cover. *For Whom the Bell Tolls* by Ernest Hemingway. "Seems fitting."

Invented by Hemingway himself, Death in the Afternoon was a simple cocktail consisting of champagne and absinthe. Its iridescent green color was also as close to glow-in-the-dark as a regular drink could get.

I narrowed my eyes, unsure whether that was a coincidence or if he was fucking with me.

He stared back, his expression inscrutable.

Dark hair. Crisp lines. Thin black frames and a suit so perfectly tailored it had to have been custom made. Kai was the epitome of aristocratic sophistication, and he'd nailed the British stoicism that went with it.

I was usually pretty good at reading people, but I'd known him for a year and I had yet to crack his mask. It irritated me more than I cared to admit.

"One Death in the Afternoon, coming right up," I finally said.

I busied myself with his drink while he took his customary seat at the end of the bar and retrieved a notebook from his coat pocket. My hands went through the motions, but my attention was split between the glass and the man quietly reading. Every once in a while, he would pause and write something down.

That in and of itself wasn't unusual. Kai often showed up to read and drink by himself before the evening rush. What *was* unusual was the timing.

It was Monday afternoon, three days and two hours before his weekly, precision-timed arrival on Thursday evenings. He was breaking pattern.

Kai Young *never* broke pattern.

Curiosity and a strange breathlessness slowed my pace as I brought him his drink. Tessa was still in the supply room, and the silence weighed heavier with each step.

"Are you taking notes?" I placed the cocktail on a napkin and glanced at his notebook. It lay open next to Kai's novel, its pages filled with neat, precise black writing.

"I'm translating the book into Latin." He flipped the page and scribbled another sentence without looking up or touching his drink.

"Why?"

"It's relaxing."

I blinked, certain I'd heard him wrong. "You think translating a five-hundred-page novel into Latin by hand is *relaxing*?"

"Yes. If I wanted a mental challenge, I'd translate an economics textbook. Translating fiction is reserved for my downtime."

He tossed out the explanation casually, like it was a habit as common and ingrained as throwing a coat over the back of his couch.

I gaped at him. "Wow. That's..." I was at a loss for words.

I knew rich people indulged in strange hobbies, but at least they were usually fun eccentricities like throwing lavish weddings for their pets or bathing in champagne. Kai's hobby was just *boring*.

The corners of his mouth twitched, and realization dawned alongside embarrassment. *Seems to be the theme of the day.* "You're messing with me."

"Not entirely. I do find it relaxing, though I'm not a huge fan of economics textbooks. I had enough of them at Oxford." Kai finally glanced up.

My pulse leapt in my throat. Up close, he was so beautiful it

5

almost hurt to face him straight on. Thick black hair brushed his forehead, framing features straight out of the classic Hollywood era. Chiseled cheekbones sloped down to a square jaw and sculpted lips, while deep brown eyes glinted behind glasses that only heightened his appeal.

Without them, his attractiveness would've been cold, almost intimidating in its perfection, but with them, he was approachable. Human.

At least when he wasn't busy translating classics or running his family's media company. Glasses or no glasses, there was nothing *approachable* about either of those things.

My spine tingled with awareness when he reached for his drink. My hand was still on the counter. He didn't touch me, but his body heat brushed over me as surely as if he had.

The tingles spread, vibrating beneath my skin and slowing my breath.

"Isabella."

"Hmm?" Now that I thought about it, why did Kai need glasses anyway? He was rich enough to afford laser eye surgery.

Not that I was complaining. He may be boring and a little uptight, but he really—

"The gentleman at the other end of the bar is trying to get your attention."

I snapped back to reality with an unpleasant jolt. While I'd been busy staring at Kai, new patrons had trickled into the bar. Tessa was back behind the counter, tending to a well-dressed couple while another club member waited for service.

Shit.

I hurried over, leaving an amused-looking Kai behind.

After I finished with my customer, another one approached, and another. We'd hit Valhalla happy hour, and I didn't have time to dwell on Kai or his strange relaxation methods again.

For the next four hours, Tessa and I fell into a familiar rhythm as we worked the crowd.

Valhalla capped its membership at a hundred, so even its

busiest nights were nothing compared to the chaos I used to deal with at downtown dive bars. But while there were fewer of them, the club's patrons required more coddling and ego stroking than the average frat boy or drunken bachelorette. By the time the clock ticked toward nine, I was ready to collapse and thankful as hell that I only had a half shift that night.

Still, I couldn't resist the occasional peek at Kai. He usually left the bar after an hour or two, but here he was, still drinking and chatting with the other members like there was nowhere else he'd rather be.

Something's off. Timing aside, his behavior today didn't match his previous patterns at all, and the closer I looked, the more signs of trouble I spotted: the tension lining his shoulders, the tiny furrow between his brows, the tightness of his smiles.

Maybe it was the shock of seeing him off schedule, or maybe I was trying to pay Kai back for all the times he could've gotten me fired for inappropriate behavior (a.k.a. talking about sex at work) but didn't. Whatever it was, it compelled me to walk another drink over to him during a lull.

The timing was perfect; his latest conversation partner had just left, leaving Kai alone again at the bar.

"A strawberry gin and tonic. On me." I slid the glass across the counter. I'd made it on a whim, thinking it'd be a funny way to lift his mood even if it was at my expense. "You look like you could use the pick-me-up."

He responded with a questioning arch of his brow.

"You're off schedule," I explained. "You'd never go off schedule unless something's wrong."

The arch smoothed, replaced with a tiny crinkle at the corners of his eyes. My heartbeat faltered at the unexpectedly endearing sight.

It's just a smile. Get it together.

"I wasn't aware you paid so much attention to my schedule." Flecks of laughter glimmered beneath Kai's voice.

Heat flooded my cheeks for the second time that night. *This is what I get for being a Good Samaritan.*

"I don't make a point of it," I said defensively. "You've been coming to the bar every week since I started working here, but you've never showed up on a Monday. I'm simply observant." I should've stopped there, but my mouth ran off before my brain could catch up. "Rest assured, you're not my type, so you don't have to worry about me hitting on you."

That much was true. Objectively, I recognized Kai's appeal, but I liked my men rougher around the edges. He was as straitlaced as they came. Even if he wasn't, fraternization between club members and employees was strictly forbidden, and I had no desire to upend my life over a man again, thank you very much.

That didn't stop my traitorous hormones from sighing every time they saw him. It was annoying as hell.

"Good to know." The flecks of laughter shone brighter as he brought the glass to his lips. "Thank you. I have a soft spot for strawberry gin and tonics."

This time, my heartbeat didn't so much falter as stop altogether, if only for a split second.

Soft spot? *What does that mean?*

It means nothing, a voice grumbled in the back of my head. *He's talking about the drink, not you. Besides, he's not your type. Remember?*

Oh, shut up, Debbie Downer.

Great. Now my inner voices were arguing with each other. I didn't even know I *had* more than one inner voice. If that wasn't a sign I needed sleep and not another night agonizing over my manuscript, nothing was.

"You're welcome," I said, a tad belatedly. My pulse drummed in my ears. "Well, I should—"

"Sorry I'm late." A tall, blond man swept into the seat next to Kai's, his voice as brisk as the late September chill clinging to his coat. "My meeting ran over."

He spared me a brief glance before turning back to Kai.

Dark gold hair, navy eyes, the bone structure of a Calvin Klein model, and the warmth of the iceberg from *Titanic*. Dominic Davenport, the reigning king of Wall Street.

I recognized him on sight. It was hard to forget that face, even if his social skills could use improvement.

Relief and an annoying niggle of disappointment swept through me at the interruption, but I didn't wait for Kai's response. I booked it to the other side of the bar, hating the way his *soft spot* comment lingered like it was anything but a throw-away remark.

If he wasn't my type, I *definitely* wasn't his. He dated the kind of woman who sat on charity boards, summered in the Hamptons, and matched their pearls to their Chanel suits. There was nothing wrong with any of those things, but they weren't me.

I blamed my outsize reaction to his words on my self-imposed dry spell. I was so starved for touch and affection I'd probably get giddy off a wink from that half-naked cowboy always roaming Times Square. It had nothing to do with Kai himself.

I didn't return to his side of the bar again for the rest of the night.

Luckily, working a half shift meant I could clock out early. At five to ten, I transferred my remaining tabs to Tessa, said my good-byes, and grabbed my bag from the back room, all without looking at a certain billionaire with a penchant for Hemingway.

I could've sworn I felt the heated touch of dark eyes on my back when I left, but I didn't turn to confirm. It was better I didn't know.

The hall was hushed and empty this late at night. Exhaustion tugged at my eyelids, but instead of bolting for the exit and the comfort of my bed, I made a left toward the main staircase.

I *should* go home so I could hit my daily word count goal, but I needed inspiration first. I couldn't concentrate with the stress of facing a blank page clouding my head.

The words used to flow freely; I wrote three-quarters of my

erotic thriller in less than six months. Then I read it over, hated it, and scrapped it in favor of a fresh project. Unfortunately, the creativity that'd fueled my first draft had vanished alongside it. I was lucky if I wrote more than two hundred words a day these days.

I took the stairs to the second floor.

The club's amenities were off-limits to employees during working hours, but while the bar was open until three in the morning, the rest of the building closed at eight. I wasn't breaking any rules by visiting my favorite room for some decompression.

Still, my feet tread lightly against the thick Persian carpet. Down, down, all the way past the billiards room, the beauty room, and the Parisian-style lounge until I reached a familiar oak door. The brass knob was cool and smooth as I twisted it open.

Fifteen minutes. That was all I needed. Then I'd go home, wash the day off, and write.

But as always, time fell away when I sat down. Fifteen minutes turned into thirty, which turned into forty-five, and I became so immersed in what I was doing I didn't notice the door creak open behind me.

Not until it was too late.

CHAPTER 2

Kai

"Don't tell me you invited me here to watch you read Hemingway for the dozenth time." Dominic cast an unimpressed look at my book.

"You've never seen me read Hemingway." I glanced at the bar, but Isabella had already moved on to another customer, leaving the gin and tonic in her stead.

Strawberries floated lazily in the drink, their vibrant red hue a shocking contrast to the bar's dignified earth tones. I typically avoided sweet drinks; the harsh burn and subdued amber of scotch was much more to my taste. But like I said, I had a soft spot for this particular flavor.

Fine, but if you change your mind, I have strawberry-flavored condoms. Magnum-size, ribbed for your—

Apologies for interrupting, but I'd like to order another drink.

Gin and tonic. Strawberry flavored.

Reluctant amusement drifted through me at the memory of Isabella's horrified expression. I'd interrupted her and her friend Vivian's condom conversation at last year's fall gala, and I still remembered the interaction in vivid detail.

I remembered *all* our interactions in vivid detail, whether I wanted to or not. She'd touched down in my life like a tornado,

11

gotten my drink wrong during her first shift at Valhalla, and hadn't left my thoughts since.

It was aggravating.

"I haven't seen you read him in person." Dominic flicked his lighter on and off, drawing my attention back to him. He didn't smoke, yet he carried that lighter around the way a more superstitious person would cling to a lucky charm. "But I imagine that's what you do when you're holed up in your library every night."

A smile pushed through my turbulent mood. "Spend a lot of time imagining me in the library, do you?"

"Only to contemplate how sad your existence is."

"Says the workaholic who spends most of his nights in his office." It was a miracle his wife tolerated him as long as she had. Alessandra was a saint.

"It's a nice office." On. Off. A tiny flame burst into life only to die a quick death at his hand. "I'd be there right now if it weren't for your call. What's so urgent you demanded I rush here on a Monday, of all nights?"

I'd requested, not demanded, but I didn't bother correcting him. Instead, I tucked my pen, paperback, and notebook in my coat pocket and cut straight to the point. "I got the call today."

Dominic's bored impatience fell away, revealing a spark of intrigue. "This early?"

"Yes. Five candidates, including myself. The vote is in four months."

"You always knew it wouldn't be a coronation." Dominic tapped his lighter's spark wheel. "But the vote is a formality. Of course you'll win."

I offered a noncommittal noise in response.

As the eldest child and presumptive heir to the Young Corporation, I'd lived with the expectation of becoming CEO all my life. But I was supposed to take over in five to ten years, not in four months.

A fresh wave of apprehension swept through my chest.

Leonora Young would never willingly cede power this early.

She was only fifty-eight years old. Sharp, healthy, beloved by the board. Her life revolved around work and hounding me about marriage, yet it'd undeniably been her on the video call that afternoon, informing me and four other executives that we were in the running for the CEO position.

No warning, no details other than the date and time of the vote.

I ran a distracted hand over the gin and tonic glass, taking strange solace in its smooth curves.

"When's the news going public?" Dominic asked.

"Tomorrow." Which meant for the next four months, all eyes would be on me, waiting for me to fuck up. Which I never would. I had too much control for that.

Though there were technically five candidates, the position was mine to lose. Not only because I was a Young, but because I was the best. My record as president of the North America division spoke for itself. It had the highest profits, the fewest losses, and the best innovations, even if certain board members didn't always agree with my decisions.

I wasn't worried about the vote's outcome, but its timing nagged at me, twisting what should've been a career highlight into a muddied pool of unease.

If Dominic noticed my muted enthusiasm, he didn't show it. "The market's going to have a field day." I could practically see the calculations running through his head.

In the past, I would've called Dante first and sweated out my worries in the boxing ring, but ever since he got married, dragging him away from Vivian for an unscheduled match was harder than prying a bone away from a dog.

It was probably for the best. Dante would see right through my composed mask, whereas Dominic only cared about facts and numbers. If it didn't move markets or expand his bank account, he didn't give a shit.

I reached for my drink while he laid out his predictions. I'd just drained the last of the gin when a burst of rich, throaty laughter stole my attention.

My gaze slid over Dominic's shoulder and rested on Isabella, who was chatting with a cosmetics heiress near the end of the bar. She said something that made the normally standoffish socialite grin, and the two bent their heads toward each other like best friends gossiping over lunch. Every once in a while, Isabella would gesticulate wildly with her hands, and another one of her distinctive laughs would fill the room.

The sound worked its way into my chest, warming it more than the alcohol she'd handed me.

With her purple-black hair, mischievous smile, and tattoo inking the inside of her left wrist, she looked as out of place as a diamond among rocks. Not because she was a bartender in a room filled with billionaires, but because she shone too brightly for the dark, traditional confines of Valhalla.

I'm afraid we don't serve glow-in-the-dark gin and tonics.

A tiny smile snuck onto my lips before I quashed it.

Isabella was bold, impulsive, and everything I typically avoided in an acquaintance. I valued propriety; she had none, as her apparent fetish for discussing sex in the most inappropriate of locations indicated.

Still, there was something about her that drew me in like a siren calling to a sailor. Destructive, certainly, but so beautiful it would almost be worth it.

Almost.

"Does Dante know?" Dominic asked. He'd finished his market predictions, of which I'd only heard half, and was now busy answering emails on his phone. The man worked longer hours than anyone else I knew.

"Not yet." I watched as Isabella broke away from the heiress and fiddled with the register. "It's date night with Vivian. He made it clear no one is to interrupt him unless they're dying—and only if every other person on their contact list is otherwise preoccupied."

"Typical."

"Hmm," I agreed distractedly.

Isabella finished her work at the register, said something to the other bartender, and disappeared into the back room. Her shift must've ended.

Something flickered in my gut. Try as I might, I couldn't mistake it for anything other than disappointment.

I'd successfully kept my distance from Isabella for almost a year, and I was well-versed enough in Greek mythology to understand the dreadful fates that awaited sailors lured in by sirens' songs. The last thing I should do was follow her. And yet...

A strawberry gin and tonic. On me. You look like you could use the pick-me-up.

Dammit.

"Apologies for cutting the night short, but I just remembered I have an urgent matter I must take care of." I stood and slid my coat from its hook beneath the counter. "Shall we continue our conversation later? Tonight's drinks are on me."

"Sure. Whenever you're free," Dominic said, sounding unfazed by my abrupt departure. He didn't look up when I closed out our tabs. "Good luck with the announcement tomorrow."

The absentminded clicks of his lighter followed me halfway across the room until the bar's escalating noise swallowed them up. Then I was in the hallway, the door shut behind me, and the only sound came from the soft fall of my footsteps.

I wasn't sure what I'd do once I caught up with Isabella. Despite our mutual acquaintances—her best friend Vivian was Dante's wife—we weren't friends ourselves. But the CEO news had thrown me off-kilter, as had her unexpected but thoughtful gift.

I wasn't used to people offering me things without expecting something in return.

A rueful smile crossed my lips. What did it say about my life when a simple free drink from a casual acquaintance stood out as a highlight of my night?

I took the stairs to the second floor, my heartbeat steady despite the small voice urging me to turn and run in the opposite direction.

I was operating on a hunch. She might not be there, and I certainly had no business seeking her out if she was, but my usual restraint had frayed beneath a more pressing urge for distraction. I needed to do something about this frustrating *want*, and if I couldn't figure out what was going on with my mother, then I needed to figure out what was going on with me. What was it about Isabella that held me captive? Tonight, that might be the easier question to answer.

My mother had reassured me she was fine during our post-conference call chat. She wasn't sick, dying, or being blackmailed; she was simply ready for a change.

If it were anyone else, I would've taken her words at face value, but my mother didn't do things on a whim. It went against her very nature. I also didn't think she was lying; I knew her well enough to spot her tells, and she'd displayed none during our call.

Frustration knotted my brow. It didn't add up.

If it wasn't her health or blackmail, what else could it be? A disagreement with the board? A need to destress after decades of helming a multibillion-dollar corporation? An alien hijacking her body?

I was so engrossed in my musings I didn't notice the soft strains of a piano drifting through the hall until I stood directly in front of the source.

She was here after all.

My heartbeat tripped once, so lightly and quickly I barely noticed the disturbance. My frown dissolved, replaced with curiosity, then astonishment as the whirlwind of notes fell into place and recognition clicked.

She was playing Beethoven's "Hammerklavier," one of the

most challenging pieces ever composed for piano. And she was playing it well.

A cool rush of shock swept the breath from my lungs.

I rarely heard the "Hammerklavier" played at its intended speed, and the stunning realization that Isabella could outperform even seasoned professionals crushed any reservations I may have had about seeking her out.

I had to see it for myself.

After a brief hesitation, I closed my hand around the doorknob, twisted, and stepped inside.

CHAPTER 3

The piano room was as grand as any other in the club, with luxurious drapes cascading to the floor in swaths of rich velvet and golden sconces glowing softly against the deep rose walls. A proud Steinway grand stood center stage, its polished black curves gilded silver by a blanket of moonlight.

Seated in front of it, her back to me and her fingers flying over the keys at a speed that was almost dizzying to witness, was Isabella. She'd entered the sonata's final movement.

A bold trill announced the start of the first theme, which twisted and stretched and turned upside down over the next two-hundred-something odd measures. Then, it was quiet, an intermission before the second theme's choir hummed into existence.

Soft, haunting, dignified…

Until the first theme crashed in again, its rushing notes sweeping over its successor's quieter existence with such force it was impossible for the second not to bend. The two themes curled around each other, their temperaments diametrically opposed yet inexplicably beautiful when conjoined, climbing higher and higher and higher still…

Then a plunge, a free-falling grand finale that nosedived off the cliff in a magnificent splash of double trills, parallel scales, and leaping octaves.

Through it all, I stood, body frozen and pulse pounding at the sheer impossibility of what I'd witnessed.

I'd played the same sonata before. Dozens of times. But not once did it sound like that. The final movement was supposed to be thick with sorrow, an emotionally draining twenty minutes that had earned it mournful superlatives from commentators. Yet in Isabella's hands, it'd transformed into something uplifting, almost joyful.

Granted, her technique wasn't perfect. She leaned too heavy on some notes, too light on others, and her finger control wasn't quite developed enough to bring out all the melodic lines. Despite all that, she'd accomplished the impossible.

She'd taken pain and turned it into hope.

The last note hung in the air, breathless, before it faded and all was quiet.

The spell holding me captive cracked. Air filled my lungs again, but when I spoke, my voice sounded rougher than usual. "Impressive."

Isabella visibly tensed before the last syllable passed my lips. She whipped around, her face suffused with alarm. When she spotted me, she relaxed only to stiffen again a second later.

"What are you doing here?"

Amusement pulled at the corners of my mouth. "I should be asking you that question."

I didn't disclose the fact that I knew she'd been sneaking into the piano room for months. I'd discovered it by accident one night when I'd stayed late in the library and exited in time to catch Isabella slipping out with a guilty expression. She hadn't spotted me, but I'd heard her play multiple times since. The library was right next to the piano room; if I sat near the wall dividing the two, I could hear the faint melodies coming from the other side. They'd served as an oddly soothing soundtrack for my work.

However, tonight was the first night I'd heard her play something as complex as the "Hammerklavier."

"We're allowed to use the room after hours if there's no one else here," Isabella said with a defiant tilt of her chin. "Which I guess there now is." She faltered, her brows drawing together in a tight V.

She moved to stand, but I shook my head. "Stay. Unless you have other plans for the night." Another involuntary glimmer of amusement. "I hear neon skate parties are all the rage these days."

Crimson bloomed across her cheeks, but she lifted her chin and pinned me with a dignified glare. "It's impolite to eavesdrop on other people's conversations. Don't they teach you that at boarding school?"

"Au contraire, that's where the most eavesdropping happens. As for your accusation, I'm not sure what you mean," I said, tone mild. "I was merely commenting on nightlife trends."

Logic told me I shouldn't engage with Isabella any more than necessary. It was inappropriate, considering her employment and my role at the club. I also had the unsettling sense that she was dangerous—not physically, but in some other way I couldn't pinpoint.

Yet instead of leaving as my good sense dictated, I closed the distance between us and skimmed my fingers over the piano's ivory keys. They were still warm from her touch.

Isabella relaxed into her seat, but her eyes remained alert as they followed me to her side. "No offense, but I can't picture you in a nightclub, much less a neon anything."

"I don't have to take part in something to understand it." I pressed the minor key, allowing the note to signal a transition into my next topic. "You played well. Better than most pianists who attempt the 'Hammerklavier.'"

"I sense a but at the end of that sentence."

"But you were too aggressive at the start of the second theme. It's supposed to be lighter, more understated." It wasn't an insult; it was an objective appraisal.

Isabella cocked an eyebrow. "You think you can do better?"

My pulse spiked, and a familiar flame kindled in my chest. Her tone straddled the line between playful and challenging, but that was enough to throw the gates of my competitiveness wide open.

"May I?" I nodded at the bench.

She slid off her seat. I took her vacated spot, adjusted the bench height and touched the keys again, thoughtfully this time. I only played the second movement, but I'd been practicing the "Hammerklavier" since I was a child, when I'd insisted my piano teacher skip the easy pieces and teach me the most difficult compositions instead. It was harder to get into it without the first movement as a prelude, but muscle memory carried me through.

The sonata finished with a grand flourish, and I smiled, satisfied.

"Hmm." Isabella sounded unimpressed. "Mine was better."

My head snapped up. "Pardon me?"

"Sorry." She shrugged. "You're a good piano player, but you're lacking something."

The sentiment was so unfamiliar and unexpected I could only stare, my reply lost somewhere between astonishment and indignation.

"I'm lacking something," I echoed, too dumbfounded to dredge up an original response.

I'd graduated top of my class from Oxford and Cambridge, lettered in tennis and polo, and spoke seven languages fluently. I'd founded a charity for funding the arts in underserved areas when I was eighteen, and I was on the fast track to becoming one of the world's youngest Fortune 500 CEOs.

In my thirty-two years on earth, no one had ever told me I was *lacking* something.

The worst part was, upon examination, she was right.

Yes, my technique surpassed hers. I'd hit every note with precision, but the piece had inspired...nothing. The ebbs and tides of emotion that'd characterized her rendition had vanished, leaving a sterile beauty in their wake.

I'd never noticed when playing by myself, but following her performance, the difference was obvious.

My jaw tightened. I was used to being the best, and the realization that I *wasn't*, at least not at this particular song, rankled.

"What, exactly, do you think I'm lacking?" I asked, my tone even despite the swarm of thoughts invading my brain.

Mental note: Substitute tennis with Dominic for piano practice until I fix this problem. I'd never done anything less than perfectly, and this would not be my exception.

Isabella's cheeks dimpled. She appeared to take immense delight in my disgruntlement, which should've infuriated me more. Instead, her teasing grin almost pulled an answering smile out of me before I caught myself.

"The fact you don't know is part of the problem." She stepped toward the door. "You'll figure it out."

"Wait." I stood and grabbed her arm without thinking.

We froze in unison, our eyes locked on where my hand encircled her wrist. Her skin was soft to the touch, and the flutter of her pulse matched the sudden escalation in my heartbeat.

A heavy, tension-laced silence mushroomed around us. I was a proponent of science; I didn't believe in anything that defied the laws of physics, but I could've sworn time physically slowed, like each second was encased in molasses.

Isabella visibly swallowed. A tiny movement, but it was enough for the laws to snap back into place and for reason to intervene.

Time sped to its usual pace, and I dropped her arm as abruptly as I'd grasped it.

"Apologies," I said, my voice stiff. I tried my best to ignore the tingle on my palm.

"It's fine." Isabella touched her wrist, her expression distracted. "Has anyone told you that you talk like an extra from *Downton Abbey*?"

The question came from so far out of left field it took a moment to sink in. "I...a *what*?"

"An extra from *Downton Abbey*. You know, that show about the British aristocracy during the early twentieth century?"

"I know the show." I didn't live under a rock.

"Oh, good. Just thought I'd let you know in case you didn't." Isabella flashed another bright smile. "You should try to loosen up a bit. It might help with your piano playing."

For the second time that night, words deserted me.

I was still standing there, trying to figure out how my evening had gone so off the rails, when the door closed behind her.

It wasn't until I was on my way home that I realized I hadn't thought about the CEO vote or its timing once since I heard Isabella in the piano room.

CHAPTER 4

Isabella

"**M**om asked about you the other day," Gabriel said. "You only come home once a year, and she's concerned about what you're doing in Manhattan..."

I frowned at the half-empty page in front of me while my brother rambled on. I already regretted answering his call. It was only six a.m. in California, but he sounded alert and put together, as always. He was probably on his office treadmill, reading the news, replying to emails, and drinking one of his hideous antioxidant smoothies.

Meanwhile, I was proud of myself for rolling out of bed before nine. Sleep proved elusive after last night's encounter with Kai, but I'd thought that maybe, just maybe, the strange experience would be enough to jar a few sentences loose for my manuscript.

It wasn't.

My erotic thriller about the deadly relationship between a wealthy attorney and a naive waitress turned mistress formed vague shapes in my head. I had the plot, I had the characters, but dammit, I didn't have the words.

To make matters worse, my brother was still talking.

"Are you listening to me?" His voice was laced with equal parts exasperation and disapproval.

The heat from my laptop seeped through my pants and into my skin, but I barely noticed. I was too busy devising ways to fill all that white space without writing more words.

"Yes." I selected all the text and cranked the font size up to thirty-six. *Much better.* The page didn't look so empty now. "You said you finally consulted a doctor about a sense of humor implant. It's experimental technology, but the situation is dire."

"Hilarious." My oldest brother had never found a single thing hilarious in his life, hence the need for a sense of humor implant. "I'm serious, Isa. We're worried about you. You moved to New York years ago, yet you're still living in a rat-infested apartment and slinging drinks at some bar—"

"The Valhalla Club isn't *some bar*," I protested. I'd endured six rounds of interviews before landing a bartending gig there; I'd be damned if I let Gabriel diminish that accomplishment. "And my apartment is *not* rat-infested. I have a pet snake, remember?"

I cast a protective glance at Monty's vivarium, where he was curled up and fast asleep. Of course he slept well; *he* didn't have to worry about annoying siblings or failing at life.

Gabriel continued like I hadn't spoken. "While working on the same book you've been stuck on forever. Look, we know you think you want to be an author, but maybe it's time to reevaluate. Move home, figure out an alternate plan. We could always use your help in the office."

Move home? Work in the office? *Over my dead body.*

Bitterness crawled up my throat at the thought of wasting my days away in some cubicle. I wasn't making much progress on my manuscript, but caving to Gabriel's "solution" meant throwing away my dreams for good.

I got the idea for the book two years ago while people watching in Washington Square Park. I'd overheard a heated argument between a man and someone who obviously wasn't his wife, and my imagination took their fight and ran with it. The story had been so detailed and fleshed out in my mind that I'd confidently told everyone I knew about my plans to write and publish a thriller.

The day after I witnessed the argument, I bought a brand-new laptop and let the words pour out of me. Except what came out at the end wasn't the shimmering diamond masterpiece I'd envisioned. What showed up were ugly lumps of coal, so I deleted them.

And the pages remained blank.

"I don't *think* I want to be an author; I *do* want to be an author," I said. "I'm just exploring the story."

Despite my current frustrations with writing, there was something so special about creating and getting lost in new worlds. Books have been my escape for years, and I *will* publish one eventually. I wasn't giving up that dream so I could become an office automaton.

"The same way you wanted to be a dancer, a travel agent, and a daytime talk show host?" The disapproval edged out Gabriel's exasperation. "You're not a fresh college grad anymore. You're twenty-eight. You need direction."

The bitterness thickened into a dry, sour sludge.

You need direction.

That was easy for Gabriel to say. He'd known what he wanted since high school. *All* my brothers had. I was the only Valencia bobbing aimlessly in the post-school waters while the rest of my family settled into their respective careers.

The businessman, the artist, the professor, the engineer, and me, the flake.

I was sick of being the failure, and I was especially sick of Gabriel being right.

"I have direction. In fact..." *Don't say it. Don't say it. Don't—* "I'm almost done with the book." The lie darted out before I could snatch it back.

"Really?" Only he could soak a word with so much skepticism it morphed into something else.

Are you lying?

The real, unspoken question snaked over the line, poking and prodding for holes in my declaration.

There were plenty of them, of course. The entire freaking thing was one giant hole because I was closer to setting up a colony on Mars than finishing my book. But it was too late. I'd backed myself into a corner, and the only way out was through.

"Yes." I cleared my throat. "I had a big breakthrough at Vivian's wedding. It's the Italian air. It was so, um, inspiring."

The only things it'd inspired were too many glasses of champagne and a massive hangover, but I kept that to myself.

"Wonderful," Gabriel said. "In that case, we'd love to read it. Mom's birthday is in four months. Why don't you bring it when you're home for the party?"

Rocks pitched off the side of a cliff and plummeted into my stomach. "Absolutely not. I'm writing an erotic thriller, Gabe. As in, there's *sex* in it."

"I'm aware of what erotic thrillers entail. We're your family. We want to support you."

"But it's—"

"Isabella." Gabriel adopted the same tone he'd used to boss me around when we were younger. "I insist."

I squeezed my phone so hard it cracked in protest.

This was a test. He knew it, I knew it, and neither of us was willing to back down.

"Fine." I injected a dose of false pep into my voice. "Don't blame me if you're so traumatized you can't look me in the eye for at *least* the next five years."

"I'll chance it." A warning note slid into his voice. "But if, for some reason, you're unable to produce the book by then, we're going to sit down and have a serious chat."

After our father died, Gabriel assumed unofficial head of household status next to our mother. He took care of my brothers and me while she worked—picking us up from school, making our doctor's appointments, cooking us dinner. We were all adults now, but his bossy tendencies were getting worse as our mother entrusted more and more of the family responsibilities to him.

I gritted my teeth. "You can't—"

"I have to go or I'll be late for my meeting. We'll talk soon. See you in February." He hung up, leaving the echo of his thinly veiled threat behind.

Panic twisted my chest into a tight knot. I tossed my phone to the side and tried to breathe through the ballooning pressure.

Damn Gabriel. Knowing him, he was telling our entire family about the book right that second. If I showed up empty-handed, I'd have to face their collective displeasure. My mom's dismay, my lola's disapproval and, worst of all, Gabriel's smug, know-it-all attitude.

I knew you couldn't do it.

You need direction.

When are you going to get it together, Isabella?

You're twenty-eight.

If the rest of us can do it, why can't you?

The phantom accusations tumbled into my throat, blocking the flow of oxygen.

Four months. I had four months to finish my book while working full-time and battling a nasty case of writer's block, or my family would know I was exactly the wishy-washy failure Gabriel thought I was.

I already hated going home every year with nothing to show for my time in New York; I couldn't bear the thought of seeing the same disappointment reflected on my family's faces.

It's fine. You'll be fine.

Eighty thousand words by early February. Totally doable, right?

For a moment, I let myself hope and believe the new me could do this.

Then I groaned and pressed the heels of my palms against my eyes. Even with them closed, all I could see were blank pages.

"I am *so* fucked."

CHAPTER 5

Kai

I leveled a cool stare at the man sitting across from me.

After yesterday's CEO bombshell and my unsettling interaction with Isabella, I'd hoped for a smooth day at work, but those hopes spiraled down the drain the minute Tobias Foster showed up unannounced.

He wore a shiny new Zegna suit, an even shinier Rolex, and a smug smirk as he inspected his surroundings.

"Nice office," he said. "Very fitting for a Young."

He didn't say it, but I could read between the lines.

I earned my office; you were born into yours.

Which was complete bull. I may be a Young, but I'd worked my way up from the bottom like every other employee.

"I'm sure yours is equally nice." I gave him a cordial smile and glanced at my watch. He'd catch the movement; hopefully, he would take a hint as well. "What can I do for you, Tobias?"

He was the head of the Young Corporation's Europe division and my biggest competition for CEO, so I'd made an exception to my no-unscheduled-meetings rule and invited him into my office.

I already regretted it.

Tobias was the worst sort of employee—good at his job but so crass and irritating I wished he weren't so we could fire him. I appreciated his competence, but he was one step away from sticking his foot so far down his mouth even the world's most talented surgeon couldn't retrieve it.

"I just wanted to drop by and say hi. Pay my respects." Tobias fiddled with the crystal paperweight on my desk. "I'm in town for a bunch of meetings. I'm sure you know about them. The Europe division is expanding so fast, and Richard invited me to dinner at Peter Luger." His laugh grated through the air.

Richard Chu was the Young Corporation's longest-serving board member and a dinosaur when it came to innovation. We'd butted heads multiple times over the future of the company, but no matter how much power he thought he wielded, he was only one vote out of many.

"I'm not surprised. Richard does enjoy a certain type of company." *The type that'll kiss his ass like it's made of gold.* Tobias's smile slipped. "Perhaps you should get going. Traffic can be quite brutal at this time of day. Would you like me to call a car for you?"

My hand hovered over the phone in a clear dismissal.

"No need." He released the paperweight and pinned with me a hard stare, all traces of fake deference gone. "I'm used to doing things for myself. But life must be a lot easier for you, huh? All you have to do is not fuck up for the next four months and the CEO role is yours."

I didn't take the bait. Tobias could talk shit all he wanted, but I was damn good at my job and we both knew it.

"I haven't fucked up in over thirty years," I said pleasantly. "I don't plan on starting now."

His phony affability slid back into place like a curtain falling over a window. "True, but there's a first time for everything." He stood, his smile oilier than a fast-food kitchen. "See you at the exec retreat in a few weeks. And Kai? May the best man win."

I returned his smile with an indifferent one of my own. Lucky for me, I always won.

After Tobias left, I reviewed the last quarter's financial reports for the second time. Print revenue down eleven percent, online revenue up nine point two percent. Not great, but it was better than the other divisions, and it would've been worse had I not doubled down on the shift to digital despite the board's protests.

A sharp ring tore my attention away from the reports.

I groaned when I saw the caller ID. My mother only interrupted my office hours to share urgent or unpleasant news.

"I have excellent news." As usual, she cut straight to the chase when I picked up. "Clarissa is moving to New York."

I flipped through my mental Rolodex. "Clarissa..."

"Teo." The clack of heels against marble emphasized her impatience. "You grew up with her. How could you forget?"

Clarissa Teo.

A vague impression of pink tulle and braces passed in front of my mind's eye. I suppressed another groan. "She's five years younger than me, Mother. *Growing up with her* isn't quite accurate."

The Teos owned one of the biggest retail chains in the UK. My mother was best friends with Philippa Teo, and our family mansions stood side by side in London's posh Kensington Palace Gardens.

"You were neighbors and attended the same social functions," my mother said. "It counts in my book. Regardless, aren't you thrilled she's moving to Manhattan?"

"Hmm." My noncommittal answer contained all the enthusiasm of a defendant sitting trial.

Despite our families' closeness, I barely knew Clarissa. I hadn't been interested in hanging out with a girl five years my junior as a kid, and an ocean separated us when we were both adults—I'd studied at Cambridge for my master's while she'd attended Harvard. By the time she returned to London, I'd already moved to New York.

We certainly weren't close enough for me to feel any type of way over her comings and goings.

"She doesn't know many people in New York," my mother

said with the subtlety of a thousand neon sparklers spelling *ask her out* at night. "You should show her around. The Valhalla Club's fall gala is coming up. She would make a lovely date."

A sigh traveled up my throat to the tip of my tongue before I swallowed it. "I'm happy to take her out to lunch one day, but I haven't decided whether I'm bringing a date to the gala yet."

"You are a Young." My mother's voice grew stern. "Not only that, you could become CEO of the world's biggest media company in four months. I've let you have your fun, but you *need* to settle down soon. The board does not look favorably on people with unsettled home lives."

"Didn't one of the board members find his wife in bed with the gardener? A married home life sounds more unsettled than an unmarried one."

"Kai."

I rubbed a hand over my mouth, wondering how my smooth, easy day had devolved into *this*. First Tobias, now my mother. It was like the universe was conspiring against me.

"I'm not asking you to propose, though it certainly wouldn't hurt," my mother said. "Clarissa is beautiful, well-educated, well-mannered, and cultured. She would make a wonderful wife."

"This isn't a dating app. You don't need to list her qualities," I said dryly. "Like I said, I promise I'll meet up with her at least once."

After a few more reassurances, I hung up.

A headache throbbed behind my temple. My mother gave me the illusion of choice, but she expected me to marry Clarissa one day. *Everyone* did. If not Clarissa, then someone exactly like her with the proper lineage, education, and upbringing.

I'd dated multiple women like that. They were pleasant enough, but there was always something missing.

Another image flashed through my mind, this time of purple-black hair and sparkling eyes and a husky, irrepressible laugh.

My shoulders tightened. I pushed the image out of my mind

and tried to refocus on work, but glints of purple kept resurfacing until I slammed my folder shut and stood.

Perhaps my mother was right. I *should* take Clarissa to the fall gala. Just because my previous girlfriends hadn't worked out didn't mean a similar relationship wouldn't work out in the future.

I was destined to marry someone like Clarissa Teo.

Not anyone else.

~

"Who the hell pissed you off today?" Dante rubbed his jaw. "You were throwing punches at me like I was Victor fucking Black."

"Can't handle it?" I quipped, sidestepping his question. I ignored the mention of a rival media group's smarmy CEO. "If marriage made you soft, let me know, and I'll find a new partner."

His glare could've melted the marble columns lining the hallway.

I suppressed a smile. Riling him up was even more therapeutic than our weekly boxing matches. I just wish he didn't make it so easy. One semi-critical mention of his wife or marriage and he reverted right back to his scowling, pre-Vivian self.

We typically boxed on Thursdays, but I'd convinced him to move our standing appointment up given yesterday's CEO vote bombshell.

"Be my guest. I'd much rather spend my evenings with Viv anyway." A short pause. "And I'm not fucking soft. We ended in a tie."

We usually did. It galled my competitive side to no end, but it was also why I enjoyed sparring with Dante so much. It was a challenge in a world filled with easy wins.

"Honeymoon stage is still going strong then?" I asked.

Dante and Vivian had recently returned from their actual honeymoon in Greece. The Dante I'd known for the better part of a decade would've never taken two weeks off from work, but his wife had accomplished the impossible. She'd transformed him into an actual human being with a life outside the office.

His face softened. "Don't think it'll ever end," he said with surprising frankness. "Speaking of which, what are you going to do about Clarissa?"

I'd told him about the CEO vote and my mother's call earlier. As expected, Dante had displayed the sympathy of a chipped boulder, but he never missed an opportunity to hound me about my mother's determination to marry me off.

"Take her out like I promised. Who knows?" I stopped at the entrance to the bar. "She could be the one. This time next month, we could be double dating and wearing matching couples' outfits in Times Square."

Dante grimaced. "I'd rather cut off my arm and feed it through a grinder."

I swallowed my laughter. "If you say so." If I convinced Vivian, she could get him to yodel naked on the corner of Broadway and Forty-Second Street. Luckily for him, I also found the idea of couples' outfits and visiting Times Square abhorrent.

We usually grabbed a drink together after our boxing matches, but he excused himself tonight for a date with his wife, so I entered the bar alone.

I wove through the room, instinctively searching for a glimpse of dimples and violet, but I only saw Isabella's blond friend and another bartender with red curls.

I settled at an empty stool and ordered my usual scotch, neat, from the blond. Teresa? Teagan? *Tessa*. That was her name.

"Here you go!" she chirped, setting the drink in front of me.

"Thank you." I took a casual sip. "Busy night. Is anyone else working today?"

"Nope. We never have more than two people working the same shift." Tessa's brows rose. "Are you looking for someone in particular?"

I shook my head. "Just asking."

Luckily, another customer soon diverted her attention, and she didn't press further.

I finished my scotch and spent the next half hour engaging in the obligatory networking and information gathering—there was nothing like a little alcohol to loosen people's tongues, which was why I had a strict three-drink limit in public—but I couldn't focus. My thoughts kept straying to a certain room on the second floor.

Not because of Isabella, obviously. I was simply bothered by how she'd outperformed me, and I couldn't rest until I'd perfected the piece.

I lasted another ten minutes in the bar before I couldn't take it anymore. I excused myself from a conversation with the CEO of a private equity firm, slipped out the side entrance, and took the stairs to the second floor.

Unlike yesterday, no music leaked into the hall. A brush of what felt perilously close to disappointment skimmed my skin until I shook it off.

I reached for the door right as it swung open.

Something—*someone*—small and soft slammed into me, and I instinctively reached an arm around her waist to steady her.

I looked down, the scent of rose and vanilla clouding my senses before my brain registered who was in my arms.

Silky dark hair. Tanned skin. Huge brown eyes that melded to mine with surprise and something else that sent an alarming rush of heat through my blood.

Isabella.

CHAPTER 6
Isabella

Kai wrapped an arm around my waist, anchoring me against his torso. It was like being enveloped in an inferno. Heat seeped through my shirt and into my veins; a flush rose to the surface of my skin, which tingled beneath the sudden, heavy weight of my uniform.

I should do *something*—apologize for running into him (even though it hadn't been my fault), step back, run the hell away—but my mind had glitched. All I could focus on was the solid strength of his body and the rapid *thud, thud, thud* of my heart.

Kai tipped his chin down, his eyes finding mine. For once, he wasn't wearing a tie and jacket. Instead, he wore a white button-down with the sleeves rolled up and the top button undone. The shirt was so soft, and he smelled so nice, that I got the inane urge to press my face into his chest. Or, worse, to press my mouth to the hollow of his throat and see if he tasted as good as he smelled.

My breath escaped through parted lips. The tingling intensi-fied; everything felt warm and heavy, like I'd been dipped in sun-kissed honey.

Kai's expression remained indifferent, but his throat flexed with a telltale swallow.

I wasn't the only one who felt the electric link between us.

The realization was enough to snap me out of my trance.

What was I doing? This was *Kai*, for Christ's sake. He was one hundred (okay, ninety) percent not my type and two hundred percent off-limits.

I wasn't going to make the same mistake as my predecessor, who'd gotten fired after my supervisor caught her giving a club member a blow job. She'd been reckless, and now she was blacklisted from working at every bar within a forty-mile radius. Valhalla took its rules—and consequences—seriously.

Plus...

Remember what happened the last time you got involved with someone who was off-limits?

My stomach lurched, and the fog finally receded enough for me to break free from his embrace. Despite the heater humming in the background, stepping out of Kai's arms was like leaving a cozy, fire-lit cabin to traverse the mountains in the dead of winter.

Goose bumps scattered over my arms, but I played it off with a casual lilt. "Are you stalking me?"

Running into him here once could've been coincidence, but twice was suspicious. Especially on consecutive nights.

I expected him to brush me off with his usual dry amusement. Instead, the tiniest hint of pink colored his cheekbones.

"We discussed this last time. I'm a member of the club, and I'm simply availing myself of its amenities," he said, the words stilted and formal.

"You've never used the piano room before this week."

A faint lift of his brow. "How do you know?"

Instinct. If Kai made regular appearances here, I'd feel it. He altered the shape of every space he entered.

"Just a hunch," I said. "But I'm glad you're coming more often. You could use the practice." I tamped down a smile at the way his eyes sparked. "Maybe one day, you'll catch up to me."

To my disappointment, he didn't take the bait.

"One can only hope. Of course..." The earlier spark turned

thoughtful. Assessing. "Last night could've been a fluke. You talk a big game, but can you duplicate the same level of performance?"

Now he was the one dangling the bait, his words gleaming like a minnow hooked to a jig head.

I shouldn't fall for it. I had to get more words in—I was woefully behind on my daily word count goal of three thousand words—and I'd only snuck in here after my shift because I'd hoped it would jump-start my creativity. I didn't have time to indulge in Kai's veiled challenges.

The practical side of me insisted I return home that minute to write; another, more convincing side glowed with pride. Kai wouldn't have challenged me if he weren't rattled, and there were so few things I was truly talented at that I couldn't resist the urge to show off. Just a little.

I released a confident smile. "Let's put it to the test, shall we? Your choice."

The weight of his gaze followed me to the bench. I opened the fallboard and tried to focus on the smooth, familiar keys instead of the man behind me.

"What did you have in mind?" I asked.

"'Winter Wind.'" Kai's presence brushed my back. A shiver of pleasure, followed by the slow drip of warmth down my spine. "Chopin."

It was one of the composer's most difficult études, but it was doable.

I glanced at Kai, who leaned against the side of the piano and assessed me with the detached interest of a professor grading a student. Moonlight spilled over his relaxed form, sculpting his cheekbones with silver and etching shadows beneath those inscrutable eyes.

The air turned hazy with anticipation.

I sank into it, wrenching my gaze back to the piano, closing my eyes, and letting the electric currents carry me through the piece. I didn't play Chopin often, so it started rusty, but just as I hit my stride, a soft rustle interrupted my focus.

My eyes flew open. Kai had moved from his previous spot. He was now seated on the bench, his body scant inches from mine.

I hit the wrong key. The discordant note jarred my bones, and though I quickly corrected myself, I couldn't lose myself in the music anymore. I was too busy drowning in awareness, in the scent of the woods after a rainstorm and the way Kai's gaze burned a hole in my cheek.

Yesterday, I'd played like no one was watching. Today, I played like the whole world was watching, except it wasn't the whole world. It was one man.

I finished the étude, frustration chafing beneath my skin. Kai watched me without a word, his expression unreadable save for a tiny pinch between his brows.

"You distracted me," I said before he could state the obvious.

The pinch loosened, revealing a glimmer of amusement. "How so?"

"You know how."

The amusement deepened. "I was merely sitting. I didn't say or do a single thing."

"You're sitting too close." I cast a pointed glance at the sliver of black leather seating between us. "It's an obvious intimidation tactic."

"Ah, yes. The secret art of sitting too closely. I should contact the CIA and inform them of this groundbreaking tactic."

"Ha ha," I grumbled, my ego too bruised to make way for humor. "Don't you have somewhere else to be instead of bothering an innocent bystander?"

"I have many other places to be." A brief light illuminated the shadows in his eyes. "But I chose to be here."

His words sank into my bones, dousing the flames of my disgruntlement.

The light flared, then died, submerged once again beneath pools of darkness. "How did you learn to play so well?" Kai switched topics so abruptly my brain scrambled to catch up.

"Most obligatory childhood lessons don't cover such difficult pieces."

Pieces of memories spilled into my consciousness. A golden afternoon here, an evening performance there.

I kept them locked in a box whenever I could, but Kai's question pried it open with distressingly low effort.

"My father was a music teacher. He could play everything. The violin, the cello, the flute." A familiar ache crept into my throat. "But the piano was his first love, and he taught us from a young age. My mom wasn't a music person, and I think he wanted someone else in the family who could connect with it the way he did."

Vignettes from my childhood floated to the surface. My dad's deep, patient voice guiding me through the scales. My mom taking me shopping for a new dress and my family crowding in the living room for my first "recital." I'd stumbled a few times, but everyone pretended I hadn't.

Afterward, my father swept me up in a huge hug, whispered how proud he was of me, and took all of us out for ice cream sundaes. He'd bought me a special triple scoop of chocolate fudge brownie, and I remembered thinking life couldn't possibly get any better than that moment.

I blinked back a telltale sting in my eyes. I hadn't cried in public since my dad's funeral, and I refused to start again now.

"'Us.' You and your siblings?" Kai prompted gently. I didn't know why he was so interested in my background, but once I started talking, I couldn't stop.

"Yes." I swallowed the swell of memories and marshaled my emotions into some semblance of order. "I have four older brothers. They went along with the piano lessons to make our dad happy, but I was the only one who truly enjoyed them. That was why he let them off the hook after they learned the basics but continued teaching me."

I didn't want to be a professional pianist. Never had, never will. There was a special magic in loving something without capitalizing on it, and I was comforted by the idea that there was at least one thing in my life I could turn to with no expectations, pressures, or guilt.

"What about you?" I lightened my tone. "Do you have any siblings?"

I knew little about Kai despite his family's notoriety. For people who'd built their fortune on dissecting the lives of others, they were notoriously private themselves.

"I have a younger sister, Abigail. She lives in London."

"Right." An image of a female version of Kai—cool, elegant, and decked out head to toe in tasteful designer clothing—flashed through my mind. "Let me guess. You both also took piano lessons growing up, along with violin, French, tennis, and Mandarin."

Kai's lips curved. "Are we that predictable?"

"Most rich people are." I shrugged. "No offense."

"None taken," he said wryly. "There's nothing more flattering than being called predictable."

He shifted in his seat, and our knees brushed. Lightly, so lightly it barely counted as a touch, but every cell in my body tensed like I'd been electrocuted.

Kai stilled. He didn't move his knee, and I didn't breathe, and we were tossed back to the beginning of the night, when the latch of his arms around my waist conjured all sorts of inappropriate thoughts and fantasies.

Tangling tongues. Sweat-slicked skin. Dark groans and breathy pleas.

The point of contact between us burned, taking our easy banter and condensing it into something heavier. More dangerous.

A blanket of static settled over my skin. I was suddenly, intensely aware of how we would look to anyone walking in. Two people crowded on the same bench, so close our breaths merged into one. A deceptively intimate portrait of rules broken and propriety discarded.

That was how it felt. In reality, we weren't doing anything wrong, but I was more exposed in that moment than if I were standing naked in the middle of Fifth Avenue.

Kai's eyes darkened at the edges. Neither of us had moved, but I had the uncanny sense we were barreling down an invisible track headed off a cliff.

Get it together, Isa. You're conversing in a piano room, for God's sake, not bungee jumping off the Macau Tower.

I dragged my attention back to the conversation at hand. "So I was right about all the lessons. Predictable." The words came out more breathless than I'd intended, but I masked it with a bright smile. "Unless you also have some exciting hobby I don't know about. Do you tame wild horses in your free time? BASE jump off the top of that tower in Dubai? Host orgies in your private library?"

Embers smoldered, then cooled.

"I'm afraid not." Kai's voice could've melted butter. "I don't like sharing."

The ground shifted, throwing me off-balance. I was scrambling for a response, any response, when a loud laugh sliced through the room like a guillotine.

The electric link sizzled into oblivion. Our heads swiveled toward the door, and I instinctively jerked my leg away from his.

Luckily, whoever was in the hall didn't enter the room. The murmur of voices eventually faded, leaving silence in their wake.

But the spell had shattered, and there was no gluing the pieces back together. Not tonight.

"I have to go." I stood so abruptly my knee banged against the underside of the piano. I ignored the pain ricocheting up and down my leg and summoned a flippant smile. "As entertaining as this has been, I have to, um, feed my snake."

Ball pythons only needed to be fed every week or two, and I'd already fed Monty yesterday, but Kai didn't need to know that.

He didn't show a visible reaction to my words. He just inclined his head and replied with a simple, "Good night."

I waited until I was out of the room and down the hall before I allowed myself to relax. What the hell was I thinking? My night had been a spectacular series of bad decisions. First, going to the piano room instead of heading home to work on my manuscript (in my defense, I usually wrote better after a piano session), then staying and semi-flirting with Kai.

My run-in with him must've knocked my good sense loose.

I made it halfway down the stairs when I ran into Parker, the bar manager.

"Isabella." Surprise lit her eyes. With her lean frame and platinum pixie cut, she bore a striking resemblance to the model Agyness Deyn. "I didn't expect to still see you here."

My shift had ended two hours ago.

"I was in the piano room," I said, electing to tell the truth. Some Valhalla managers got testy about employees using the facilities even in accordance with the rules, but Parker knew about my hobby and encouraged it.

"Of course. I should've known." Her eyes twinkled.

Parker was a gem, as far as managers went. A thousand times better than Creepy Charlie or Handsy Harry from my previous places of employment. Besides my friends Vivian and Sloane, she was also one of the few people in New York who knew—and kept—my secret. For that, I would always be grateful.

"I didn't get a chance to tell you earlier, but congratulations on your upcoming work anniversary." A smile warmed her face. "I'm glad I have you on my team."

Warmth sloshed in my stomach, eroding some of my earlier guilt. "Thank you."

Take that, Gabriel. He might not have faith in me, but my manager said I was one of her "best employees."

Parker's words followed me all the way across town to my apartment, where Monty snoozed in his vivarium and my manuscript sat, seventy-nine thousand words short of its eighty-thousand word target.

Bartending paid the bills, but like with piano, I wasn't interested in it as a career. Still, it felt good to be good at something. Parker had worked at Valhalla for years; she'd seen plenty of people come and go, and she was impressed by *me*.

I couldn't let her down.

That meant keeping my nose clean, staying focused, and staying far, far away from a certain British billionaire.

But when I climbed into bed that night and fell into a fitful sleep, my dreams had nothing to do with work and everything to do with dark hair and stolen touches.

CHAPTER 7

Isabella

"Romantic comedies are overrated and unrealistic." Sloane frowned at the montage of cute dates and passionate kisses flickering across her TV screen. "They're setting people up for failure with false hopes of happily ever afters and cheesy grand gestures when the average man can't even remember their partner's birthday."

"Uh-huh." I grabbed another handful of extra buttered popcorn from the bowl between us. "But they're fun, and you still watch them."

"I don't watch them. I—"

"*Hate*-watch them," Vivian and I finished in unison.

We were curled up in Sloane's living room, gorging on junk food and half paying attention to the cheesy Christmas rom-com we'd picked for the night. Some people might say it was too early for Christmas movies, but those people would be wrong. It was October, which meant it was practically December.

"That's what you say every time." I popped a fluffy kernel into my mouth, taking care not to drop any crumbs on my laptop. "You're not *entirely* wrong, but there are real-life exceptions. Look at Viv and Dante. They're proof lovestruck men and cheesy grand gestures exist in real life too."

"Hey!" Vivian protested. "His gestures weren't cheesy. They were romantic."

My brow arched in challenge. "Buying you dumplings from the thirty-six best restaurants in New York so you can choose which one you like best? I'd say it's both. Don't worry." I patted her with my free, non-popcorn-filled hand. "I didn't mean it in a bad way."

If anyone deserved extra love and cheesiness in their life, it was Vivian. On the outside, her life seemed perfect. She was beautiful and smart and owned a successful luxury event planning company. She was also heiress to the Lau Jewels fortune, but the money came with a price—she'd had to grow up with Francis and Cecelia Lau, who were, for lack of a better word, total assholes. Her mother constantly criticized her (though less so than before) and her father disowned her after she stood up to him.

Francis was the main reason Vivian and Dante's relationship had had such a rocky start, but luckily, they'd moved past it and were now so sickeningly sweet together my teeth hurt every time I was in their vicinity.

Freaking dumplings. It was so cute and depressing at the same time. I'd never dated anyone who cared enough to remember my favorite food (pasta), much less buy me multiples of it.

If I weren't terrified of inadvertently summoning the devil (thanks to my lola, who took great pains to instill the fear of God in her grandchildren), I'd make voodoo dolls of my worst exes.

Then again...I eyed my laptop.

I had something better than voodoo dolls. I had my words.

"You know what? *Maybe*..." I straightened, my fingers already moving before my brain had the chance to catch up. "I can incorporate Dante and Viv's date in my book somehow."

This was the part I loved about writing. The lightbulb moments that unraveled new sections of the story, bringing it closer to completion. Excitement, motion, *progress*.

It'd been a week since Gabriel's call. I'd yet to hit my daily word counts, but I was getting closer. That morning, I wrote a whopping eighteen hundred words, and if I squeezed in a thousand or so more before movie night ended, I'd meet my target.

Sloane's brows dipped in a frown. "Dumplings in an erotic thriller?"

"Just because it hasn't been done doesn't mean it *can't* be done." My February deadline loomed ever closer, and I was willing to try anything at this point.

"Perhaps one of the characters can choke on one," Vivian suggested, seemingly unfazed by my morbid take on her husband's romantic gesture. "Or they can lace the dumplings with arsenic and feed them to an unsuspecting rival, then dissolve the body with sulfuric acid to hide the evidence."

Sloane and I gaped at her. Out of the three of us, Vivian was the *least* likely to hatch such diabolical ideas.

"Sorry." Her cheeks pinked. "I've been watching a lot of crime shows with Dante. We're trying to find a normal hobby for him that doesn't involve work, sex, or beating people up."

"I thought he outsourced that last part," I half joked, tapping out an obligatory sentence about arsenic. Dante was the CEO of the Russo Group, a luxury goods conglomerate. He was also notorious for his questionable methods of dealing with people who pissed him off. Urban legend said his team beat a would-be burglar to the point where the man was still in a coma years later.

I'd be more concerned about the rumors if he didn't love Vivian so much. One only had to look at him to know he'd rather throw himself off the Empire State Building than hurt her.

Vivian wrinkled her nose. "Funny, but I meant his boxing matches with Kai."

My typing slowed at the mention of Kai's name. "I didn't know they boxed."

He was so neat and proper all the time, but what happened when he stripped away the civility?

An unbidden image flashed through my mind of his torso, naked and gleaming with sweat. Of dark eyes and rough hands and muscles honed through hours in the ring. Glasses off, tie loosened, mouth crushed against mine with heady carnality.

My body sang with sudden heat. I shifted, thighs burning from both my laptop and the fantasies clawing their way through my brain.

"Every week," Vivian confirmed. "Speaking of Dante, he's picking me up soon for dinner at Monarch later. Do you guys want to join us? He's friends with the owner, so we can easily update the reservation."

"What?" I asked, too disoriented by the sharp left turn in my thoughts to catch up to the new topic.

"Monarch," Vivian repeated. "Do you want to come? I know you've been dying to eat there."

Right. Monarch (named after the butterfly, not the royals) was one of the most exclusive restaurants in New York. The wait-list for a table was months long—unless, of course, you were a Russo.

Sloane shook her head. "I have to pick up my new client tonight. He lands in a few hours."

She ran a boutique public relations firm with a roster of high-powered clients, but she usually outsourced her errands. Whoever it was must be *really* important if she was picking them up herself, though she looked distinctly unhappy about the task.

I pushed my laptop off my thighs and lifted my hair off my neck. A welcome breeze swept over my skin, cooling my lust.

"Count me in," I said. "I don't have work tonight."

I didn't love playing third wheel, but I'd be an idiot to turn down a meal at Monarch. It'd been on my restaurant bucket list forever, and it would be a good distraction from my unsettling Kai fantasies.

I couldn't wait to tell Romero—about dinner, not Kai. Besides engineering, my brother's greatest joy in life was food, and he was going to die when—

Wait. Romero.

"Oh my God, I totally forgot!" The adrenaline of remembering a forgotten task surged through me, erasing any lingering thoughts about a certain pesky billionaire. I reached forward and pulled my backpack onto my lap. "I promised Rom I'd give this to you guys to try."

After some rummaging, I triumphantly fished out a high-tech, beautifully ribbed, bright pink dildo.

Two brand-new packaged toys sat at the bottom of my bag, but I liked to show off the goods first, so to speak.

Romero was a senior design engineer at Belladonna, a leading adult toy manufacturer, which was a fancy way of saying he made vibrators and dildos for a living. They relied on testers for early feedback, and somehow, he'd roped me into recruiting my friends for the task.

It wasn't as weird as it sounded on paper. Romero was a total science geek; if you placed a naked supermodel and the newest design software in front of him, his priority would be mastering the software. To him, there was nothing sexual about the toys. They were simply products that needed perfecting before they hit the market.

That being said, *I* didn't test out his designs. Even Romero agreed that would be too creepy, but my friends and acquaintances were fair game.

"No." Sloane pressed her lips together. "I don't need another dildo. I have a whole cabinet of those things, and they take up valuable space."

Like her office, clothing, and pretty much everything else in her life, Sloane's apartment was an exercise in stark minimalism. Besides the television and, well, us, the only sign of life in her white-on-white living room was the oblivious goldfish swimming in the corner. The previous tenant had left it behind, and Sloane had been threatening to flush the Fish (yes, that was its name) down the toilet for the past two years.

"But this is state of the art," I argued, shaking the dildo. "You're one of Romero's most trusted reviewers!"

Unlike Vivian, who softened her feedback with encouraging

words, Sloane specialized in scathing evaluations that dissected each product down to the bone. This was the same woman who wrote multipage critiques of every romantic comedy she watched; her capacity for preempting strangers' hurt feelings hovered somewhere in the negative thirties. On the flip side, if she said she liked something, you knew she wasn't bullshitting you.

After more cajoling, threatening, and bribing in the form of a promise to watch every new Hallmark rom-com with her, I convinced Sloane to continue her reign as Belladonna's most feared and revered tester.

I was still coming down from the high of winning an argument with her when the doorbell rang.

"I'll get it." Vivian was in the bathroom and Sloane was busy scribbling in her notebook—based on how aggressively she was writing, the poor movie was getting eviscerated—so I scrambled off the couch and made my way to the front door.

Thick dark hair, broad shoulders, olive skin. A quick twist of the doorknob revealed Vivian's husband, looking every inch the billionaire CEO in a midnight-black Hugo Boss shirt and pants.

"Hi!" I said brightly. "You're early, but that's okay because the movie just finished. You know, the male lead kind of reminds me of you. Super grumpy with daddy issues and a perpetual frown—until he finds the love of his life, of course."

Actually, the male lead had been a cinnamon roll, but I liked to poke fun at Dante whenever possible. He was so serious all the time, though his disposition had improved dramatically since he married Vivian.

A flush crawled across his sculpted cheekbones and over the bridge of his nose. At first, I thought I'd annoyed him so much he was having a heart attack right there in the hallway, but then I noticed two things in rapid succession.

One, Dante's gaze was fixed on my right hand, which still held the prototype toy from Belladonna. Two, he wasn't alone.

Kai stood behind him, tie straight and suit neatly pressed, his appearance so perfect it was hard to believe he engaged in a sport as brutal as boxing.

My eyes dropped to his hands, searching for bruised knuckles and bloody cuts, but I only saw crisp white cuffs and the glint of an expensive watch. Not a single wrinkle or piece of lint.

Would he exert the same level of fastidious control in the bedroom, or would he abandon it for something more uninhibited?

Both possibilities sent a heady rush through my veins. My grip instinctively tightened around the toy, and I lifted my gaze in time to see Kai's attention drift from my face to the fuchsia dildo with the agonizing speed of a slow-motion car crash.

Silence engulfed the hall. Perhaps it was my imagination, but I could've sworn the dildo vibrated a little despite not being plugged in, like it couldn't contain its excitement from all the attention.

While Dante looked like he'd swallowed a wasp, Kai's expression didn't flicker. I might as well have been holding a piece of fruit or something equally innocuous. Still, heat scorched my cheeks and the back of my neck, making my skin prickle.

"We were testing this," I said. The guys' eyes widened, prompting a hasty clarification. "*Not on each other*. Just...in general. To see how many speeds it has."

Dante shook his head and rubbed a hand over his face. Meanwhile, the corner of Kai's mouth twitched, as if he were constraining a smile.

A bubble of laughter cascaded over my shoulder. I dropped my free hand from the doorknob, turned, and glared at Vivian, who'd returned from the bathroom and was watching me flounder with far too much amusement for a supposed best friend.

"I can't believe you didn't tell me I was still holding this," I said, waving the dildo in the air. Dante let out a choked noise that landed somewhere between a sputtering car engine and a dying cat. "Friends don't let friends answer the door with phallic accessories. Don't come running to me if your husband keels over from cardiac shock."

"How is it my fault?" Vivian protested between laughs. She appeared wholly unconcerned by her husband's imminent demise. "I was in the bathroom. Blame Sloane for not warning you."

I glanced at my other traitorous friend. She'd moved on from her film critique and was glaring at her phone like it'd personally produced, directed, and starred in her most hated rom-coms.

Interrupting Sloane when she was in a foul mood was like tossing a hapless gazelle in front of an enraged lion. *No, thank you*. I liked my head right where it was.

"Kai, are you joining us for dinner?" Vivian asked, drawing my attention back to the hall. Her laughter had finally subsided. She moved next to her husband, who wrapped a protective arm around her waist and dropped a soft kiss on the top of her head. A pang of envy wormed its way into my gut before I banished it. "Like I told the girls, we can easily change the reservation."

"Maybe another night. Dante and I had a meeting nearby, and I just came up to say hi." Kai's gaze flicked toward me for a split second. An answering thrill rippled beneath my skin. "I don't want to crash your date."

"Nonsense. You won't be crashing at all," Vivian said. "Isa's joining us, so it'd actually be perfect. Seating four is easier than seating three."

My shoulders stiffened. The *last* thing I wanted was to sit through an entire meal with Kai. I'd done it before, at a dinner party Dante and Vivian hosted right after they returned from their honeymoon, but that was different. That had been before the piano room. Before dangerous fantasies and accidental touches that tilted my world off its axis.

Kai's eyes rested on mine again. An invisible steel door slammed down around us, shutting out the rest of the world and cocooning us in a bubble of whisper-light breaths and colliding heartbeats.

Goose bumps rose on my skin. But whereas I struggled to maintain a semblance of calm, he regarded me the way a scholar would examine an old but thoroughly forgettable text. A hint of interest, tempered by a sea of indifference.

"In that case," he said, the words like velvet in his cultured voice, "I'm happy to help."

An unwelcome surge of anticipation leaked into my veins, but it was dampened by unease. Dante and Vivian always got lost in their own world, which meant I was facing at least two hours of Kai's uninterrupted company.

"Excellent." Vivian beamed, looking happy over something as simple as a group dinner.

I opened my mouth, then closed it. My desire to experience Monarch warred with trepidation over a night with Kai. On one hand, I refused to let him ruin a bucket list item for me. On the other...

"Guys, I have to go." Sloane came up beside me, so quiet I hadn't heard her approach. Sometime in the past five minutes, she'd tossed a camel Max Mara coat over her blouse and pants and swapped her slippers for a pair of sleek leather boots. "My client landed early."

She nodded a curt greeting at the men and handed me and Vivian our bags, effectively dismissing us.

We were too used to her work emergencies to be offended by her abrupt announcement. Sloane wasn't the warm and fuzzy type, and her face should be stamped next to the dictionary entry for *workaholic*, but if things went to shit, I knew I could count on her. She was fiercely protective of her friends.

"Who is it anyway?" I asked, discreetly dropping the dildo back into my backpack while she locked the door. "Anyone we know?"

Most of her clients were business and society types, but she took on the occasional celebrity like British soccer star Asher

Donovan and the fashion model Ayana (one name only, à la Iman).

"I doubt it," Sloane said as we walked to the elevator. "Unless you follow the *lazy playboys* section of the society pages closely." Her voice seeped with cold disdain.

Okay then. Whoever the client was, he was clearly a sore subject.

Vivian and I fell into step with her while the guys brought up the rear. Normally, I'd pester her for more information, but I was too distracted by the soft footfalls behind me.

The clean, woodsy scent of Kai's cologne drifted over me in a warm rush of air. I swallowed, tingles of awareness scattering over my back. It took every ounce of willpower not to turn around.

No one spoke again until we reached the elevator. The oak-paneled car was built for four at most, and in our jostling to squeeze into the tight space, my hand grazed Kai's.

A golden streak of heat shot through me, electrifying every nerve ending like live wires in the rain. I pulled away, but the phantom thrills remained.

Beside me, Kai stared straight ahead, his face carved from stone. I almost believed he hadn't felt the touch until his hand, the one I'd inadvertently brushed, flexed.

It was a small movement, so quick I would've missed it had I blinked, but it grabbed hold of my lungs and twisted.

The air compressed from my chest. I quickly tore my eyes away and faced forward like a teen who'd been caught watching something inappropriate. The hammering of my heart reached deafening decibels, drowning out Dante, Vivian, and Sloane's chatter.

Out of the corner of my eye, I saw Kai's jaw tense.

The two of us stood there, unmoving and unspeaking, until the doors pinged open and our friends spilled out into the lobby.

Kai and I hesitated in unison before he nodded at the exit in a universal *after you* sign.

I held my breath as I brushed past him, but somehow, his

scent still infiltrated my senses. It muddled my thoughts so much I almost walked into a potted fern on our way out, earning myself strange looks from Vivian and Sloane.

I suppressed a groan, the next two hours stretching in front of me like an endless marathon.

This is going to be a long night.

CHAPTER 8

Kai

I hadn't planned on tagging along with Dante after our meeting, but when he mentioned the Monarch reservation, I'd been curious. My job included checking out the most buzzworthy places in the city, and I'd been putting Monarch off for too long.

Certainly, my decision to abandon a relaxing night in for the somewhat tedious fine dining scene had nothing to do with Dante's casual comment about picking Vivian up from girls' night with her friends.

Sloane had departed for the airport, leaving me and Isabella in the back seat of Dante's car while the newlyweds cozied up in front. Of all the nights, Dante had to choose tonight to drive instead of relying on his chauffeur.

Silence suffocated the air as we inched through Manhattan traffic, interrupted only by the soft patter of rain against glass.

Isabella and I sat as far apart as humanly possible, but it wouldn't matter if the Atlantic Ocean itself separated us. My senses were imprinted with the smell and feel of her—the lush sensuality of roses mixed with the rich warmth of vanilla; the brief, tantalizing glide of her hand against mine; the static charge that clung to my skin every time she was near.

56

It was maddening.

I answered an email about the DigiStream deal and slid my phone into my pocket. I'd been working on acquiring the video streaming app for over a year. It was so close I could taste it, but for once, my thoughts were consumed with something other than business.

I glanced at Isabella. She stared out the window, her fingers drumming an absentminded rhythm against her thigh, her face soft with introspection. Her backpack sat between us like a concrete wall, dividing my runaway thoughts from her unusual quiet.

"How many speeds does it have?"

The drumming stopped. Isabella turned, confusion stamped across her features. "What?"

"Your test at Sloane's house." The memory of her answering the door with that ridiculous pink toy in hand pulled at the corners of my mouth. "How many speeds does it have?"

Although I disapproved of Isabella's distressingly common lack of propriety, part of me was charmed by it. She was so completely, irrepressibly *herself*, like a painting that refused to be dulled by time. It was enthralling.

Color glazed her cheekbones and the tip of her nose. Unlike Vivian's refined elegance or Sloane's icy blond beauty, Isabella's features were a bold, expressive canvas for her emotions. Dark brows pulled together over eyes that sparked with defiance, and her full, red lips pressed into a firm line.

"Twelve," she said, her tone sweet enough to induce a cavity. "I'm happy to lend it to you. It might help loosen you up so you don't die of a stress-induced heart attack before age forty."

I'd much rather have you loosen me up instead.

The thought was so sudden, so absurd and unexpected, it robbed me of a timely response.

First and foremost, I did not require *loosening up*. Yes, my life was quilted with neat squares and perfectly delineated lines, but that was preferable to chaos and whimsy. One wrong tug at the latter, and everything would unravel. I'd worked too hard to let something as unreliable as a passing fancy ruin things.

Second, even if I *did* need to loosen up (which, again, I did not), I would do so with anyone *but* Isabella. She was off-limits, no matter how beautiful or intriguing she was. Not only because of Valhalla's no fraternization rule but because she was going to be the death of me in one way or another.

Still, lust rushed through my veins in all its raw, hot glory at the thought of dipping my head over hers. Of tasting, testing, and exploring whether she was as uninhibited in the bedroom as she was outside it.

Isabella's brows formed questioning arches at my prolonged silence.

Fuck. I tamped down my traitorous desire with an iron will cultivated from years at Oxbridge and wrestled back control over my faculties.

"Thank you, but on my list of items I'd never borrow, adult toys rank at the top," I said, my placid tone a deceptive shield for the storm brewing inside me.

She shifted to face me fully. Her skirt slid up, baring another inch of perfect, bronzed skin.

My blood burned hotter, and a muscle flexed in my jaw before I caught myself. Who wore skirts without tights in the middle of an unseasonably cold October? *Only Isabella.*

"What else is on the list?" She sounded genuinely curious.

"Socks, underwear, razors, and cologne." I rattled off the answers, keeping my eyes planted firmly on her face.

Those expressive dark brows hiked higher. "Cologne?"

"Every gentleman has a signature cologne. Pilfering someone else's signature would be considered the height of rudeness."

Isabella stared at me for a full five seconds before a burst of laughter filled the car. "My God. I can't believe you're real."

The throaty, unabashed sound of her mirth hit me somewhere in the chest and spread like melting butter through my veins.

"If that were the case, fragrance brands would go out of business left and right," she said. "Imagine if every product only had one customer."

"Ah, but you're overlooking an important part of what I said." The arch of my brow matched hers. "I said every *gentleman*, not every person."

She rolled her eyes. "You are such a snob."

"Hardly. It's a matter of comportment, not status. I meet plenty of CEOs and aristocrats who are anything but gentlemen."

"And you think you're an exception?"

I couldn't help it. A wicked smile touched my lips. "Only in certain situations."

I spotted the instant my meaning registered. Isabella's high color returned, washing her face in a lovely bloom of pink. Her lips parted in an audible breath, and despite my better instincts, dark satisfaction curled through my chest at her reaction.

I wasn't the only one tortured by our attraction.

She opened her mouth right as the engine cut off, swallowing her words and abruptly severing our link.

We'd arrived at Monarch.

I hid a twinge of disappointment when a valet hurried over to us and took the keys from Dante. By the time I turned back to Isabella, she'd already exited the car.

I released a controlled breath and tucked the wayward emotion into a padlocked box before following her into the building.

It was better that I didn't know what she'd been about to say. I shouldn't have slipped up and teased her in the first place, but there was a growing civil war between my logic and my emotions where Isabella was concerned. Luckily, Dante and Vivian were too deep in newlywed land to notice anything amiss.

The elevator whisked us up to the top floor of the skyscraper, where Monarch overlooked the sprawling expanse of Central Park.

Since we were early for our reservation, the maître d' offered us complimentary glasses of champagne while we waited in the well-appointed entryway. I was the only one who declined. I wanted a clear head tonight, and God knew Isabella's presence was intoxicating enough.

My phone lit up with two new emails—a follow-up about DigiStream and logistics for the upcoming executive leadership retreat. Things had been suspiciously quiet since my mother announced the CEO vote, but I'd bet my first edition set of Charles Dickens novels that at least one of the other candidates would make their move at the retreat.

"Kai?"

I glanced up. A somewhat familiar-looking woman stood in front of me with an expectant smile. Late twenties, long black hair, brown eyes, a distinctive beauty mark at the corner of her mouth.

Recognition clicked into place with a breath of surprise.

Clarissa, my childhood neighbor and, judging by the number of articles she'd forwarded me regarding Clarissa's philanthropic efforts and accomplishments, my mother's first choice for daughter-in-law.

"Sorry, I realize it's been a long time since we last saw each other." She laughed. "It's Clarissa Teo. From London? You look almost exactly the same—" Her eyes flicked over me in appreciation. "But I realize I've changed quite a bit since the last time we saw each other."

That was an understatement. Gone was the awkward, braces-wearing teen I remembered. In her place was an elegant, polished woman with a beauty pageant smile and an outfit straight out of a society magazine.

I declined to mention I'd googled her last week, though she looked almost as different in person as she did from her teenage years. Softer, smaller, less stiff.

"Clarissa. Of course, it's so good to see you," I said smoothly, masking my surprise. According to my mother's unsolicited updates, she wasn't supposed to arrive in New York until next week. "How are you?"

We made small talk for a few minutes. Apparently, she'd moved to the city earlier than planned to help with a big, upcoming exhibition at the Saxon Gallery, where she was in charge of artist relations. She was staying at the Carlyle until they finished renovations at her new brownstone, and she was nervous about moving to a new city but lucky to have found a mentor in Buffy Darlington, the well-respected grande dame of New York society, whom she was meeting for dinner tonight. Buffy was running late because of an emergency with her dog.

I'd had dozens of similar conversations over the years, but I feigned as much interest as possible until Clarissa started comparing the pros and cons of Malteses versus Pomeranians.

"Forgive me. I forgot to introduce you to my friends." I cut her off neatly when she paused for a breath. "Everyone, this is Clarissa Teo, a family friend. She just moved to the city. Clarissa, this is Dante and Vivian Russo and Isabella Valencia."

They exchanged polite greetings. Full name introductions were common in our circles, where a person's family said more about them than their occupation, clothes, or car.

More small talk, plus a hint of awkwardness when Clarissa slid a quizzical glance at Isabella. She'd recognized Dante and Vivian, but she clearly didn't know what to make of Isabella, whose violet highlights and leather skirt were the antithesis of her own classic neutrals and pearls.

"We should catch up over lunch soon," Clarissa said when the maître d' announced our table was ready, saving us from further stilted chatter. "It's been too long."

"Yes, I'll give you a call." I offered a polite smile. "Enjoy the rest of your night."

My mother had already given us each other's number "just in case." I wasn't looking forward to another round of small talk, but encounters with old acquaintances after a long time were always strange. Perhaps I wasn't giving Clarissa enough credit. She could very well be a brilliant conversationalist.

"Ex-girlfriend?" Isabella asked as we walked to our table.

"Childhood neighbor."

"Future girlfriend then."

A small arch of my brow. "That's quite a leap to make."

"But I'm not wrong. She seems like the type of woman you'd date." Isabella took her seat next to Vivian, directly across from me. Her words contained no judgment, only a stark matter-of-factness that rankled more than it should've.

"You seem quite interested in my love life." I snapped my napkin open and laid it across my lap. "Why is that?"

She snorted. "I'm not interested. I was just making an observation."

"About my love life."

"I'm not sure you *have* a love life," Isabella said. "I've never heard you talk about women or seen you at the club with a date."

"I like to keep my *private life* private, but it's nice to know you've been keeping such close tabs on my alleged lack of female company." My mouth curved, an automatic response to her adorable sputter before I wrangled it into a straight line.

No smiling. No thinking anything she does is adorable.

"You have an overinflated sense of your own importance." Isabella canted her chin higher. "And FYI, the private life excuse only works for celebrities and politicians. I promise there are fewer people interested in your paramours than you think."

"Good to know." This time, my smile broke free of its restraints at her tangible indignation. "Congratulations on being one of those lucky few."

"You're insufferable."

"But imagine how much more insufferable I'd be if I were a celebrity or politician."

A glint of amusement coasted through Isabella's eyes. Her cheeks dimpled for a millisecond before she pursed her lips and shook her head, and I was struck with the overwhelming urge to coax those dimples out of her again.

Beside us, Dante and Vivian's heads swiveled back and forth like spectators at a Wimbledon match. I'd almost forgotten they were there. Dante's brows knotted in confusion, but Vivian's eyes sparkled suspiciously with delight.

Before I could investigate further, our server approached, bread basket in hand. The cloud of tension hovering over the table dissipated, and as dinner progressed, our conversation eased into more neutral topics—the food, the latest society scandal, our upcoming holiday plans.

Dante and Vivian were heading to St. Barth's; I was undecided. I usually returned to London for Christmas, but depending on how things went with DigiStream, I might have to stay in New York.

Part of me relished the idea of a quiet season with only work, books, and perhaps the occasional Broadway show to keep me company. Big holiday gatherings were highly overrated, in my opinion.

"What about you, Isa?" Vivian asked. "Are you heading back to California this year?"

"No, I'm not going home until February for my mother's birthday," Isabella said. A brief shadow crossed her face before she smiled again. "It's so close to Christmas and Lunar New Year that we usually wrap all three celebrations together into one giant weekend. My mom makes these *amazing* turon rolls, and we go to the beach the morning after her party to unwind..."

I brought my glass to my lips as she talked about her family traditions. Part of me hungered for insights into her background the way a beggar hungered for food. What had her childhood been like? How close was she to her brothers? Were they similar to Isabella, or did their personalities diverge as siblings' so often did? I wanted to know everything—every memory, every piece and detail that would help solve the puzzle of my fascination with her.

But another, larger part of me couldn't forget the shadow. The brief glimpse of darkness beneath the bright, bubbly exterior. It called to me like the light at the end of a tunnel, heralding salvation or damnation.

A booming laugh from another table pulled me out of my spiral.

I gave my head a tiny shake and set my glass down, annoyed by how many of my recent waking moments were occupied with thoughts of Isabella.

I reached for the salt in the middle of the table, determined to enjoy my meal like it was a normal dinner. Isabella, who'd ceded the conversation to Vivian's recounting of her and Dante's sailing adventures in Greece, reached for the pepper. Our hands brushed again, a facsimile of our elevator graze.

I stilled. Like the first time, an electric shiver ran up my arm, burning away logic, rationality, *reason.*

The restaurant faded as our eyes locked with a near audible *click,* two magnets drawn together by force rather than free will.

If it were up to free will, I would continue with dinner like nothing happened because nothing *had* happened. It was simply a touch, as innocent as an accidental bump on the sidewalk. It shouldn't have the power to turn my blood into liquid fire or reach inside my chest and twist my lungs into knots.

Fuck.

"Excuse me." I abruptly stood, ignoring Dante's and Vivian's startled looks. Isabella dropped her hand and refocused on her food, her cheeks pink. "I'll be right back."

A bead of sweat formed on my brow as I strode through the dining room. I pushed my shirtsleeves to my elbows; I was burning up.

When I reached the bathroom, I removed my glasses and splashed ice-cold water on my face until my pulse slowed to normal.

What the hell was happening to me?

For a year, I'd successfully kept Isabella at an arm's length. She was the opposite of everything I considered proper, a complication I didn't need. Her flamboyance, her chattiness, her incessant talk about sex in public venues...

Her laugh, her scent, her smile. Her talent for piano and the way her eyes light up when she's excited. They were the most dangerous kind of drug, and I feared I was already sliding down the slippery slope of addiction.

I let out a soft groan and wiped my face dry with a paper towel.

I blamed that cursed Monday two weeks ago. If I hadn't been so caught off guard by the CEO vote's announcement and timing, I wouldn't have sought out Isabella at Valhalla. If I hadn't sought her out, I wouldn't have overheard her in the piano room. If I hadn't overheard her in the piano room, I wouldn't be taking refuge in a public restroom, trying to hold myself together after a two-second touch.

I allowed myself another minute to cool down before I put on my glasses, opened the door—and ran straight into the devil herself.

We collided with the force of a football tackle—my arm around her waist, her hands braced against my forearms, the air vibrating with a disturbing sense of déjà vu.

My heartrate surged even as I silently cursed the universe for constantly throwing us at each other. Literally.

Isabella blinked up at me, her eyes like rich pools of chocolate in the dim light. "I was right," she said. Her playful voice contained a hint of breathiness that wound its way through my chest in smoky tendrils. "You *are* stalking me."

Christ, this woman was something else.

"We happened to exit the restroom at the same time. It could hardly be classified as stalking," I said with infinite patience. "Might I remind you I left the table first? If anything, I should ask if you're stalking me."

"Fine," she acceded. "But what about when you followed me to the piano room? *Twice*?"

A dull throb sprang up behind my temple. I suddenly wished I'd never agreed to dinner. "How many times are you going to bring that up?"

"As many times as it takes for you to give me a straight answer." Isabella stood on tiptoes, bringing her face closer to mine. Every muscle in my body tensed. "Kai Young, do you have a crush on me?"

Absolutely not. The mere idea was absurd, and I should've told her so immediately. But the words wouldn't come out, and I hesitated long enough for Isabella's eyes to widen. Their teasing glint dimmed, giving way to what looked like alarm.

Irritation ignited in my chest. I wasn't romantically interested in her—my interest was intellectual, nothing else—but was the prospect *that* terrible?

"We're not in high school," I said, voice tight. "I don't get crushes."

"That's still not a straight answer."

My back teeth clenched. Before I could inform her that my response had, in fact, been a straight answer if she read between the lines, a low buzz filled the air, followed by an ominous flicker of lights. A low, collective murmur swelled in the dining room.

Isabella stiffened, her fingers curling around my biceps. My pulse thudded against my veins. "What is—"

She didn't get a chance to finish her sentence before another buzz traveled the hall, high-pitched and angry, like a saw tearing through wood.

Then, with a final, sputtering flicker, the lights died completely.

CHAPTER 9

Isabella

A few screams from the dining room shredded the restaurant's hushed elegance into tatters. I gasped—not at the cries or the sudden death of light, but at the weight of a solid, muscled male body caging me against the wall.

One minute, I was teasing Kai as payback for his toy question in the car; the next, I was pressed flush against him, chest to chest, thigh to thigh, my lungs inundated with the heady scent of wood and citrus.

Our proximity carried me back to last week, when we'd found ourselves in a similar position in the piano room. Only this time, it was no accident.

The world went hazy at the edges as we stood there, frozen, Kai's body forming a protective shield over mine. No words, just the rapid rise and fall of our breaths and the adrenaline leaking into the air like battery acid. It ate away at the fog until my senses sharpened enough to distinguish shapes in the darkness.

I tipped my chin up, my heart giving another unsteady thump when I saw Kai staring back at me. It was too dark to make out the individual contours of his face, but that didn't matter. I'd already committed them to memory—the elegant slash of his cheekbones, the sculpted ruthlessness of his mouth, the heat simmering beneath the cool veil of dark, inscrutable eyes.

The lights had gone out—nothing nefarious, but shocking enough to trigger a flight-or-fight response—and his first instinct had been to shield me.

My heart squeezed. I fisted a handful of tailored cotton and swallowed past the dry husk of my throat. Despite the power outage, electricity sizzled around us, one spark away from catching fire.

Kai shifted, his arm curling around me like he could sense the tension creeping into my frozen muscles. At first glance, he might appear soft, all quiet politeness and scholarly charm, but he had the body of a fighter. Hard and lean, corded with muscles draped in the most elegant of fabrics. A wolf disguised in sheep's clothing.

And yet, my inner alarms remained silent, my body pliant. For all the theoretical danger he posed, I'd never felt safer.

A buzz and the darkness vanished as suddenly as it'd materialized. Light seared my eyes; when I blinked away the disorientation, my dreamy, cocooned haze evaporated alongside it.

Kai and I stared at each other for an extra beat before we pulled back with the haste of people who'd accidentally touched a hot stove.

Oxygen rushed into my lungs, amplifying the thunder in my ears.

"We should head back—"

"They're probably wondering where—"

Our voices tripped over each other in a cacophony of noise. Flags of color glazed Kai's cheekbones, and his jaw tightened before he inclined his head toward the end of the hall.

Neither of us spoke during our walk back to the dining room, but the air weighed heavy with unspoken words. The side of my body facing him tingled with awareness. I hated how he could do that—make me feel so much when I'd vowed not to feel anything again toward men like him.

Rich, good-looking, and far too dangerous for my mental and emotional health.

"There you are," Vivian said when we returned to our table. "Wasn't that wild? I'm glad the restaurant was able to fix the outage so quickly."

In reality, the power outage had lasted less than five minutes, but time stretched so languorously when Kai and I were alone that I was genuinely surprised the restaurant seemed so *normal*. The earlier screams had subsided as quickly as they'd erupted, and other than a few rattled-looking diners, everyone was carrying on as if the blackout never happened.

"Do you know what caused it?" I smoothed my napkin over my lap and avoided looking at Kai, afraid even the tiniest glance would expose the tumultuous emotions whirling inside me.

The stab of jealousy at seeing him with Clarissa earlier, the breathlessness when we'd touched, the sensation of sinking into a deep, warm bath I never wanted to get out of when he held me. I shouldn't be feeling any of those things, but I'd never been great at sticking to *shoulds*.

It was damn hard to keep someone out of my mind when life insisted on pushing us into each other's path whenever possible.

"I'm guessing it was an electrical issue, but they have a backup generator." Dante shook his head. "Of all the fucking nights for something like that to happen, it had to be tonight."

"It didn't disrupt our meal too much," Vivian said, always the voice of reason. "I'm glad it wasn't anything serious. The restaurant offered everyone a complimentary reservation that..."

I tuned her out. I was too busy making sure no part of my body touched Kai's above or below the table. Judging by the stiff set of his shoulders, he was doing the same.

Nerves rattled in my stomach. *Dammit.*

I reached for my wine and took a big gulp, ignoring Vivian's glance of surprise. I wasn't a big wine person, but I had at least one more hour in Kai's company.

I needed all the help I could get.

CHAPTER 10

Isabella

The rest of dinner at Monarch passed without incident, but that was the last time I saw Kai for another week.

He didn't show up for his usual Thursday night drink at the bar, and I told myself I didn't care. There'd been a time when I would've taken Kai's aloofness as a challenge and dove headfirst into a forbidden fling, but I wasn't that girl anymore.

No, the *new* Isabella was responsible. Focused. She had direction, and she would prove her oldest, know-it-all brother wrong if it killed her.

"Stop ignoring his calls, Isa." Felix walked past with an armful of fuzzy red tubes. "You know he won't stop until you answer."

My phone vibrated with another insistent buzz, underscoring his point.

I ignored it, as I had all morning. I'd learned my lesson after picking up Gabriel's last call and getting saddled with a ridiculous deadline for my book.

I bet my favorite black leather boots he was calling to check on my progress. Unlike normal people, Gabriel texted for emergencies and called for bullshit, so I wasn't worried about a health scare for Mom or an earthquake destroying our family home in California.

"That's precisely why I'm not answering," I told Felix. "I like to imagine his face getting all red and sweaty like that time I shrunk his favorite dress shirt when he came home from college."

My second-oldest brother laughed and shook his head.

Of all my siblings, he was the one I was closest to. Not in terms of age (that would be Romero) or temperament (that would be Miguel), but in terms of sheer compatibility. Unlike anal-retentive Gabriel, Felix was so laid-back no one would believe he was a renowned artist.

He lived in L.A.'s hip Silver Lake neighborhood most of the year, but he kept a small art studio/apartment in New York since he had so many shows here. He'd landed yesterday and was busy putting the final touches on his sculpture for some big art show next month.

Since I hated working in silence, I'd crashed his studio time with my laptop, a bag of Sour Patch Kids, and a ruthless determination to finish chapter ten before my shift. I was finally making progress on my book, and I wanted to wring out every bit of momentum before it inevitably fizzled out on me.

"Be nice, Isa. It's probably nothing." Felix twisted two of the red tubes into a double helix shape. He'd tried to explain the sculpture's symbolism earlier, and I'd nearly passed out from boredom. As much as I loved him, I wasn't built for that type of art appreciation. "I bet he wants to know what you're buying Mom for her birthday so we don't accidentally double up."

I hadn't told him about the manuscript ultimatum, and I'm guessing Gabriel hadn't either.

"We won't. The day we come to an agreement on anything, including gifts, is the day hell experiences an Arctic freeze." I switched topics before Felix could probe further. He was the peacemaker of the family, so he was always trying to wrangle us into some semblance of harmony. "Speaking of Mom's birthday, are you bringing your new girlfriend?"

"Maybe," Felix said noncommittally. He went through girl-friends like candy, so it wouldn't surprise me if he had a new one by the time February rolled around. "What about you? Mom's been banging on about your love life since..."

Him.

The unspoken word hung between us like a guillotine poised to drop. It dug into my bones, excavating memories long buried beneath piles of guilt and shame while a thick lump clinched my throat.

The clink of ice against glass. The gleam of a signet ring beneath the lights. The echoes of a deep voice whispering all the words I'd wanted to hear.

I love you. I miss you. We'll go away, just the two of us.

A fantasy that ended in tears, blood, and betrayal. Two years later, I was still grappling with the fallout from my younger self's stupid decisions.

The lump expanded, pressing against my nose and the backs of my eyes until the studio blurred.

I blinked away my tears and typed a random word just so I had something to do. "No. I don't bring guys home anymore."

For a brief, unbidden moment, dark eyes and a crisp British accent flashed through my mind before I batted them away.

Kai and I weren't lovers. We weren't even friends. He had no business invading my thoughts like that.

When I looked up again, Felix was watching me with his signature knowing stare. "It's been two years," he said gently. "You can't let that asshole ruin your trust in relationships forever."

I shook my head. "That's not it." He'd shared similar senti-ments before, and my lies tasted less bitter every time I uttered them. It wasn't that I didn't trust relationships as a concept; it was more that I didn't trust myself. But he didn't need to know that. "I've been busy. You know, with work and the book."

I could tell he didn't believe me, but in true Felix fashion, he didn't press the issue. "Well, if you change your mind, let me know. I have single friends."

That pulled a genuine smile out of me. "You're the only brother I know who would willingly set up their sister with a friend. Also thanks, but no thanks. I would rather die."

I shuddered at the thought of sleeping with anyone who was associated with a family member in any way. I was a firm believer in the separation of church (the sanctity of my sex life) and state (surveillance from my mother and overprotective brothers).

"I'm an excellent judge of character," Felix said, unfazed by my disgust. "I wouldn't set you up with someone you wouldn't like."

"I'm not worried about that because you're not setting me up with anyone." I glanced at the top corner of my screen and cursed when I saw the time. "Shit! I have to go. I'm going to be late for work!"

So much for finishing chapter ten.

I scrambled off the couch, shoved my laptop into my bag, and rushed to the exit. Felix's studio was downtown; Valhalla was uptown. It'd take me at least forty-five minutes to get there via subway, barring any delays or disruptions.

"You're coming to my exhibition, right?" Felix called after me. "They're finalizing the guest list today."

I waved a hand over my shoulder. "I'll be there!"

By the time I swiped my card at the nearest subway station, I was out of breath and drenched with sweat beneath my coat. Parker was laid-back about most things, but she was a tyrant when it came to punctuality. She'd fired my predecessor for showing up ten minutes late after a train fire.

Luckily, the transportation gods were on my side, and I made it to Valhalla Club with minutes to spare.

My relief was short-lived, however, because when I stepped behind the counter, I immediately caught Tessa's worried expression. She widened her eyes at me and flicked them toward the bar.

I followed her gaze, down...down...all the way to the man

seated with a smug smile and eyes fixed on me like a predator spotting prey.

Oh, fuck.

~

"Isabella." The cold, oily voice sent a thousand invisible insects skittering over my skin. "You're looking lovely tonight."

"Thank you." My smile was tight enough to double as a Victorian-era corset. "What can I get for you, Mr. Black?"

Victor Black assessed me with those flat dark eyes. He was the CEO of Black & Co., a media company whose tabloids made the *National Enquirer* look like Pulitzer material. He technically belonged to Valhalla's D.C. chapter, but he visited New York often. Unfortunately.

"Sex on the Beach." A grin snaked across his face. The army of insects bred and multiplied. "My favorite."

"Coming right up." I ignored the obvious double entendre and went to work making the drink. The sooner I finished, the sooner I could get away from him.

Late thirties, slicked-back hair, flashy clothes. Victor was objectively decent-looking, but something about him always gave me the creeps. Maybe it was the way he looked at me like he was envisioning the dirtiest things he could get away with doing to me, or maybe it was the relentless come-ons despite my obvious disinterest.

Tessa sent me a sympathetic look from down the bar. She knew how much I disliked him, but he always insisted on having me serve him when he was here, so there was nothing she could do.

"What are your plans for this weekend?" Victor asked. "I'm in town until Monday, and I know of a few interesting events coming up."

I'm sure you do. I bet they involved little to no clothes and high hopes for his overeager dick.

"I'm working," I said, which was the truth. I got the best tips on the weekends, so I always said yes to Fridays and Saturdays.

"I'm sure you could take a night or two off."

My smile could've frozen the inside of a volcano as I handed him his drink. "Unfortunately, I have bills to pay, so no, I can't." It was as rude as I allowed myself to be toward a club member. Most of them were petty and egotistical enough to get someone fired because of a "bad attitude," including Victor.

"There are other ways to pay your bills." Victor deliberately brushed my hand when he took the glass from me. A shiver of disgust ran down my spine. "For example, I can be quite generous in certain situations."

His meaning was clear.

Waves of nausea tossed in my stomach like a ship during a storm. I would rather fucking die than ever let Victor Black put his hands on me.

"Thank you for the thought, but as I'm sure you know, fraternization between members and employees is a flagrant violation of Valhalla's rules." My frosty reply contrasted with the anger simmering in my veins. I wished I could toss the nearest drink in his face or, better yet, slap him so hard it knocked the slimy thoughts right out of his head, but like I said, I had bills to pay and a job to keep. "Now, if that's all, I have other customers who require my attention."

I only made it two steps when his hand latched around my wrist.

The nausea intensified, coupled with a surge of adrenaline that pounded in my ears. It took every ounce of willpower not to deck him in the face with my free hand.

"Rules don't apply to me," Victor said casually, as if he weren't holding me hostage in a room full of witnesses. Arrogance gleamed bright and cold in his eyes. "I can—"

"Let her go, Victor." A familiar smooth, aristocratic voice sliced through my tension like a freshly honed blade through silk. "It's unbecoming to manhandle someone, even for you."

Victor's face darkened, but he wasn't stupid enough to cause a scene with another member. He dropped my hand and turned.

Kai stood behind him, tie pin-straight, handkerchief crisply folded in his jacket pocket, and eyes diamond-hard as they pinned the other man against his seat.

Warmth rushed to the pit of my stomach, erasing some of my disgust at Victor's touch.

"It's nice to see you taking advantage of our intraclub network," Kai said, his voice deceptively pleasant despite the quiet fury rolling off him in waves. "But I would be remiss not to remind you of our no-harassment policy. Violate it, and your network access will be terminated. Violate it with the wrong person, and you'll be permanently banned from Valhalla." A polite smile, colder than the northernmost reaches of the Arctic. "You know what happens to excommunicated members, don't you?"

Victor's lips thinned. I didn't know what happened to excommunicated members, but the threat was enough to quiet him despite the murderous resentment brimming in his eyes.

"Perhaps you should take a breather elsewhere in the club." Kai smoothed a hand over his tie. "There's a lovely jazz performance happening in the music lounge."

I didn't relax until Victor disappeared through the exit, leaving a trail of choked bitterness in his wake.

Kai took his vacated seat. A buzz sparked in the air, and my heart twisted into a position that would've made my old yoga teacher proud.

"Thank you," I said quietly. "You didn't have to do that."

Most people would take the rich, powerful person's side even if they were in the wrong. Others would simply turn a blind eye, especially for something as "small" as a wrist grab. I was female, a minority, and an employee. I held the least amount of power in situations like the one with Victor, and while what Kai did was the bare minimum in some respects, the sad truth was that a majority couldn't even do that.

"I don't know what you mean," Kai said, his tone mild. "I simply reminded him of the club rules, per my duty as a member of the managing committee."

A smile edged onto my lips. "Taxing work."

"Positively grueling. But I try my best."

"So grueling you missed your standing appointment here last Thursday?" The words fell out of their own accord. I wished I could snatch them back the instant they left my mouth, but it was too late.

The remnants of Kai's stony expression melted, revealing a flicker of warm pleasure that had my toes curling in my boots.

"Keeping tabs on me again, Isabella?"

The velvety way he said my name was almost indecent, conjuring images of lazy afternoons and silken sheets. Of hands sliding up my thighs and kisses trailing down my neck, his mouth doing wicked things to my body while he thrust inside me. Over and over, until—

Fuck.

Heat ignited between my thighs. My fingers curled around the counter, but I shrugged off his question and forced myself not to break his knowing stare. "Only so I can avoid you. Anyone who translates classics into Latin for fun terrifies me."

A laugh crinkled the corners of his eyes, and my pulse jumped in response. It was turning into a Pavlovian situation at this point. Anytime Kai did something, my traitorous body reacted like it'd been struck by lightning.

"I'm happy to report there'll be no translations today, but if it makes you feel better, I work on genre fiction too. I translated a Nora Roberts novel once. It was a refreshing change of pace."

"It doesn't, but thank you for that detail. Come back to me when you've translated dinosaur erotica."

Kai blinked. "I'm sorry?"

"Never mind." I didn't want to push him too far, too fast. The poor man would probably have a heart attack if he discovered some of the books floating outside his literary bubble. "You know, you never told me why you came in on a Monday the other week."

It'd been nagging at me since it happened. I had more important things to worry about, but not knowing the reason bothered the hell out of me, like trying and failing to remember the name of a song that sat on the tip of my tongue.

Kai recovered admirably fast from my dinosaur erotica quip. "Does it matter?"

"Maybe not in the grand scheme of things, but I'm a bartender, which means I'm also a good sounding board and therapist." I poured his scotch and slid the glass across the counter. "A few days ago, I consoled a ramen noodle heiress because she couldn't find her driver in the rain and had to use her hundred-thousand-dollar handbag as a makeshift umbrella. The worst part was..." I lowered my voice. "The bag was a super special limited edition, and the designer refused to make her another one."

"Ah, the classic handbag dilemma," Kai said sympathetically. "What a tragedy."

"The gravest kind. We should alert the Red Cross."

"You call, I'll email. We should cover all the bases for a case of this magnitude."

My smile blossomed into a full-fledged grin. I hated to admit it, but Kai was tolerable when he wasn't being an uptight stick in the mud. More than tolerable, in fact.

"I'll answer your question, but I have to warn you, my secrets aren't as interesting as you presume." He took a sip of his drink. "I learned my company's CEO vote is happening earlier than I'd expected." His words sparked a hazy memory of a *Wall Street Journal* article I'd read a few weeks ago. I usually skipped straight to the style section, but Kai's photo had been front and center on the website. I couldn't resist a peek, which I soon regretted. The article had been boring as hell.

"How much earlier?" I asked.

"Years. I hadn't expected to take over until I was forty."

Kai was only thirty-two.

"Well, that's a good thing, right?" I reasoned. "It's like an early promotion."

Provided he won the vote, which he likely would. I had a feeling Kai Young never lost at anything.

A corner of his mouth tipped up. "That's one way of looking at it, but if you knew my mother, you'd know she would never give up power this early. She says everything is fine, but..."

His eyes clouded, and my breath stilled when I pieced together the rest of his sentence. "You're worried she's sick."

A pause, then a slight dip of his chin.

"She won't tell me if she is," he said. "Not until she can't hide it anymore. She hates being pitied more than anything in the world."

A deep, unsettling ache unfurled behind my ribs at the strain in his voice.

There was nothing more gut-wrenching than losing a parent. I wasn't sure what was worse—the long, drawn-out wait for the inevitable, as with terminal diseases and illnesses, or the sudden rupture of a family, as with accidents and cruel strokes of fate.

Sometimes, I wished my father had been sick. At least then, we would've been prepared instead of having him yanked from us without warning.

One minute, he was there, his face filled with loving indulgence as I begged him to take me to Disneyland for my birthday. The next, he was gone. His hopes, his fears, his dreams and memories all reduced to a hollow shell of a body lying among twisted heaps of rubber and metal.

Maybe it was selfish of me. I wouldn't have wanted him to suffer, but I also never got to say goodbye...

I swallowed the knot of emotion in my throat and forced a smile. I could wallow in the past later, when there wasn't someone else who had more pressing concerns sitting in front of me.

"There could be dozens of other reasons why she's stepping down early," I said in an attempt to make Kai feel better. "For instance, she could be getting blackmailed. Or maybe she met a hot young stud on vacation and wants to spend the rest of her days cavorting with him in the Bahamas instead of listening to boring sales reports." I paused, my brow furrowing. "Your parents are divorced, right?" I remembered reading something to that effect online. "If they aren't, forget what I just said and stick with the blackmail."

"They're separated, but close enough." A ray of amusement peeked through the cloud in Kai's eyes. "It's odd that I'm hoping for blackmail, isn't it?"

"Nope. It's the most easily solvable out of the options, and I'm guessing you don't want to think about your mom's sex life."

Kai blanched.

"Right. Well, if it does end up being blackmail, let me know after you've dealt with it. I need some good ideas for my book."

Those knowing dark eyes sharpened. "What book?"

Shit. I hadn't meant to let that slip, but it was too late to take it back.

"I'm writing an erotic thriller." I tucked my hair behind my ear with a self-conscious hand. I didn't like talking about it with anyone except Sloane and Vivian. They wouldn't judge me, but some people got so uppity about genre fiction. Either that, or they would ask me a million questions about my agent, publisher, and release date, none of which I had. "I've been working on it for a while, but I'm stuck."

I'd made decent headway since Gabriel's call. It was more than what I'd written in the past two months, but it wasn't enough. Not if I wanted to finish before my mom's birthday.

Kai's eyes fastened on mine. To my surprise, I only saw curiosity and a touch of sympathy. No judgment. "Stuck on which part?"

"Everything." I didn't know why I was telling him this, but something about today felt different from our previous interactions. Easier, more comfortable. "The plot, the characters..." *What I want to do with my life.* "Sometimes it feels like I forgot how to string a few words together, but I'll figure it out."

Maybe if I said it enough times, it would come true.

"I'm sure you will." A faint smile touched Kai's lips. "You chose well. Of all the genres, erotic thriller suits you best."

My eyes narrowed. "Was that an insult or a compliment?"

"It's however you want to take it," he said in that infuriatingly enigmatic tone. "So why did you choose writing? I must admit, I pictured you in a more...social profession."

It was a small, stupid thing, but the fact that he called it my profession even though I hadn't published anything made my heart squeeze a little.

For that alone, I let his earlier ambiguous comment slide. "I wasn't a big reader growing up, but I was going through a hard time a few years ago and needed something to take my mind off what was happening." Work stress, the flaming fallout from my last breakup, seeing all my high school friends get engaged and realizing my father would never walk me down the aisle...it hadn't been a good time. "One of my old coworkers lent me her favorite thriller, and the rest is history."

Some people escaped into romance, others into fantasy, but I found thrillers oddly comforting. Sure, I was lost in life and scraping by on minimum wage in one of the most expensive cities in the world, but at least I wasn't trapped in a cabin with a psychopathic husband or on the run from a serial killer who was obsessed with me.

It was all about perspective.

"Now all I have to do is finish my own," I said. "Then I can quit and kick Victor Black in the balls without worrying about losing my job."

Kai's smile notched up another inch, but his eyes remained serious behind his glasses. "You'll finish it." He said it with such unflinching certainty that my heart stilled for a split second.

"How do you know?" I hated the note of self-doubt in my voice.

I'd always been the social butterfly, the person who cheered my friends on and pushed them to step outside their comfort zone. But there were nights when I lay awake, stripped of all confidence and pretense, wondering who the hell I was and what I was doing. Had I chosen the wrong path? Was there even a right path for me, or was I destined to drift through life like an aimless ghost? No meaning, no purpose, just day after day of routine and drudgery. A life wasted on bad decisions and short-term highs.

The familiar vise of anxiety clamped around my chest.

"I know," Kai said, his calm voice pulling me out of my poorly timed existential spiral. "Because you're too strong not to. You might not think so, but you are. Also..." A glint of mischief cracked his sober expression. "You tell great stories, condom varieties notwithstanding."

He laughed when I tossed a cocktail napkin at him.

Heat seared my cheeks, but it was nothing compared to the warmth flooding my veins.

I was seeing a different side of Kai, and I liked it. Too much.

More than I should.

CHAPTER 11

I took Clarissa to the Valhalla Club's annual fall gala for our first date. It was a risky move, considering how big the event was, but I couldn't put it off any longer. The messages from my mother piled up by the day, and I needed to take my mind off a certain brunette with a penchant for impropriety and a smile that'd lodged itself into my consciousness.

So far, it wasn't working.

"This branch is so different from the London chapter." Clarissa swept her eyes around the gilded ballroom. Last year's gala theme focused on the Roaring Twenties; this year's paid homage to ancient Rome, complete with towering marble columns, a miniature Colosseum, and free-flowing wine. "Our parties are less... ostentatious."

"New York is Valhalla's flagship. They like to show it off." I glanced at the far side of the room. A crowd had already formed around the bar, blocking my view of whoever was on duty tonight.

I'd resisted checking whether Isabella was working the gala earlier, but now, I wished I'd given in to my earlier temptations.

Clarissa was perfectly nice. Unlike our awkward reunion at Monarch, our conversation tonight had flowed easily from our favorite hidden gems in London to the latest world news since I picked her up half an hour ago. She also looked stunning in a pink Roman-style gown and diamonds; more than a few guests had cast admiring glances at her on our way in.

Unfortunately, no matter how hard I tried to focus on Clarissa, my attention remained divided between the woman standing next to me and the woman who'd taken up residence in my thoughts.

My jaw tightened at the memory of Victor's sleazy hands touching Isabella. I wasn't one for violence outside the boxing ring, but seeing him grab her had incited a dark, burning rage that'd made me want to tear his arm off and feed it through a wood chipper.

Thankfully, he'd returned to D.C. and wasn't in attendance tonight, or I'd be thrown out of Valhalla myself for murdering another club member.

I ran a hand over my mouth and forced my mind elsewhere. It was neither the time nor the place for violent fantasies.

For the next hour, Clarissa and I circulated the room as I introduced her to the other members. Some she already knew. The international jet set was small, and they gathered at the same glittering social events every year: Cannes, the Legacy Ball, the Met Gala, New York and Paris Fashion Week. The list went on.

Dante and Vivian were here, as were the Laurents, the Singhs, and Dominic and his wife Alessandra. Even the Serb made an appearance, though he left after only a few minutes. I was surprised he'd showed at all; the unsmiling, unspeaking tycoon rarely showed his face in public. He'd joined Valhalla last year, and I hadn't heard him talk once. I made a valiant effort to avoid the bar, but when Clarissa excused herself to use the restroom, I couldn't resist a quick look. The crowd had cleared, and I found myself scanning the length of the room for a flash of distinctive purple.

Blonde hair, red hair, silver...violet.

My breath stilled. Isabella stood at the end of the bar, talking to Vivian. High ponytail, sparkling eyes, unfettered grin. Somehow, she made her simple black uniform look better than any of the expensive designer dresses on display tonight.

My feet took me across the room before my brain could protest.

In a rare change of pace, Isabella spotted me before I could overhear her talking about something inappropriate—glitter condoms, perhaps, or a modern reenactment of ancient Roman orgies—and her voice petered off as I approached.

A strange stab of disappointment pierced my gut.

"Hey, Kai." Vivian smiled, resplendent in a floor-length aqua gown and diamonds befitting the Lau jewelry heiress. "You have perfect timing. I was just about to find Dante. You know him. Can't leave him alone for too long." She slid off her seat. "Have fun. Isa, I'll see you at Sloane's on Thursday."

She disappeared into the crowd before Isabella or I could get a word in.

An awkward silence bloomed in her wake. I smoothed a palm over my tie, needing something to do with my hands. My tuxedo was custom-tailored, but it suddenly felt too tight, like it could barely contain the heavy drum of my heartbeat.

I'd dined with presidents, negotiated with CEOs, and vacationed with royalty, but none had shredded my composure the way Isabella did.

"So where's your date?" she asked, not looking at me as she worked on a drink.

Who—right. Clarissa. "She's in the restroom." I recovered quickly from my near misstep. "I figured it would be a good time to check in on you. Make sure you're not distributing certain...party favors illegally on club grounds."

"Ha ha." Isabella rolled her eyes, but a smile curved her mouth. "What did I tell you the other night? I *knew* you and Corissa would end up dating."

"Her name is Clarissa, and we're on a date, not dating. There's a difference."

"You know what they say. The road to dating is paved with dates." Her tone was casual, but I detected an undercurrent of tension.

"Jealous?" I drawled, more pleased by the thought than I should've been. Dark, amused satisfaction coasted through me at her telling scowl.

"Hardly. You two are perfect for each other. You're both so... proper."

"You say that like it's an insult. Where I come from, propriety is a virtue, not a vice."

"You mean the Rupert Giles school of life?" Isabella wrinkled her nose. "I can only imagine."

I couldn't contain a grin. "A *Buffy* reference. Why am I not surprised?" She reminded me a lot of the titular nineties character. Often underestimated because of her looks and stature, but fiercely intelligent with a spine of steel beneath the delicate exterior.

"Because you know I have taste," she said primly. She handed me the drink she'd been working on. Strawberries. Pink. "Tradition."

The idea of sharing a tradition with Isabella, even one as silly as a cocktail, pleased me even more than her potential jealousy, but I kept my voice bland as I took a sip. It was the perfect balance of sweet and tart.

"So we're on a tradition basis now," I drawled. "I'm flattered."

"Don't be. I have traditions with everyone, including my oversexed neighbor and the barista at my local coffee shop." Isabella's dimples flashed at the quizzical tilt of my brows. "Whenever my neighbor disrupts my sleep with his *activities*, I blast Nickelback and sing along off-key until I kill their mood. Usually takes about ten minutes. I like to think I'm doing the women a favor because their moans do *not* sound real. There's nothing worse than performing vocally without getting paid in the form of orgasms."

A laugh bubbled into my throat even as my blood heated at

the sound of the word *orgasms* leaving her mouth. "And the barista?"

"His girlfriend is Filipino. He wants to learn Tagalog for her, so I teach him a new phrase every morning when I come in for my coffee. He's getting pretty good."

My smile softened at the mental image of Isabella teaching someone random Tagalog phrases at the register. It sounded exactly like something she would do. Beneath all the sass and sarcasm, she had a heart of gold.

"In that case, I'm honored to be part of such an illustrious roster." I paused. "Minus the oversexed neighbor."

"Lucky you."

Isabella's grin kicked my pulse into overdrive. I tried to stop it, but control slipped through my fingers like wisps of smoke.

It always did where she was concerned.

"I'm so sorry."

The shock of hearing Clarissa's voice snapped my defenses back into place. I straightened, taking in Clarissa's flushed cheeks and apologetic expression.

"This is terribly rude of me, but I have to leave early," she said. "An emergency came up at the gallery. One of our featured artists pulled out of the upcoming exhibition."

A shameful breath of relief cooled my lungs. "You don't have to explain. Work comes first."

Clarissa glanced at Isabella. Recognition sparked in her eyes, but she didn't say anything. Instead, she gave me a hesitant smile. "Rain check on our date?"

"Of course," I said after the briefest of hesitations.

"The old work excuse," Isabella said after Clarissa disappeared into the crowd. "You must be a terrible date."

I ignored the obvious bait. The truth was, I was tempted to leave early too. I'd already talked to everyone I wanted to see, and after years of attending similar balls, I was unimpressed with the pageantry. I'd rather go home and lose myself in a book, except...

I've been working on it for a while, but I'm stuck...

All I have to do is finish my own...

How do you know?

My jaw tensed as my conversation with Isabella two weeks ago played on a loop in my mind. Her career aspirations were none of my business, but she'd looked so lost in that moment, and she'd sounded so sad...

"When does your shift end?" The question left my mouth of its own accord.

"In about an hour." Isabella's brow formed a questioning arch. "Why?"

Don't do it, a voice of reason warned. *This is a terrible idea. You should not tell her about—*

"Meet me at the main staircase after you're off," I said. "I have something to show you."

∼

ISABELLA

I had a history of making bad decisions when it came to men, so it was no surprise I showed up at the stairs after my shift. If we got caught, I'd be in deep shit. Not Kai, of course, since his status protected him from any consequences. But me, a lowly employee? I'd be tossed off Valhalla's premises faster than I could say *double standard*.

Still, curiosity was a demanding beast, and it held me firmly in its clutches as we walked up the stairs and down the second-floor hallway.

"You're not luring me to a black site where you can chop me into pieces, are you?" I asked. "Because that's not how I'd prefer to spend my Saturday night. I have a strong aversion to physical pain."

Kai slanted a disbelieving glance at me. "You've been doing too much thriller research."

"Nope, just listening to a lot of true crime podcasts." Which I supposed was the same thing. "It never hurts to be cautious."

"I promise we're not going to a black site. That's reserved for Tuesday nights."

"Ha ha. Hilarious," I grumbled, but I fell silent when we stopped in front of a familiar door.

"The library." Disappointment cut a swath through my nerves. "That's it?"

I liked the library as much as the next person, but after expecting a maze of secret passageways or a fancy hidden room, it was a bit of a letdown.

A small smile touched Kai's lips. "Have faith."

Valhalla's library soared two stories to an elaborate cathedral ceiling engraved with the founding families' crests. Rolling ladders and filigreed spiral staircases connected the main floor to the upper level, which bristled with leather-bound books and priceless tchotchkes.

I followed Kai up one of those staircases to the mythology section, where he skimmed his fingers over a shelf of books so old their titles were barely legible. He stopped on a battered copy of *The Iliad*, twisted the gold lion statuette on a nearby table with his other hand, and pulled out the book before reshelving it.

"What are you..."

The soft creak of the bookcase swinging open swallowed the rest of my words. My jaw unhinged.

Oh my God.

Plush purple carpet muffled my footsteps as I stepped inside, feeling like I'd been dropped into the middle of a movie about some rich, eccentric billionaire who enjoyed befuddling his heirs with riddles and secret passageways.

So the surprise *was* a hidden room. And not just any hidden room, but the hidden room of my dreams.

A beautiful rolltop desk and chair occupied the right wall, complete with a vintage typewriter and Tiffany glass lamp that drenched the room in a soft amber glow. On the opposite wall, an antique leather trunk served as a table for piles of old magazines and assorted knickknacks. A cozy-looking couch sat in the middle of the room, piled high with cushions and a red cashmere throw.

A dreamy sigh escaped. I usually preferred noise and chaos over peace and quiet, but I could wrap myself in that blanket and stay here forever.

"My great-grandfather built this room when Valhalla was founded," Kai said, closing the door behind us. "He was the most introverted of the founders, and he wanted a place where he could be alone and no one could find him. Only the managing committee knows it exists, and only my family knows how to open it."

"And me," I said softly, turning to face him.

Kai paused. "And you."

The words sank so deep into my skin my breath couldn't find its way around them. "Aren't you afraid I'll tell someone?"

He leaned against the wall, the picture of casual elegance, his eyes never leaving mine. "Will you?"

I held his gaze for a moment before giving my head a slow shake. My nerves buzzed like live wires in the rain, scattering sparks of awareness through my body.

Two people. A secret room.

Our presence here seemed painfully intimate, like a pair of star-crossed lovers' last rendezvous or a forbidden glimpse inside someone's diary.

A smile ghosted Kai's mouth. "The room isn't a treasure trove. There are no priceless artifacts or stores of gold here. But if you wanted a quiet place to write..."

The sparks of awareness melted into a golden, honeyed warmth.

I didn't work well in silence. My doubts and second-guessing festered in the absence of company, growing claws and fangs that shredded my creativity into ribbons.

But Kai's gesture was so thoughtful I didn't have the heart to tell him, so I simply smiled through the blossoming ache in my chest.

"Thank you. This is..." I faltered, unsure how to express the emotions sweeping through me. I couldn't remember the last time someone had done something so considerate for me without expecting anything in return. Not when it came to my writing, which even my friends sometimes treated as a hobby more than anything else. "This is amazing."

The warmth of his attention settled on my back as I walked through the room, taking in the details, the decor, and the different titles on the shelves. To my surprise, they weren't limited to the classics. There were children's books, academic texts, romance novels and fantasy doorstoppers. Dostoyevsky and Austen sat next to Chinese classics such as *Journey to the West* and *Dream of the Red Chamber;* Neil Gaiman and George R. R. Martin occupied the shelf below Judy Blume and Beverly Cleary. The eclectic collection spanned an impressive range of cultures, genres, and eras.

"We're missing dinosaur erotica," Kai said with a completely straight face. "I'll have to remedy that oversight soon. If you have any recommendations, feel free to send them to me."

I shot him a narrow-eyed glance. "You like poking fun at me, don't you?" I accused over a bubble of suppressed laughter.

Another ghost of a smile, followed by a wicked gleam that had my pulse skyrocketing.

"Do I look like someone who would do such a thing?" Kai pushed off the wall and walked toward me, his stride easy but powerful, like a panther leisurely contemplating its next move.

The space between us collapsed, as did any glimmer of levity when he stopped in front of me. His body heat was a living, breathing thing, clouding my mind and stealing my focus until my world consisted of nothing except dark eyes, soft wool, and the clean, expensive scent of citrus and wood.

Goose bumps rose on my sensitized skin.

"You're right. You and *fun* don't belong in the same sentence," I managed. My head swam like I'd been downing drinks all night instead of serving them. "I can't recommend any of the books I read to you. They're too wild. You might go into cardiac shock."

Kai regarded me with a lazy, dangerous amusement that I felt all the way to my toes.

"Do you think I'm boring, Isabella?" The question came out soft. Dark. *Suggestive,* like he was ruminating over all the ways he could prove me wrong. It trailed down my spine and left delicious little bursts of electricity in its wake.

The air shifted and thickened. Every *tick* of the clock pounded in rhythm with my heart, dragging me closer toward the precipice of no return.

I shook my head, attempting to form a coherent response. "You said it. Not me."

My voice didn't sound like mine. It was too thin, too breathless, but Kai's proximity had snuffed out the oxygen in the room. I couldn't breathe fast enough or deeply enough to sustain a clear head.

"I see," he murmured. "I don't suppose I can change your mind." Gone were the crisp edges and formal syllables. In their place were velvet and smoke, whispering silent promises against my skin and compelling me to tilt my face up. Just a fraction, just enough to meet his gaze full on and see the heat glinting beneath pools of dusky clarity.

Heaviness gathered low in my belly, thick and molten.

I shouldn't be here. Not with him, and not like this. But I was intoxicated, and he was beautiful, and the world had blurred into a lovely, hazy dream I didn't want to wake up from.

Would it be so bad to indulge myself *once* after years of abstinence? To see whether that stern, sculpted mouth would soften into something more sensual when pressed against mine?

My lips parted. Kai's eyes dropped, and time slowed as it always did when we were alone.

I didn't resist the downward drift of my eyelids. My body pulled taut with anticipation for the moment when I'd find out if that glacial sophistication would melt with a kiss.

But the moment never came.

I heard a low curse. Then the delicious cocoon of warmth vanished, replaced with a sharp breeze of air. Coldness bathed my arms and chest.

By the time my eyes flew open, the bookcase had already swung shut behind him.

Kai was gone.

CHAPTER 12
Kai

" **I** s there a reason we're doing this here instead of at the club?" Dominic cast a disdainful look around the simulation room. It was the best money could buy, with the latest state-of-the-art technology, a glass case of autographed golf paraphernalia, and a full wet bar, but he looked thoroughly unimpressed. "Valhalla has better facilities. This is adequate at best."

"Don't be a snob." I uncapped a bottle of single-malt scotch. "Sometimes, a change of scenery is necessary."

Dominic, Dante, and I were gathered at the new entertainment complex in Hudson Yards for our semi-regular lunch and exchange of information. I supplied the news and whispers, Dominic the market insights, and Dante the corporate wheelings and dealings. It was a mutually beneficial relationship all around, though we'd yet to find a meeting spot up to par with Dominic's standards.

The quiet foster kid with the chip on his shoulder had come a long way since his days in the Ohio projects. Dominic had the most expensive taste of anyone I knew, and I'd grown up with people who hadn't blinked an eye at shelling out tens of millions of dollars on objectively questionable art.

"And sometimes, people use change as an excuse to avoid a

certain location," Dante drawled from his seat along the wall. "You haven't set foot in the club for three weeks unless it was for boxing."

I poured the alcohol into a glass and avoided his eagle-eyed gaze. "I have other responsibilities besides loitering at the club. The holiday season is a busy time of year."

"Hmm." The sound weighed heavy with skepticism.

I ignored it. I wasn't lying about my workload. It was the week before Thanksgiving, which meant I had a tight window left to close the DigiStream deal before everyone signed off for the holidays. My team had stressed the importance of completing the deal before the end of the year for various financial reasons. It wouldn't be a total disaster if negotiations spilled over into January, but I didn't settle for "not a disaster" when it came to business. I wanted the deal sealed before the CEO vote.

Of course, Dante wasn't wrong. I'd avoided Valhalla like the plague since the fall gala. Since the night I took Isabella to my hideaway—my favorite place at the club, which I'd never shown anyone—and almost kissed her.

I tossed back my drink. The scotch burned a path down my throat but couldn't erase the memory of those big brown eyes and lush, red mouth.

One tiny dip of my head and I could've tasted her. Discovered for myself whether her lips were as soft as they looked and whether she tasted as sweet as I imagined.

Heat rippled through me. I set my jaw and brushed it off.

Thank God reason had prevailed before I gave in to my baser instincts. It would've been poor form to take one woman on a date, then kiss another woman the same night, even if the former had already left.

It would've been worth it, an insidious voice sang.

Shut up, another voice snapped. *You never know what's good for you.*

I rubbed a hand over my face. Great. Now I was silently arguing with myself. *Damn Isabella.*

Dominic finished his round at the simulator. I took his place, eager for a distraction. I wasn't a huge fan of golf, but DigiStream's CEO loved it, and I wanted to brush up on my skills for our post-Thanksgiving game at Pine Valley.

I'd just lined up my shot when Dominic's phone dinged.

"Kai."

Something in his voice snapped my senses into high alert. I straightened, a cold rope of dread twisting through my gut when I saw both Dominic and Dante staring at their cells with grim expressions.

Did something happen to my mother? Maybe she was sick after all; she'd collapsed and been rushed to the hospital. Or perhaps it was my sister and newborn nephew, who were flying to Australia today. There'd been a plane accident, or a fire, or...

My dread solidified into ice as worst-case scenarios flipped through my head at lightning speed.

I reached for my phone and scanned the headlines blaring across my screen. Not my family. Relief loosened the fist around my heart, but it was short-lived.

DigiStream co-founder Colin Whidby rushed to the hospital after a drug overdose...

Tech superstar and DigiStream CEO Colin Whidby in critical condition...

"Jesus fuck." Dante verbalized my sentiments as only Dante could. "That's some bad timing."

"You don't say." I didn't indulge in profanity often, but the temptation to curse pushed against my lips as the implications sank in.

I knew Colin had a nasty drug habit; so did half the people on Wall Street. I didn't like it, but I also didn't police my business associates' personal lives. They could do whatever they wanted as long as they weren't hurting other people or the bottom line. Plus, of the two co-founders, Colin had been the most amenable to the deal. His co-founder Rohan Mishra had resisted until Colin brought him around. Now, I either had to deal with Rohan or postpone closing talks until next year, likely *after* the CEO vote had already happened.

Dammit.

Even without the CEO position at stake, the DigiStream deal was essential. The board might not believe me, but the video streaming service was the future of news as the world shifted from traditional media apparatuses to citizen-driven reporting.

And now, the deal that would cement my legacy was in jeopardy because a twenty-four-year-old tech bro couldn't keep his nose out of cocaine long enough to sign a contract that would've made us both legends.

"Go," Dante said, accurately reading my mood. "Let us know if you need anything."

I responded with a curt nod, my initial panic rearranging itself into to-do items and checklists. By the time I hit the lobby, I'd already sent flowers to Colin's hospital room via my assistant, reached out to Rohan's office to set up a call, and assembled my team for an emergency meeting at the office.

The actions took the edge off my adrenaline, and when I stepped out into the crisp fall air, I'd regained my usual cold, practical clarity.

Colin was in the hospital, but he wasn't dead. DigiStream was still operational, and Rohan had sat in on all the meetings. I didn't need to catch him up on the latest developments. He might need more wooing, but the deal was in both our interests. Even someone as stubborn as him could see it.

I might be able to salvage the deal before the holidays after all. If I didn't, I'd still become CEO.

Everything would be fine.

I reached the main intersection and was about to hail a cab when a familiar laugh hit me square in the chest.

I wasn't conscious of stopping. All I knew was, one minute, I was moving; the next, I was frozen, watching as Isabella walked toward me. Her face was alight with animation as she talked to the vaguely familiar-looking guy next to her. Her ruby-red coat popped against the black-clad masses teeming on the sidewalk, but even without it, she would've been the brightest spot of the day.

She laughed again, and a sliver of something green and unpleasant curled in my chest.

I tensed, awaiting our eventual encounter. She was only a few steps away.

Closer.

Closer.

Closer...

Isabella walked past, still deep in conversation with her companion.

She hadn't even noticed me.

"Isabella." Her name came out sharper than I'd intended.

She glanced back, her face blanking for a second like she was trying to remember who I was.

My irritation doubled alongside the suspiciously-like-jealousy-but-couldn't-possibly-be-jealousy tendrils snaking through my veins.

"Oh! Hi." The blankness gave way to a surprised smile. "Kai Young outside the Upper East Side. I never thought I'd see the day."

"Miracles happen every day." I assessed the man beside her with a cool once-over. Late twenties or early thirties. Tall, lanky, with curly brown hair and a distinct European artist vibe amplified by his plaid scarf and ink-stained fingers.

I disliked him on sight.

"This is Leo Agnelli," Isabella said, following my gaze. "He's the author of one of my favorite books, *The Poison Jar*. Have you read it?"

That was why he looked familiar. Leo had been the darling of the literary world a few years ago. He was still well-known, but his two-year hiatus from publishing had stunted his momentum. Rumor had it he was working on a new book, but nothing had been confirmed.

"Yes."

Isabella was too busy gushing about him to notice my unenthused reply. "I joined a local writing group to see if it would help with my block. Today was my first meeting, so imagine my surprise when Leo showed up!"

"I'm friends with the organizer," Leo explained. "I'm in town for some meetings, and I dropped by to say hi."

"Perfect timing." Isabella's dimples flashed. "It's like fate."

"How fortuitous." I didn't understand her excitement over Leo. He was good, but he wasn't *that* good.

Unlike most writers who stuck with one or two genres, Leo's works spanned literary, contemporary, and historical fiction. *The Poison Jar* was the most introspective piece in his catalog, and Isabella hated lit fic.

They carried on like I hadn't spoken.

"Are your meetings about your next book?" she asked.

"Some of them," Leo said with a grin. "I'm working on a travel memoir about the two years I spent abroad."

So the rumors about a new project were true. Normally, I would've texted my books and culture editor with the news, but I was too distracted by the way Isabella's face lit up at the confirmation.

"Yes! I read your guest column in *World Geographic*. I can't believe you went diving in Silfra," she breathed. "That's one of my top bucket list items."

My jaw tensed as she rambled on about his adventures. Personally, I didn't think they were a big deal. So what if Leo went diving between tectonic plates? He didn't *discover* the Silfra Fissure, for Christ's sake.

Isabella brushed a strand of hair out of her eye. Her tattoo peeked out from the sleeve of her coat, and I tried not to think about tracing its lines and swirls with my tongue.

I had a meeting to get to, but I couldn't leave her alone with Leo. His timing was too suspicious. He just *happened* to be in town for meetings? Likely story. What if he was a stalker or, worse, a serial killer?

My phone buzzed with a new message from my assistant informing me the Whidby crisis response team was onsite. I reluctantly pulled my attention away from Isabella and typed out a quick response.

Me: *I'll be a few minutes late, but have them put together an initial crisis plan. Finance, legal, everything. I want bullet points when I arrive.*

Alison: *Consider it done.*

Isabella was still gushing over Leo's travels when I looked up again.

Climbing Mount Kilimanjaro. Bungee jumping from Victoria Falls. Sailing through the Drake Passage to Antarctica.

Was he a writer or Indiana fucking Jones?

Unmistakable jealousy gnawed at my gut. She'd never smiled at me the way she was smiling at him, and I couldn't help but wonder if she'd let him kiss her the way I almost had.

I shouldn't have left her in the library. My sense of self-preservation and propriety had kicked in at the last minute, but for once in my life, I wished they hadn't.

Finally, I couldn't take it anymore. My mouth opened before my brain could stop me. "There's a big event this Saturday. It's the VIP opening for a new piano bar in the Meatpacking District," I said when Isabella paused for breath. "I have an extra ticket, if you're interested in attending."

It wasn't hiking Mount Everest, but it was an exclusive event. Leo wasn't the only one who could have fun.

"Oh." She blinked, clearly caught off guard given how our last interaction had ended. It'd been three weeks since I left her in the library without so much as a goodbye. It wasn't my finest moment, but she had a way of pulling both the best and worst out of me. "Um, thanks for the invite, but I have to work—"

"Hina Tanaka is the opening act." I banked on the hope that Isabella would know who she was. Hina was one of the top pianists in the world, and she hadn't performed in the United States in years.

"Oh." This time, Isabella's face lit with excitement. "Well, I think I can find someone to cover for me."

"Apologies, but I only have two tickets," I told Leo with a forced, polite smile. "Otherwise, I would offer you an invitation as well."

"No worries," he said easily. "I'm not a big piano guy anyway." He checked his watch. "I'm meeting my agent in half an hour so I have to run, but it was nice meeting you. Isabella, I'll send you the signed copy of *The Poison Jar* when I get home."

"He's a bit full of himself, isn't he?" I said after Leo left. "All that bragging about his travels."

Isabella slanted a strange look at me. "*Leo*? He's one of the most down-to-earth people I've ever met."

"Yes, well, you only met today. How do you know your assessment of his character is accurate?"

She crossed her arms over her chest. "Are you sick? Because you're behaving very strangely."

She wasn't wrong. I was acting like an ill-mannered boor, but I couldn't stop myself. Seeing her laugh and converse so easily with Leo had triggered my worst caveman impulses.

"I'm not sick. I'm—" I caught myself and took a deep, calming breath. "I'm late for a meeting. But send me your address and I'll pick you up at seven on Saturday."

"No need. I can meet you at the club." Isabella paused. "You're not going to leave me there without saying goodbye, right?"

A flush singed my cheeks at the indirect reference to what'd happened in the secret room. "No."

"And this isn't a date?"

"Of course not."

It was simply a friendly gathering of two acquaintances at a predetermined time and location.

I said a curt goodbye and called Alison on my way back to the office. "I'll be there in twenty minutes," I said. "In the meantime, please reschedule my dinner with Russell on Saturday. Tell him a personal emergency came up."

I was supposed to take our company's visiting COO out this weekend, but plans changed.

"Of course. Is everything okay?"

"Yes, everything's fine, but I changed my mind about the piano bar opening. RSVP yes for me and a plus-one. Thank you."

I hung up. I should have been brainstorming strategies to manage the DigiStream crisis, but as the cab sped toward midtown Manhattan, I couldn't stop my mind from fast-forwarding to the weekend—or my pulse from hammering at the anticipation of a completely innocent, one hundred percent platonic non-date.

CHAPTER 13

Isabella

The piano bar occupied a hidden, speakeasy-style basement in the Meatpacking District, nestled in between a coffee shop and the type of trendy boutique that sold ripped jeans for eight hundred dollars a pop.

Twin bouncers the size of mountains screened invites. Past them, a narrow flight of stairs led to a lavish room that looked like something out of 1920s Chicago, with exposed brick walls, crystal chandeliers, and red velvet booths curved around tables of well-dressed, well-heeled guests in sleek designer eveningwear. An imposing five-tiered wall of liquor anchored one end of the space, while a stage with a grand piano occupied the other.

It was stunning and exclusive and a throwback to headier times.

It was also incredibly, mind-numbingly boring.

I stifled a yawn as another pianist took the stage. The night had started promisingly enough with a dazzling performance from Hina, who'd opened the show early so she could catch her flight to Japan—apparently, she'd agreed to perform at the last minute as a favor to the club's owner—but the rest of the hours had inched by second by torturous second.

I liked piano, but I didn't want to sit through set after set of classical music. I needed *action*.

I drained the rest of my drink and glanced at Kai, who watched the show with an attentive expression. His profile was all clean lines and sculpted cheekbones, classically handsome in a way that evoked smoky jazz lounges and Old Shanghai glamour.

Charcoal tailored suit molded to broad shoulders, crisp white shirt against tanned skin, the subtle, expensive scent of cologne.

Warmth and whiskey pooled in my stomach. My body tightened with annoying appreciation as I leaned over, holding my breath so I didn't inhale more of that delicious scent than necessary. I was convinced he'd laced his cologne with drugs.

"How many more songs are left?" I whispered. I would die if there were more than two.

"Five." Kai didn't take his eyes off the stage.

Five? Cold dismay doused the warmth.

I shouldn't even be here. Tessa had agreed to cover my shift tonight, but I hated asking people for last-minute favors. Plus, voluntarily agreeing to a night out with Kai Young? Sheer insanity, especially after our almost-kiss and his abrupt departure.

I hadn't seen him for three weeks after, and I was sure he'd been avoiding me. That hadn't stopped my heart from fluttering when I saw him downtown the other day or prevented a whisper of satisfaction from snaking through me at his obvious dislike of Leo.

Perhaps I'd imagined it, but I could've sworn he'd been jealous.

The thought evoked a strange thrill beneath my skin.

"Are you enjoying the performances? Besides Hina's," I amended. "Be honest."

Kai finally glanced in my direction. The full width of the table separated us, but the impact of his attention still sank into my body, filling every inch with uncomfortable warmth.

I crossed and uncrossed my legs, oddly breathless. I was dying for a shot of tequila, but all thoughts of alcohol fled when his eyes dipped to my bared thigh. The slit of my dress had fallen open, and my skin burned under his dark, inscrutable scrutiny.

The noise from the rest of the bar faded like someone had turned the volume down on the radio. It took an ungodly amount of willpower not to shift my leg so even more thigh was exposed to his heat...or to cover myself up so I wasn't tempted to do anything stupid.

Like agree to a piano bar date when you'd vowed to stay away from him? the irritating voice in my head taunted.

Shut. Up.

I had a bad habit of reneging on my promises to myself. It wasn't a great attribute, but I owned it; though I didn't particularly like being called out on it.

The current sonata ended, followed by a wave of polite applause.

Kai dragged his gaze up to meet mine again. The slow-spreading burn followed, gliding over my hips, my waist, my breasts, and my neck before settling on my cheeks. I wore one of the slinkiest dresses in my collection—a little burgundy velvet number that I'd thrifted at the Looking Glass boutique—but I might as well be trekking across the Sahara in a full-length parka.

Sweat beaded on my chest and forehead. Good thing I hadn't ordered that tequila shot, or I might burst into flames right here in the middle of Tchaikovsky's "Piano Concerto No. 1."

Something passed through Kai's eyes. "The performances are fine," he said in response to my long-forgotten question. His neutral tone gave nothing away, but when he faced forward again, I caught the quick flick of his eyes to his watch.

The tiny movement shocked me out of my stupor.

"Oh my God," I breathed, all ill-advised lust forgotten. "You're bored."

Normally, I'd be offended because hello, I was excellent company, but we'd barely talked all evening. His boredom had nothing to do with me (I hoped) and everything to do with two hours of mind-numbing classical music.

Kai's mouth pressed into a straight line. "I am not. This is delightful."

"You're such a liar." Laughter bubbled from my throat, drawing glares of condemnation from the table next to us. I ignored them. "You just checked the time."

"Checking the time isn't a direct correlation to boredom."

"Yes, it is." I'd checked the time no less than a dozen times since Hina's performance ended. Who could blame me? No dancing, no talking, no song requests. I might as well be in church, for Christ's sake. "Admit it. You're not enjoying yourself."

"I will do no such thing." Kai paused, then added, "Besides, the performances are almost over. We can go elsewhere after if you'd like."

It was as much of an admission as I would get out of him. *Men and their pride.* They would rather die than admit they were wrong. Meanwhile, *I* would die if I had to spend another minute listening to a mournful song without lyrics.

"Why don't we go elsewhere now?" I suggested. "The night is young, and you've shown me your New York. Let me show you mine."

A frown notched between his brows. "This is hardly my New York, and it would be rude to leave early."

"No, it wouldn't. We've stayed long enough to pay our respects." I nudged his knee with mine. His shoulders visibly stiffened beneath the sharp lines of his suit. "Come on. Live a little, Young. I promise it won't kill you."

"No, but you might," he muttered.

I stayed silent, letting my puppy-dog eyes do the talking. They were the same eyes that'd gotten me out of trouble when I played dress-up with my mother's clothes as a preteen and accidentally ripped her favorite dress. She'd only grounded me for, oh, two weeks instead of the rest of my life.

After a minute of silence, Kai released a weary-sounding sigh. "What did you have in mind?"

My innocent, pleading expression melted into a grin.

Success! Isabella, one. Kai, zero.

I flipped through my mental calendar of events for a good spot to take him. A nightclub was too generic, a sex dungeon too wild. What kind of place would take him out of his comfort zone without sending him into—*aha.*

My mind screeched to a halt at a certain weekly gathering miles away. My brother had introduced me to it, and the more I thought about it, the more perfect it was.

My grin widened. *Thank you, Felix.*

"It's a surprise," I said, evading Kai's question. "Do you trust me?" I was already sliding out of the booth and heading toward the exit, my blood fizzing with excitement.

I couldn't wait to get out of here and see Kai's face when I brought him to the site.

"Not particularly." But he followed me, his face stamped with suspicion. He handed our coat check ticket to the attendant. She returned less than a minute later with my patchwork trench—one of my prized Goodwill finds; I'd snagged the genuine leather piece for less than twenty-five bucks—and Kai's custom-made Delamonte. "This activity wouldn't happen to be illegal or illicit in any way, would it?"

"Of course not." I placed a hand over my chest, insulted. "I'm offended you would even ask. When I participate in illegal activities, I do it myself. I'm smart enough not to involve coconspirators."

Another, even wearier sigh.

"Fine." Kai slipped on his coat. "But if it involves glow-in-the-dark anything, I'm leaving."

CHAPTER 14

Isabella

Forty minutes later, our cab rolled to a stop in the industrial bowels of Bushwick.

"No," Kai said flatly, staring at the building before us. Cracked windows glinted in the moonlight and graffiti turned the red stone exterior into a riot of colors, cartoons, and curse words. It was dark save for a row of lights blazing on the top floor. "This looks like the type of place where serial killers stash their victims' bodies."

"And you say *I* listen to too much true crime." I slid out of the backseat and stifled a grin when Kai paid our driver with a pained expression. He could complain all he wanted, but he was here and he wasn't leaving, or he would've asked the driver to take him home. "I promise, there were no dead bodies the last time I checked. *But* that was over a month ago, so I can't guarantee things haven't changed since then."

"If I'd known you were such a comedy fan, I would've brought you to the Comedy Cellar instead."

"It was a lack of foresight on your part, but perhaps next time," I quipped, implying there would be a next time.

My stupid, overly hormonal heart thumped at the prospect.

Kai and I hadn't discussed our almost-kiss yet. After three

weeks, what happened in the library seemed like a fever dream, the product of exhaustion and fantasies bleeding into real life. Looking at him now, so rigid and proper in his four-thousand-dollar coat, it was hard to imagine him ever losing control like that.

"Perhaps." Kai eyed the warehouse's black metal front door like it was infested with cholera. Someone had spray-painted three giant boobs on it, along with the word *Titz* in fluorescent yellow. "How charming."

"It is." I shrugged off my disappointment at his lack of response to my *next time* remark and typed the security code into the keypad. A second later, the door buzzed open. "You know what they say. Third boob's the charm."

Kai coughed into his fist. If I didn't know better, I could've sworn he was hiding a laugh.

The door shut with a clang behind us. We walked down the dimly lit hall and took the elevator up to the top floor, where a woman with blue pigtails and black lipstick sat on a stool by the entrance. There were no rooms in the building; each floor was comprised of one giant, loft-like space, and she looked inordinately small against the cavernous backdrop.

She glanced up from her sketch pad long enough to check our IDs and my membership card before waving us past.

The studio was empty save for the woman at the door and a skinny, goateed blond rubbing blue paint over his torso like it was baby oil. Everyone was probably downstairs, but I wanted to ease Kai in before I threw him into the deep end.

He stopped at the edge of the tarp covering the gray concrete floor. A temporary wooden wall stood in the middle of the room, covered with white floating canvases and paint-filled balloons hung on push pins. Detachable tabs locked the canvases in place. Next to the wall, a rolling bar cart held drinking glasses, several bottles of clear alcohol, and a jar brimming with folded slips of paper.

Kai's eyes moved from the balloons to the bar to the blond

artist, who was now doing yoga stretches on his corner of the tarp. Quite a sight, considering he wore nothing except paint and a pair of loose-hanging shorts.

A faint grimace crossed Kai's face when the blond shifted into a killer praying mantis pose. "Isabella."

"Yes?" I said brightly.

"What, exactly, did you bring us to?"

"A creative community! It's like one of those paint and wine places, but better." I gestured at the wall, where bright trails of paint snaked over a few of the canvases and dripped onto the tarp. "Have you ever watched *The Princess Diaries*? With Anne Hathaway? There's this scene with Mia and her mom after she finds out she's actually a princess..."

He stared at me.

"Never mind. The point is, this is very similar to what they did in the movie. Your goal is to puncture those balloons with a dart so the paint spills onto the canvas and creates an abstract piece of art. If you miss, you have to pick a slip of paper from that jar and answer the question truthfully or take a shot of Violet's Special Moonshine. Violet is the owner of the studio," I clarified. "Her moonshine is no joke. The last time someone took more than three shots, they ended up streaking across Bushwick and singing the national anthem at the top of their lungs. Got arrested for indecent exposure, but their boss's daughter's best friend bailed him out because they were having an affair—"

"Isabella," Kai said again.

"Hmm?"

"Unnecessary detail."

Fair enough. Not everyone found the sex lives of random New Yorkers as interesting as I did. Maybe because they were *having* sex and not confined to hearing about it through friends and strangers.

To his credit, Kai didn't immediately turn and walk out the door at the prospect of throwing darts at balloons all night. Instead, he averted his gaze from the artist yogi, took off his coat, and draped it over a nearby chair.

An irritating wisp of relief curled through me. I shouldn't care whether he stayed. I didn't enjoy his company that much.

I placed my coat over his and retrieved two smocks from the hooks lining the wall on our right.

"How did you find out about this place?" Kai rolled up his sleeves and accepted the smock I handed him.

I darted a glance at his forearms. Tanned, muscled, corded with sexy veins and a light smattering of dark hair...

An electric shiver ghosted down my spine before I yanked my eyes away. *New Isabella does not drool over random men's forearms. No matter how hot they are.*

Kai lifted a brow, and I remembered belatedly that he'd asked a question.

"My brother Felix told me about it." I removed my heels and fastened the smock around me, all the while keeping my gaze planted on the canvases. It was safer that way. "He's an artist, and he likes to come here when he's feeling stuck. He says being surrounded by other creatives in a low-stakes environment helps jog ideas loose." Felix's method for getting unstuck had never worked for me, but I liked how fun the exercise was. Sometimes I paired up with another person for the questions part; other times, I was content with just throwing darts. "He lives in L.A., but he visits New York often and knows all the underground places."

"An artist. A writer. Creative family." Kai's warmth brushed my side as he came up beside me. Even in an ugly black smock, he looked aristocratic, like a prince among commoners.

He plucked a dart from the nearby tray and handed it to me.

I took it gingerly. Our hands didn't touch, but my palm tingled like they had. "That's only me and Felix," I said. "The rest of my brothers aren't into the arts. Gabriel, the oldest, runs our family business. Romero is an engineer, and Miguel teaches poli sci at Berkeley." A wry smile. "A lot of Asian families push their children into law, medicine, or engineering, but my parents were big on us doing what we wanted as long as it's not illegal or unethical. *Habulin mo ang iyong mga pangarap.* Chase your dreams. Our family motto."

I left out the part about us having to achieve said dreams by age thirty due to a certain written clause. It was my parents' way of ensuring we didn't jump from passion to passion because we couldn't make up our minds. *The way I had for the past oh, ten years.*

If we didn't settle into a career path by thirty, then...

I swallowed the lump of unease in my throat. *It'll be fine.* I had time. If there was one thing that motivated me more than the prospect of money, fame, and success, it was the chance to prove my brother wrong.

"Are you?" Kai asked.

"What?"

"Chasing your dreams."

Of course. The answer sat on the tip of my tongue, but something prevented me from saying it out loud.

My eyes met Kai's for a single, knowing beat before I looked away. My heart rattled behind my ribcage, but I tried my best to ignore it. Instead, I focused on a balloon, aimed, and threw my dart as hard as I could. It glanced harmlessly off the wood.

I sighed. *Typical.* I'd been coming here for months, and I'd only hit my target twice.

"You pick." I gestured at the jar of paper. "I'm too busy wallowing in my lack of hand-eye coordination."

Miguel and Gabriel had gotten all the athletic genes in the family. It was so unfair.

Kai's gaze sparked with amusement, but he didn't argue. He plucked a slip from the jar and unfolded it. "What's your biggest fear?"

It was a generic question with plenty of generic answers—clowns, losing more people I loved, being alone. All things that had kept me up late at night, especially after I watched *It*. But the answer that came out of my mouth had nothing to do with killer clowns or dying by myself on some stranded road.

"A life without purpose." Embarrassment warmed my cheeks. The reply sounded so generic, like something a college freshman would spout in philosophy class, but that didn't make it any less true.

"It's not a concrete fear, like falling onto the subway tracks or having an air conditioner fall on my head," I said, naming two of the most common worries New Yorkers had. A faint curve touched Kai's lips. "But I don't know. The thought of dying without achieving *something* is..." *Depressing. Suffocating. Terrifying.* "Stressful. Especially in a city like New York, you know? Everyone here seems to know what they're doing or at least what they *want* to be doing. They live for a purpose, not survival."

I couldn't articulate why that bothered me so much. I just knew that sometimes, I scrolled through social media, consumed with envy over all the engagement, promotion, and insert-other-big-life-change announcements. I didn't begrudge my friends their happiness; I was truly thrilled when Vivian got married and when Sloane landed a big client. But I wished I had something of my own to share besides jokes and gossip. Something substantial that would consume my thoughts at night and drive away the restless, amorphous anxiety that plagued me whenever I was alone too long.

The curve on Kai's mouth straightened. "You do have a purpose," he said. Instead of sounding annoyed by my rambling, he spoke with a familiar certainty. *You'll finish it.* "It's to share your stories."

It was what I wanted. But if that was my real purpose, wouldn't I be better at it?

I bit back my uncertainty. I'd shared enough of my messy internal angst for the night. I didn't want to spend my Saturday wallowing in self-pity.

"You're right. Anyway." I tore my eyes away and refocused on the canvases. "Enough boring existential crisis talk. Your turn."

The warmth of Kai's gaze touched my face for an extra second before he faced forward. I was dying to ask him a question, but of course, his dart flew straight and true. It punctured one of the balloons with the precision of a laser-guided missile, as did his next throw, and the one after that. Half an hour later, I'd missed all of my shots while he'd missed none.

"There's no way." I gaped at the paint-splattered wall with disbelief. "You're cheating!"

Kai quirked a dark brow. "How would one cheat at darts?"

I opened my mouth, then closed it, stumped. *Damn him.* Why did he have to look like that *and* be good at everything he did? God truly had favorites.

"If I knew, I would've hit the target myself," I grumbled. "Fine. Let's switch it up since you're clearly some sort of inhuman dart-throwing machine." I gestured at the balloons. "If I make this next throw, you have to answer a question. It's unfair that you know all these things about me when I barely know anything about you."

He gave an elegant shrug. "Seems fair."

I plucked another dart from the box and narrowed my eyes at the wall. *I can do this.* How hard could hitting one teeny, tiny balloon be?

I took a deep breath, aimed, threw...and watched as the dart thudded on the ground without touching a single inch of wood, canvas, or latex.

Dammit. My shoulders slumped. *Not even close.*

"I'm starting to think you're missing on purpose," Kai said, sounding amused.

I scowled. "Not all of us are gifted with..." My voice trailed off when he stepped behind me, close enough my hair brushed his chest. My heartbeat wavered. "What are you doing?"

"Teaching you how to throw so we don't end the night with a

twelve-zero score." The crisp breeze of his voice skimmed my neck. "Landslide victories are hardly victories at all."

The studio was so large it carried a chill despite the overworked radiator in the corner, but Kai's body heat drove every ounce of it away. "This isn't a competition."

"Everything's a competition." Kai placed his hands on my hips and angled my body so I stood diagonally to the wall. "This is the standard stance. It makes it easier to position your center of gravity and aim." He reached next to us for a dart and slid it into my hand, closing his palm over it so he could guide my arm up. My back pressed against his front and sent tingles of excruciating awareness down my spine. "You don't want to grip the dart too tightly. Too much pressure will disrupt its balance..."

I usually tuned out technical explanations, but to my surprise, Kai's calm, steady instruction clicked after a while. Maybe it was the accent. It made everything better.

"Ready?" The word grazed the sensitive spot above my ear.

Goose bumps peppered my arms. I nodded.

Kai removed his hand from mine but kept a light touch on my back while I drew my right hand back, aimed, and fired.

Close...

Closer...

Bright blue paint burst from a balloon and spilled over an empty canvas.

I stared at it, my brain too stunned to register what happened.

Did I just...

"Oh my God," I breathed. The first prickles of realization appeared in my stomach. "I did it. I did it!"

I squealed, jubilation overtaking my shock. Without thinking, I turned and threw my arms around Kai's neck, my chest bursting with pride. Landing a dart throw was a small accomplishment, but it felt bigger somehow. It was proof that, with a little guidance and support, I could achieve the seemingly impossible.

It wasn't much, but after so many failures and blocked paths, I'd take any encouragement I could get.

"Careful, or we're going to be the ones covered in paint." Kai laughed. His hands came up around my waist, steadying me. I'd almost knocked us to the ground in my excitement. "So what's the question?"

"Hmm?" I asked, still high from my victory. Even surrounded by acrylic, he smelled good. Whatever he paid for his "signature scent," it was worth it.

"The question you want to ask me now that you hit the target," he prompted.

Right. My teeth sank into my bottom lip. I was torn between instant gratification and taking my time to come up with something good. Asking him about his fears or most embarrassing moment seemed like a missed opportunity to dig deeper.

"Can I save the question for later?"

"That goes against the rules you set out earlier."

"They weren't rules, they were guidelines. Besides..." I flashed an impish smile. "Rules are meant to be broken."

"Why am I not surprised to hear you say that?" Kai sighed. "Fine. One question of your choosing, to be determined at a later date."

"Thank you." I beamed. "See? Not everything is black and white. There's hope for you yet."

"Good to know. I was getting worried," he said dryly.

My arms were still around his neck, his hands still on my waist. My initial burst of excitement had faded, and my breaths slowed to match his.

Our smiles gradually faded as a spark of something other than amusement came to life in his eyes. The air settled around us, thick with electricity, and I felt a heady pull to stand on my tiptoes and—

A loud humming chased the sparks away. Kai and I jerked our heads toward the corner, where the blond artist/yogi was meditating on the floor. I'd completely forgotten he was there.

He wasn't paying attention to us, but the spell had shattered.

We dropped our arms from each other and stepped back. Awkwardness rushed to fill the new space between us.

"Well," Kai said stiffly, his cheekbones tinted with a dull brick-red. "This was an enjoyable if unexpected end to the evening. Thank you for the...enlightening experience. Shall I call a car to bring us both home?"

My brows dipped. "What do you mean, bring us home?"

"It's past midnight. I assume you're tired."

Most parties didn't start until midnight in New York, and I was anything but tired.

Kai was giving both of us an easy out.

If I were smart, I'd take it, but the thought of going home to an empty apartment filled me with trepidation. I loved Monty, but I couldn't exactly converse with a snake.

"Exactly. It's midnight, which means the night is still young." A new smile filled with mischief stole across my face. "I haven't shown you the real draw in the building yet."

I almost laughed at how fast Kai's face paled.

"Do I want to know?"

"Probably not, but you'll find out anyway." I removed my smock and tossed it in the dirty laundry bin. "Let's go. We can get our canvases later. We don't want to miss the fun."

He looked like he had a different word in mind than fun, but he followed my lead and removed his smock, albeit with obvious reluctance. We left our coats in the studio and took the elevator to the basement.

"Brace yourself," I said when the steel car thudded to a stop.

The line of consternation between Kai's brows deepened. "What..."

The doors opened, and a powerful wave of noise drowned out the rest of his words. His consternation morphed into visible horror. This time, I couldn't contain my laugh.

During the day, the basement was a glorified storage room. But at night? It was the hottest, most exclusive party in Brooklyn.

No name, no advertisements, just good music, cheap drinks, and shattered inhibitions.

The Hulk-like bouncer recognized me on sight. He was a big fan of Felix's, and he stamped our hands with the entry symbol before waving us past with a toothy grin.

"Is this...a rave?" I couldn't hear Kai clearly over the music, but his appalled expression told me all I needed to know about his feelings toward raves.

"Of course not!" I shouted. "Raves have more drugs!"

Another laugh broke free from my throat. He looked like he'd swallowed a lemon whole.

"Come on!" I grabbed his wrist and pulled him toward the bar. It wasn't fancy like Valhalla's, but the drinks were strong and the prices cheap. Sometimes, that was all we needed.

It took us a while to push through the sweaty, gyrating crowd, but we eventually made it to the other side. The bar's alcove provided enough shelter from the music for people to hear each other without shouting. I ordered two of the house specials and handed one to Kai.

"First round's on me." I lifted my plastic cup. Like I said, not fancy, but I wasn't drinking the container. "To stepping out of comfort zones."

Kai hesitated, eyeing the drink the same way he'd eyed the door earlier, like it might kill him if he got too close. For a second, I thought he was going to refuse, but then he shook his head, muttered something that looked suspiciously like *fuck it* (if my lip-reading skills were anything to go by), and tapped his cup against mine.

"To stepping out of comfort zones."

We tipped our heads back and downed the drinks at the same time. The fiery burn of bourbon scorched its way into my stomach. It tasted awful, but the resulting buzz was worth temporarily murdering my taste buds.

"Jesus." Kai grimaced. "What did they put in this? Battery acid?"

"Don't ask. Sometimes, ignorance is bliss." I dragged him back to the dance floor.

He rubbed his free hand over his face. "You're going to be the death of me one day."

I beamed, touched by the idea that I was powerful enough to cause someone's death. Figuratively, not literally. I enjoyed reading about murder, not committing it.

It took several songs and shots, but Kai eventually relaxed enough to act like a normal person instead of a disapproving head-master at a school dance.

I laughed with delight when he spun me out, then pulled me back in. He was actually a pretty good dancer once he removed the stick from his ass.

"Not bad."

"Not bad?" He arched a mock offended brow. "I won my university's annual dance competition four years in a row. Show some respect."

I rolled my eyes. "Of course you did."

His talent was *being* talented. It was extremely annoying, but I found it hard to hold onto my anger when he was smiling down at me with that boyish gleam in his eyes.

He'd always been beautiful, with his elegant planes and chiseled lines, but tonight he looked different. More real, like he'd shed enough layers for his true self to peek through.

The music slowed, taking on a sultry, hypnotic beat. Our bodies shifted to match, swaying with a sensual rhythm that had my pulse throbbing in my ears. For the second time that night, our smiles faded as a familiar awareness crept between us.

The lights glinted off his glasses, flashing blue, then green, then red and blue again. His sweat-dampened shirt clung to his broad shoulders, and a lock of thick, dark hair fell over his eye, tousled by an hour of dancing. I had the sudden urge to brush it back from his forehead.

My pulse pounded harder, overpowering the music.

The boyish gleam in Kai's eyes was gone. All the banked heat and desire we shouldn't acknowledge blazed in its stead.

Shouldn't. What a strange word, considering I couldn't think of a single reason why we shouldn't do anything. In fact, I couldn't think much at all.

A woozy headiness filled me when his hand slid up my back and around my neck. His head dipped, and my chin tilted up like a flower leaning toward the sun.

Our breaths mingled for a single, breathless moment.

Then his mouth was on mine, and my mind emptied completely. Nothing else existed except *this.* The heat, the pleasure, the firm pressure of his lips and soft glide of his tongue against mine.

My fingers slid into his hair while I tipped my head back further, giving him as much access as possible. He tasted like whiskey and mint and, God, *him.* Something so delicious and indescribable I wanted to drown in it.

A moan slipped from my mouth to his. He answered with a tortured groan of his own, his hands tightening around my hip and nape in a way that had heat kindling between my thighs.

My first kiss in two years. It should've felt strange or at least a little uncomfortable, but it didn't. Instead, it felt completely, perfectly *right.*

My bones liquefied. If he hadn't been holding me up, I would've melted right there in the middle of the dance floor.

There was no denying it. Rigid, proper Kai Young, of the posh accent and boring hobbies, was an incredible kisser.

I would've been happy staying in that dark, sweaty basement forever, but an explosion of noise tore us from our bubble with the subtlety of a sledgehammer-wielding giant.

We startled apart as the music segued from smooth R&B to upbeat pop rock.

Kai and I stared at each other, our chests heaving. The change in tempo killed the haze clouding my brain, and a slow horror seeped into my consciousness when I realized what just happened.

"We should—"

"It's late—"

Our words stumbled over each other, lost beneath the frenetic beats. It didn't matter. I knew what he wanted to say because the same words echoed through my head.

What have we done?

CHAPTER 15

Isabella

I'd kissed Kai.

Boring, buttoned-up Kai. Always overhearing me say the most inappropriate things Kai. Member of the Valhalla Club Kai. And I'd *liked* it.

The world had truly turned upside down.

I wiped the counter, my movements slow and distracted as memories from Saturday night unwound through me like an invisible spool of silk. Kai and I had left the club after grabbing our coats and canvases and taken separate cabs home without saying a word. Four days had passed since then, but my mind couldn't stop replaying our kiss.

It wasn't just the physical act itself. It was the way I'd *felt,* like being in Kai's arms was the safest place I could be. I'd kissed plenty of guys before, but ours was the only one that clicked.

Either that, or I'd been really, really drunk.

I sighed and glanced around the empty room. It was the day before Thanksgiving, which meant the club was a dead zone. Usually, I loved this shift because I got paid for little to no work, but the silence was driving me crazy.

Thirty more minutes. Then I could take my laptop to my favorite café and write. I hadn't forgotten about the February deadline, but I'd been so distracted I hadn't had time to dwell on it.

I caught a flash of gray out of the corner of my eye. I looked up, and the air died in my lungs.

Kai. He walked in like he owned the place, which, as a managing committee member, he kind of did.

No jacket, no tie, only a white dress shirt with the sleeves rolled up and suspenders running crisp lines down to a pair of perfectly tailored charcoal pants. He was back to his usual polished self, except for the tiny frown marring his forehead.

I forced oxygen past the knot in my chest.

We hadn't talked or seen each other since our kiss, and I'd underestimated the impact his presence would have on me. If I hadn't stopped moving altogether when he entered, I would've accidentally knocked one of the three-hundred-dollar Baccarat glasses to the ground.

Our eyes connected. A different, heavier silence fell over us, the kind woven from forbidden memories and unspoken words.

Kai reached the bar and took the seat across from me; I poured a glass of scotch and pushed it toward him without a word.

He brought it to his lips, his throat working with a sexy swallow.

I didn't have other customers to distract me, so I just watched him, lazy tendrils of desire curling in my stomach even as the silence expanded between us.

He set the glass down, and we observed each other warily like we were gauging the other's expression for the right thing to say.

"Why aren't you in London?" I finally asked after what felt like hours but was probably only minutes. "For Thanksgiving."

The corner of his mouth quirked, melting some of the tension. "The British don't celebrate Thanksgiving."

Right.

"Besides..." The frown reappeared for a split second between his brows. "I have a work crisis to deal with."

"Over a holiday weekend?"

"Crises are unaccommodating that way. They have little respect for human schedules." Amusement gilded his reply.

"So you're just going to work the entire weekend? That's so depressing." A pang hit my chest when I pictured Kai pulling all-nighters at his computer while everyone else celebrated with their families.

I shouldn't feel sorry for him. He earned more in a day than most people earned in a year, but he was still human. Everyone deserved time off.

"It's not as bad as it sounds. I enjoy my job." He rubbed a thumb over the rim of his glass. "And you? How are you spending the holidays?"

"Writing, shopping, and preparing for Christmasbirthdaynew-yearpalooza in February. I know, it's a mouthful," I said when his mouth quirked again. "But we're too lazy to come up with a better name." I hesitated, then added, "So we'll both be in the city this weekend."

I wasn't sure why it mattered. It wasn't like we were going to invite each other over to our houses for four days of food, sex, and shopping. Right?

Kai gave a slow shake of his head. "I have a red-eye flight to San Francisco tonight," he said. "Part of the work crisis management."

"Oh." Disappointment sank like a weight in my stomach.

"Have you visited the library again?" He abruptly switched topics. "For your writing?"

"Not yet." It reminded me too much of him. Even if it weren't so quiet, I doubted I could write in there. "Maybe one day."

"I see." This time, he was the one who looked disappointed.

Silence lapsed again, punctuated by the hum of the heater. God, this was torture. Why couldn't I simply say what I wanted to?

Because it's a bad idea. Because it's against the rules. Because—
I get it. Shut up.

Kai hesitated. "About Saturday—"

"It was a mistake." I interrupted him before he could state the obvious. "I know. You don't have to say it. We shouldn't have done...what we did."

His frown deepened. "That's not what I was going to say."

I faltered. "It's not?"

The clock ticked in the ensuing quiet. My heartbeat ticked right alongside it, rising and falling with the tide of emotion threatening to sweep me under.

"No." A muscle worked in his jaw. "Unless you truly think it was a mistake."

"I..." On one hand, it was a mistake. Kai and I came from different worlds. His role as Young heir probably involved marriage to a proper society heiress like Clarissa. Getting even more involved with him was a sure path toward heartbreak. I'd been there, gotten the T-shirt, and I never wanted to go back.

On the other hand...

I swallowed. I didn't know what Kai and I currently had, but the thought of severing it cleaved through me like a scythe.

"You don't have to answer now." Kai stood and nodded at his empty glass, his expression unreadable. "Put it on my tab. I'll be upstairs."

By the time my brain processed his words, he was already gone.

I'll be upstairs.

His parting statement played on a loop while I cleaned and closed out the bar. He had no reason to tell me that unless...

You don't have to answer now...I'll be upstairs.

A choice. I could go home, pretend the kiss never happened, and move on with my life.

Or I could go upstairs.

New Isabella should do the smart thing and choose option

one, but it was obvious by now that no version of me was good at doing what she *should*.

I locked the bar door behind me and made my way to the second floor. A part of me knew I was risking my job by doing this. Unfortunately, that part was so faint I could barely hear it over the drum of my heart.

I could rationalize away my attraction to Kai all I wanted, but the truth was he made me feel more alive than anything else had for years.

I stopped in front of the piano room and rested my hand on the doorknob. The drumming in my chest intensified. *No going back now.*

I opened the door, stepped inside…and there he was, lounging against the side of the piano in a deceptively casual pose.

Dark hair, dark eyes, devastation inked onto every inch of him.

Even if he hadn't dropped the upstairs hint, instinct would've guided me to him. The melding of gazes in a crowded ballroom, a chance meeting in a quiet hallway…no matter where we were, an invisible force drew us together like magnets to steel.

Our eyes locked.

Emotion flickered over Kai's face. It was there, then gone, like a ship passing in the night, but it was enough.

It pulled me toward him at the same time as he straightened, his body lined with tension.

Five steps.

Four.

Three.

Two.

One.

I halted inches away from him, my mind and pulse gone haywire. I didn't say a word. I didn't have to; my presence was telling enough.

His throat flexed.

A breath passed, and then—we collided.

Hands. Lips. Teeth.

His mouth crushed against mine, my fingers tangled in his hair, and urgency ignited between us until my limbs were heavy and weak with desire.

This time, there was no crowd, no music, only the desperate, frantic need to get as close to him as possible.

My back slammed against the side of the piano. I gasped, more at the thick, insistent press of Kai's arousal against my thigh than the impact. Pain didn't register. My blood was liquid fire, burning away any sensations except pleasure, want, need.

Kai's body molded against mine. He bracketed me with his arms, and a moan rose in my throat when he drew my bottom lip between his teeth and tugged.

The stiff, reserved CEO was gone. In his place was someone who kissed like a man possessed, filled with filthy promises and wicked intent.

My hands roamed over warm skin and sculpted muscles, feverish with want. We were pressed so tightly together I could feel the wild beats of his heart, but it wasn't enough.

Kai groaned when I arched into him, craving *more.*

"I was right. You *are* going to be the death of me," he muttered.

He pulled back. A protest climbed my throat, but it quickly died when he took off his glasses and tossed them to the side before kissing me again, even deeper this time, his mouth exploring mine so expertly all rational thought dissolved. Strong, warm hands swept up the backs of my thighs and lifted me onto the piano. One stayed on my thigh, sliding up and around until it brushed the wetness soaking my underwear; the other stole beneath my top and bra to palm my breast.

"Please." My half gasp, half whimper would've been embarrassing had I been in my right mind.

I couldn't draw enough oxygen into my lungs. My head grew light, every ounce of consciousness arrowing to the heat building in my center.

"And here I thought I'd never hear you beg." Kai's silken murmur traveled the length of my spine and dropped between my legs. It pulsed with an empty ache as he pushed my panties to the side and rubbed a thumb over my sensitized clit.

My vision hazed.

I didn't see when he pushed my top up and closed his mouth around my nipple, or when he pushed a finger deep enough inside me to make me cry out. Time lost all meaning as he consumed me, licking and sucking and playing me with ruthless precision until I writhed with mindless pleasure.

I was practically lying on top of the piano at this point, and a sharp cry tore from my throat when he pressed the most sensitive spot inside me. I thrashed and bucked, my hand accidentally hitting the exposed ivory keys.

Discordant notes spilled into the air, masking the existing, filthy symphony of moans, whimpers, and the wet sounds of his fingers plunging in and out of me.

My arousal dripped down my thighs and onto the Steinway's lacquered top. I was nothing but sensation, lost in a rhythm that was both too much and not enough.

"That's it, love." Gravel transformed Kai's soft words into a rough command. "Be a good girl and come for me."

That was all it took.

My orgasm scorched through me like gasoline set ablaze. Higher, hotter, crashing over me in wave after wave until I was so spent I could do little more than lie there, limp and spent while Kai cleaned me up.

Languid contentment spread through me as he wiped my thighs with something soft—a handkerchief, maybe—and gently tugged my clothes back into place.

"Well, that's one way to celebrate Thanksgiving," I said drowsily. "Much better than the Macy's parade."

His soft laugh blanketed my skin. "Technically, it's Thanksgiving Eve."

Kai helped me off the piano and onto my feet, though my knees were so weak I wobbled a bit before I regained my balance.

Sometime between giving me one of the best orgasms of my life and now, he'd put his glasses back on. His hair was mussed from my hands, and flags of color stained the crests of his cheeks, but he was still far more put together than I was.

"If you have the clarity of mind to know what day it is, something's wrong." I dropped my eyes to where his arousal tented his pants. My throat dried, and a fresh wave of heat coasted through my stomach. "When is your flight again?"

Do we have time for a second round? The real meaning behind my question wasn't lost on either of us.

Heat darkened his eyes, followed by a rueful smile. "I have a conference call in half an hour. Last one before the holiday. Apparently, it's the only time that works for everyone."

He was turning down sex for a *business call?*

I tried not to look too insulted.

"We'll talk next week when we have more time," Kai said. "This was...that is, I didn't expect..." He faltered, looking so adorably flustered that I couldn't hold on to my annoyance.

He was right. The day before Thanksgiving wasn't the best time for a deep dive on whatever we had. He'd fingered me in the piano room of the club where I worked, for Christ's sake—the same club that would throw me out on my ass and blackball me if people found out what happened.

I needed time to think about what to do next when I wasn't riding a post-orgasmic high.

The inklings of dread returned. How did I always find myself in these situations?

By making bad decisions, a voice sang in my head. *By never having a plan and ending up in places you don't want to be.*

I didn't bother refuting it. I couldn't if I tried.

"Makes sense." I tucked a strand of hair behind my ear, suddenly feeling unsure. Our tension had exploded spectacularly after weeks, maybe even months, of buildup, and now we had to deal with the aftermath. The problem was, I always sucked at cleanup. I was forever getting into messes with no vision of how to get myself out.

Kai and I lapsed into silence as we finished straightening the room and ourselves out. He seemed as lost for words as I was, though he could just be mentally prepping for his call, I thought sourly.

I exited the room first, but I didn't make it two steps before I came to an abrupt halt. My stomach dropped several inches.

There was someone in the hall.

Tall, broad, and utterly terrifying, the behemoth of a man stared down at me, his face expressionless. His eyes were an icy, unsettling blue, so pale they were almost colorless. His dark hair was cropped short, and a vicious scar slashed diagonally across his face from eyebrow to chin, bisecting it into two otherwise flawless halves. If it weren't for the scar and those shiver-inducing eyes, he could've made a killing as a model with those cheekbones.

My gaze dipped, and a jolt ran through me at the sight of thick red burns twisting around his neck like a rope. Unlike the flat coldness of his stare, the burns seemed to pulse with rage under my scrutiny, as if they were seconds away from leaping off his skin and strangling me.

An answering pressure wrapped around my throat. The amount of pain he must've endured to get those scars...

His eyes sharpened into icicles. I expected him to call me out on my admittedly rude staring, but he simply gave Kai a curt nod before stepping around me and disappearing around the corner.

The encounter had lasted less than twenty seconds, yet the icy touch of his glare shivered on my skin.

"Who was that?" Whoever it was, he was definitely a club member—and he'd seen me and Kai exit the piano room together.

My heart thudded with panic.

"Vuk Markovic, better known as the Serb. He doesn't like people using his given name." Kai didn't elaborate, but his tone told me there was more to the story than he was letting on.

"Don't worry about him. He won't say anything. He keeps to himself."

I chose to believe him, if only for the sake of my sanity.

I glanced over my shoulder as we walked toward the stairs. The hall was empty, yet I couldn't shake the chill crawling over the back of my neck—the type you got when someone was watching you.

CHAPTER 16

I spent my Thanksgiving weekend in a hotel, alternating between work and Isabella. Specifically, fantasizing about Isabella while *trying* to work.

I had a multibillion-dollar deal on the line, and all I could think about was the woman who'd crashed into my life and blown it into a thousand smithereens.

The kiss. The piano room. The two best and worst decisions of my life.

Even now, days later, my mind echoed with Isabella's cries as she came all over my hand. I'd attended countless symphonies, orchestras, and performances headlined by the best and brightest in the music world, but no song had ever sounded as sweet.

"You're not even paying attention." Dante's irritated voice sliced through the memory like jagged glass through silk.

"Hmm?"

He threw an exasperated stare my way. "I'm trying to help you, asshole. The least you can do is listen. Isn't that why we're having this meeting?"

We'd arranged a brainstorm in his office over lunch. Outside our weekly boxing matches, where we had free rein to pummel each other as much as we liked, we often consulted each other on business matters. Granted, I couldn't take his advice half the time because his solutions bordered on illegal, but it was nice to have an objective third-party sounding board.

"No. I simply missed your cheerful, optimistic personality." I lifted my water in a mock toast. "You brighten my day."

"Fuck off." He snorted, but a shadow of a smile played over his mouth. "Mishra still refusing to meet with you?"

"So far, but he'll cave." Colin Whidby was still in the hospital, but his condition had stabilized. He'd pull through. The problem was, he wouldn't be back on his feet for another few months. The longer we waited, the greater the chance of something going wrong.

My team and I had been working around the clock to close the DigiStream deal before the end of the year, but it was looking less and less likely. Rohan Mishra, the other co-founder, was digging his heels in on certain clauses in the contract and refusing to meet in person. One face-to-face meeting was worth a dozen phone calls.

Dammit, Whidby. If he'd kept his nose out of cocaine long enough to sign the papers, we wouldn't have this problem. If I screwed up this deal, I would be the laughingstock of the business community. Reputation tarnished. Legacy gone.

My skin itched at the thought.

And yet, despite what was at stake, I couldn't focus. What happened at Valhalla last week had embedded itself in my psyche like a tree digging its roots into fresh soil. It split my attention, dragging half my mind toward glory and the other toward endless replays of last Wednesday afternoon.

The scent of rose and vanilla. The beautiful flush of Isabella's skin. The throaty gasp of my name interspersed with her moans.

Heat prickled my skin.

"If you're really stuck, I know a guy," Dante said, pulling my attention back to the present again. "He can dig up information that'll have Mishra folding in no time."

Right. Mishra. DigiStream. *Focus.* "Don't tell me it's Harper," I said with a small grimace.

Christian Harper, the CEO of Harper Security, was Dante's go-to guy for all things tech and security related. We were acquaintances, but he was closer with Dante, who'd been his first client back in the day and was far more comfortable with his black-hat methods. I preferred staying on the right side of the law. My reputation was stainless, and I intended to keep it that way.

Dante shrugged. "You know he can get the job done."

I shook my head. "I can handle Mishra on my own." Frankly, I was a touch insulted he thought I'd have to stoop to blackmail to get the other man to sign.

I didn't lose. Not when I put my mind to something. One way or another, the DigiStream deal *would* happen.

"It's your deal," Dante drawled. "But don't say I didn't give you a solution."

A knock interrupted us, followed by the soft creak of the door opening.

Dante straightened. I didn't have to turn to know who'd entered; there was only one person who made his eyes light up like that.

"Hi, Vivian," I said without looking up from my lunch.

She laughed. "Hi, Kai."

Dante's wife came around the desk and bent to give him a kiss on the cheek. He turned his head at the last minute so his mouth caught hers instead. Vivian's cheeks flushed, and my tuna roll suddenly tasted tooth-rottingly sweet.

"My meeting ended early, so I thought I'd surprise you for lunch," she said a touch breathlessly. She placed two white takeout bags on the desk and gave me an apologetic glance as Dante pulled a chair up next to his. "I didn't realize you had an appointment. I can come back—"

"No need," he cut in. "The meeting's over. Kai has another appointment after this." He flicked a glance at me. "Close the door on your way out, will you?"

Vivian frowned. "Don't be rude. Look at his plate. It's still half-full."

"He can't eat all of that. He's on a diet." Dante gave me a pointed stare. "Right?"

"Actually, I'm quite hungry today," I drawled. "One should never let sushi from Masa go to waste, though I am curious about what Vivian brought. It smells wonderful."

If looks could kill, Dante's glare would've incinerated me on the spot. I returned it with an innocent smile.

After boxing and translation, provoking him was my favorite pastime.

"Burgers, fries, and shakes from Moondust Diner," Vivian said, pulling the items out of the bags. "Stay. There's enough for all of us, and we haven't talked since Monarch."

I pretended not to hear Dante's warning growl. I'd already blocked out the hour for our meeting. It would be rude to rebuff Vivian's generous hospitality.

"If you insist," I said. "I do love a good burger."

I was going to pay for that in the boxing ring later, but I wasn't worried. Dante and I were evenly matched, and it was worth it for the look on his face.

Vivian and I chatted while he scowled. She owned a luxury event planning company, and she had plenty of stories about wild requests and demanding clients, many of whom were mutual acquaintances.

I listened politely, asking and answering questions where needed, but I couldn't stop my mind from straying to a specific connection we had.

Vivian and Isabella were best friends. Had Isabella mentioned what happened last week to her? Vivian wasn't acting any differently toward me, so I assumed Isabella hadn't said a word to her friends.

I wasn't sure whether to be relieved or offended.

"By the way, I won't be home until late tonight," Vivian told Dante. "I'm going out with the girls. We're trying to break Isa's man ban."

My water went down the wrong pipe. I choked out a cough while Dante's brows pulled together.

"What the hell is a man ban?"

"She hasn't dated anyone in two years because of an...unpleasant experience with an ex," Vivian explained. "We figured it's time to break her dry spell."

Absolutely fucking not. Her dry spell has been broken. By me.

My reaction was so sharp, so visceral, that it knocked the breath from my lungs. I had no frame of reference for the dark, irrational possessiveness coursing through my blood or the crimson tinting my vision at the mere thought of another man's hands on Isabella. I was not a jealous person, and one kiss and orgasm did not a relationship make.

But it didn't matter. When it came to Isabella, all my previous mores went out the window.

"Does she want to break the ban, or is this an intervention?" I checked my phone, my tone indifferent, but my muscles tensed in anticipation of Vivian's reply.

"I'm sure she does. She said she wanted to at our wedding, but in classic Isa fashion, she drank too much champagne and fell asleep before it happened." Vivian laughed. "Anyway, her birthday is coming up, so we figured it would be a good time to take her out."

"Where are you going?" I asked casually.

Dante's eyes cut in my direction. I ignored his laser scrutiny and focused on Vivian.

"Verve. It's a new club downtown," she said, seemingly oblivious to her husband's growing suspicion. "Isa's been talking about going since it opened."

"Laurent's place. I've heard of it." The Laurents built their empire on restaurants, but they were expanding into other areas of hospitality. "I didn't know her birthday was so soon."

"December nineteenth. A Sagittarius through and through, as she'll tell you," Vivian said with a smile.

"Why the sudden interest in Isabella?" Dante asked. "Finally looking to give your mother the daughter-in-law she so desperately wants?"

I glared at him. Sometimes, I missed the days when all he did was scowl and punch people. Now he had jokes.

"No," I said coolly. "I'm inquiring about an acquaintance I see quite often. It's social courtesy—something you might want to brush up on."

"Ah, of course. My mistake." If Dante's smirk were any bigger, it'd fall off his face. The bastard was having a field day. Payback for me staying and interrupting his alone time with Vivian, no doubt.

It didn't matter. He could gloat all he wanted, but he had no proof I was interested in Isabella. It wasn't like I was going to show up at Verve and drag her away from potential suitors like some territorial caveman.

I had more pride than that.

CHAPTER 17

A wave of heat, alcohol, and noise slammed into me the minute I stepped into Verve.

In my defense, I truly hadn't planned on visiting the club that night. I disliked packed spaces, drunken foolishness, and migraine-inducing remixes, all of which nightclubs possessed in spades.

However, as a Young Corporation executive and publisher of *Mode de Vie,* the world's preeminent fashion and lifestyle magazine, it was my job to keep a pulse on the city's hotspots. I wouldn't be doing my due diligence if I didn't experience Verve myself, would I?

The deep bass of the latest hit song rattled my bones as I pushed my way through the crowd. Everywhere I looked, I was assaulted with noise and people—women in tight dresses, men in tighter jeans, couples engaged in dancing that looked more like fornicating. No signs of Isab—of anyone I knew yet.

Not that I was looking for anyone in particular.

I made it halfway to the VIP lounge when one of the clubgoers bumped into me and nearly spilled her drink on my shoes.

"Oops! Sorry!" she squealed, her eyes bright in a manner that could only be attributed to drugs, alcohol, or both. She clutched my arm with her free hand and looked me over. "Oh, you're cute. Do you have a girlfriend?"

"How about we find your girlfriends instead?" I suggested. I gently freed myself from her grip and steered her toward her friends at the bar (easily identifiable since they wore the same bachelorette party sashes as my erstwhile admirer). I flagged down the bartender. "A bottle of water for the lady, please."

By the time he returned, she was already busy taking shots with some suit in an off-an-rack Armani.

I doubted she'd drink the water, but I left it there anyway. Being the only sober person in a club was like babysitting a room full of strangers.

I ordered a scotch for myself, already regretting my decision to come here when a familiar voice cut through the noise.

"Kai? Is that you?"

I turned, my gaze honing in on the brunette with glossy caramel hair and blue-gray eyes. My face relaxed into a smile.

"Alessandra, what a pleasant surprise. I didn't take you for the clubbing type."

Dominic's wife returned my smile with a small one of her own. Objectively, she was one of the most beautiful women I'd ever met. She looked like a younger version of her mother, who'd been one of Brazil's biggest supermodels in the nineties. But despite, or perhaps because of, her looks and marriage to one of the richest men on Wall Street, she always carried an air of melancholy around her.

Dominic was my friend, but I wasn't blind to his faults. He was about as romantic as a rock.

"I'm not, but Dom is busy with work, and it's been so long since I've had a girls' night..." She shrugged, a brief flicker of sadness passing through her eyes. "I thought it would be nice to get out of the house. Lord knows I spend enough time there."

Girls' night. A seed of suspicion sprouted in my stomach, but I kept my tone as casual as possible. "You don't have to explain. I understand." A pause, then, "Who are you here with?"

"Vivian and her friends. We met at last year's fall gala and stayed in touch. When she found out I didn't have any plans tonight, she invited me to come out with them." Alessandra tilted her head toward the elevator. "Do you want to join us? We have a table in the VIP lounge."

Vivian and her friends. Meaning Isabella.

The knowledge lit a match in my blood, but I suppressed a visible reaction. "I don't want to intrude on a girls' night out."

"You won't be intruding. The whole point of the night is to meet the opposite sex. Well, not me and Vivian since we're married," Alessandra amended. She twisted her wedding ring around her finger. "But Sloane and Isabella have been fending off advances all night. Well, Sloane has been fending off and Isabella has been accepting." She laughed. "She must've danced with half the single men here already."

Something dark and unwanted flared in my chest.

"How lovely," I said, my voice clipped. I forced an easy smile over the urge to demand the name of every single fucker who'd touched her. Normal me would've been appalled at the violent turn in my thoughts, but I hadn't been normal since the moment I laid eyes on Isabella.

A burst of rich, creamy laughter spilled through the air, shattering my concentration.

I glanced up with a touch of annoyance. I'd been making decent progress on my translation of The Art of War *before I'd been rudely interrupted.*

I scanned the bar, my eyes settling on the one person I'd never seen before. Purple-black hair, tanned skin, incredible curves poured into Valhalla's signature black staff uniform. Silver earrings glinted in her ears, and when she lifted her hand to brush a lock of hair out of her eye, I spotted the dark swirls of a tattoo on her inner wrist.

Her coworker said something, and another burst of mirth

poured out of her. Even if it hadn't, I would've known she was the laugh's owner. She radiated the same wild, uninhibited energy.

She talked with her hands, her face animated. I didn't know what she was saying or why I was staring, but every time I tried to look away, her presence demanded my attention like a rainbow in a sky of gray.

A whisper of unease threaded through my gut.

Whoever she was, I could tell, without even exchanging a single word with her, that she was going to be trouble.

"Kai?" Alessandra's voice grounded me back in the club.

I blinked away the memory and slipped on an easy smile. *Focus.* "But I think I'll join you after all. I'd much rather spend the evening with friends than strangers."

"Perfect." She returned my smile. "Vivian will be happy to see you."

We made small talk as we took the elevator up to the third floor, but I was only half paying attention.

I hadn't reached out to Isabella since Thanksgiving Eve. One, I'd been swamped with work, and two, I'd needed time to sort through my thoughts.

The rational side of me insisted I leave things as they were. No good would come of pursuing her any further, especially with the board watching my every move. I couldn't afford a scandal before the CEO vote, and everything about Isabella—from her indecent conversation topics to her ability to storm through every defense I'd erected with nothing but a smile—screamed scandal. The *irrational* side of me, however, didn't give a fuck.

For the first time in my life, the irrational side was winning.

When Alessandra and I entered the VIP lounge, my eyes automatically scanned the room for a pair of familiar dimples and dark hair.

Nothing.

Vivian and Sloane sat at a corner table, but Isabella was nowhere in sight.

She could be in the restroom or getting another drink...or

she could be dancing with someone somewhere else in the club.

Green spread in my blood like poison.

I'd never been jealous of anyone in my life. I didn't need to be; I'd always been the fastest, smartest, most accomplished person in the room. I barely paid attention to the competition because there *was* no competition.

But in that moment, I was so fucking jealous of a hypothetical person I couldn't breathe.

I attempted to marshal my runaway emotion into a neutral expression as I approached the table. I wasn't sure I succeeded; it was too thick and consuming, like smoke billowing from a wildfire.

"I hope you don't mind, but I brought a guest." Alessandra took the seat next to Vivian, whose eyebrows winged up when she saw me. "I saw Kai downstairs and figured the more, the merrier."

"I'm here for research," I said, preempting Vivian's question. "*Mode de Vie* is featuring Verve in an article about Manhattan nightlife."

Note to self: tell Mode de Vie's *entertainment editor to run an article on Manhattan nightlife and mention Verve.*

"I see." Amusement glided across her face. "Well, like Ále said, the more, the merrier. I hope you find some good tidbits for your... article."

"You're doing the research yourself?" Sloane leaned back and assessed me with cool, skeptical eyes. Alessandra and Vivian were dressed for a night out, but Sloane's tight bun and wide-legged pantsuit looked like they came straight from the office. "Isn't that something reserved for junior writers, not division presidents?"

"I prefer a hands-on approach to projects I'm interested in."

"Such as those pertaining to city nightlife."

My smile tightened. "Yes."

"Interesting." She looked like she was gearing up for a second round of interrogation, but fortunately, a burst of laughter from a nearby table caught her attention before she could grill me further. Her eyes snapped to her right, and her expression iced so quickly I felt the chill in my bones. "You've got to be kidding me."

I followed her glare to the group lounging in the booth across from us. It consisted of celebrity offspring, wild-child socialites, and a few hangers-on, one of whom was booted unceremoniously from his seat for the latest arrival.

His back was to me, but I'd recognize the tattoos anywhere. There was only one person who'd ink a rival family's crest on his bicep.

Xavier Castillo, the youngest son of Colombia's richest beer magnate.

Sloane stormed over to his table. He turned, a grin forming on his face despite her obvious displeasure. I couldn't hear what they were saying, but judging by her hand gestures and his irreverent expression, I was minutes away from witnessing a murder.

Alessandra's brows knitted. "Is that Xavier? I thought he was in Ibiza."

I was as surprised as she was to see him in the city. He usually whiled away his days on a yacht, surrounded by models and other hedonistic heirs. His father had built his company from the ground up, but Xavier's ambition hovered somewhere south of zero.

"He moved to New York a few weeks ago. He's Sloane's newest client." Vivian winced when Sloane jabbed a finger at his chest, her eyes sharp enough to pierce stone. Xavier yawned, seemingly unfazed. "They're having some growing pains."

After another terse exchange, Sloane stalked toward the exit. "I'll be right back," she said grimly as she passed our table. Xavier followed her, managing to look bored and amused at the same time.

He nodded a greeting at me and winked at Vivian and Alessandra, who watched them leave with a wry smile.

"And then there were three," she said. "So much for girls' night."

"Speaking of which, where's Isabella?" I asked casually. As

fascinating as Sloane's client problems were, I didn't care to specu-late about what she was doing with—or to—Xavier, though I wouldn't put it past her to stab him with a stiletto.

"She's on the second floor." Vivian took a demure sip of her drink. "This *gorgeous* guy asked her to dance, and we wanted to give them some alone time, so we didn't follow her. Wasn't he beauti-ful, Ale? He looked a bit like Asher Donovan."

Alessandra's frown deepened. "He wasn't *that* beautiful…"

Vivian stared at her, hard. That strange silent communication women shared must have happened, because Alessandra's face soon relaxed. Her eyes darted toward me. "But yes, I suppose he was quite handsome. Isabella certainly thought so."

My teeth clenched so hard it hurt. "You let her go off with a stranger? When was the last time she checked in? He could be *drugging* her right now."

Didn't they read the news? Crime was up. New date rape drug variants hit the streets every week. They were Isabella's friends! They should have been looking out for her, not foisting her off on every Asher Donovan look-alike who passed by.

Donovan wasn't even that good-looking, for fuck's sake.

"She's an adult. She can make her own decisions," Vivian said calmly. "Isa is smart enough to take care of herself. Besides, the whole point of tonight was to find her a one-night stand."

"Or more," Alessandra added.

Vivian's eyes twinkled. "Or more."

Neither seemed to grasp the severity of the situation.

Irritation crawled into my chest and fed the restlessness bubbling beneath my skin. "Excuse me." I stood so abruptly I almost knocked the glasses off a passing bottle server's tray. "It was lovely seeing you both, but I should take a look around the club. For research."

"Of course." Vivian's smile widened. "Good luck with your article."

I left them in the lounge, Vivian looking oddly smug while Alessandra simply looked bemused.

I was too impatient to wait for the elevator, so I took the stairs to the second floor. My phone buzzed with a call from Dominic on my way down; I ignored it, though his timing was curious. He never called this late, and he was supposed to be in the office. Dominic rarely paid attention to anything except numbers when he was in work mode.

But all thoughts of why he might be calling me at midnight melted away when I reached my destination. Unlike the spacious VIP lounge, the second floor teemed with drunk twenty- and thirty somethings. Reggaeton blasted through the room, and the air dripped with sex, alcohol, and sweat.

Finding Isabella so soon defied all odds, considering how packed the club was. But I turned my head, and there she was. Even in a crowd of hundreds, she stood out like a sunflower in a field of weeds.

Face flushed, eyes sparkling, cheeks dimpled with an unfettered smile. Her hair tumbled down her back in loose waves, and the urge to wrap my fist around all that raven and violet silk burned through me. One tug and she'd be mine, her mouth ripe for the taking, her neck bared for my teeth and tongue.

I hardened, my mind alive with fantasies it had no business entertaining. I'd locked my less desirable impulses into foolproof boxes over the years, but one glance at her and the bolts disintegrated like parchment in flames.

Isabella's laugh carried over the music to my ears. She tilted her head up to look at the man in front of her. Brown hair, ill-fitting shirt, the professionally whitened teeth of a politician or car salesman. *Beautiful, my ass*. He looked like a fucking douchebag.

My desire morphed into the flinty edge of jealousy. It glinted, one spark away from a fire, when he snaked an arm around her waist and whispered something in her ear.

Isabella must've felt the heat of my stare because instead of replying, she turned her head toward me. Our gazes collided, hers bright with surprise, mine undoubtedly dark with emotions I'd rather not examine too closely.

Her smile faded, and I heard the catch of her breath from across the room.

It should've been impossible, but I was so attuned to her I could single out her tiniest movement in a club full of people.

Car Salesman said something to her again. She broke our stare, but my feet were already moving, carrying me across the floor and to her side.

"There you are, darling." I placed a hand on Isabella's back, right above the asshole's arm, which was still curled around her waist. My polite smile masked the vicious dose of possessiveness pouring through my blood. "You didn't tell me you made a new friend."

The man's eyes narrowed. He didn't take his arm off Isabella. "Who the hell are you?"

"Someone who'll rearrange your already pitiful face if you don't leave in the next ten seconds," I said pleasantly. "In case your knockoff Patek Philippe can't tell the time correctly, that would be right about now."

Ten seconds was generous. I'd wanted to slam my fist into his jaw the moment I saw him.

Blotches of red formed on his face. "Fuck you. I—"

The man lapsed into silence when my smile sharpened. I didn't enjoy violence outside the ring, but I would gladly knock his teeth out and feed them to him.

My pulse roared with bloody anticipation.

He must've read the intentions scrawled over my face because he quickly dropped his arm, mumbled an excuse, and scurried off.

"What the hell was that?" Isabella demanded. She shrugged off my hand and glared at me. "You scared off my date!"

A muscle ticked in my jaw. "It's not a date if you didn't show up with him."

It occurred to me someone from Valhalla might see us, but my peers didn't frequent places like this. Even if they did, they would be in the VIP lounge, not on the general dance floor. But honestly, I was too riled up to give a fuck. The entire managing committee could've been standing next to us, and I'd still be focused on Isabella.

She canted her chin up. "It is if I *leave* with him."

"If that was all it took to scare him away, he doesn't deserve you," I said coolly. "If you'd left with him, you would've had to endure two minutes of assuredly unsatisfying fornication on a dirty mattress without a bed frame, so you should thank me. Given how he ran off, I doubt he could find enough rhythm to clap along to a basic nursery song, much less make your night worthwhile."

Isabella's jaw unhinged. She stared at me for a long moment before dissolving into laughter. "Wow. Fornication? Who talks like that?"

"Am I wrong?"

"I wouldn't know. Like I said, you scared him off before I could confirm how—" Her sentence broke off in a gasp when I wrapped my arm around her waist and pulled her to me.

"Do you think you would've enjoyed your time with him, Isabella?" I asked softly. "Would you have screamed for him like you did for me when I had my fingers buried inside your sweet little pussy? When you rode my hand until it was soaked with your release? I can still hear your cries, love. Every damn second of every day."

A dark flush colored her cheeks, swallowing her earlier amusement. Her eyes blazed with a fire that matched the one wreaking havoc on my good sense. "Stop."

"Stop what?" My free hand slid from her waist to the small of her back. The warmth of her skin seared into my palm, branding me.

"Stop saying things like that."

The noise should've overpowered her breathless words, but I heard her as clearly as if we were in an empty room.

Her throat flexed with a swallow when I grazed my knuckles

147

up the bare expanse of her back. Her dress dipped to just above her waist, and her skin glided like silk beneath my touch.

"Things like what? The truth?" I lowered my head, my mouth brushing the shell of her ear. "If there's one thing I regret, it's walking away before we finished what we started in the piano room."

If we had, maybe the memory of her wouldn't have tortured me so much the past week. Maybe it would've satiated this savage, clawing need to etch myself in her so deeply I was the only man she could think of.

I'd abandoned an evening with my books for a nightclub, for Christ's sake. If that wasn't a sign of my irreversible spiral, nothing was.

A shiver rippled through her. Her head fell back when my lips skimmed down to her earlobe and nipped. "Kai..."

The breathy sound of my name on Isabella's lips snapped whatever control I had left.

Lust surged through me, sweeping every piece of logic and rationality aside.

Few things in life were certain, but this I knew—if I didn't have her soon, and if she didn't want me as desperately as I wanted her, I would fucking die.

"Go upstairs and tell your friends you're leaving." I curled my hand around the back of her neck, my voice so low and dark I hardly recognized it. "You have five minutes, sweetheart, or you'll find out firsthand that I'm not always the gentleman you think I am."

CHAPTER 18

Isabella

I didn't remember what excuse I gave my friends for leaving early. I didn't remember much at all, really, about how I ended up here with Kai at half past midnight, my heart in my throat and my body thrumming with nerves.

We were at the Barber, a bar that looked like, well, a barber shop, if barber shops served alcohol in faux shampoo bottles and employed DJs who looked like they could moonlight as models.

Unlike the chaos of Verve, this place screamed exclusivity. Engraved admission wristbands, sensual music, air redolent with the perfumes of the lucky few who knew this place existed. We were only a few blocks from the club, but it was like we were in a different world.

Anticipation fluttered beneath my skin as Kai and I passed through a velvet curtain separating the main floor from the VIP area. He was a good foot taller than me, yet our steps fell in perfect rhythm. Every once in a while, his shirtsleeve would graze my skin, or my hair would tickle his arm. Neither of us visibly reacted, but every little touch dripped into the tension already simmering around us.

You have five minutes, sweetheart, or you'll find out firsthand that I'm not always the gentleman you think I am.

Pressure ached between my legs. After last week, I had no doubt Kai was capable of quite a few ungentlemanly things. I both loved and hated how much the prospect turned me on.

My anticipation scattered into head-to-toe tingles when the curtain closed behind us, cocooning us in a room that looked like... another barbershop. Black-and-white checkered tiles covered the floor, and black-cushioned swivel seats anchored personal bar stations. Instead of brushes, hair dryers, and gels, the stations boasted glasses, garnishes, and alcohol.

The room was oddly empty, but my heart jerked in surprise when Kai walked over to a station and knocked on the mirror. It slid open, revealing a bartender in a bow tie. He handed Kai two bottles, and the mirror shut again.

I couldn't decide whether the setup was incredibly cool or disturbingly creepy.

Kai's gaze sparked with amusement at whatever he saw on my face. He handed me one of the bottles, which I accepted without a word.

We hadn't spoken to each other since we left Verve, but instead of cooling my desire, the silence amplified it. Without conversation to distract me, my mind spun off into a dozen directions—toward the basement in Bushwick, where we'd kissed for the first time; the piano room at Valhalla, where he'd given me one of the best orgasms of my life; and the dance floor at Verve, where his appearance had skyrocketed my pulse more than I cared to admit.

I didn't take my eyes off his as I tilted my head back and downed the drink. Kai's expression seeped with lazy interest, but his gaze scorched like I was standing too close to a fire.

"What were you doing at Verve?" I finally spoke, my curiosity overtaking my fear of upsetting the delicate balance between us. "You don't strike me as the clubbing type."

Vivian had mentioned something about article research, which I didn't believe for a second. Presidents of multibillion-dollar companies didn't run around doing grunt work.

Kai observed me with those dark, knowing eyes. "Don't ask questions you already know the answer to, Isabella."

A shiver ghosted over my skin. God, the way he said my name was indecent, like a wicked lover stealing kisses in shadowed corners. Smooth silk layered over dark velvet. Deceptively proper yet dizzyingly sensual.

I'd told him to stop, but in truth, I was addicted to his voice, his touch, every single thing about him. And the way he looked at me made me think I wasn't the only one spinning out of control.

"Come here." The soft command skated down my spine.

My feet moved before my brain could protest. One step, two steps, three, until our bodies nearly touched. His body heat licked at my skin and singed the edges of my resistance.

"We shouldn't be doing this," I breathed. "It's against Valhalla's rules."

That was what I kept telling myself. I clung to the rule the way a shipwreck survivor would cling to a piece of driftwood. It was my lifeline, the only thing keeping me from drowning beneath the ferocious waves of my desire. But the pull of the tide was too great, and I could already feel my arms fatiguing. One more undertow, and I was a goner.

"I know," Kai said, as calmly as if we were strolling through Central Park. "I don't give a damn about the rules."

My heartbeat tripped. "That's unlike you." The words came out so fast they almost blended together, but I kept talking, afraid that if I stopped, I would drown. "I thought you worshiped rules like they're your religion. It's the British education, isn't it? I bet Oxbridge is quite rigid when it comes to that type of thing. Don't you—"

"Isabella."

I forced a swallow down my throat. "Yes?"

"Shut up and let me kiss you."

And there was an undertow.

I didn't have time to think. One minute, I was standing; the

151

next, Kai had crushed his mouth to mine, and my bones dissolved with such embarrassing speed I would've melted to the floor had he not been holding me up.

Our kiss in Brooklyn had been a sweet, tentative surprise. This one was deliberate, delivered with such aching, targeted precision that it obliterated all my defenses in one fell swoop.

The hand fisting my air. The sensual firmness of his mouth. The dizzying heat and scent of him.

Every weakness of mine, plundered and stroked into submission.

My head grew light, and I didn't resist when Kai maneuvered us to a chair. Part of me noted we were still in public, despite the empty room, and someone could come in at any second, but that hardly seemed important when he was fisting my hair like that and tugging on my bottom lip just so.

Every shiver melted into the next until I was racked with one long, ceaseless shudder of pleasure.

Then he pulled back, and I inhaled a shallow breath before I found myself on his lap. I didn't know how we ended up in that position, but I wasn't complaining. Not when his mouth scored a fiery path down the side of my neck and his arousal pressed flush against my back, driving the oxygen out of my lungs again.

I ground against him, chasing the orgasm that shimmered on the horizon like a mirage. Close enough to touch, but too far to claim.

"Spread your legs for me, love." Kai's murmur dripped honey into my veins. *God, that accent.*

I obliged. Pressure built between my legs as his hand trailed lazily up my inner thigh until they reached my soaked thong. The force of my need squeezed a low, embarrassing whine from my throat. He'd barely touched me, and I was already a mess.

"Just like that." He coaxed the straps off my shoulders with his other hand and gently tugged my dress down. I wasn't wearing a bra, and every brush of air against my tight, sensitized nipples sent an answering jolt to my core. I squirmed, desperate for more friction, but I couldn't get enough leverage in my position. "Let me feel how wet you are."

He pushed my underwear to the side.

"Kai." I gasped when he pushed two fingers inside me. Sweat beaded on my forehead at the agonizingly sweet stretch. "We can't..." My sentence evaporated when he palmed my breast and squeezed. He rubbed a thumb over my nipple while his fingers delved deeper.

My head fell back even as lust and caution warred for dominance. Nothing except a velvet curtain separated us from the rest of the bar. Someone only had to push the drape aside to get a wanton view of me sitting half-naked in Kai's lap, dress pushed to my waist, legs spread and skin flushed while he played me like a toy.

"Someone will hear." A humiliating whimper clawed through the air when he buried his fingers to the hilt and pressed a thumb against my swollen clit.

Tiny bursts of fireworks erupted beneath my skin. Low, rhythmic bass saturated the air, but my heart pounded so loud I was sure people could hear it from across the island.

"No, they won't." Kai sounded maddeningly calm, like he was dissecting an academic text instead of finger fucking me in semi-public. "Do you want to know why?"

I shook my head. My teeth dug into my bottom lip with such force the taste of copper spilled over my tongue.

"Because you're not going to come," he said softly. He pinched my nipple, hard, in warning emphasis. Twin streaks of pleasure and pain forced another whimper from my throat. Arousal dripped down my thighs and onto his expensive, perfectly pressed pants. "That would be highly inappropriate, considering we're in public."

The velvet curtain rustled. A stranger's laugh coasted perilously close to where we sat, but I couldn't bring myself to care.

My entire body thrummed with need. I was ravenous with it, hungry and hollow for something only Kai could give.

It went beyond the physical. I'd had sex with other men before, but I'd never *wanted* like this. Like I would die if I didn't have him inside me soon.

"Please." The word splintered on a broken moan when he dragged his thumb over my clit.

Slow. Firm. Utterly exquisite in its torture.

I tried to twist around to face him, but he locked an arm around my waist and caged me in place.

"I didn't say you could turn around." His mouth returned to my neck. The words inked into my skin with each featherlight kiss.

My breath stalled. "Do people always do what you say?"

I felt him smile against the curve of my shoulder. "Yes."

The simple response shouldn't have been so hot, but fuck, it was. And I was tired of waiting.

I finally gathered enough strength to pull his arm from my waist. He let me; I wasn't naive enough to think I could've bested him if he'd tried.

With one smooth twist, I straddled his lap. My bare breasts brushed the soft white cotton of his dress shirt.

Kai's breathing was steady, his expression placid, but his eyes blazed with so much intensity it threatened to consume us whole.

Not so unaffected after all.

The knowledge gave me the confidence to forge ahead. "Funny. I'm also used to people doing what I say."

Amusement leaked into his gaze. "Are you going to order me to do something, Isabella?"

"Yes." I leaned forward, pressing my breasts against his chest. His amusement vanished, leaving pools of darkness in their wake. "Fuck me."

A beat passed.

Kai didn't move.

Lines of tension corded his jaw and neck, but he remained deathly still when I reached up to take off his glasses.

I wanted to see him without any extra barriers between us.

I dropped the glasses on the counter behind me with a soft clatter.

It was a tiny sound, but it finally triggered a reaction.

Kai stood so abruptly I almost fell off his lap. He swallowed my gasp with a punishing kiss, and every thought blinked out of existence.

Hands. Lips. Teeth.

I couldn't tell where his ended and mine began. It didn't matter. All that mattered was *this*. The taste and feel of him, headier and more potent than any drug.

My arms wound around his neck, and he hiked my legs around his waist as he pushed me up against the nearby wall.

His earlier precision hung in tatters around us. This was pure, unadulterated lust, and there was no room for anything as neat as rational thought.

Kai kissed his way to my chest, his mouth a hot brand against my skin. A shudder rolled through me when he took a nipple in his mouth, licking and tugging and teasing until I was close to shattering.

His hands gripped my hips with bruising force; my teeth sank into the curve between his neck and shoulder with desperate want. We were sweat and heat and wild abandon, and I never wanted it to end.

He removed one of his hands from my hip. I dimly heard the metal rasp of a zipper, followed by the crinkle of foil.

The hot, hard head of his cock nudged against my pussy. I shifted my hips with a pleading whine, but he didn't *move*, dammit.

"Look at me," Kai said roughly.

I tipped my chin down and blinked the haze from my eyes. Shock and something more primal speared through me.

Lust had stripped away Kai's refined veneer. It carved harsh lines in his face, tautening the sculpted planes of his cheekbones and turning his eyes into pools of black.

I hardly recognized him, yet the heavy, insistent ache between my thighs responded to this version of him with reckless abandon.

Desire melded our gazes together as he pushed inside me, inch by torturous inch. It felt unbearably intimate, but I didn't look away until he bottomed out and my eyes instinctively shut with a gasp.

Pain prickled at me, followed by a white-hot burst of pleasure. I'd had toys to keep me company the past two years, but none of them had been so big or buried so deep. The unrelenting stretch drove the oxygen from my lungs, and my body involuntarily bucked and twisted as I struggled to accommodate him.

"Please." I wasn't sure whether I was begging him to stop or make me come. Both. Neither. It didn't matter. All I knew was I craved something only he could give, and I desperately hoped he could figure it out on his own because I couldn't so much as remember my name right now.

Kai gripped my thighs to hold me in place while he withdrew. Slowly, until just the tip of his cock was inside me. Then he thrust back in. Deeper. Faster. Harder.

Any remaining coherence shattered as he fucked me against the wall with so much force it rattled my bones. Everything blurred. My nails dug into his shoulders as squeals and whimpers poured out of me, mingling with his grunts and the deep, rhythmic bass of the music.

My entire body was on sensory overload. No matter how much I took, it wasn't enough. *More. I need more*.

Kai's teeth grazed against my neck. "Still think I'm boring?" His taunt whispered into my ear in time with a particularly savage thrust.

White-hot sensation ripped through me. Tears leaked from my eyes, and I bucked like an unbroken filly, wild and out of control. Heart pounding, fingers clawing, mouth falling open in a reckless cry that abruptly cut off when he slammed his hand over my mouth. The muffled remnants of my scream leaked around his palm.

"Shh." Kai's voice was soft, almost gentle in contrast with the merciless way he fucked. "We don't want someone to come in and see your sweet little pussy getting wrecked by my cock, do we?"

The unexpectedly vulgar words, delivered in such an aristocratic accent, tipped me over the edge.

"God, *Kai*."

My orgasm tore through me, unfolding in wave after wave of mindless, toe-curling pleasure. The world blanked in one suspended, breathless moment before I crashed back into reality.

The smooth, deep thrusts grew erratic. His breath hissed between his teeth, and I clung to him, too dazed to do anything more than hold on when he finally came with a loud groan.

Our chests heaved as we held each other in the comedown. If it weren't for the wall braced against my back, we might've both collapsed to the floor.

Oh my God. I tried to speak, but my vocal cords wouldn't work. I was too exhausted and satiated.

Eventually, our heartbeats returned to normal. Kai withdrew and gently set me on my feet before disposing of his condom and straightening our clothing.

"You know..." He smoothed my dress back down over my thighs with a thoughtful expression. "This might be the longest I've heard you go without talking."

His chest rumbled with laughter when I snapped out of my sex-induced trance and gave him a mock glare.

"Don't act so smug," I said. "It's simply the result of having sex for the first time in two years. You're not the sex god you think you are."

It was a blatant lie, but I couldn't let his ego inflate any further lest he float off into space. *Then* where would I get my orgasms?

"Interesting." Kai retrieved his glasses from the bar station and put them on. "That's not what you said when you were coming all over my cock."

Heat scorched my cheeks even as my stomach tingled at his words. "You're insufferable." I flicked a wary glance at the exit. "We're lucky no one saw us."

The possibility of getting caught had added an undeniable thrill, but *actually* getting caught would've been disastrous.

"They wouldn't have. Security knows not to let anyone back here until I give them the signal," he said with a shrug. "Five hundred dollars goes a long way toward motivation."

My jaw unhinged. "You had someone standing guard the entire time?" And he'd led me to believe we were one drunken partygoer away from flashing the entire club. Unbelievable.

"Of course. I couldn't very well have someone walking in on us."

"Because photos of the Young heir engaging in carnal activities at a bar would put his CEO candidacy at risk."

"No. Because if anyone saw you like that, I'd have to kill them." He said it so simply, so casually, it took a moment for the words to sink in.

Once they did, the air vanished from my lungs.

It suddenly hit me that I'd had sex with *Kai Young*. In the back of a bar, no less. If anyone told me I'd be in this situation mere weeks ago, I would've laughed in their face.

Now my man ban lay in pieces at our feet, and I was in danger of getting caught in the post-sex trap, a.k.a. reading more into the situation than what was there.

Old Isabella would've gone along with it and taken whatever scraps she could get. Sometimes, ignorance was bliss, especially when you were young, inexperienced, and desperate for love or some approximation thereof.

But I'd walked that road, and it'd led me somewhere I never wanted to visit again. So even though I hated being the person who initiated serious talks right after sex, I cut straight to the point. Our relationship was too complicated to let things linger without clearing the air.

"So what happens next?" My heart pounded so hard it almost bruised.

A quizzical line formed between Kai's brows.

"This." I gestured between us. "Us. What are we doing?"

"Recovering from excellent orgasms, I presume."

The full weight of disappointment anchored my stomach. "You're too smart to play dumb," I said, hurt by his cavalier attitude.

I'd broken a years-long vow to myself for him, and he couldn't take me seriously enough for one meaningful conversation.

Kai's smile gradually dissolved. His eyes searched my face; whatever he saw made him wince.

"You're right. I'm sorry," he said quietly. "But I thought you knew."

This time, I was the confused one. "Knew what?"

"That there's no going back after this." His admission was a warm breath on my skin. "You should've never let me take you, Isabella. Because now that I have, I won't be able to let you go."

CHAPTER 19
Kai

I was fucked, both literally and figuratively.

If Isabella had dominated my thoughts before we had sex, she'd utterly consumed them after. It'd been a week since I took her to the Barber, and not a minute had passed without the memory of her taste haunting me.

I rubbed a hand over my mouth and tried to focus on my mother's closing speech. It was the last day of the company's annual leadership retreat, which took place in our Manhattan office this year. High-level executives had flown in from all over the world for four days of seminars, workshops, and networking, all of which I'd breezed through.

I may have been distracted, but I could still outsell, outsmart, and outperform every other member of the Young Corporation with my eyes closed.

My phone buzzed with a new text.

"...lean into your individual strengths as leaders to build an even bigger, better company that reflects the direction of the market..." My mother's voice faded in and out as I checked my messages.

Isabella: *are you alone right now?*

A small smile curved my lips.

Me: *No. I'm at the company retreat.*

I hadn't seen her since the retreat started, but we texted every day. Our conversations consisted mostly of memes and funny videos (sent by her), interesting articles and food recommendations (sent by me), and flirtatious subtext (sent by both of us). Normally, I wasn't a huge fan of long text conversations because they inevitably lost their point, if there was one in the first place, but I looked forward to her messages with embarrassing anticipation.

Isabella: *perfect. then i have a picture for you;)*

A photo popped up on-screen. I instinctively swiped my phone off the table, but to my relief and disappointment, it wasn't anything scandalous.

Isabella lounged on the couch in the library's secret room, her cheeks dimpled with a mischievous grin and her hair fanning around her in a spray of amethyst-tinted silk. Her free hand clutched a bottle of Mexican Coke.

Isabella: *behold, a future bestselling author working hard*

My smile ticked up another inch.

Me: *I see that. Your hands must be tired from typing on your invisible keyboard.*

Isabella: *first of all, brainstorming is working too, judgy mcjudge*

Isabella: *second of all, i've come up with an incredibly detailed sex scene that i was going to tell you about*

Isabella: *but since you're being so rude, i'll keep it to myself*

Heat raced to my groin, but I marshaled my emotions into a neutral expression.

Me: *Perhaps you should spend an equal amount of time on proper punctuation and capitalization. I've heard they're necessary skills for writers...*

Isabella: *...*

Isabella: *how dare you*

Isabella: *im texting you not writing a college thesis*

Isabella: *and yes i removed all the punctuation on purpose*

Isabella: *i hope it triggers you :)*

A laugh rustled my throat, the soft noise unnaturally loud in the silence.

The meeting. Fuck.

I looked up to find the rest of the room staring at me. My mother wore a disapproving frown, which meant I would get an earful later.

"Is there something you'd like to share?" Tobias drawled from his kiss-ass seat next to her. "An exciting new deal, perhaps? Things finally work out with DigiStream?"

On his other side, Richard Chu smirked. Typically, board members didn't attend the leadership retreats, but the CEO voting committee had opted in this year so they could "better evaluate their options."

Richard's presence was the only reason Tobias was bold enough to call me out. The little sleaze hid behind his board bene-factor like a child hiding behind his mother's skirts. It was probably why Richard liked him so much; he knew he could con-trol him.

"We're on track to close soon," I said smoothly. "Big deals like DigiStream take time. I understand this is not an area you're experi-enced in, but that's what these retreats are for. Learning."

Tobias's smirk didn't budge. "It's funny you should say that." The glint in his eyes sent the first trickle of unease down my spine. His ego was so fragile he reacted to the slightest insult, but he'd absorbed my public barb without batting an eye. "You may not have big news today, but I do." He ran a hand over his tie, his tacky gold watch gleaming smugly beneath the lights. "I'm happy to announce that, after months of closed-door negotiations, we've reached a deal with Black Bear Entertainment."

The words swirled in the air for a stunned moment before the table erupted with noise. Only my mother, one other CEO candi-date, and I remained silent.

Black Bear Entertainment was one of the most prolific enter-tainment companies in the world. Its acquisition would add a huge, diverse slate of much-needed content to our subscription video service, which was historically one of the company's weakest divisions. We'd been trying to shore it up for years.

As the current CEO, my mother must've already known about the deal. I wasn't worried about it overshadowing DigiStream, which would be worth at least three times more once it closed, but Tobias beating me to a flashy announcement galled the hell out of me. I'd heard inklings he was pursuing Black Bear; I hadn't expected him to succeed.

I slid a glance at the other silent candidate. Paxton James lounged next to Richard with an unreadable expression. Besides me, the executive vice president of business development was the youngest person in the room. He was sharp, witty, and innovative. Of all the candidates, I liked him the most, though I knew better than to underestimate him the way I had Tobias. He acted like he didn't want the CEO position half the time, but he hadn't climbed the ranks so quickly without a healthy dose of ambition.

He was likely lying low and evaluating what the Black Bear bombshell meant for his odds in the vote.

I studied the other candidates for their reaction to Tobias's news.

Laura Nguyen, our Chief Communications Officer, sat rigid-backed, her disdain barely concealed by a tight smile. She'd skyrocketed the Young Corporation's public profile over the past five years, and she disliked Tobias even more than I did. Proof she had good judgment when it came to press *and* people.

Next to her, Russell Burton slunk down in his seat. He'd served as the company's Chief Operating Officer for over a decade. The quiet, unassuming father of two was the type of man who dealt better with systems than people. His candidacy was a formality after so many years of competent service, but judging by how green he turned every time someone brought up the vote, he would rather jab a steak knife in his eye than take on the burden of CEO.

"Congratulations." My voice cut through the din. The room

fell silent again, and I offered Tobias a courteous smile. "The acquisition is a great boon for the company. I'm excited to see where it goes."

I didn't give him the satisfaction of a bigger reaction. There were no benefits to acting petty and jealous. I wasn't even jealous, merely annoyed.

The meeting officially adjourned. Low chatter and the scratch of metal against carpet filled the room as everyone rushed out for happy hour. The post-retreat gathering was optional, but no one ever missed the opportunity to hobnob.

We'd reserved the bar down the street, and for the next two hours, I circulated the room while trying not to think about Isabella. I'd much rather spend the evening with her, but I had to put in my face time.

Paxton sidled up to me during a lull and cut straight to the chase. "You think Black Bear will move the needle for Tobias?"

"Yes, but not enough."

"Don't write him off so easily. He's a tricky bastard."

I slid a glance at my companion. Beneath that easygoing demeanor were the instincts of a shark. "Reminds me of someone else I know."

Paxton grinned, not bothering to deny it. "I'm here for the ride. EVP of a Fortune 500 company before the age of thirty-five? Not bad for a kid from Nebraska. CEO would be nice, but I'm not banking on it. That being said..." He nodded at where Tobias was holding court with Richard and two other voting committee members. "I have a low tolerance for that particular brand of bullshit. If it can't be me, I'd much rather it be you."

I examined him over my glass. "You want an alliance."

"An agreement," he corrected. "Alliance sounds so formal. But I'll be straight with you. Two electors are leaning my way right now. It might not sound like a lot, but in the event of a tie, every additional vote counts. I can convince them to swing their vote to you."

"You'll do this out of the goodness of your heart, I presume," I said dryly.

"That, and the promise of a promotion," Paxton said without missing a beat. "President of Advertising Sales when Sullivan retires. He already has one foot out the door, and you know I have the chops for it."

"Getting ahead of yourself, aren't you? Sullivan has a good five years left in the company."

Paxton gave me a droll look.

Fair enough. Sullivan was more checked out than a bag of groceries at Citarella. Our advertisers loved him, but I gave him two years tops before he left.

"We've talked enough shop this past week," I said. "Enjoy the drinks and food tonight. We'll discuss any business matters later."

I left my response purposely vague. I liked Paxton as a person, but I trusted him as far as I could throw him.

"Of course." He raised his glass, seemingly unfazed by my lukewarm reception to his proposal. "Looking forward to it."

The festivities wound down around nine. The company's leadership trickled out one by one until only a handful were left.

Finally. I could make my excuses and leave without seeming rude. I'd had enough networking to last me for the next year.

"Kai." My mother stopped me on my way out. "A word."

I suppressed a sigh. *So close.*

I followed her to a quiet corner of the bar, out of the direct eyesight of the remaining executives.

The professional smile she'd worn all evening had melted away, leaving lines of tension in its wake.

"Don't worry," I said. "The Black Bear deal will be nothing compared to DigiStream when it goes through. The board knows that."

She arched an elegant dark brow. With her smooth skin and rich black hair, courtesy of London's top esthetician and colorist, she could pass for someone in her late thirties instead of late fifties. "*Will* it go through?"

"Of course," I said, insulted she'd even ask. "When have I ever failed?"

"Word has it Mishra isn't budging and Whidby is at risk of being permanently removed as CEO. If I hear these things, so does the board. They aren't pleased."

My shoulders tensed. "I know. I have contingencies for all of those scenarios."

"I'm sure you do, but that's not enough." My mother pursed her lips. "This isn't just about deals, Kai. CEO elections aren't as clear-cut as profit and loss statements."

"I'm aware."

"I don't think you are." Her voice lowered. "Getting voted in isn't about merit. It's about politics. Your last name is both an advantage and a detriment. Some board members favor you because you're a Young and they value stability. But others resent you for that very reason. They're using the DigiStream delay and your…modern views regarding the future of the company to advocate for fresh blood. That faction is growing louder by the day."

A chill swept through the air and sank into my bones. "What are you trying to say?"

"I'm saying you need to stop coasting on your name and record and start placating some of your naysayers, or you could very well lose the vote."

The word *lose* tore through me like a fanged beast.

History remembered the winners. The losers faded into obscurity, their names lost over time like statues rubbed smooth by too many hands. Dead in every way, as if they'd never existed.

Pressure suffocated my chest.

"I'm not going to lose," I said, my voice colder than intended. "I never do."

"Make sure you don't." My mother didn't look entirely convinced. "I've already said more than I should. I'm supposed to be neutral, but this is our family name on the line. Imagine what people will say if a Young loses the CEO position of Young Corporation. We'll never recover from the shame."

She fixed me with the same no-bullshit stare that had enemies and allies alike trembling before her. "Campaign for the job, Kai. Do what it takes to make them happy. I know you think it's beneath you, but don't let your pride get in the way of winning. Not unless you want Tobias giving you orders from the corner office."

My stomach revolted.

I hated the word *campaign* almost as much as the word *lose*. It was so...undignified. The fake smiles, the ass-kissing, the platitudes both parties knew but didn't acknowledge as lies.

But my mother knew exactly which buttons to push; I would rather swallow a vial of poison than take a single order from Tobias Foster.

The frigid night air cooled my anger when I stepped outside. Still, unease roiled beneath my skin, and returning home to my apartment didn't hold the same appeal it usually did.

I took out my phone and opened my latest message thread.

Me: *Are you still at Valhalla?*

I should've been tapped out on socializing, but talking to Isabella never drained me the way talking to other people did.

Isabella: *Nope, I just got home*
Isabella: *I don't have a shift tonight...*

The implied invitation was clear.

Me: *I'll be there in twenty minutes*

CHAPTER 20

Isabella

T he doorbell rang at five to ten, exactly twenty minutes after I texted Kai my address.

My heart flipped when I opened the door and found him standing in the hall, hair tousled and cheeks ruddy from the wind. Seeing him in person for the first time in almost a week was like taking the first gasp of air after holding my breath for too long.

Cool euphoria flooded my lungs.

"Hi," I said breathlessly.

A smile curved his lips. "Hi."

"Did anyone ever tell you your punctuality is terrifying?"

"Not in so many words, no." He gave a casual shrug. "If it's an issue, I can leave and come back—"

"Don't you dare." I grabbed his wrist and dragged him, laughing, into the apartment. "And don't look so pleased with yourself. I just didn't want my apartment cleanup to go to waste."

Kai looked even more pleased. "You cleaned up for me? I'm flattered."

Blood rose to my neck and chest. If he touched me right now, he'd probably burn himself. *It would serve him right.* "I didn't say that. It was due for some tidying up anyway. The timing is pure coincidence."

"I see."

"Anyway." I ignored the knowing gleam in his eyes and deliberately turned my back to him. I swept an arm around the freshly tidied space. "Welcome to my humble abode. Six hundred square feet of rent-controlled luxury, right in the heart of the East Village."

I'd lucked out on my studio apartment. A friend of a friend had lived here before they moved back to Arizona, and I'd snagged it before it went on the market. Sixteen hundred dollars for a downtown location with decent natural lighting, in-building laundry, and no roach or rat infestation? By New York standards, it was a steal.

Kai came up beside me and surveyed the little touches I'd added to make the apartment homier—the collection of shot glasses I'd acquired on my travels, the electric keyboard stashed beneath the window, the oil portrait Vivian and Sloane had commissioned as a joke for one of my birthdays. It depicted Monty as a Victorian aristocrat wearing a white ruffled collar. It was the most ridiculous thing I'd ever seen, and I loved it.

The studio was probably the size of Kai's closet, but I was inordinately proud of it. It was mine, at least for as long as I could pay rent, and I'd made it my home in a city that chewed up and spit out starry-eyed newcomers faster than they could unpack their suitcases.

"This apartment is very you," Kai observed, his warm, amused gaze alighting on the golden vase of peacock feathers by the door.

Something fluttered in my chest. "Thank you."

Then, because it would be rude for me not to introduce the true lord of the house, I walked over to the vivarium and retrieved the ball python lounging amid the greenery.

"Meet Monty." I'd bought him a few months after I moved to New York. Ball pythons were incredibly low maintenance and cheap to care for, which made them perfect for my bartender schedule and salary. Monty wasn't as cuddly as a cat or dog, but it was nice to come home to a pet, even if all he did was eat, drink, and sleep.

He slithered over my shoulder and peered curiously at Kai, whose mouth flickered with a smile.

"Monty the python. Cute."

"My father was a big *Life of Brian* fan," I admitted. I wasn't as devoted a fan, but I liked puns and my father would've gotten a hoot out of it, had he still been alive.

"Interesting. I figured you'd be a Pomeranian girl."

"Because I'm adorable with great hair?"

"No, because you're small and yappy." Kai's smile graduated into a laugh when I swatted his arm.

"Be nice, or I'll sic Monty on you."

"Quite a threat, but I'd be more concerned if he were a viper instead of a friendly ball python," Kai drawled.

As if to prove his point, Monty rubbed his head against Kai's outstretched hand.

"Traitor," I grumbled. "Who's the one that feeds you?" But I couldn't suppress my own smile at the adorable sight.

Most people were terrified of snakes because they thought they were ugly or venomous or evil. Some snakes were, but judging an entire species by a few bad apples was like judging all humans by the serial killer population. It was grossly unfair, and I had a soft spot for anyone who treated Monty respectfully instead of looking like they wanted to call animal control on him the first chance they got.

After a few minutes, I placed Monty back in his vivarium, where he yawned and happily curled into a ball. He was well socialized and had a higher tolerance for being held than other snakes, but I tried not to stress him out with too much contact from strangers.

"How was the retreat?" I washed my hands and turned back to Kai, who rinsed after me. "Four days of leadership training sounds like a special torture method conjured in the depths of corporate hell."

bright on the company skyscraper that it could be seen for miles. How could he lose?

"Office politics." He gave me a brief overview of the situation, which didn't lessen my ire.

"That's stupid," I said when he finished talking. "Why do rich people like having their asses kissed so much? Doesn't it chafe after a while?"

The side of Kai's mouth twitched. "Excellent questions, darling. I assume the answers are their ego and yes, it does chafe, but they don't care." His fingers laced with mine over the sheets. "However, I appreciate your umbrage on my behalf."

"Your mom could be wrong," I said, though it seemed unlikely. Making nice with self-centered board members wasn't the end of the world, but it was annoying Kai had to resort to flattery when his record should've spoken for itself. "Did you ever figure out why she's stepping down so early?"

"No. She won't tell me until the time is right. Which, knowing her, could be never."

"What about your father? What does he think?" Kai never talked about him. While Leonora Young ran her media empire in the spotlight, her husband was a far more mysterious figure. I'd only seen one or two photos of him.

"He's in Hong Kong. He runs a financial services business there, separate from the Young Corporation. My parents are separated," Kai clarified when my brows winged up. His mother lived in London, which was a long way from Hong Kong. "They have been for ten years, but they make the occasional public appearance together when necessary. Their separation is an open secret."

"That's a long time for a separation with no divorce."

"They resent each other too much to be together but love each other too much to break up. Plus, dividing their assets would be too complicated," Kai said dryly. "It's not a healthy situation for anyone involved, but Abigail and I are used to it, and it's pretty tame as far as dysfunctional families go."

Considering Vivian's father blackmailed Dante into marrying

her before they actually fell in love, I'd say that was an understatement.

"Why did they separate?" I curled up against Kai's chest, letting his voice and steady heartbeat lull me into contentment.

I preferred nights out more than nights in, but I could lie here and listen to him talk forever. He rarely opened up about his personal life, so I wasn't taking a single second of this for granted.

"My mother worked too much, my father grew resentful, so on and so forth." Kai sounded detached, as if he were recounting another family's history instead of his own. "Almost embarrassing, really, how cliché the reason is, but clichés exist for a reason."

"True," I murmured. My father had quit his teaching job to raise my brothers and me while my mother worked. He hadn't resented her, but even he had displayed the occasional flash of irritation when she'd missed yet another dinner or outing in the early days of her career.

"Enough about me," Kai said. "How did the rest of your writing session go?"

"Um...good," I hedged. I'd tried drafting in the secret room, but as expected, I couldn't get much done in the silence. Blasting music through my headphones had helped only a little bit. "Like I said, I did more brainstorming than writing. But that counts too."

"Hmm." Kai dipped his head and trailed a lazy kiss over my shoulder. "I remember you mentioning something about a detailed sex scene..."

Fresh heat kindled in my stomach. "And I remember I'm not telling you a single thing about it because you were so rude," I said primly.

"My sincerest apologies. I shouldn't have offended you so." He stroked my breast with his free hand. Pleasure lanced through me and manifested in the form of a gasp. "Perhaps there's a way I can make it up to you..."

There was, and he did, over and over again until the stars blinked out and the first murky hint of dawn crept through the window.

CHAPTER 21

The next week passed in a blur of sex, work, and more sex. When I wasn't with Isabella, I was busy putting together my campaign strategy. It was a necessary evil, but other than sending personalized Christmas gifts to the voting members, I didn't have to implement it until after New Year's. Everyone was too checked out during the holidays.

I did, however, have to fulfill other social obligations. As much as I would've liked to spend all my free time with Isabella, the illicit nature of our relationship meant I couldn't take her to any of the functions I was invited to, including the Saxon Gallery's big winter exhibition.

I accepted a welcome glass of champagne from the hostess and scanned the exhibition. Usually, the gallery catered to the downtown crowd, but the big names at its winter showcase had pulled in quite a few uptown and international VIPs. I spotted Dante and Vivian walking hand in hand through the exhibit. The supermodel Ayana floated through the room in an ethereal wash of red tulle while Sebastian Laurent held court in the corner.

Even Vuk Markovic made one of his once-in-a-blue-moon appearances, though he didn't appear inclined to interact with anyone. He stood in the corner, his wintry eyes dissecting the other guests like a scientist examining bugs beneath a microscope.

"Kai, I'm so glad you could make it." Clarissa appeared next to me, looking elegant but a touch frazzled in a black cocktail dress and headset. She was the gallery's director of artist relations, and I would've skipped the event altogether had she not invited me personally. I hadn't seen her since the fall gala, but I felt guilty enough about leading her on that night that I'd accepted.

"Of course. The exhibition looks great," I said. "You and the rest of the team did a wonderful job."

We made small talk for a while before an awkward silence descended between us.

Our conversations were never as comfortable or thrilling as those with Isabella, but we'd talked easily enough at the gala. However, Clarissa appeared distracted tonight, like her mind was floating a thousand miles from her body.

"I can't chat too long. I have to make sure the artists have everything they need. Creative types can be quite temperamental." She smiled, but there was a strange note in her voice. Her gaze roved around the gallery like she was searching for someone before it settled on mine again. A curious resolve hardened her features. "We should get drinks sometime soon. I still owe you a rain check for leaving the Valhalla gala early."

"Happy to," I said, though I felt a bit uneasy about agreeing to what she probably thought was a date when I was involved with Isabella. "Let me know when you're free."

After she left, still with that distracted expression stamped on her face, I cut a diagonal path toward Dante and Vivian. I only made it halfway before someone bumped into me and nearly knocked the drink from my hand.

"I'm so sorry!" A familiar voice yanked my gaze to my right. "I—Kai?"

"Isabella?"

We stared at each other, our faces mirror images of astonishment. She'd told me she also had an event tonight, but never in a million years had I expected to see her here. A black velvet dress poured over her curves, revealing miles of tanned skin, while black stiletto boots brought her closer to my eye level. She was clearly a guest, albeit one dressed more for an East Village underground party than a Chelsea gallery exhibit.

"What are you doing here?" Isabella recovered first.

"I could ask you the same question."

"I'm here with my brother. He's...somewhere." She waved a hand around the room. "I lost him a while ago, but there's plenty of wine and snacks to keep me busy."

"I see that." Amusement edged out my surprise. Her free hand carried a plate piled so high with hors d'oeuvres it resembled the Leaning Tower of Pisa. "Are you sure you picked up enough food, love?"

A faint wash of pink edged Isabella's cheeks and the tip of her nose. "As a matter of fact, no. I was just about to get more when *someone* got in my way."

"How rude of them."

"Very. No one has manners these days."

"A sign of our imminent societal collapse, no doubt." My mouth curved into a lazy, appreciative smile as I tipped my chin down. "On a less ominous note, you look beautiful. It's a good thing you didn't put that on before I left, or neither of us would be standing here right now."

I'd spent the day at her apartment before going home to change for the event. Now, I wished I'd stayed through the night. I had some ideas for what we could be doing that rivaled any of the artists for creativity.

Isabella's mock indignation melted beneath a deeper blush. The air thickened with something warm and honeyed before she shook her head. "Shh." Her eyes darted around the room. "Someone will hear you. Dante and Viv are *right there*."

"Dante and Vivian are too busy making moon eyes at each other to notice anything else."

But Isabella was right. Though we were having an innocent

conversation—for now—drawing any additional attention to us would be unwise. Vuk was already suspicious after seeing us leave the piano room together. Luckily, the man never spoke and never involved himself in others' business unless he had to, but we wouldn't always be that lucky.

One of the other guests broke free from his companion and arrowed straight toward me. He was the arts and culture reporter from the company's flagship paper, which meant I had to entertain him.

"There's an alcove in the back of the gallery, behind the wave sculpture," I murmured as the reporter closed in. "Meet me there in an hour."

Isabella didn't respond. She turned away, but not before I saw the answering gleam in her eyes.

For the next fifty-five minutes, I mingled half-heartedly before I excused myself to use the restroom. Instead of making a right toward the lavatory, I slipped into the back alcove. The exhibition took place in the main room, so this particular area was quiet save for the low hum of the heater. A deconstructed wave sculpture hid the alcove from passersby, making it the perfect spot for a rendezvous.

Isabella was already waiting when I entered.

"I was joking the first two times, but this is no coincidence. You *are* following me," she teased.

I closed the distance between us with three long strides. "You have quite a high opinion of yourself, Ms. Valencia."

Her grin bloomed further, carving beautiful dimples in her cheeks. "But is it unwarranted?"

"Not at all."

Her answering breath brushed my chest. The scent of rose and vanilla teased my senses, and I was sure even the goddesses of myth had never smelled so divine.

My palms tingled with the desire to wind my fist around those silky dark waves and map every curve and valley of her body—the elegant column of her neck, the smooth curve of her shoulder, the indent of her waist, and the flare of her hips. Velvet and silk, ripe for the taking.

The need pulsed like a living thing inside me, but I kept my arms at my sides, as did she. Sneaking away at an event filled with our peers and journalists was dangerous enough, but trying to stay away from her was like asking the ocean to stop kissing the shore.

Impossible.

My chin tipped down while hers canted up, bringing our eyes together. We didn't speak. We didn't touch. And yet this was the highlight of my night.

"I'm tempted to leave before the official artist speeches," I murmured. "But that would be impolite of me, wouldn't it?"

"Possibly." Isabella swallowed when I tucked a stray strand of hair behind her ear. I couldn't help it; I needed some form of contact with her before I went crazy. "But politeness is overrated."

Good, because there was nothing polite about the thoughts running through my mind right now.

"Well, this is unexpected."

The oily voice doused our warm intimacy more effectively than a bucket of ice water. My hand dropped, and Isabella and I jerked apart like marionettes yanked in different directions.

"Kai Young and the help canoodling at a public event. I never thought I'd see the day."

Victor Black stood in the alcove entrance. His eyes gleamed with malicious delight as they roved between me and Isabella. He must've just arrived; I hadn't seen him earlier.

A rope of dread wound tight around my chest.

Technically, Isabella and I weren't doing anything wrong, but Victor had a talent for spinning innocent situations into tawdry, bestselling bullshit.

"We're not at Valhalla," Isabella said coldly. "I'm a guest here. If you'd like someone to direct you to the exit, I recommend checking with one of the staffers wearing clearly marked badges."

"My mistake. It's so easy to forget when you're dressed like a hooker." Spite slicked Victor's smile as his attention swiveled toward me. "No wonder you were so upset when you saw me talk—"

I crossed the room quicker than he could react. The rest of his sentence dissolved into a pained grunt when I slammed him against the wall with my forearm pressed against his throat.

"Second mistake of the night, Black," I said quietly. "Do not disrespect *any* woman like that when I'm in the room." *Especially not Isabella.*

Cold fury wedged jagged shards in my chest and washed the room in crimson. Victor's features morphed into a map of vulnerable points—the eyes, the nose, the jaw and temples. A well-aimed strike could shatter any and all of them.

Isabella's presence was the only thing keeping me semi-leashed. An outsized reaction would confirm Victor's suspicions, and the short-term satisfaction of rearranging his face would pale next to the long-term consequences.

He must've come to the same conclusion. Despite the twinge of fear bleeding into his eyes, he didn't back down.

"Of course." His voice came out high and reedy thanks to his pinned throat. "You're right. Surely the great Kai Young is too smart to do something as stupid as fraternize with a Valhalla *bartender* this close to the CEO vote." He choked out another pained breath when I pressed my arm tighter against his neck.

"Kai."

The crimson receded from my vision at the sound of Isabella's anxious voice.

I dropped my arm and glared at Victor. He straightened and coughed before continuing, "Voting members are real sticklers when it comes to scandal. One of the chief executive candidates for Greentech lost the position a few years ago because of an affair with the nanny. Fifteen years of hard work, down the drain."

I remembered. The scandal had dominated the news for months.

The difference was, I wasn't married. I could date whoever I wanted.

Tell that to Valhalla and the board, an insidious voice whispered.

I gritted my teeth. Triumph slowly replaced the apprehension on Victor's face. He'd hit his target, and he knew it.

"You're a CEO," Isabella said, coming up beside me. "So obviously, corporate boards don't care that much about scandals. Didn't your car get blown up earlier this year?"

Victor's face flushed scarlet. The fiery destruction of his Porsche had made headlines in the spring. He never found the person responsible, but his list of enemies was miles long. It could've been anyone.

Normally, I abhorred the senseless destruction of property, but I found it hard to summon sympathy for him. No one died. The only things hurt were his ego, his car, and his reputation, not that the latter had been great to begin with.

"Isa!" A man in a linen shirt and pants entered the room, cutting off Victor's response. "There you are. I was looking for you."

I recognized him immediately as Oscar, one of the gallery's featured artists. Tall and lean, with shoulder-length black hair tied in a ponytail and a string of puka shells adorning his neck, he looked like he should be hanging ten in Hawaii instead of headlining an exclusive art exhibit in Chelsea.

He brushed past a surprised-looking Victor and draped an arm over Isabella's shoulders. My spine pulled taut.

"I'm giving my speech soon. Thought I'd bring you up there with me, considering you inspired one of the pieces."

She wrinkled her nose. "No, thanks. I hate speeches, and this is your night."

The brewing violence from earlier had dissipated, replaced with another type of tension.

"Isabella, I wasn't aware you knew Oscar," I said with a tight smile, fighting the urge to yank his arm off her.

"We more than know each other. He's one of my favorite people on the planet." She beamed up at him.

A muscle ticked in my jaw. "How lovely."

And what am I? Chopped liver?

I didn't like the jealous, territorial caveman I became whenever I saw her smiling at another man, but nothing about my attraction to her had ever been rational.

Isabella blinked at my curt tone before amusement crept into her eyes. "Oscar is—"

"Oh, I'm so sorry!" A beautiful Asian woman came to an abrupt halt next to the wave sculpture. Victor had disappeared. I hadn't noticed him leave, but good riddance. "We didn't mean to interrupt. We weren't, um, expecting anyone to be back here." A delicate rose colored her cheeks.

Next to her, a familiar-looking man with brown hair and icy green eyes surveyed us like it was our fault for interrupting them even though we were here first.

Typical Volkov.

"Alex, Ava, good to see you." I masked my irritation over Oscar and Isabella with a smile. *Why is his arm still around her shoulders?* "I didn't know you were in the city."

"Ava wanted to see the exhibit, so here we are." Other than a touch of softness on his wife's name, Alex Volkov's voice was cold enough to send the temperature of the room plummeting.

The notoriously aloof real estate billionaire possessed the warmth of an Arctic ice cave, but he'd mellowed considerably since he started dating Ava a few years ago.

We were friendly, if not friends. He owned the skyscraper housing Young Corporation's New York headquarters as well as half the street where I lived. I regarded him the same way I did Christian Harper, but at least with Alex, I knew what I was getting. Christian was a wolf dressed in custom-tailored sheep's clothing. Dante had offered several more times to have him dig up dirt on Rohan Mishra and the other CEO candidates, and I'd declined every time.

Dante was comfortable pushing ethical boundaries, but I refused to win by cheating. There was no glory in false victories.

Speak of the devil.

"There's a secret party back here and no one invited us? I'm offended." Dante's deep drawl preceded his appearance around the corner with Vivian by his side. "I was wondering where everyone went."

"I believe the vast majority of guests are still in the main exhibition area," I said dryly, wondering how my intimate meeting with Isabella had devolved into this circus.

Then, as if the room wasn't crowded enough, Clarissa swept in like a storm, her expression severe.

"Uh-oh." Oscar finally dropped his arm from around Isabella's shoulders. "I think I'm in trouble." He didn't sound particularly concerned.

"There you are," she said in a clipped voice. "Your speech is in three minutes. You have to come with me. Now."

I'd never heard Clarissa sound so irritated, though to be fair, I hadn't talked to her in years before she moved to New York.

"I'll be there." Oscar didn't move. She didn't budge.

After a moment of silence, he sighed and followed her out. The rest of the room trickled out after them.

I fell back so I could walk next to Isabella.

"You two seemed friendly," I said. "How do you know each other again?"

Her eyes danced with renewed laughter. "Kai, Oscar is my brother. His real name is Felix, but he used our father's name as his artist pseudonym. It's his way of paying homage."

Her brother?

A wave of shock rippled through me. I glanced at the back of Oscar's—Felix's—head. "How..."

Despite his dark coloring, Oscar/Felix was obviously white. Isabella was Filipino.

"His parents died when he was a baby," she said. "My parents were his godparents before they legally adopted him. He's been part of the family since before I was born." Her dimples popped up again. "See? No reason to be jealous."

Heat touched my skin. "I wasn't jealous."

"Of course not. You look at every man like you want to rip them to shreds and barbecue them."

"If we weren't in public," I said, my voice low and calm, "I'd put you over my knee and punish you for your insolence alone."

Isabella's breath audibly hitched. "You wish."

A smile edged my lips, but it was a Pyrrhic victory because not being able to follow through on my threat was as torturous for me as it was for her.

We poured into the main exhibition room, where Oscar/Felix had already commenced his speech.

I slid a hand into my pocket and tried to focus on his words instead of the woman standing next to me. A cool rush of surprise flooded me when my fingers brushed against what felt like a scrap of paper.

I discreetly retrieved and unfolded it. The other guests were too busy listening to the artists' speeches to notice the way I stiffened when I read the note.

No name, no signature, only two simple sentences.

Be careful. Not everyone is who they seem.

CHAPTER 22

Isabella

Both Kai's company and Valhalla emptied out in the second half of December, giving us plenty of leeway to sneak around to our hearts' content. Everyone had fled to St. Moritz or St. Barth's, but we avoided the city hotspots out of an abundance of caution.

Instead, we made good use of my bed—the one furniture item I'd splurged on—and the club's various nooks and crannies. Occasionally, we indulged in out-of-the-way date destinations: the New York Botanical Garden in the Bronx, tiny dumpling and tea shops in Flushing, an underground comedy show in Harlem.

They were areas I would've never visited on my own due to time and distance, and I loved exploring them with Kai. However, my favorite spot was still, hands down, the place where it all began.

I stepped into our secret room. The bookcase clicked shut behind me, and my heart fluttered when I saw Kai was already there. He sat in the armchair, reading one of those boring classics he loved so much. In his shirt and suspenders, with the sleeves rolled up and his glasses perched on the end of his nose, he looked like the world's sexiest professor.

"If my lecturers looked like you in college, I would've spent way more time in class instead of playing hooky at the beach," I said.

Kai saved his spot with a bookmark and set the book aside before glancing up. "Hooky at the beach?" he said with a disordinate amount of interest. "I don't suppose you have photos of you there to back up your claim. For verification purposes, of course."

"Of course," I said in a solemn tone. "No photos, but I have something better." I swept a hand over my front. "I found this trench at my favorite vintage store. Looks appropriately spyish, don't you think? Perfect for sneaking around."

Kai looked disappointed. "I suppose," he said dubiously. "It's certainly...a style."

"Hmm." I tilted my head with a thoughtful frown. "Perhaps you'll like it more when you see what I'm wearing underneath..."

I untied my belt, revealing the black lace-and-silk teddy I'd changed into after my shift. It retailed for a mind-boggling price, but thanks to Vivian, I had an evergreen friends and family discount at Delamonte, one of the luxury brands in Dante's portfolio.

Kai stilled, his gaze fastening on the flimsy material like a predator locking onto prey.

The coat fell to the floor as I walked toward him, my heels gliding with ease over the plush carpet.

"I thought we could play a game today." I straddled his lap and wrapped my arms around his neck.

"What type of game?" He sounded remarkably calm, but his breathing accelerated when I pressed my mouth to his jaw.

"The one where you're not allowed to touch me until you come." I kissed my way down his neck to the hollow of his throat. He smelled so delicious I wanted to wrap him around me like a blanket. "If you do, you lose, and you have to read only books of my choosing for a month."

Kai was so stressed about DigiStream and work. Hopefully this would loosen him up.

"And if I win?" The words turned smoky in the thickening air.

"If you win..." I hooked my fingers around his suspenders and straightened. "I'll do whatever you want for twenty-four hours."

His eyes gleamed with dark interest. "Whatever I want?"

A streak of fear mixed with a potent shot of arousal. "Yes."

It wasn't an offer I would've given anyone else, but I trusted him. He wouldn't take advantage of the situation.

Besides, I had no intention of losing.

Kai leaned back. A shutter fell over his expression as he observed me with the detached interest of a professor examining a student or a king observing a peasant.

Do your best, his eyes challenged.

My heart thrummed behind my ribcage as I released his suspenders and slid his shirt buttons from their plackets. Slowly, one by one, until his torso was bared and I could taste the heat of his bare skin.

Our breaths and the soft ticks of the clock filled the room.

Kai possessed the mind of a scholar but the body of an athlete. Lean and chiseled, its sleek muscles the result of boxing instead of gym work.

I flicked my tongue against his nipple and smiled at his resulting shudder.

I continued my journey down the defined ridges of his chest and abs until I reached his belt. It took me less than a minute to remove the barriers and free him from his confines.

His cock sprang out, thick and veined and already leaking precum. My mouth watered at the memory of how it tasted and felt.

"God, I can't wait to take you down my throat," I said huskily.

I stacked my hands on his impressive length and swirled my tongue around the head, savoring the shudder that ran through his body.

I loved giving blow jobs to Kai. Nothing turned me on more

than seeing him lose control and knowing I was the one in charge of his pleasure. I could give, take, and withhold as I pleased.

I had no intention of withholding today.

I bobbed my head up and down, licking and sucking and taking him deeper each time. I looked up, the ball of heat in my stomach coiling tight at the naked intensity on Kai's face. His jaw clenched so tight I could see the muscle spasm.

Deeper...deeper...

His cock hit the back of my throat. I choked, my eyes watering as my gag reflex kicked in. Drool leaked from the corners of my mouth and dripped down my chin.

My clit throbbed in time with my escalating pulse. I desperately wanted to touch myself, but if I did, I'd cave and beg for him to fuck me again.

Kai's knuckles turned white around the armrests. He hadn't made a sound since the game started. There was something so fucking hot about the wet, sloppy sounds of my blowjob filling the silence while he so clearly strained against the leash of his control.

Spots danced in front of my vision, and I finally pulled back with a gasp. Oxygen flooded my lungs, making me light-headed, but it evaporated again at Kai's next words.

"I didn't say you could pull back." His voice carried a preternatural calm. "Keep sucking, Isabella."

The command poured through me like molten lava. I was supposed to be the one calling the shots, but my resistance disintegrated before it even fully formed.

I obeyed, taking him to the hilt again.

"Fuck." His groan ran straight to the ache building between my legs. "Just like that, sweetheart. You take my cock so beautifully."

He didn't touch me, but his words of encouragement acted in his stead. They were a fist in my hair, guiding me up and down with increasing speed. They were hands on my breasts and fingers manipulating my clit until my wetness matched the mess of tears, drool, and precum smearing my face.

Kai's head tilted back. The tendons in his neck strained, and his harsh breaths mingled with my chokes and gurgles until he finally came down my throat.

"Swallow every drop. That's it." His fingers tangled in my hair. "You look so pretty on your knees with your mouth full of my cum."

I moaned. A tiny beacon of pride glowed in my chest, and it was only after I swallowed thoroughly that I sat back on my haunches.

"Good girl," Kai murmured, smoothing a hand over my head.

The pride glowed brighter, but not enough to make me forget the purpose of the game.

"You touched me," I breathed, my voice raw from my exertions. "At the end. You lost."

Amusement leaked into his gaze. "I touched you after I came, love. Which means I won."

"That's..." I faltered, unsure. I'd been so lost in my ministrations I hadn't paid attention to the timing.

Kai tightened his grip on my hair before releasing it. "Pick a book."

"What?" I blinked, disoriented by the sudden and baffling change in topic.

"A book." He nodded at the leather-bound tomes lining the shelves. "Pick one."

Curiosity compelled me to select a book at random.

"Open it."

I opened it to a page in the middle. Coincidentally, I'd chosen Jane Austen's *Pride and Prejudice,* one of the few classics I enjoyed.

"Now bend over the couch and spread your legs."

My confusion ramped up even as heat crawled through my blood, lighting me on fire. In this position, I was bared to him, the tiny scraps of my lingerie doing little to hide my swollen arousal or the juices drenching my thighs.

"We're going to play a new game." Kai stepped behind me. "It's simple. If you can read a full page out loud without stopping or stuttering, I'll let you come."

"What..." I gasped when he slipped the flimsy silk to the side and brushed a feather over my clit. *Where the hell did he get a feather?*

Another brush, and where he found it suddenly didn't matter.

A moan climbed up my throat. I tried to push back against him, but his other hand braced my hip, forcing me to still.

"Start reading, Isabella." Iron underlaid his voice. "Or we'll be here all day."

He's sadistic. That was the only thought running through my mind as I attempted to read the page while he tortured me with the feather. It was firm enough to spark jolts of pleasure but too flexible to induce an orgasm no matter how much I bucked and ground against it.

"Mr. Darcy, with grave propriety, requested..." The feather brushed a particularly sensitive spot, and my sentence trailed off with a whimper. Tiny shivers rippled down my spine.

They turned into a shocked yelp when Kai's palm landed on my bare ass with a sharp slap. There was a breath-rattling sting of pain, followed by a slow bloom of heat.

"Start over," he ordered with the stern command of an unforgiving professor.

I did, but I never made it more than two paragraphs before I paused or stuttered. Every mistake earned me another slap until my eyes welled with tears and I squirmed with mindless abandon. Pain and pleasure blurred into one delicious, agonizing burn.

I was barely paying attention to the text anymore. It got to the point where every word out of my mouth alternated with a hard spank.

"Please," I sobbed. "I can't...I need..."

"Yes, you can." Kai's voice was as unyielding as his punishment. He shoved two fingers into my dripping, exposed cunt.

Oh God. My insides knotted; my breaths came out in heavy, whining pants. *So close*. If he would only move. I would...I could...

"Unless you're messing up on purpose." He kept pushing until he was knuckles deep inside me. "Does this turn you on, Isabella? Getting bent over and punished like a dirty schoolgirl?"

"No. Yes. I don't know," I moaned, too dizzy and turned on to think properly. Tears leaked down my cheeks when he twisted and curled his fingers inside. I bucked again, but it was no use. I couldn't get enough friction to light the simmering fuse in my stomach. "I need to come...let me come...*please*."

But no matter how much I begged and pleaded, Kai refused to yield.

"You can come once you complete your assignment. That's the game." He withdrew his hand and resumed his exquisite, feathery torture. "You like those, don't you? Now start from the top."

I didn't know how, but eventually, I mustered enough willpower and presence of mind to read the page without messing up. The words poured out, faster and faster, before reaching a breathless crescendo on the last sentence.

Kai's fingers slammed inside me again. His thumb pressed against my clit, and his other hand delivered a sharp, final slap on my ass.

My orgasm ripped through me in one brutal, mind-numbing tear. My entire body bowed from the intensity; bursts of light exploded behind my eyes as the book clattered out of my limp hands and hit the cushion with a faint thud.

When I floated back down an eternity later, I was still racked with shudders from how hard I came. The echoes of my screams lingered in the air, bringing a wash of mortification to my cheeks.

"Perfect." Kai's voice softened. He was himself again, not the cruel, demanding master who'd forced me to dance on the razor's edge of orgasm for God knew how long. Strong, gentle hands smoothed and kneaded away the burn. "I knew you could do it. A-plus work, Ms. Valencia."

"Fuck you," I mumbled, too spent to infuse my words with much venom. "I can never read Austen the same way again."

Kai turned me around and pressed a smiling kiss on my pout. "Look on the bright side. Whenever you come across an obstacle, you know it can't be harder than reading a full page of *Pride and Prejudice* out loud while someone's trying to make you come."

A simultaneous laugh and groan slipped past my lips. "You're the only person I know who can turn sex into some weird motivational life lesson."

"It's a special talent, along with my fluent command of Latin and ability to produce amazing orgasms."

"Huh. I don't know about *amazing*..."

I squealed when he picked me up and tossed me on the couch. "Do you need another lesson?" he threatened, his eyes dancing with a playful light that made my heart melt. Sex and banter aside, my favorite version of Kai was the relaxed, comfortable one. He was so stressed all the time, and it made me happy to see him happy.

"Maybe. I've never been great at school." He didn't resist when I pulled him down next to me and draped an arm and leg over him like he was a giant teddy bear. Drowsiness hit with the suddenness of a lightning bolt. I yawned and snuggled closer to him. "But let's..." Another yawn. "Rest first. Have to recharge." I mumbled the last sentence into his chest.

Kai and I settled into a comfortable silence. The past few weeks had been a whirlwind of mind-blowing sex and swoonworthy dates, but they didn't hold a candle to the quiet moments in between. I could lie here next to him and listen to his heart beat forever.

"What are you doing for Christmas?" Kai asked after a while. He played absentmindedly with the ends of my hair, and warmth seeped through me at the casual intimacy of his touch.

"Binge-watching cheesy rom-coms and butchering my mom's

traditional Christmas recipes," I said. "One of these days, I *will* make buko pandan as good as hers. What about you?"

"Binge-watching cheesy action movies and ordering takeout," he quipped. Another silence fell. Then, he asked, so quietly I almost didn't hear him, "Why don't you spend it with me?"

My eyes snapped up to his. "What?"

"Spend Christmas with me. We'll both be in the city, and we can come to a compromise about the movies."

My heart stuttered beneath the blow of my surprise.

Sex and dating was one thing. Spending the holidays together was another. My family may have pushed our celebration back for logistical purposes, but Christmas was sacred to us. Who we spent it with mattered.

Plus, Kai and I were already treading a fine line with our relationship. We were having fun now, but we came from different worlds. It was only a matter of time before everything exploded in our faces.

My chest pinched at the thought.

On the other hand...if what we had was destined to end, wouldn't it make sense to enjoy every second while it lasted?

Don't overthink. Do what feels right. My father's advice drifted, unbidden, through my mind.

He'd been talking about music, but the same principle applied here.

I made a snap decision. It wasn't what New Isabella should do, but New Isabella could shove it.

I brushed my lips over Kai's with a smile. "I'd love to spend Christmas with you."

CHAPTER 23

K*AI*
   As much as I looked forward to spending the holidays with Isabella, we had one more occasion to celebrate before Christmas. She insisted we roll both into one, but I wasn't having it.

"It's your birthday. It should be celebrated separately." I wrapped my arms around her waist and tucked my chin between her neck and shoulder. We sat on my bed, her back pressed against my front, our bodies loose and languid after her birthday party earlier that night.

"We already celebrated." Isabella yawned. Her friends had rented a private room at an exclusive Italian restaurant, followed by a VIP experience at a nearby nightclub. "We don't need to do it twice."

"Tonight was your friends' idea. It's not the same." Vivian had invited me out of courtesy, but her friends didn't know about us, which meant we spent the night acting like simple acquaintances. I couldn't kiss her, dance with her, or talk with her like I wanted. But she'd been happy, which was what mattered. "Name your wish," I said, rubbing a lazy thumb over her skin. She was so warm and soft I could've held her here, like this, forever. "Anything you want."

Isabella twisted her head to look at me. "Really? Anything?"

"Paris for breakfast and Barcelona for dinner? I could have my jet ready in an hour."

Her laugh brushed my chest. "Kai, we are *not* going to Europe tomorrow."

"I know. We'd go tonight."

She pulled back to look at me fully. "Stop. We're also not flying to Paris tonight."

My mouth tugged up at the disbelief painted across her face. "Why not? It's the weekend." It was selfish, but I wanted to hoard all her smiles and laughs for myself. Since that wasn't possible, I'd settle for making her smile the most. Her friends had their turn; now, it was mine. "We'd get there in time for breakfast croissants and a stroll in Montmartre. We could people watch, browse the books at Shakespeare and Company, go vintage shopping in the Marais..."

I spun a seductive portrait of Paris, my anticipation already spiking at the thought of a weekend getaway. No prying eyes, no unbreakable rules. Just us, enjoying the city together.

Isabella's expression wavered for a split second before cementing with refusal. "Tempting, but I want something else. Something more normal."

"Like a private performance at the Lincoln Center?" That was even easier than flying to Europe.

"*No.*" Isabella's eyes gleamed with mischief, and that was when I knew, beyond a shadow of a doubt, that I'd made a horrendous mistake. "I want to go to Coney Island."

~

ISABELLA

Located on the southern tip of Brooklyn, between SeaGate and Brighton Beach, Coney Island was known for its amusement park, beaches, and boardwalk. During the summer, it swarmed with people, but in the winter, the rides shut down and the area turned into a ghost town.

That was what made it the perfect date spot for, say, a couple who was trying to stay under the radar.

"What do you think?" I chirped. "Isn't this fun?"

"*Fun* isn't the first word that came to mind," Kai said dryly. He was dressed like a normal person today in a sweater and jeans. Yes, the sweater was cashmere, and yes, the jeans probably cost more than an average person's monthly rent, but at least he'd ditched the suit and tie.

As sexy as he looked in business attire, he looked even better in casual wear.

"Oh, come on," I said. "The beach sucks during the winter, but the hot dogs were good, right?"

"We could've gotten hot dogs in the city, love."

"Not the same. Coney Island hot dogs hit different."

Kai responded with a half-amused, half-exasperated glance.

We were walking down the boardwalk, the amusement park on one side and the Atlantic Ocean on the other. It wasn't that cold today compared to the previous weeks, but I didn't protest when he wrapped an arm around my shoulders and drew me closer.

Warmth radiated through my body. I bit my lip, trying and failing to constrain a cheesy smile.

Paris sounded dreamy, but this was what I wanted. A nice, normal date where we could be a nice, normal couple. As much as I loved a good adventure, I thought normality was highly underrated.

"Thank you for coming here with me," I said. "I know it's not Europe, but I thought a more casual outing would be nice. It's been a hectic few weeks."

Kai's face softened. "When I said *anything*, I meant it. That includes visiting Coney Island." His mouth twisted with a small grimace.

A laugh burst between my lips. "Don't be a snob. You sound like I'm making you swim the Atlantic in the dead of winter."

"One, I'm an excellent swimmer even in extreme temperatures. Two, I'm not a snob. I simply have exacting taste."

"If by exacting, you mean *boring*, then you're correct."

Our playful banter continued to the New York Aquarium, where I had a little too much fun with the interactive "touch tanks." After much begging and cajoling, I convinced Kai to dip his hands in the water and touch the sea life.

"Are you afraid of fish?" I asked, suppressing another laugh at his wary expression.

"No, I'm not *afraid* of fish, but their texture—" He stopped when he saw my wide grin. "You're a menace."

"Maybe, but I'm also the birthday girl, so what I say goes. Now, how do you feel about octopi?"

For the next four hours, I dragged Kai around Coney Island. After the aquarium, we went ice skating and drank a few too many pints at a local brewery.

He wasn't a Brooklyn or beer type of guy, but aside from the fish incident, he didn't complain once. By the time we finished our day with jumbo slices from a well-known pizzeria, he almost looked like he was enjoying himself.

"Admit it," I said around a mouthful of cheese and pepperoni. "You *did* have fun."

"Because of you." Kai plucked a pepperoni off his slice and placed it on mine. He hated the topping and I loved it, which meant we were pizza partners made in heaven. "Not because of this place."

Butterflies swooped in my stomach. How did he manage to say the perfect thing every time without even trying?

That was one of the things I loved most about him. He was thoughtful and caring because that was who he *was*. There was no ulterior motive.

"So how does this birthday rank compared to your others?" he asked after we polished off our food and started walking again.

The sun was hanging low over the horizon, and we wanted to head out before sunset.

"Pretty damn high. In fact..." I stopped on the boardwalk and turned to loop my arms around his neck. I stood on tiptoes and gave him a soft kiss. "It was perfect. Thank you."

"You're welcome." His mouth brushed mine. "Happy birthday, love."

He'd presented with me a beautiful gold and amethyst necklace earlier, but his best gift was accompanying and spending time with me here.

An unshakeable warmth settled in my bones. It didn't matter that it was winter or that my face was raw from the wind. I would've floated away on a cloud of sunny bliss had Kai not been holding my hand.

"The first part of my birthday wish came true," I said when we resumed our walk. "Let's see about the second part." Unfortunately, it wasn't something money could buy.

Kai gave me a quizzical look. "What's the second part?"

"To make buko pandan as good as my mother for Christmas. I've been trying for years." I pictured myself puttering around the kitchen in an adorable apron and Kai's amazed expression when he ate my masterpiece of a dessert. "It'll happen. Just wait."

CHAPTER 24

Kai

Isabella did not, in fact, make buko pandan as good as her mother.

I'd never tasted the Valencia matriarch's famed recipe, but one bite of the cold dessert told me all I needed to know.

"I don't understand." Isabella stared at the delicacy with dismay. "I could've sworn I got the ratio of ingredients right this time! How does my mom do it?"

She flopped onto the kitchen stool in a fluff of reindeer-print wool and despair. She looked so adorable I couldn't repress a smile, despite the delicacy of the situation.

"I'm afraid there are certain superpowers only mothers have." I added an extra heap of marshmallows to a steaming mug of hot chocolate and pushed it toward her. "Cooking traditional recipes being one of them."

Isabella took a morose sip of the sugar-laden drink. "Is it that bad?"

Yes. I was fairly certain that the usually sweet dish wasn't supposed to be so...salty. But while I operated on a general principle of honesty, wild horses couldn't drag this particular truth out of me.

"It's perfectly edible." I stirred milk into my tea and prayed she didn't ask me to elaborate or, God forbid, take another bite. "However, it's Christmas. We should be enjoying the day instead of, ah, cooking. Why don't I order food instead?"

She acquiesced with a sigh. "That's probably a good idea."

I hid my relief and placed the order on my phone.

We were supposed to tackle her mom's Christmas recipes last night, but we got...distracted after she'd showed up at my front door wearing a red dress. Granted, the dress had been modest by Isabella's standards, but it didn't matter. She could wear a potato sack and the sight would still hit me in the gut.

It was quite concerning. I had half a mind to fund research on her baffling impact on me during my next round of scientific donations.

We migrated from the kitchen to the dining room, which my housekeeper had decorated with a massive flocked Christmas tree after Thanksgiving. White marble reindeer sculptures, sleek gold wreaths, and a row of snowy velvet stockings added to the festive atmosphere.

"This is so beautiful." Isabella ran her hands over the stockings. "If I were you, I'd never take these down."

Warmth sparked in my stomach.

I asked for the same decor every year. Changing it annually was a waste of time and efficiency, and I'd never thought much about it. But seeing them through her eyes made me appreciate the details just a little more.

"I could keep them up," I said. "But then there'd be no fall decor, Halloween decor, Lunar New Year decor..."

"Good point." She dropped her hand with another sigh. "I hate how you keep making those."

Our food arrived with surprising speed, and after some debate over Netflix versus board games, we settled into increasingly competitive rounds of Scrabble over cinnamon roll pancakes, champagne donuts, eggs Benedict, and sweet potato hash.

"Vizcacha? Are you kidding?" Isabella slapped her palm

against the board when I won the third round in a row. "How do you *come up* with these words?"

"You came up with *quetzals* in the last round," I pointed out.

"One, I visited Guatemala in college, and two, I still lost." She narrowed her eyes. "Are you cheating?"

"I don't need to cheat," I said, offended. "Cheating is for the intellectually lazy and dishonest."

Isabella came close to beating me a few times, but we finished with a final score of five to zero. I almost let her win at the end, but she wouldn't take kindly to a pity loss from me. Plus, the thought of willingly giving up a victory curdled like bile in my stomach.

Other than her vizcacha outburst, she took the outcome in stride.

"I have something for you," she said after we finished our food and put away the Scrabble board. "I know we didn't say anything about presents, but I saw this and couldn't resist."

She reached into her bag and handed me a brown paper-wrapped package. It read *To Kai. Merry Christmas!!* in her signature loopy cursive. Red hearts dotted the *i*'s and matched the red bow.

A pang pierced my gut at the sight of the hand-drawn hearts.

I unwrapped the present methodically, taking great care not to rip the paper or the bow. The wrapping fell away, revealing a book unlike any I'd encountered before.

I stared at the cover, too flummoxed to form a coherent response. "Is this..."

"A signed copy of *A Raptor Ripped My Bodice,* the latest dino erotica by Wilma Pebbles," Isabella confirmed. "It's a hot commodity since Wilma only sells a small number of autographed books every year. I literally had three screens up at the same time so I could snag one before they sold out. Congratulations." Her dimples deepened. "Your literary collection is now complete. Also, you have something new to translate when the board pisses you off. I bet it'll be more relaxing than translating Hemingway."

If the hearts had cracked the outer wall of my defenses, the present—and her explanation—demolished it beyond repair.

I'd received countless gifts in my life. A customized Audi for my sixteenth birthday; a limited-edition Vacheron Constantin watch when I was accepted into Oxford; a penthouse atop the Peak in Hong Kong when I graduated from Cambridge with my master's. None of them touched me as much as a flimsy paperback of velociraptor erotica.

"Thank you," I said, trying to make sense of the odd tightness in my chest. I sincerely hoped I wasn't in the early throes of a heart attack. That would ruin Christmas forevermore for all parties involved.

"Wait, that's not all." Isabella pulled a manila envelope from her bag.

"Does the raptor have a brother who also enjoys a good bodice rip?" I teased.

"Ha ha. As a matter of fact, he *does,* but you're not ready for the kinks in *that* book. No. This is, um, my manuscript so far." Isabella handed the envelope to me with a noticeably nervous expression. "I'm not sure whether it counts as a gift since I can't guarantee it's good, but you wanted to read it, so here it is. Just promise you won't read it until *after* I'm gone."

Forget what I said about the book. Isabella trusting me with her work in progress was...

Fuck. I swallowed past the creeping pressure in my throat.

"I promise." I tucked the envelope beneath Wilma Pebbles and retrieved a box from beneath the tree. Most of the gifts were for show; only two were exceptions. "On that note, I also have a surprise for you. It seems we were on the same page about presents."

Isabella's face lit up. "I *love* surprises." She took the box and shook it gently. A rattling sound ensued. "What is it? Makeup? Shoes? A new laptop?"

I laughed. "Open it and find out."

Isabella didn't have my hang-up about preserving the wrapping paper. She tore through the metallic foil without hesitation, revealing a simple black box.

An unfamiliar rush of anxiety shot through me when she removed the lid and went utterly still.

"Oh my God," she breathed. "Kai..."

Sitting in the box, nestled in a bed of tissue paper, was a vintage 1960s typewriter. The manufacturer went out of business decades ago, and there were less than a dozen of its products still circulating in auction rooms and antique shops. I'd paid a king's ransom to refurbish and restore it to functionality before Christmas, but it was worth it.

"You said you keep deleting what you write, so I thought this would help." I tapped the side of the box. "No delete option on a typewriter."

"It's gorgeous." Isabella ran her fingers over the keys, her eyes suspiciously bright. "But I can't accept it. It's too much. I bought you *dinosaur erotica,* for God's sake. This is in no way an equal trade."

"It's not a trade. It's a gift."

"But..."

"It's rude to decline a host's gift in his own house," I said. "I can show you the exact reference page in my etiquette manual if you don't believe me."

"Do you really have...you know what? I don't want to know." She shook her head. "I believe you." She leaned over and kissed me, her face soft with emotion. "Thank you."

"You're welcome." I cupped her face with one hand and deepened the kiss, trying to ignore the inappropriate thoughts creeping through my brain. Like how natural waking up next to her was or how this was the most at peace I'd felt in months. Or like how I could spend every Christmas with her, just the two of us, and be happy.

They were thoughts I had no business entertaining. Not when I couldn't promise anything more than what we had in the moment.

My stomach twisted. I pushed aside the bubble of unease and leaned back. "Before I forget, there's something else." I nodded at the box. "Check the sides."

After some rustling, Isabella retrieved a smaller, slimmer box. It was roughly the size of a Kindle but twice as thick due to the attached keyboard.

"It's a digital typewriter," I explained. "Much easier to travel with."

"Why am I not surprised you thought of everything?" she teased. She squeezed my hand, her face softening. "Thank you again. These are the best gifts I've ever received, except for maybe the Monty painting."

"Understandable. It's hard to beat an oil portrait of a nineteenth-century serpentine aristocrat."

"Exactly."

Our gazes caught and lingered. A thousand unspoken words crammed into the small space between us before we looked away at the same time.

We'd had sex multiple times over the past twenty-four hours, yet it was the small moments that felt the most achingly intimate.

A hand-drawn heart.

A simple thank you.

An intangible, pervasive sense that this was where we were meant to be.

"Let's watch a movie," Isabella said, breaking the tension. "It's not really Christmas without a holiday movie marathon."

"You choose." I dropped a soft kiss on her forehead and stood, trying to ease the returning pressure in my lungs. "I'll make popcorn. But *no* movies with royalty." After the relentless news coverage of Queen Bridget and Prince Rhys of Eldorra's fairytale love story the past few years, I was all royaled out.

"But that's almost all of them!" Isabella protested. "Don't give me that look...ugh, fine. I hope you don't have anything against bakers, or we're *really* out of luck."

A smile tugged on my lips as I entered the kitchen and started the popcorn maker. It was easier to breathe when I wasn't around her. It should've been a relief, but the rush of oxygen was almost disconcerting.

I'd just poured the popcorn into a bowl when my phone rang. *Unknown number.*

I would've brushed it off as a telemarketer, but I'd paid an exorbitant sum to effectively block cold calls, and no one had my personal cell number except for a select few friends, family, and business associates.

"Hello?"

"Merry Christmas, Young."

My spine stiffened with surprise at Christian Harper's smooth, distinctive drawl. I didn't bother asking how he got ahold of my number. He had a knack for ferreting out private information, which was why Dante used his services so much.

"Merry Christmas," I said, coolly polite. "To what do I owe the pleasure?"

"Just wanted to see if you had a chance to open my gift yet. I believe a messenger hand delivered it yesterday."

My mind flashed to the skinny, dark-haired messenger and the small box he'd handed me. I meant to open it yesterday, but Isabella had arrived right after.

I hadn't thought much about it since similar gifts poured in every year, but now, a trickle of unease slithered down my spine.

"What is it?"

"Open it and find out," he said in an eerie mirror of what I'd told Isabella earlier.

I remained silent. The day I opened an unsolicited package from Christian Harper was the day I walked through Times Square naked of my own free will.

Christian sighed, managing to infuse the sound with equal parts boredom and amusement. "It's a present from a mutual friend. A little chip with everything you need to secure your position as one of the youngest CEOs in the Fortune 500 come late January. You're welcome."

The implication hit like a crate of bricks.

"Blackmail," I said flatly.

I was going to *murder* Dante. He was the only mutual friend who would do something like this. He had good intentions, but his methods were questionable at best.

"Insurance," Christian corrected. "Dante said you would be too morally pure to use it, but it never hurts to have leverage in your back pocket. I don't care either way, but don't say I never gave you anything. Now, if you'll excuse me, I have to get back to my girlfriend. Enjoy the holidays."

He hung up before I could answer.

"Everything okay?" Isabella asked when I returned to the living room with our snacks. "That took a long time."

"Yes." I settled next to her and banished Christian's call to the back of my mind. It didn't matter that he'd sent the equivalent of an information nuclear bomb; I was never going to use it. "Everything's fine."

CHAPTER 25

Isabella

" Tf you type any faster, you'll sprain your wrist," Sloane said
without looking up from her computer. "Slow down."

"I can't slow down. I have less than a month to finish
this book, and I only have"—I checked my word count—"forty
two thousand, six hundred and four words, several hundred of
which are placeholders."

It was the week after New Year's. People were back from the
holidays, and the Upper West Side café where Sloane and I had set
up camp buzzed with activity. She had a client meeting nearby in
an hour, and I needed somewhere noisy where I could focus.

Normally, I used Vivian's office as my writing space while she
did admin work, but it was an offsite day for her. So here I was, my
butt planted on a wooden stool, my heart racing, and my hands
jittery from four cups of espresso as I attempted to wrangle my
manuscript into shape.

The holidays had been a dream. I ate, slept, and floated through
the city with Kai by my side and not a care in the world. But now
that they were over and Manhattan had resumed its snarling, frenetic energy, the sheer impossibility of my task loomed before me
like Mount Everest.

Forty thousand words in three weeks. *God*, why hadn't I been more disciplined about my writing before?

Because you were distracted.

Because you always run from the hard stuff.

Because it's easy to keep pushing the hard stuff to tomorrow until there are no tomorrows left.

Panic and self-loathing formed a tight knot in my throat.

Across from me, Sloane tapped away, her face a mask of cool efficiency. We were roughly the same age, and she owned her own super successful business. So did Vivian. How come they had their shit together and I didn't? What was their secret?

I had a steady paycheck and a decent lifestyle, but I was merely surviving while they were thriving. I didn't begrudge my friends their success; however, the weight of my failures sat all too heavy on my chest. *Why can't I show up for myself where it really counts?*

"How are things with Xavier?" I asked. I needed a distraction or I'd spiral into a wasteland of productivity. Nothing blocked my creativity more than creeping self-doubt. "Is he still alive, or have you murdered him and stashed his body in the trunk of your car?"

"Alive for now, but ask me again in twenty-four hours," Sloane muttered. "I'm one irreverent quip away from hacking him to pieces with a butcher's knife. It'll be bad PR for me, but I can spin it. He's insufferable."

The Lululemon-wearing blonde next to us glanced up and slowly inched toward the other side of the long, communal table.

"Why did you take him on as your client if you hate him so much?" Sloane had been complaining about him since the day she picked him up from the airport. I thought they would've learned to get along by now, but her irritation seemed to expand by the day.

"Favor to his father." Her curt tone disinvited further probing. "Don't worry. I can handle Xavier Castillo. His stupid smile and dimples and joke gifts *will not*"—she jabbed at her keyboard—"deter me from my duties."

My eyebrows skyrocketed. I had never, in all the years I'd known her, seen Sloane so heated.

"Of course not." I paused. "What are your duties again?"

"*Being a professional*—" She sucked in a deep breath, held, and released before smoothing a hand over her perfect bun. Her voice leveled off. "Repairing, cultivating, and maintaining his reputation as a *valuable* member of society, not a spendthrift playboy with zero goals or ambition."

"Well, if anyone can do it, it's you," I said cheerfully, wisely skipping over the reality that Xavier was, in fact, a spendthrift playboy with no discernible aspirations. "I have faith in you."

"Thank you."

Sloane and I lapsed into silence again.

I wasn't sure whether my words were any good, but I kept typing.

Kai hadn't said anything about the chapters I'd given him on Christmas, which didn't help my anxiety. Had he read them yet? If yes, why hadn't he mentioned it? Were they *that* bad? If no, why not? Maybe he wasn't actually interested in reading them. Maybe I put him in an awkward position by foisting a half-finished, unedited manuscript on him. Should I ask him about it, or would that make things even more awkward?

"Isa." There was a strange note in Sloane's voice.

"Hmm?"

Ugh, I should've stopped with the dinosaur erotica. What was I thinking?

"Have you looked at the news?"

"No, why? Did Asher Donovan crash another car?" I asked distractedly.

No response.

I looked up. A cold sensation crawled down my spine at Sloane's neutral expression. She only wore that look when something was very, very wrong.

She silently turned her laptop around so I could see her screen.

The *National Star*'s distinctive red and black text splashed across its website. Lurid headlines and unflattering celebrity photos dominated the page, which wasn't unusual. The trashy tabloid was famous for...

Wait.

My eye snagged on a familiar dress. Long sleeves, emerald-green cashmere, a hem that skimmed the tops of my thighs. A fifteen-dollar steal from the depths of the Looking Glass boutique's basement.

I'd worn it on a date with Kai two weeks ago.

My stomach bottomed out.

They weren't photos of celebrities. They were photos of *us.* Kai and me on Coney Island. Us strolling through the New York Botanical Garden, our heads bent close in laughter. Him feeding me a custard tart at a dim sum restaurant in Queens. Me exiting his apartment building, looking thoroughly mussed and slightly guilty.

Dozens of photos capturing some of our most intimate moments. We thought no one we knew would be in such out-of-the-way places, but obviously, we were wrong.

My skin flushed hot and cold. The muffin I ate for breakfast threatened to climb up my throat and ruin Sloane's pristine MacBook.

I'm so dead.

Once the club saw this, it was over. I'd lose my job and probably get blacklisted from working at any bar within a fifty-mile radius. Even worse, if the reporters did *any* digging, they'd find out—

"Breathe." Sloane's crisp voice sliced through my fog of panic. She slammed her laptop shut and pushed a glass of water in my hand. "Drink this. Count to ten. It'll be okay."

"But..."

"Do it."

In terms of comfort and warmth, she wasn't the greatest. She *was,* however, excellent at crisis management. By the time I gulped down the water, she'd already typed up a ten-point bullet plan for defusing the bombshell.

Step one: discredit the source.

"It's the *National Star,* which helps," she said. "No one takes that rag seriously. Still, it'll be good to—"

"Aren't you mad?" I interrupted. Liquid sloshed in my stomach, making me queasy. "About me keeping the Kai thing a secret from you and Viv?"

Sloane rolled her eyes. "Isa, please. Anyone with a working brain can see you two have the hots for each other. I'm only surprised it took you so long to do something about it. Besides, I understand why you didn't tell us. It's a delicate situation, given your job. That brings me to my second point. Valhalla will—"

She was interrupted again, this time by the buzz of my phone.

Parker. Speak of the devil.

My stomach plummeted further. "Hold that thought." I sucked in a lungful of air and braced myself. "Hello?"

So. Dead.

"Isabella." My supervisor's voice clinked over the line like jagged ice cubes. There wasn't a trace of her usual warmth. "Please report to Valhalla as soon as possible. We need to talk."

Half an hour later, I walked into the Valhalla Club's executive office with a pile of concrete blocks in my stomach.

Reserved for the reigning head of the managing committee, which rotated between sitting members every three years, the mahogany-paneled office resembled a cross between a Georgian library and a cathedral. A massive dark desk dominated the far end of the room.

Vuk Markovic sat behind it with the stiff posture of a displeased general surveying his troops. He must be the current head of the committee. I didn't pay attention to club politics, so I didn't even know who the committee members were besides Kai and

Dante—both of whom, I noticed with a jolt, were seated across the desk from Vuk. They occupied the chairs on the right; Parker sat on the left, her face tight.

Every pair of eyes swiveled toward me when I entered.

Self-consciousness prickled my skin. I avoided Kai's gaze as I walked over, afraid any eye contact would unleash the pressure building in my chest.

"Isabella." Parker nodded at the chair next to her. "Sit." She was the lowest-ranked person in the room, but she kicked off the meeting by cutting straight to the chase. "Do you know why you're here?"

I tucked my hands beneath my thighs and swallowed a lump of dread. There was no use playing dumb. "Because of the photos in the *National Star*."

Parker glanced at Vuk. Those pale, eerie eyes watched me with unnerving focus, but he didn't say a word.

"The club has a strict non-fraternization rule between members and employees," Parker said when he didn't speak up. "It is clearly stated in your employment contract, which you signed upon being hired. Any violation of said rule—"

"We weren't fraternizing." Kai's even voice cut off the rest of her sentence. "Isabella and I have mutual friends. We see each other often outside the club. Dante can attest to that."

My head jerked, unbidden, in his direction. He kept his attention on Parker, but I could practically *feel* the tendrils of comfort wrapping around me.

A messy knot of emotion tangled in my throat.

"It's true." Dante sounded bored. "Kai and I are friends. Isabella and my wife are best friends. You do the math."

I wasn't sure why he was here. Kai, I could understand since this involved him too. Maybe Dante was a character witness? We technically weren't on trial, though I felt like we were.

Either way, I was grateful for his support, even as guilt wormed through my gut. Kai and I had wittingly broken the rules, and now other people were being dragged into it.

Parker paused, clearly trying to figure out how to respond without being taken for an idiot—the photos revealed far more intimacy than that between casual acquaintances—or pissing off her employers.

"With all due respect, Mr. Young, you and Isabella were alone in those photos," she said carefully. "You were spotted holding hands—"

"I was simply guiding her over a rough patch of ground," Kai said, his tone so smooth and confident it almost concealed the absurdity of his excuse. "We met several times over the holidays to plan a surprise party for Vivian's birthday."

"You were planning a surprise party for *Vivian Russo* on Coney Island?" Parker asked doubtfully.

A short but pregnant pause saturated the room.

"She likes Ferris wheels," Dante said.

Another, longer pause.

Parker glanced at Vuk again in an obvious plea for help. He didn't answer. Now that I thought about it, I'd never heard the man utter a single word.

It didn't escape my notice that I was the one in the hot seat even though Kai and I were *both* in the wrong. But he was a rich, powerful VIP and I wasn't. The difference in treatment was expected, if not necessarily fair.

"The photos aren't proof we broke the non-fraternization rule," Kai said. "It's the *National Star*, not the *New York Times*. Their last issue claimed the government is harvesting alien eggs in Nebraska. They have no credibility."

Parker's mouth thinned.

My guilt thickened into sludge. I liked my supervisor. She'd always been good to me, and she'd kept my secret all this time. I hated putting her in such a tough position.

"I understand, sir," she said. "But we simply can't let the matter go unaddressed. The other members—"

"Let me worry about the other members," Kai said. "I'll—"

"No. She's right." My quiet interruption ground their argument to a halt. My heartbeat clanged with uncertainty, but I forged ahead before I lost my nerve. "I knew the rules, and the details don't matter. What matters is how it looks, and it doesn't look good, for us or the club."

Kai stared at me. *What are you doing?*

The silent message echoed loud and clear in my head. I ignored it, though a warm ache twisted my heart at how adamantly he was trying to defend me. He didn't lie, but he had. For me.

"What I'm trying to say is, I know what I did," I said, focusing on Parker. *It's just a job.* I could get another one. It probably wouldn't have the same benefits, hours, and pay, but I'd survive. And if Gabriel gave me shit for changing employers again...well, I'd cross that bridge when I came to it. "And I'm willing to accept the consequences."

There was a time when I would've been happy to let others fight my battles for me, but it was time I took responsibility for my actions.

Kai's stare burned a hole in my cheek. Next to him, Dante straightened, revealing a spark of intrigue for the first time since I entered the room. His presence was clearly out of loyalty to Kai and not any particular interest in my future at Valhalla.

Parker sighed, the sound laced with regret. I was one of her best employees, but she was a stickler for the rules. As my manager, she took the heat for my fuckups.

She looked to Vuk for confirmation. His chin dipped, and though I'd been expecting it, *asking* for it, her next words still punched a hole in my gut.

"Isabella, you're fired."

CHAPTER 26
Kai

I didn't follow Isabella after she left. Instinct screamed at me to comfort her, but reason stayed my hand. There were too many eyes on us right now; I didn't want to risk dragging her deeper into this mess.

Plus, I had about a hundred other people to placate before I could focus on my personal life.

Reporters, board members, company execs, friends and family...my phone had been ringing off the hook since the photos exploded across the internet that morning. I wasn't a movie star or rock star, but there were still plenty of people interested in the lives of the rich and scandalous. Bonus points if the scandal affected the future of one of the world's largest and most famous corporations.

"What were you thinking?" My mother's fury roared across the line, undeterred by the thousands of miles separating New York and London. "Do you understand what you've done? We're weeks out from the vote. This could destroy *everything*."

A migraine crawled over my skull and squeezed. I stared out the window of Valhalla's conference room, my stomach churning with a cocktail of emotions.

I had no doubt Victor Black was behind this mess. The

National Star was his publication, and the bastard was petty and vindictive enough to send someone to tail me after I bruised his ego.

"They're innocent photos," I said. "And it's the *National Star*. No one takes the *Star* seriously."

It was the same excuse I'd used earlier. Unfortunately, my mother wasn't as easily swayed as Parker.

"*Innocent* would be photos of you reading to children on World Book Day, not cavorting around New York with that *woman*," my mother said coldly. "A bartender? Really, Kai? I set you up with someone like Clarissa and you choose a run-of-the-mill gold digger? She has purple hair, for heaven's sake. And *tattoos*."

Anger chased behind my shame, incinerating it in one fiery burst. "Don't talk about her like that," I said, my voice lethally quiet.

My mother fell silent for a moment. "Don't tell me you've *fallen* for her." A hint of derision tainted her words.

Of course not.

The denial sat on the tip of my tongue, but no matter how hard I pushed, it wouldn't budge.

I liked Isabella. I liked her more than anyone I could remember. But there was a vast ocean of difference between *like* and *fallen*. The former was a safe, clearly marked path. The latter was an abrupt, potentially fatal crash off the side of a cliff, and I wasn't ready to take that leap.

I didn't know how to categorize my feelings for Isabella. All I knew was the thought of never seeing her again felt like a serrated blade slicing through my chest.

"We can still salvage this. Like you said, it's the *Star*." My mother moved on from her original line of questioning. She didn't press the Isabella issue, likely because she was afraid she'd get an answer she wouldn't like. "Lean in on its unreliability. Reassure the board. And, for God's sake, stop seeing that woman."

My grip strangled my phone. "I'm not breaking up with her."

The past few months had been a shitshow. Isabella was the only bright spot in my life right now. Remove her, and...

Fuck.

I loosened my tie, trying to ease the sudden pressure in my chest.

"Be serious." My mother switched from English to Cantonese, a sure sign she was pissed. "You're willing to throw your future away over a girl? Everything you've worked for. Your career, your family, your *legacy*."

My teeth clenched. "You're blowing this out of proportion. They're just photos." Not even risqué ones, at that.

Dammit, I should've taken more precautions. I'd been arrogant, careless. So sure no one would ever catch on.

What had I been thinking?

That's the problem. You weren't.

I'd been too distracted by Isabella, and it'd come back to bite us both in the ass.

My mind flashed back to the note I'd received at the Saxon Gallery. I'd brushed it off as a prank, but perhaps there was more to it than I originally thought. The timing seemed awfully suspicious.

Be careful. Not everyone is who they seem.

Who could they be talking about? Victor? Clarissa? Someone else at the gallery?

"They're just photos now," my mother said, drawing my attention back to her. "Who knows what else will come out? It only takes a spark to start a fire, and *any* scandal, no matter how small, could lose you crucial votes."

The pressure expanded, dimming my vision. I couldn't focus. My usual cold clarity had vanished, leaving a whirlwind of tumult in its wake. There were a thousand voices in my head, clamoring to edge the others out like commuters shoving their way onto a rush-hour train.

Keep her. Leave her.

"I'll fix it."

"You only have—"

"I know how much time I have." I rarely snapped at family. Asian children simply did not talk back to their parents, no matter how grown up or successful they were. But if I didn't get off the phone in the next five minutes, I would explode. "Like I said, I'll fix it. In two weeks, the photos will be a mere memory and I'll be voted in as CEO."

The other option was too awful to contemplate.

Losing. Taking orders from Tobias. Becoming a laughingstock. The taste of ashes filled my mouth.

"I hope so." My mother didn't acknowledge my rare loss of temper; there were bigger things at stake. "Or you'll go down in history as the Young who lost control of his family's empire. Remember that the next time you feel like running around town with your new girlfriend."

After I hung up, I sent the rest of my calls to voicemail and took a car to Isabella's house. I had the driver follow a winding route in case I was still being tailed, but it didn't matter much if I was. The photos had done their damage.

Isabella looked remarkably calm when she opened the door.

"I'm okay," she said before I could ask. If it weren't for the redness tipping her nose and rimming her eyes, I might've believed her. "It's just a job. I'll find another one. See? I've already started looking." She gestured at the job search site pulled up on her computer. "I'm thinking about adding *photogenic even in candid photos* in the special skills section." A small wobble betrayed her joke.

I didn't smile. "Isa."

"I've been fired before. Not as many times as I've quit but, you know, the end result is the same." A semblance of a smile strained across her face. "What's one more failure on the books? It doesn't—"

"Isa."

"It doesn't matter in the grand scheme of things. The only shitty part is if Parker blacklists me with other bars. She knows everyone in the New York nightlife industry. I don't *think* she will—"

"Isabella." I opened my arms. "Come here, love."

She fell silent, her eyes glassy. Her chest heaved from her rapid-fire rambling, and she didn't move for a long, drawn-out second.

Then her face crumpled, and she fell into my open arms with a quiet sob that ripped through me like shrapnel. I pressed a kiss to the top of her head and held her as she cried, wishing I didn't feel so damn helpless.

No one was above Valhalla's rules, not even the managing committee. I could easily find her another job or pay her bills so she didn't *have* to find new employment, but that wouldn't go over well. She was too independent to accept anyone's charity. Besides, I knew Isabella well enough to know her termination from Valhalla was not the root issue here.

She confirmed it less than a minute later when she lifted her head, her eyes red and swollen from her tears.

An ache clawed its way into my chest and stabbed at my heart.

"I'm sorry." She hiccupped. "This is so stupid. I totally didn't mean to cry all over your really nice and probably very expensive shirt." She rubbed her thumb over the mascara-stained cotton like it would magically erase the black marks.

"It's just a shirt." I grasped her wrist, stilling her. "And it's not stupid. You've had a...taxing day."

"Kai Young, the king of understatement." Isabella's watery smile dissolved almost as soon as it formed. "It's not even the getting fired part that gets me. I mean, obviously I'm upset, but part of me expected it to happen. I just..." Her throat bobbed with a hard swallow. "I feel like such a failure. My mom's birthday is in a few weeks, my book isn't done yet, and I'll have to go home and tell my family I got fired. It's worse because they've been so supportive. Well, besides Gabriel, but that's another story. They've had faith in me this entire time, and I keep letting them down."

"You're not letting them down. There's no time limit to success, and they're your family," I said. "They want you to be happy."

"I'm happy when I'm with you or my friends. But when you leave and I'm alone, I just feel...lost. Like I don't know where I'm supposed to be in life." The last word came out as an achingly vulnerable whisper.

The ache intensified, creeping into my bones and veins like poison without a cure. I had billions in the bank and the most powerful people in the world on speed dial, but I'd never felt so powerless.

"You're not alone," I said softly. "You have me."

If it were anyone else, they'd have to pull the words out of me with pliers. But with Isabella, the admission floated as easily between us as a gust of air.

Her eyes brightened with a fresh sheen. A tear streaked down her cheek, and I brushed it away with my thumb, wishing I could offer more than words and a promise. I'd give anything to see her happy—truly happy, not just happy in the moment. No fears, no anxieties, just the freedom to bloom to her fullest potential.

"We'll be lost together." A smile edged my lips. "Lucky for you, I have an excellent sense of direction."

"Funny, because I don't have *any* direction." Her expression dimmed further before she shook her head. The tense melancholy retreated an inch. "Every man thinks they have a great sense of direction. I bet you refuse to ask for help even when you *are* lost." Isabella sniffled out a laugh. "Anyway, enough about me. What about you? The board must be freaking out about the photos. I'm not exactly CEO partner material." Concern swallowed the fleeting humor in her eyes. "It's not going to affect the vote, is it?"

Her question grabbed hold of my heart and squeezed. She was the one who'd gotten fired, and she was worried about *me*.

In that moment, I wanted to hunt down every person who'd ever made her feel like she was a failure, a disappointment, or anything less than fucking perfect.

"It's caused some complications, but they're nothing I can't handle." I smoothed away the furrow in her brow with a kiss. "Don't worry about me, love."

"I know we should've been more careful," she said quietly. "But is it bad that I don't regret what we did?"

"No." My lips traced the curve of her cheek to the corner of her mouth. "Because I don't either."

I'd replayed and dissected the past three months dozens of times since the photos surfaced. The piano room, the holidays, our first "date" in Brooklyn and subsequent library rendezvous... they were reckless, yes, but they were also the only patches of sunlight in the overwhelming grayness of my life. I hadn't noticed how muted my world was until Isabella burst in, full of life and color and energy, like a rose blossoming in the middle of an arid desert.

I wouldn't trade any of my moments with her for all the calm and peace in the world.

I thought I abhorred chaos, but somehow, somewhere along the way, I'd grown to love it.

"What are we going to do?" Isabella whispered. "*The Star* could still have people following us..."

"I've taken care of that." The special team I'd hired immediately upon seeing the photos could ferret out a tail faster than a bloodhound could find a bone. It should've been enough, but impulse and a desperate desire to wipe the worry from her face pushed my next words out of my mouth. "Let's go away."

She startled at my words. "What?"

"Let's go away for the weekend. Take a break, recharge and regroup." The more I thought about it, the more I liked the idea of a strategic withdrawal to somewhere warm, away from prying eyes and the icy claws of the city. "My family owns property in Turks and Caicos. No one will bother us there."

Isabella stared at me like I'd suggested walking barefoot to California. "We can't just *leave*."

"Why not?"

"Because!" For once, she was the caution to my spontaneity. "You're already in hot water over the photos. Even if your tail doesn't follow us there, someone could see us and sell more pictures to the tabloids."

"They won't. Trust me." I nodded at her computer. "You have to finish your book and find a new job. I have to put out a hundred fires and craft a new strategy for the CEO vote. We can work on them together. It'll be our version of an executive retreat."

Isabella hesitated.

"You'd be surprised how much a change in scenery can unlock your creativity," I said. "Think about it. Would you rather work in an overcrowded Midtown café or on a beautiful tropical island?"

"I don't go to cafés in Midtown. They're too depressing." She was caving. I could see it in her eyes. "Are you sure no one will see us?"

"Positive."

"God, what a fucking day." She shook her head, a burble of hysterical laughter escaping from her throat. "I woke up, got fired, and now I'm thinking about running away to Turks and Caicos."

"To be fair, there's no better time to run away than after getting fired," I said. "Unlimited vacation days."

My mouth curved when she let out another small yet genuine laugh. My professional life might have been going up in flames, but the sight of Isabella's smile had a way of righting my world, if only for a time.

"Twist my arm, why don't you?" Her eyes contained a lingering trace of sadness, but their usual sparkle was making a slow, steady return. Isabella didn't see it, but she was the strongest, most resilient person I knew. "If you ever tire of the executive life, you should go into travel sales. You'd make a killing."

My smile inched up another millimeter. "I'll keep that in mind."

"Now for the real question." Isabella grinned, and a rush of unsettling warmth filled my stomach. "What does one pack for a weekend getaway in the Caribbean?"

CHAPTER 27

Isabella

When Kai said his family owned property in Turks and Caicos, I'd pictured a breezy beach mansion with wicker furniture and nice gardens. I hadn't pictured an *entire freaking island*.

Dubbed Jade Cay for the color of its surrounding waters, the island spanned over four hundred acres of lush vegetation, pristine beaches, and exotic wildlife. The Balinese-style main residence occupied the highest point on the island, offering spectacular three-hundred-sixty-degree views of the Caribbean and all the amenities of a five-star luxury resort. Eight bedrooms, three wraparound terraces, two infinity pools, a private chef who made the most delicious lobster I'd ever tasted.

I could live and die here happy.

Kai and I flew in yesterday afternoon. We spent the night getting settled, but today, we were off and running. The morning had been a blur of writing (me), calls (him), and brainstorming (both of us). Kai was right; toiling over my manuscript in tropical paradise was much better than toiling over it in the wintry hell of post-Christmas New York.

We were currently taking a lunch break on the uppermost terrace, and I'd never felt more relaxed, even with my deadline looming on the horizon like a thundercloud. Here, surrounded by the ocean and sunshine, I could almost forget the *Star* photos and getting fired.

Sometime between the main course and dessert, Kai excused himself to use the restroom and returned with a slim black folder in hand.

"Put that away," I said, nudging his foot with mine beneath the table. "No work during meals, remember?"

"It's not work in the traditional sense. It's a present." His eyes came alive with laughter when I perked up like a dog hearing the word *walk*.

"A present? For me?"

"You've said you were having issues with writer's block, so I did some research and put together a list of ways to overcome the block." He handed me the folder. "I confirmed with several neuroscientists that these methods are scientifically sound."

I nearly choked on my freshly squeezed grapefruit juice. "You consulted with a team of *neuroscientists* about my writer's block?"

He shrugged. "I donate a significant sum to various scientific organizations every year. As such, they're happy to indulge some of my more personal requests."

I opened the folder and scanned the suggestions. Most of it was advice I already knew from trawling the web. Meditating, setting aside a block of time every day for creative play, using the Pomodoro technique, so on and so forth. There were a few I hadn't seen before, but it wouldn't matter if Kai had handed me a packet of introductory yoga class flyers.

He'd taken the time to research solutions and consult neuroscientists, for Christ's sake. My previous boyfriends thought they were doing me a favor when they picked up pizza on their way to my house.

The last time someone did something so thoughtful without expecting anything in return was when a certain billionaire showed me his family's secret room and offered it as a writing space.

My throat constricted with emotion. I dipped my head and blinked back an embarrassing sting. The last thing I wanted was to start bawling over my crab and rice. I'd already cried once in front of Kai this week; twice would be overkill.

I flipped the pages noisily while I wrangled my runaway emotions. The pressure in my throat eased as I stopped on the second to last item.

"Engage in frequent and rigorous sexual activity when feeling stuck," I read aloud. "Orgasms stimulate creativity, among other things." I slanted a suspicious look at Kai, who returned it with an innocent one of his own. "Huh. I wonder who came up with that one."

His grin spread as slow and molten as warm honey. "No need to wonder. It's scientifically proven, my love."

My love.

Around us, the world fell eerily quiet. No birds chirped. No waves crashed against the distant shores. Even the wind came to a standstill.

Kai had called me *love* many times before, but he'd never called me *his*.

One word. Two letters.

Sometimes, they made all the difference.

Kai's smile slipped into a line of realization. Tension crept between us, twining around my torso and settling in my chest like a concrete weight.

It wasn't unpleasant, but it was the type of silence so drenched in meaning that it drowned out any admissions lurking beneath the surface. We weren't ready for those conversations.

I changed the subject before the pause stretched into must-acknowledge territory.

"Well, let's see how your other suggestions fare before we test the orgasm theory," I said lightly. "What about you? How are negotiations with Mishra going?"

DigiStream was one of the many fires Kai had to put out due to the *National Star* photos. I thought it was hypocritical of them to care so much about who he spent his free time with when *their* CEO got hospitalized for a drug overdose, but what did I know? I was just a bartender. *Ex*-bartender, if I didn't find a new job soon.

Kai shifted, and just like that, the world came roaring back. The bird and ocean sounds returned, and the wind blew strands of hair across my face. Tension melted like pools of ice beneath the sun.

"They removed Whidby as CEO two days ago," he said. "Mishra officially replaced him and is closing ranks, which means I'm basically back to square one. It's chaos over there."

"Why is he so reluctant about the deal when his co-founder was so ready to sign?" Kai and I didn't talk about his work often. He said it would bore me, and I wholeheartedly agreed, but I was genuinely curious about the DigiStream deal.

"Whidby was easy. He wanted the money. Mishra is a purist. He doesn't want to relinquish control of DigiStream to a corporation who will, quote, unquote, *gut it.*"

I chose my next words carefully. "*Will* you gut it?"

"Not exactly. Their success stems in large part from their culture and team dynamics. I don't want to ruin that," Kai said. "But all acquisitions require some form of change from both the buyer and the seller. Their operations have to be streamlined to fit in with the rest of the company."

"That's the sticking point," I surmised.

Kai dipped his chin in affirmation. "The biggest one. Mishra is worried about the integration. He wants a deal where DigiStream operates exactly the way it does now. Obviously, that's not possible. Even if I agreed, the board members won't. They have to approve the strategic plan for all new acquisitions."

"Is there a way to offer concessions on specific changes he's worried about instead of a blanket agreement?"

Kai's brows winged up. "Perhaps. The details are a bit complicated, but we were working on a similar plan before Whidby's ouster sidelined negotiations." A small smile touched his lips. "And you say you don't like talking business."

"I don't. It puts me to sleep ninety percent of the time. You're lucky this conversation falls into the remaining ten percent." His laugh brought an answering smile to my face, but it faded when I ventured into my next question. "I'm not saying this will happen, but hypothetically, what happens if you don't win?"

"I keep my title and position, but I'll be a laughingstock." His face cemented into stone. "The other candidates can go back to their jobs and carry on because they were long shots anyway. I'm a Young. I'll forever be known as the person who lost his family's company to an outsider."

"You'll still be a major shareholder," I pointed out. I'd looked it up. Kai controlled over a quarter of the company's shares, second only to his mother.

"It's not the same." A muscle ticked in his jaw before it smoothed. "People remember leaders, not voters."

"I think people will remember you regardless," I said. "You've broken records even as a non-CEO, and there are plenty of chief executives who are shitty at their job. Your accomplishments matter more than a title."

Kai's expression softened. He opened his mouth, but my phone rang and cut him off before he could respond.

Surprise and confusion sparked at the caller's name. "It's Alessandra."

We were friendly, but I couldn't think of a reason why she'd call me out of the blue.

"Take it," Kai said. "It must be important if she's calling on the weekend."

In the end, curiosity won out. I walked to the other side of the terrace and answered the call. "Hey, Ale."

"Hey. Are you free to talk right now?"

I glanced at Kai and my half-eaten lunch. "For a bit. What's up?"

"I realize this may be presumptuous of me, so I apologize in advance." A trace of embarrassment colored her voice. "But I heard you and Valhalla have, er, parted ways, and you're looking for a new job."

I perked up. "I am. Do you know someone who's looking for a bartender?"

"No. However..." Her pause carried the hesitation of someone debating their next words. "I *am* looking for an assistant. I don't want to go through an agency. I'd rather have someone I know and trust, which is why I thought of you."

Disappointment threaded through my stomach. "I appreciate that, but I have to be honest. I would make a terrible PA. I can barely keep on top of my calendar, much less someone else's."

"Oh no, not a personal assistant," Alessandra said quickly. "A business one. I should've been more clear."

My brows pulled together. "I didn't know you had a business."

"I don't. Not yet, hence the need for an assistant." She let out an awkward laugh. "I have a lot of ideas, but I need help implementing them. Vivian mentioned you worked at a startup once? So you have an idea of what it's like to build something from the ground up."

"That's overselling what I did," I said dryly. "I worked as a marketing assistant, and I was only there for a few months. I couldn't stand all the fintech bros." I drew my bottom lip between my teeth. I needed a new job, but I didn't want to promise something I couldn't deliver. "Honestly, Dominic would be more helpful. He built a multibillion-dollar firm from scratch." *And he's your husband.*

I kept that last part to myself. Alessandra didn't talk about her marriage much, but I could tell there was trouble in paradise.

"The same multibillion-dollar firm keeps him too busy to help with little projects like this." A current of sadness ran beneath her light tone before it disappeared. "I'll be honest. I like you, and I think we would work well together. I can offer a competitive salary and flexible hours so you have time to work on your manuscript."

My heart skipped, then sank. It was a great offer, but what did I know about starting a business and being an assistant? Nothing. I didn't want to start another job only to fail miserably again. I'd be better off sticking to what I knew.

"How about this?" Alessandra said quickly. "I'll email you the details, and you can think it over. I am looking to onboard someone soon, so if you can give me an answer within the next week or two, that would be great."

After another beat of hesitation, I agreed.

I hung up and returned to the table, where I finished my lunch and relayed her offer to Kai. His eyebrows flew up when I mentioned Alessandra was starting her own business, but he didn't express the same reservations I had about the job.

"You should accept," he said. "Ale's a good person, and working for her will almost certainly be better than any bartending gig in the city."

"But I've never been a business assistant." My stomach twisted. "What if I fuck it up and destroy her company before it even takes off?"

"You won't." As always, his steady, confident voice loosened some of the knots. "Have as much faith in yourself as you do others, Isa."

I wish I could, but faith was easier when I didn't have a hundred *what-ifs* tearing it apart.

Kai must've detected the turmoil raging inside me because he pushed back his chair and stood.

"No more work today," he said, holding out his hand. "Let's enjoy the island. I have something to show you."

For the next four hours, Kai and I indulged in all the perks of having a secluded tropical island to ourselves. We snorkeled, rode Jet Skis, and luxuriated in waters so clear I could see the scales on the fish swimming around us. When the sun dipped toward the horizon, we dried off and took the scenic route back to the main house.

"This is the most cliché thing I've ever done," I said. "A long, sunset walk on the beach? You might as well slap us on the cover of a honeymoon brochure and call us *that generic couple*." A dreamy sigh drifted past my lips. "I love it."

If it were any other man and any other island and any other sunset, I would've hated it. What was interesting about a walk? *Nothing*.

But this was Kai. Brilliant, gorgeous, thoughtful Kai, with the lazy half smiles and knowing eyes that saw parts of me even I couldn't find. A deep golden glow drenched the island, lending it a dreamlike haze, and I was quite sure, in that moment, that there was absolutely nothing I would rather do than walk side by side with him.

"I had a feeling you would," he said with one of those smiles I loved so much. I couldn't believe I once thought he was stuffy and boring. Well, okay, I could believe it, but I'd since amended my opinion. "But I haven't shown you the best part yet."

"This isn't the part where you whip out your dick and try to seduce me on the beach, is it?" I teased.

"Darling, if I wanted to seduce you on the beach, you'd already be screaming around my cock," Kai drawled, his casual tone at odds with his dirty words.

Heat crawled over my cheeks and tugged at my stomach. "You have quite a high opinion of your skills."

"It's the inevitable outcome of sustained, raving feedback, I'm afraid."

I wrinkled my nose and bumped my hip against his as we reached a rocky outcropping toward the end of the beach. "Egomaniac."

Kai laughed. "I've been called worse." He stopped at the largest rock. "We're here."

I stared dubiously at the weathered limestone formation. *This* was what he wanted to show me? It looked like every other beach rock. "Oh. It's so, um, jagged."

"Not the rock, love," he said, his voice dry. "*This.*"

It was then that I noticed the carvings—the letters C+M etched on the side facing away from the ocean, inside a heart. It was the type of sweet, cheesy declaration one would expect to find in a high school bathroom, not a private island in the Caribbean.

"I found it a few years ago," Kai said. "That was when my family bought the island. I don't know who C and M are since they don't match the initials of the island's previous owners, but I like to think they're living happily together somewhere."

I brushed my fingers over the rough-hewn rock face. For some reason, the simple, heartfelt carvings made my heart twist. "Kai Young, a secret romantic. Who would've thought?"

"It's the dinosaur erotica you gifted me for Christmas. It's opened my eyes to a whole new world of romance."

"Shut up." I laughed, then paused. "Did you really read it?"

A grin stole over his lips. "You'll never know."

He still hadn't said anything about my manuscript. At this point, I'd rather he forget all about it. If he thought it sucked, I didn't want to know.

"I don't know how old the carvings are, but they've lasted at least half a decade," Kai said, his face sobering with contemplation. "They should've eroded by now. Whoever C and M are, they've left their mark."

Like Kai, I hoped the mysterious couple was sipping mai tais and strolling the beach together somewhere in the world. Even if they weren't, the carvings were an unexpected monument to the love they once had. Proof that, no matter what happened, there'd been a time and place where they loved each other so much they immortalized it in stone.

Kai reached into his pocket and pulled out a chisel.

"What are you doing?" I asked, semi-alarmed. Where did he even *find* a chisel?

"Thinking we should give our anonymous friends some company." He held out the tool. "Shall we?"

My heart thumped. After a moment's hesitation, I took the chisel and gingerly pressed the tip against the rock. Moisture had softened the limestone, making it easier to manipulate.

Kai and I took turns carving until clear letters took shape. We didn't have to discuss the message; we already knew.

K + I, inside a heart.

It was hands down the cheesiest thing I'd ever done, but that didn't stop a wonderful, aching pressure from pressing against my rib cage.

The etching wasn't a ring. It wasn't a promise. It wasn't even a love declaration in the normal sense of the word. Yet somehow, the fact that we'd made our mark on the world together meant more to me than any of those things.

It was small, but it was ours, and it was perfect.

Kai's hand found mine. Our fingers interlaced, and the pressure ballooned until I thought I might burst.

"I'm liking secret romantic Kai more and more," I said, swallowing past the lump in my throat. I attempted a lighthearted tone. "If this is the result of dino erotica, expect more Wilma Pebbles in your future."

"Good. I've already finished translating the first into Latin."

My eyes snapped to his laughing ones. "Are you ser—"

He cut me off with a kiss, and the rest of my words melted beneath the insistent heat of his mouth.

The holidays in New York. The sanctuary of a hidden room. An island nestled in the heart of the Caribbean.

Magical pockets of time and space that belonged only to us.

And as the sun died brilliantly on the horizon, and the shades of our kiss transformed into the cool blues of dusk, I found myself wishing I could stay in this particular moment, with this particular man, forever.

CHAPTER 28

Isabella

The rest of our weekend passed in a lovely haze of work and play. I took Kai's writer's block suggestions and actually implemented them instead of reading them over and over like the benefits would somehow transfer through osmosis.

I quickly found out meditating wasn't for me, but the creative play suggestion helped. So did the orgasm one, much to his (and my) satisfaction.

By the time we returned to New York, I'd written twenty-five thousand words and debated Alessandra's job offer to death. In the end, I accepted.

Kai was right. I needed to have more faith in myself. Plus, she was offering a *great* salary, and I had zero motivation to trawl through job search sites.

Once I accepted, things moved quickly. Three days after my return, I started my first day of work as Alessandra's business assistant (actual business name pending). Kai was in California again for DigiStream talks, but I woke up to an oh so encouraging voice note from him that morning.

Remember, you read a full page of Austen while getting spanked. If you can do that, you can do anything.

He had a point, but that didn't stop nerves from buffeting my stomach as I followed Alessandra through her apartment.

The Davenports lived in a sprawling modern penthouse in Hudson Yards, complete with floor-to-ceiling windows, a floating glass spiral staircase, and a private terrace with a plunge pool and fire pit. It was absurdly large for two people, and it brimmed with so many priceless items I was afraid of touching anything lest I accidentally break a two-million-dollar Fabergé egg.

"What type of business are you interested in starting?" I asked.

I probably should've confirmed *before* I accepted the job, but beggars couldn't be choosers, and I'd had other priorities in Turks and Caicos. Namely, food, writing, and copious amounts of sex.

"You'll see," Alessandra said with a mysterious smile. She was possibly the prettiest person I'd ever met, but an air of melancholy tempered her beauty.

"It's not meth, is it?" My New Year's *Breaking Bad* marathon with Kai flashed through my head.

Her laugh chimed like silver bells in the wind. "Sadly, chemistry has never been my strong suit." She opened the door at the end of the hall. "No, it's something a little more, um, creative."

The first thing I noticed when I stepped inside was the smell. Lush and fragrant, it instantly transported me back to the climes of the Caribbean. The second was the array of colorful bouquets lining the table and windowsill. Finally, my eyes were drawn to the far wall, where a gallery of pressed flowers hung in elegant wooden frames.

"Oh, wow," I breathed. I wasn't sure what I was expecting, but I hadn't expected *this*.

"It's a silly hobby," Alessandra said, her cheeks reddening. "I'm not curing cancer or anything, but it's fun, and it helps me pass the time while my husband is working."

"It's not silly. These are *gorgeous*." I brushed my fingers over the glass frame protecting a huge pressed herbarium on black paper. "How long did it take you to make this?"

"About a month if you include the drying time. That one is one of my favorites. They're all night-blooming flowers, hence the black background." Alessandra drew her bottom lip between her teeth. "I sometimes gift these to friends. People seem to like them, so I thought, why not open an online shop? A small one."

"That's an amazing idea."

She didn't need the money, but she was clearly passionate about the art. I counted at least a dozen pressed flower artworks in the room. She must've been doing this for at least a year.

Her face relaxed. "Thank you. I'm glad you think so. It's much better than meth, no?"

I laughed. She was right. We were going to work well together.

Since it was my first day, we spent the next two hours ironing out my schedule, logistics, and expectations. Neither of us really knew what we were doing, but we had fun figuring it out together.

We agreed to a tentative list of tasks, to be amended if and when necessary. I would assist with research, marketing, and administrative tasks, including brainstorming business names. Alessandra wanted to keep things low-key to start, but once we got our bearings and ironed out the logistics, she'd hire more people. Until then, it was a two-person show.

I didn't have set hours. As long as I met my deadlines, I could work whenever and wherever I wanted.

"That being said, you're welcome to work here if you'd like." Alessandra gestured around the apartment. We were back in the living room, which was so massive it could easily host a Super Bowl game. "Don't feel obligated, but if you get tired of being alone, my door's always open."

"I might take you up on that offer. I hate working alone." I hesitated, debating whether to ask my next question. "Are you sure Dominic won't mind?"

She gave me a sad smile. "He won't even notice."

Their marriage was none of my business, but I couldn't help

feeling a pang of sympathy. *Money can't buy happiness*. It was cliché, but it was true.

My eyes landed on the wedding photo propped up on the mantel. "That's a beautiful shot of you two."

Their physical features hadn't changed much over the years—Alessandra possessed the same flawless skin and stunning bone sculpture, Dominic the same golden hair and chiseled jaw—yet I hardly recognized the people in the photo. In it, Alessandra's face glowed with joy, and her new husband gazed down at her with obvious adoration. They looked young and happy and so incredibly in love.

It was difficult to reconcile them with the cold Wall Street titan dominating the business papers and the quiet, melancholic woman before me.

"Thank you." Alessandra's smile took on a strained quality. She didn't look at the mantel. "Speaking of photos, we should create social media accounts, right? I'm not great at photography, but I can hire a professional..."

I went along with her obvious deflection. It was her marriage. If she didn't want to talk about it, I wasn't going to push her.

When I left her house another two hours later, it was late afternoon and I was riding high from our meeting. I had a shit ton of work to do on top of finishing my manuscript, but after getting fired, it was nice to feel useful again.

The ping of a news alert punctured my high as I entered the nearest subway station. I'd set up news alerts for my name against Sloane's advice. I couldn't help it; I *needed* to know what people were saying.

I pulled my phone out of my pocket. I expected more tabloid rumors about me and Kai, maybe even someone who'd caught us together in Turks and Caicos. His staff had been the only other people on the island, but one never knew. Sleazy outlets like the *National Star* had eyes and ears everywhere.

But the most recent wave of headlines had nothing to do with our impromptu getaway and everything to do with me. Specifically, my family and my background.

Bile coated my throat.

Oh, fuck.

CHAPTER 29

Colin Whidby had been my primary liaison for DigiStream negotiations until his hospitalization and subsequent ouster. Charismatic, gregarious, and prone to hyperbole, he was the type of startup founder who graced magazine covers and was featured in viral interview clips.

Rohan Mishra was his opposite. Quiet, calm and methodical, the twenty-four-year-old wunderkind observed me with obvious skepticism.

I'd finally convinced him to agree to another sitdown, but our talks weren't progressing any further than they had over email and videoconferencing.

"You have the user base and technology, but you don't have the ability to scale as quickly as your business demands," I said. "Your current audience is concentrated in the US, Canada, and pockets of Europe. We can take you global. Our presence in emerging markets—"

"I don't give a fuck about emerging markets," Rohan said. "I told you. It's not about the money. Colin and I built this company from the ground up. We dropped out of Stanford and worked our asses off to get it to where it is today. He may have been impressed by all the zeroes you're throwing around, but I'm not. I've done my research, Young. You think I'm going to roll over and let some vulturish corporation sweep in and tear us apart the way you did to Black Bear?"

Goddammit, Tobias.

My jaw clenched. The ink hadn't even dried on the Black Bear contract before he'd pushed through "significant restructuring." Mass layoffs, destroyed morale. It was a mess.

"I'm not the one running point on Black Bear," I said. "I assure you, DigiStream will be integrated seamlessly under my watch."

"It doesn't matter whether it's you or someone else running point. It's all the same." Rohan shook his head. "You look out for your bottom line, not anyone else's. With Whidby gone, the company needs stability, not more change."

Frustration chafed beneath my skin.

Goddamn Whidby. I should get the phrase tattooed, given how many times it crossed my mind.

"Give me a list of specific concerns," I said. "Layoffs, team restructuring, workplace culture. We'll hammer them out. We've been in negotiations for over a year, and you and I both know a merger would be a boon to both companies. This is a billion-dollar deal hinging on a few small details."

"Small but important." Rohan tapped his fingers against his armrest. "I've seen the tabloids, and I've heard the rumors. Your selection as CEO isn't guaranteed."

My spine stiffened. I'd put out the most urgent fires while I was in Turks and Caicos, but there were plenty of smaller blazes left unchecked. My mother had found out about Jade Cay, which was why I'd been avoiding her calls all week. I had to follow up with Clarissa, who'd left me a cryptic voicemail over the weekend, and Paxton, who'd reached out again with an alliance offer. With the way things were going, I was seriously considering it.

"Honestly, I didn't think you were the playboy type," Rohan said, his eyes sharp. "Sneaking around with a bartender? Very unlike the image you've previously portrayed."

Irritation hardened my jaw. If there was one thing I hated almost as much as losing, it was being called a fake. "I didn't realize my personal life factored into our talks."

"It shouldn't, but given the mess with Whidby, I'm sure you understand why I'm hesitant to do business with someone who's embroiled in scandal."

"I was dating an employee, not doing drugs," I said flatly. I used the past tense deliberately, if not truthfully. No one needed to know about my continuing relationship with Isabella until after the vote. "She's no longer employed at Valhalla, which renders the point moot."

"Perhaps." His fingers tapped faster.

Sneaking around with a bartender? Very unlike the image you've previously portrayed.

I could read between the lines. Rohan didn't care about Isabella per se. The tabloid gossip had thrown my character into question, and he was worried about being deceived.

Unfortunately, no matter how much I tried to reassure him, he didn't budge.

"We can resume our last round of talks after the vote," Rohan said after half an hour of fruitless back-and-forth. "I'm not signing anything until I'm sure the new CEO will honor the terms, both in spirit and on paper. I can't risk it, and like you said, we've been in negotiations for a while. If you're voted in and we still can't come to an agreement, then I'm sorry. The deal is dead."

I left Rohan's office and headed straight to my hotel bar for a stiff drink. My head pounded with a vicious migraine, which my scotch did nothing to alleviate.

Four months ago, I'd had the DigiStream deal locked in, the CEO position within reach, and my pesky emotions in check. Now, my control over my professional and personal lives was unraveling faster than the seams of a worn-out coat.

The downward slide started the moment I walked upstairs and heard Isabella playing the "Hammerklavier" at Valhalla. If I'd stayed at the bar that day, I might've been in an entirely different situation right now.

The problem was, if I'd stayed at the bar, Isabella and I would've remained acquaintances. No secret room, no Brooklyn date, no Christmas movie marathons or island getaways or the dozens of small moments that had made the otherwise hellish months bearable.

My gut twisted.

I rubbed a hand over my face and tried to focus my thoughts. I was here for business, not to wallow over *should haves* and *what-ifs*.

My phone lit up with a news alert.

I glanced at it, then froze.

"Kai Young's Mistress's Lies Exposed!" the *National Star* gloated.

A sour feeling spread in my stomach. I clicked on the headline and was greeted with a giant photo of Isabella working at a dive bar. She wore hot pants, a tiny crop top, and a big smile as she leaned over the counter. Several frat boy types ogled her cleavage.

I couldn't see their full faces, but I had the sudden, visceral urge to hunt them down and gouge their eyes out.

I swallowed my anger and scrolled to the actual article.

Bartender, plaything, and...millionaire heiress? You read that right! Kai Young's latest fling is no innocent employee caught in the web of a predatory employer. [Read our article on how the seemingly "nice" billionaire heir abused his power at the exclusive Valhalla Club to coerce the younger woman into a relationship].

We did a little digging into the poor girl's past and discovered Isabella Valencia is not so poor after all. In fact, she's the only daughter of Perlah Ramos, the founder and CEO of the Hiraya boutique hotel chain. The wily matriarch kept her maiden name while her children took her husband's last name...

Shock splashed ice down my spine. Hiraya Hotels? I was drinking in one of their properties right this second.

The Valencia brood boasts several talented children, including Ramos's eldest son and Hiraya COO Gabriel, an award-winning engineer, a tenured professor at UC Berkeley, and celebrated artist Oscar (né Felix Valencia). No wonder their youngest child—and only daughter—kept her real identity under wraps! Other than a string of short-lived bartending stints and even shorter-lived odd jobs, she has embarrassingly few accomplishments to her name. It must be hard, getting outshone that much by her siblings.

Except for Oscar, the Ramos/Valencia family is notoriously press-shy. Perlah Ramos hasn't given an interview in more than eight years. That explains why no one made the connection to Isabella earlier, but that doesn't explain why the snobbish Kai Young stooped to messing around with the help. Heiress or not, she's far from his usual Ivy League-educated type.

We're guessing the youngest Valencia is quite talented in other ways that don't involve her brain...

I'd read enough.

Fury outpaced shock in a heartbeat. Crimson splashed across my vision while a swift, white heat burned through my veins.

Fuck California and DigiStream. I was going to sue the *National Star* into oblivion and dismantle Black's media company, piece by piece, until even vultures wouldn't touch its rotting carcass. Then I was going to track Victor Black himself down and murder him.

"Kai Young?"

An unfamiliar voice interrupted my increasingly and alarmingly violent thoughts.

I looked up. A man around my age stood next to me, his suit and tie as neatly pressed as the ones lining my closet.

Recognition doused the rising flames of my anger.

I didn't have to ask who the newcomer was. They had the same dark eyes, full lips, and olive skin. She burst with life and color while he looked like he'd been sucking on a rotting lemon since he escaped from the womb, but the similarities were undeniable.

"Gabriel Valencia, COO of Hiraya Hotels." Isabella's brother gave me a thin smile. "We need to talk."

~

Fifteen minutes later, I settled into a chair in Gabriel's office.

Hiraya Hotels was headquartered in Los Angeles, but it operated hotels throughout the state. As COO, Gabriel must have an office in most, if not all, of them.

We eyed each other warily across his desk.

It wasn't how I'd pictured meeting Isabella's family, but at least he'd interrupted me before I committed several felonies and a murder.

"First, I must apologize for the unorthodox manner in which I approached you," Gabriel said stiffly. "We place utmost value on our guests' privacy. However, I'm notified whenever a VIP checks into any of our hotels. Given the circumstances, you must understand why I sought you out when I saw your name."

"By circumstances, I assume you mean the *National Star* hit pieces?" I refused to call them articles. Articles required a modicum of objectivity; the most recent publication was libel. Once my lawyers were through with them, there wouldn't be much of the *Star* left. I'd make sure of it.

Victor got his short-term victory, but he'd made a crucial long-term mistake.

Gabriel's mouth flattened further into a granite line. "Because of you, photos of my sister are splashed all over that rag. They're dragging my family's name through the mud and hounding our hotels, our corporate offices, our personal lines." As if on cue, his office phone rang with a shrill noise. He ignored it. "The article just went live, and it's already started."

"I'm sorry you're dealing with harassment, but that's a *National Star* issue," I said calmly. "I didn't leak those photos to them, nor did I have anything to do with their most recent publication."

The one where they revealed that Isabella was an heiress to the Hiraya Hotels fortune.

I'd been so incandescent over the disgusting lies that I'd overlooked the bombshell. Now, the realization over Isabella's identity sank in with diamond clarity.

Why had she kept it a secret? Did her friends know the truth, and I was the only one in the dark?

Unease formed a knot in my chest.

"Perhaps not, but she wouldn't be in this situation if it weren't for you," Gabriel said. "We've never met, but I know your reputation. I thought you were above taking advantage of your employees."

My jaw tightened. This was the third time my character had been called into question today, and I was getting damn sick of it.

"I didn't take advantage of her," I said coldly. "It was a consensual relationship. I have never coerced a woman into doing anything they didn't want to."

"Was or is?"

I paused. I didn't know how Isabella wanted to handle things with her family, but my silence was answer enough.

Gabriel's nostrils flared. "She's dated men like you before," he said. "Rich, charming, used to getting what they want. Happy to keep her a secret until shit hits the fan. Isabella seems tough, but she's a romantic at heart, and as her brother, it's my job to protect her, including from herself. She has a habit of making bad decisions."

My hand closed around the edge of my armrest. Punching my girlfriend's brother in the face probably wasn't the best move, but I hated how he infantilized her. She might've kept secrets from me, but after meeting Gabriel, I could understand why. I wouldn't want anyone to know I was related to him either.

"She's an adult." I strove for calm. "Her decisions, good or bad, are her own. You don't have any right interfering in her life."

"I didn't before and look what happened. That mess with Easton. Getting fired from Valhalla. Getting involved with *you*." Gabriel drummed his fingers on his desk. "Do you want to explain to me why you—the Young heir—are running around New York City with my little sister when you could have any woman you want?"

Because she's beautiful, smart and funny. Because seeing her smile is like watching the sun rise, and being with her is the only time I feel alive. No other woman compares.

"The fact you have to ask," I said quietly, "proves how much you undervalue her."

I caught the briefest glimpse of surprise before Gabriel's expression shuttered again. "You might think you're different from the other men, but you're not," he said. "Stay away from Isabella. She doesn't need another opportunistic asshole ruining her life. This is your first and last warning."

"And if I don't?" I asked pleasantly.

His cool expression matched mine. "You'll find out what happens soon enough."

The threat barely touched me. Gabriel could try to browbeat me all he wanted, but I'd dealt with much worse than overprotective brothers. If Isabella wanted me gone, she'd tell me herself. She didn't need other people fighting her personal battles for her.

However, one thing Gabriel said stuck with me through the rest of the afternoon and well into the night.

Who the hell is Easton?

CHAPTER 30

Isabella

I holed up in my apartment and ignored all my calls, texts, and emails for two whole days. They were relentless—my family, my friends, the media. Some meant well, others less so. Regardless, I couldn't scrounge up the energy to face any of them.

The only time I interacted with the outside world was through my work with Alessandra, who thankfully kept our exchanges professional and didn't ask about the *National Star* revelations. After the identity reveal, the tabloid continued publishing articles and rumors, most of which were blatant lies.

I went to rehab for a cocaine addiction (I'd volunteered there during college). I'd slept with previous employers to get hired (they fucking *wished*). I had an orgy with an entire MLB team after the World Series a few years back (I served them during their celebratory night out and had *one* round of drinks with them).

The claims were so ridiculous I dismissed them out of hand. If someone was gullible enough to think I had a secret orgy-induced love child stowed away in Canada, that was their problem.

However, the truths were much harder to swallow.

Other than a string of short-lived bartending stints and even shorter-lived odd jobs, she has embarrassingly few accomplishments to her name...

Heiress or not, she's far from his usual Ivy League-educated type.

Nausea curdled my stomach.

I tucked one hand beneath my thigh and bounced my knee as Kai returned from his kitchen with two mugs of tea.

Dark circles shadowed his eyes, and his normally neat hair was tousled, like he'd run his fingers through it one too many times. Tension bracketed his mouth and lined the broad planes of his shoulders.

My heart wrung itself at his obvious exhaustion.

He'd returned to New York that afternoon and texted me asking to meet. It was the first time we'd spoken since the latest round of *National Star* hits, which didn't bode well for us.

I accepted the tea in silence.

Kai sat next to me on the couch, his brows furrowed.

"How are you doing?" he asked.

An embarrassing wave of emotion crested at the sound of his voice. He'd been gone for less than a week, but it felt like a lifetime.

"I'm okay." I let out a weak laugh. "I became famous while you were gone. Celebrity takes its toll."

He didn't smile at my lame attempt at a joke. "I'm dealing with Black. The *Star* will retract its stories."

My forced humor slipped. "But not the one about my family," I said quietly. "That one's true."

A muscle flexed in his jaw. "No. Not that one." He set his drink on the coffee table and rubbed a hand over his face. "Why didn't you tell me?"

"Because I..." I faltered. "I don't know. I've kept it a secret for so long that it didn't even cross my mind to say anything. I know it seems like a silly thing to hide, but my family is *extremely* private. The past week must be killing them."

Guilt and shame bubbled in an unsettling stew in my stomach. "When I first moved to New York, I was pretty wild, and I didn't want my actions to reflect poorly on them. If people knew who I was, I would've been all over the gossip sites. I also swore I wouldn't rely on my family's name and money to make my way, and I haven't. Some people might think I'm stupid for not taking advantage of what I had, but I didn't want to be one of those rich kids who lived off their parents' wealth without *doing* anything."

My mother had kept our personal lives out of the press for decades. Even Felix, my most high-profile brother, focused on his work in interviews. I wanted to explore the city and just *live* without worrying about sullying the family name, and I didn't want people to treat me differently because I was an heiress.

No scrutiny, no expectations, no pressure.

It worked...until it didn't.

"Did anyone know before the piece?" Kai asked, his face unreadable.

"Viv and Sloane." I curled my hands around my mug and took solace in the warmth. "They found out organically when my mother dropped by for a surprise visit a few years ago. Sloane recognized her. Parker knew too since she ran my pre-employment background check, but she promised not to say anything."

My trust fund was both a blessing and a curse. I didn't have access to it yet; it would kick in if and when I "settled" into a career I loved, as determined by my mother and Gabriel. If I was still floating from job to job by the time I turned thirty, I forfeited the money to charity.

Theoretically, it was nice knowing I had money to fall back on. In reality, the age stipulation amplified the pressure. I tried not to think too much about it because when I did, I couldn't breathe.

It wasn't even about the trust fund as much as it was about the symbolism. If I lost it, it would mean I had failed, and failing when every door was open to me felt like a special kind of hell.

"I spoke to your brother when I was in California."

Kai's admission snapped me out of my spiraling self-pity.

My head jerked up. "*What?*"

I listened with mounting disbelief and anger as he explained what happened, from Rohan Mishra's ultimatum to Gabriel's appearance at the bar.

No wonder he looked so stressed. The past few days had been as shitty to him as they had been to me.

"He had no right," I fumed. "He had absolutely *no* right to ambush you like that."

"He's your brother. He's protective," Kai said mildly.

Protective? Gabriel had better learn to protect himself because I was going to strangle him with one of those stupid silk ties he loved so much.

"He also mentioned someone named Easton." Kai's gaze remained steady while my blood solidified into ice. "Who is that?"

My heart pounded in my ears.

Forget strangulation. That was too good for my brother. I was going to make him watch while I shredded every suit in his closet with garden shears before suffocating him alive with the scraps.

A bitter taste welled in my throat. My first instinct was to lie and say I didn't know anyone named Easton, but I was tired of living in the shadow of what happened. I'd let that asshole dictate too much of my life for too long. It was time to let go of the past, once and for all.

"Easton is my ex. The last man I was with before you and the reason I didn't date anyone for two years." The bitterness spilled into my chest and stomach. "I met him at a bar. I wasn't working that night, just having fun and meeting new people. I was by myself since Sloane and Vivian were both out of town, and when he approached me, I thought he was perfect. Smart, good-looking, successful."

Kai's eyes darkened, but he remained silent while I talked.

"Our relationship took off quickly. Within two weeks of meeting, he was taking me on weekend getaways and buying me all these expensive gifts. I thought I loved him, and I was so blinded by my infatuation that I didn't pick up on the red flags that are so clear in hindsight. Like the way he only took me to remote places for our dates, or how I never met his friends and co-workers because he wanted me 'all to himself' for a while longer." I grimaced at my younger self's naivety. "He spun his excuses into romantic intentions when the truth was so simple. He had a wife and two kids in Connecticut."

A bitter sound, half laugh and half sob, scored my throat. "What a cliché, right? The proverbial married cheater with the family stashed away in the suburbs. But that wasn't the worst part. The worst part was when said wife walked in on us in the middle of sex."

Kai blanched.

"Yeah, I know. She suspected he was having an affair, and she hired a private investigator to tail him. That night, she'd had a little too much to drink. Got aggressive when the P.I. sent her husband's location to her. She showed up, screaming and crying. As you can imagine, I was horrified. I had no idea..." I forced oxygen past my tightening lungs. "Easton and his wife got into a huge argument. I tried to leave because my presence was making things worse, and that was when she...she took out a gun."

I still remembered the cold glint of metal beneath the hotel lights. The bone-deep terror that'd robbed me of breath and the cold, pervasive silence that'd fallen over the room like a white sheet over a corpse.

"Easton and I both tried to talk her down, but she was too drunk and upset. The next thing I knew, he was trying to wrestle the gun away from her. It went off by accident, and it..." My breathing shallowed.

Screams. Cries. Blood. So much blood.

"The bullet somehow hit her. She's alive, but she'll never walk again." The knowledge smashed through me like a wrecking ball, scattering jagged splinters and shattered grief through my chest. "She didn't—I mean, she shouldn't have taken out the gun, but she was...it wasn't her fault. Her husband cheated on her *with me*, and she's the one suffering for it."

A sob racked my shoulders. I hadn't talked about it in so long. Even my friends didn't know the full truth of what happened. They just thought I'd had a bad breakup with a cheating asshole.

Talking about it with Kai broke the dam on my emotions, and everything—the guilt, the anger, the horror, the shame—rushed over me like a flood sweeping over a plain.

Kai engulfed me in his arms and held me as I cried. Easton, Valhalla, the *National Star*, my manuscript deadline...every fuckup and mistake I made over the past few years. They poured out of me in a river of grief until I was hollow and aching.

"It wasn't your fault," he said quietly. "You didn't know. You didn't make him cheat on her, and you didn't make her bring the gun. You're as much a victim of the situation as anyone else."

"I know, but it *feels* like my fault." I pulled back, my voice raw from my sobs. "I was so stupid. I should've caught on..."

"People like that are expert cheats. You were young, and he took advantage of that. It wasn't your fault," Kai repeated firmly. He brushed a stray tear from my cheek. "What happened to him?"

"Last I heard, he moved to Chicago before his business went bankrupt and he's estranged from his kids. They're over eighteen now, and I don't think they ever forgave him for what happened with their mother."

I didn't know where Easton was now. Hopefully rotting in the pits of hell.

"I see." Kai's expression sent a dart of trepidation down my spine.

"Don't track him down," I said. "I mean it. I just want to leave him in the past, and I don't want you to get in trouble."

A hint of amusement bloomed at the corners of his mouth. "What do you think I'm going to do to him if I do, hypothetically, track him down?"

"I don't know." I wiped my cheeks with the back of my hand. "Maim him?"

"That's certainly crossed my mind," Kai muttered. "I—"

The gentle chime of the doorbell interrupted him.

I stiffened again as Kai and I exchanged wary glances. We were lying low until the CEO vote—I snuck in through the building's back entrance earlier—and an unexpected visit these days was more cause for alarm than celebration.

A shimmer of dread threaded through me as Kai answered the door. Had a tabloid reporter somehow gotten past security? Should I hide?

A faint murmur of voices leaked from the entryway. I couldn't hear his exact words, but Kai's surprised tone came through loud and clear.

He reentered the living room a minute later, his face grim.

My stomach dropped to the floor when I saw who was behind him. I suddenly wished it *were* a tabloid reporter; that would've been infinitely preferable to the newcomers.

I'd never met them in person, but I recognized their pictures from the news.

Leonora and Abigail Young.

Kai's mother and sister.

CHAPTER 31

Kai

The four of us sat in the living room—Isabella and me on one couch, my mother and Abigail on the couch opposite us.

We faced each other like opposing armies on the battlefield, each waiting for the other to fire the first shot. A plague of tense silence engulfed the room. The only sound came from the clock standing sentry in the corner, as unmoved and passionless as a god observing the petty quarrels of humans.

Tick. Tock. Tick. Tock.

I knew my mother would show up eventually. Leonora Young was incapable of relinquishing control over my personal life. However, I hadn't expected her to drag my sister with her. Abigail looked like she would rather be trekking through the Andes in the winter than sitting here.

"I heard your meeting with Mishra went poorly." My mother cut straight to the chase. Other than a telltale tightening of her features when she first saw Isabella, she hadn't acknowledged her presence since she arrived. "Luckily, I have good news that might counteract the DigiStream problem. Tobias is out. He withdrew his candidacy an hour ago."

Shock burned away my knee-jerk defensiveness at the Mishra comment. "He *withdrew?* Why?"

"He didn't give a reason. He simply said he didn't feel like he was the right fit for the role at this time."

It didn't make sense. He had the Black Bear deal, and we were a little over a week away from the vote. Of all the other candidates, Tobias was the *least* likely to throw in the towel. He wouldn't drop out this close to the finish line unless...

An inkling of suspicion formed in my stomach.

The photos. The withdrawal.

The two leading candidates hit within weeks of each other and close enough to the election that we had little time to rally. Perhaps it was a coincidence, but the timing was awfully convenient.

However, I kept my face neutral while my mother continued. I didn't want to throw accusations out until I had more than my instincts backing me up.

"This is a good thing," my mother said. "I like Tobias, but he was your biggest competition. His votes are up for grabs, which means you need a last-minute campaign push."

"We were here to check on you anyway after everything that happened," Abigail added. "The Tobias news came at the perfect time. Now, we can brainstorm how to get those votes together."

"Abby." I leveled her with an even stare. "You hate talking business."

She was a professional socialite. Her campaign experience started and stopped with chairing a gala committee. My mother probably forced her to come so she could convince me to break up with Isabella. She knew I wouldn't listen to her, but I might listen to my sister.

"I can still have ideas," Abigail countered. "You're my brother. I want you to win."

"The first order of business is generating good press," my mother said, cutting off our back-and-forth. Once Abigail and I started, we could argue for hours. "I've arranged for a public date with you and Clarissa."

Next to me, Isabella stirred for the first time since we sat down. My hands clenched into fists, but I forced myself to relax until my mother finished talking.

"She was understandably hesitant, given the situation you put her in, but she agreed. This will help quash rumors about you and your...friend." Her eyes flicked over Isabella with disdain. "Not that you seem particularly worried about the tabloids catching you together."

She was right. Even after the *National Star* scandal, I'd been careless about sneaking around with Isabella.

If I were smart, I'd cut off contact with her until after the vote, but she had a way of scrambling my brain. Perhaps that was part of the problem. Whenever I was with Isabella, the world seemed... brighter. It could be burning down around us and it wouldn't matter as long as she was there.

"First, I'm not going on a date with Clarissa," I said coolly. "It's wrong to lead her on. Second, Isabella is sitting right here."

"Is it leading her on?" My mother arched a sculpted brow and switched to Cantonese. "Your infatuation with Isabella will pass, and you'll realize Clarissa is a much better fit for you when it comes to breeding, education, and temperament. You may think I'm overbearing, but I'm your mother. I only want what's best for you. I've seen too many wayward children make terrible mistakes to allow you to do the same. Look at the Gohs. Their daughter ran off with that *awful* pool boy only to get knocked up and swindled out of her inheritance. Her poor parents haven't been able to show their faces in society since."

"Clarissa and Isabella aren't dogs," I said in Cantonese, striving for calm. "We can't put them side by side and compare their breeding. However, if we did, might I remind you Isabella is the heiress to Hiraya Hotels? She's not some lowly bartender, as you originally thought."

I wasn't upset at Isabella for hiding her family background

256

from me. I was initially hurt that she hadn't trusted me enough to tell me her secret, but I understood why she did it. Honestly, her family reveal made our relationship an easier sell to both my family and the board. A Young dating a bartender was scandalous. A Young dating an heiress was par for course.

My mother's lips thinned. "It's not about the wealth. It's about suitability. She—"

"Don't you think Kai should be the one who determines the suitability of his partner?" Isabella cut in. She smiled at the flare of surprise on my mother's face. "I'm Filipino Chinese. I speak English, Tagalog, Hokkien, Mandarin, and Cantonese. I'm surprised you didn't think of that, given all your *education* and breeding."

I wiped a hand over my mouth, hiding my grin. A similar smirk tugged at Abigail's lips.

We loved our mother, but we also loved seeing people call her out. It didn't happen often.

She recovered with remarkable speed, as Leonora Young always did. "Then you should know why you and my son make a poor match," she said in a voice like ice water. "If it weren't for you, we wouldn't be in this...predicament. A Young has helmed our company since it was founded more than a century ago. I refuse to let a tawdry infatuation ruin our legacy."

"It's funny," Isabella said. "You want Kai to run a Fortune 500 company, yet you treat him like a child who can't make his own decisions. How do you reconcile those two things?"

My grin widened.

I should've been thinking about DigiStream, Tobias's suspicious withdrawal, and getting my family out of my apartment as soon as possible, but all I could think about at that moment was how much I wanted to grab Isabella and kiss her.

My mother was, understandably, less impressed by Isabella's comeback. "How dare you talk to me that way?" She turned furious eyes on me, her cheeks stained red with outrage. "Is *this* the type of woman you're willing to throw away your future for?"

"No one is throwing away anything." I ruthlessly corralled my amusement into a straight line. "Isabella isn't responsible for any of this. It takes two to maintain a relationship. She didn't force me to date her, nor did she tip her hand to the *National Star*. She's as much a victim of Victor Black as anyone else."

"Speaking of Victor, what are you going to do about him?" Abigail asked. She despised him almost as much as I did after the *Star* insinuated she was siphoning charity funds years ago.

"I'm taking care of it." I'd ignored his machinations in the past because they weren't worthy of my attention, but he'd gone too far. By the time I was done with him, he wouldn't have a company *or* reputation left.

"We'll discuss your private relationship later," my mother said, her expression stiff. She must've realized she couldn't get through to me with Isabella sitting right there. "However, our public statement maintains there was *never* a relationship and that the photos are innocent. Tobias's withdrawal puts you in the lead again, but we can't be complacent. We need to go on the media offensive."

As the current CEO, she shouldn't have been strategizing with me, but our family's reputation was at stake. Leonora Young wasn't a rule breaker by nature, but when pushed, the ends always justified the means.

"You think going on a date with Clarissa should be part of that offensive," I said flatly. Without thinking, I curled my hand over Isabella's. Hers rested in her lap, the skin ice cold. She was more nervous than her earlier bravado let on.

A wave of protectiveness crested in my chest. I gave her hand a small squeeze, which she returned.

My mother's mouth pursed. "Yes. Clarissa understands the nature of the date and has agreed to help. We need to rehabilitate your image. Every little bit helps, especially this close to the vote."

"I hardly think—"

"You should do it."

Three pairs of shocked eyes swung toward Isabella, including mine.

"Excuse me?" I said, sure I'd heard wrong.

"You should do it," she repeated. "You and Clarissa both know it's not a real date, which solves the problem of leading her on. It's a PR stunt, and if it helps you win the vote, then it's worth doing."

A shadow of approval crossed my mother's face. "For once, we're in agreement."

"It's a good idea," Abigail chimed in. "One date equals at least a week of press."

Jesus Christ.

I disliked the idea of using Clarissa to further my own means. It was tacky, but I knew how the media worked. Every little bit did help.

"Fine," I said, wondering how my work life had devolved from mergers to publicity stunts. "One date. I'll do it."

I only hoped it didn't come back to bite me in the ass later.

Two days after my mother and sister's visit, I gritted my teeth and paid Richard Chu a visit in his Fifth Avenue home. After the initial rancor following their surprise arrival, the four of us, Isabella included, had put aside our differences to iron out my plan for the next two weeks. Step one was the PR date with Clarissa. Step two was a face-to-face with the company's most powerful board member.

Like my mother said, Tobias's withdrawal eased some of the pressure, but I couldn't afford complacency.

"This is a surprise." Richard folded his hands across his stomach and regarded me with amusement. A touch of triumph gleamed in his eyes, making my stomach turn. "The intrepid Kai Young seeking me out in *my* home. What an honor."

My jaw locked, biting back a snappish reply.

I hated the old, musty scent of his office.

I hated the smug look on his face.

Most of all, I hated having to slink to him for help, like a stray dog begging for scraps.

Part of me would rather jump off the Brooklyn Bridge than bend the knee, but there was more than my pride at stake. At least that was what I kept telling myself.

"We have much to discuss." My smile masked my distaste. "I'm sure you'll agree."

"Funny how you'd like to talk now that your future is on the line." Richard raised a bushy gray brow. "You certainly didn't want to listen to me when I told you we're moving too fast with all this digital noise."

Because your advice is more outdated than your taste in decor.

His office could be plunked whole in a museum for late twentieth-century artifacts and no one would bat an eye.

"Since Tobias is out of the running, it's in both our interests to work together," I said, deflecting from his pointed remark. "You and I both know I'm the best person for the job. Paxton is too inexperienced, Russell is too docile, and Laura is talented at communications but doesn't have the range for CEO. Meanwhile, I've been preparing for this since I was born. You may not like me, but you still want what's best for the company. That would be me leading it."

Richard snorted. "There's nothing like the arrogance of youth. Fine." He spread his hands. "Since you came all this way, let me hear what you have to say."

I bristled at his patronizing tone, but I forced myself to ignore it.

I laid out my proposal. It was simple. If he promised me his vote, I would appoint him as senior adviser during my first year as CEO, which would give him considerable influence over the company's initiatives. The first year, especially the first one hundred days, were crucial for a new CEO. That was when they set the tone and priorities for their leadership going forward.

Bringing Richard into my inner circle was a significant concession on my part, but it was the only way to alleviate his concerns and secure his vote.

"Interesting," he said after I finished. "I'll think about it."

My spine locked. He'd *think* about it? Heat simmered slow and thick in my veins. "This is the best offer you'll get."

I wasn't going to beg. Not anymore than I already had.

Richard gave me an enigmatic smile. "I'm sure." He stood and held out his hand in an obvious dismissal. "Good to see you, Kai. Best of luck with the vote."

I kept my calm during the elevator ride and the walk through the lobby, but the frigid January air blasted the doors off my control. Frustration surged, unchecked, through my blood.

Me: Are you free for a match tonight?

Dante answered less than a minute later.

Dante: Emergency?

Me: Friendly request

Dante: Right. See you at 7

Dante: Btw you owe me. I was supposed to watch a movie with Viv tonight

Me: I'm sure your twentieth rewatch of Stardust would've been as scintillating as the first

Dante: Fuck off

I pocketed my phone, my anger easing with the promise of a guaranteed fight later. Some people went to therapy; Dante and I punched each other. It was faster, more efficient, and doubled as a workout.

I climbed into my waiting town car and instructed the driver to take me back to the office.

Richard thought he was a kingmaker, but I could win without him.

I was Kai Young.

I never lost.

CHAPTER 32

Isabella

I couldn't do it. Even with my flexible work hours, Kai's neuroscientist-approved writer's block busters, and the prospect of facing Gabriel's smug *I knew you were bluffing* expression, I couldn't finish my book in time.

My mother's birthday was less than a week away, and every time I sat at my new typewriter, I froze. It wasn't a matter of deleting anymore; the words wouldn't come, period. I was only a few chapters short, but my brain was too crammed with other concerns—the *National Star* vultures, my awful meeting with Kai's mother, the uncertainty of my relationship with Kai and, most of all, his recent date with Clarissa.

I was the one who told him it was okay. I knew it wasn't real and that the date was purely for PR purposes, but that didn't stop me from playing the comparison game when the photos hit the society pages earlier this week. Kai and Clarissa having a romantic dinner at an Italian restaurant. Kai and Clarissa walking down the street, holding hands. They were both elegant and sophisticated—the perfect match.

A better match than you and him, an insidious voice whispered.

My stress and insecurities piled up like a dam, blocking the flow of creativity until I was starved for inspiration.

Since I couldn't find a way past the block, I threw myself into work for Alessandra instead. It was a lot easier building someone else's dream than mine. There was less risk, less investment, less fear of failure.

We came up with a name for her business—Floria Designs, in a nod to both the flowers and Florianópolis, her favorite city in Brazil. I set up the social media accounts, designed a basic website, and created a seller account on Etsy. We pored over business plans, marketing strategies, and financial statements.

Sometimes I stayed at Alessandra's house until ten or eleven at night, but I never caught a glimpse of Dominic. It was like he didn't even live there.

"He spends most of his time in his office," Alessandra said when I asked her about it over breakfast one day.

"It seems like a waste to spend this much money on a beautiful house and not enjoy it." The more time we spent together, the more comfortable I was talking about things other than work.

I didn't want to pry, but I had a feeling Alessandra needed someone to vent to.

"The penthouse cost him twenty-five million," she said. "The office makes him over three billion. Which do you think he cares about more?"

I had no answer to that.

We ate in silence, both lost in our own thoughts, before she spoke again. "How are you doing? Big day today."

The bread turned to ash on my tongue. "I'm okay. Just nervous for Kai."

After months of waiting and planning, the Young Corporation's CEO vote was finally here. I'd set an alert for the results, but my phone had been silent all morning.

"He'll win," Alessandra said. "I can't imagine them choosing anyone else. He's a Young."

"I know, but it'll be nice to confirm." An unsettling feeling churned in my gut, which I blamed on last night's heavy dinner.

She was right. Kai was miles ahead of the other candidates. I had no reason to worry.

According to Kai, the board had bought the Clarissa photos hook, line, and sinker. We'd refrained from meeting in person since his family's surprise visit. It was too risky, given the heightened scrutiny after the Clarissa stunt, so we'd settled for calls and texts.

Not seeing him in person didn't help my general plague of anxiety, but I was more worried *for* him than anything else. If he lost…

Don't go there. He's not going to lose.

Breakfast continued in a similarly muted manner. Alessandra and I usually had plenty to talk about, but we were both too distracted to make good company.

I glanced at my phone for the twentieth time that morning. *Nothing*.

"Let's go over the social media plan again," Alessandra said after we finished eating. "It'll help take your mind off other matters."

"True. There's nothing like the promise of social media fame to distract me." I fought the urge to google *Young Corporation*. What was taking them so long? The voting committee had been deliberating since the morning, and it was mid-afternoon in London already. Maybe my news alerts were broken. "We'll be one of those companies that's fun and snarky online, like Wendy's. I know!" I snapped my fingers. "We can start a mutually beneficial internet war with another pressed flowers company. There'll be more florals and drama than an episode of *Bridezillas*. Who wouldn't want that?"

Doubt suffused Alessandra's expression. "I don't know if that's the best—"

Our phones vibrated at the same time, cutting her off.

We stared at each other for a second before we scrambled to

check the news. My heart ricocheted when I glimpsed the name of Kai's company filling my screen.

This was it.

The CEO vote results were in.

CHAPTER 33

Dante slammed his fist into my jaw. My head snapped back, and the taste of copper filled my mouth.

It should've hurt, but adrenaline blunted the impact. I shook it off and returned his hit with one of my own. The vicious hook caught him high on the chest, eliciting a pained grunt.

Perspiration coated my face and torso. We'd been at it for over an hour. My muscles screamed with agony, and the scent of blood, sweat, and testosterone clogged my nostrils. Once my adrenaline crashed, I was going to be out for at least a day.

I'd worry about that later. For now, I narrowed my focus onto beating Dante and off of a certain meeting in London. Neither the current CEO nor the candidates were allowed in the room during deliberations, so I was flying blind until the election committee announced their decision.

I landed another punch on Dante's cheek; he caught me in the ribs.

Again and again, the familiar rhythm of our jabs and hooks was almost enough to drive the vote to the back of my mind.

Almost.

"You could've saved yourself the torture of waiting if you'd used what I gave you," he panted, dodging an uppercut. "I literally delivered the position to you on a silver platter. Or in a manila envelope, if we're being technical."

It was the first time he'd acknowledged sending Christian's Christmas "gift."

"I told you, I don't need to stoop to blackmail." The thought of using the information had crossed my mind after the photos of me and Isabella first surfaced, but I'd dismissed it as quickly as it came.

Resorting to blackmail was the same as admitting defeat. It meant I wasn't good enough to win on my own.

"It's not blackmail. It's insurance." Blood leaked out of a cut on Dante's brow, and the beginnings of a bruise darkened his jaw.

Vivian was going to give me hell later for the battered condition I'd return her husband in, but I doubted I looked much better. Today's session was a cathartically brutal one.

"Funny. That's exactly what Harper said."

"And he's right." Dante paused with a grimace. "Don't tell him I said that. Bastard's ego would shoot through the fucking roof."

I snorted. "I would think you'd be against blackmail, given what happened with Vivian's father."

His face darkened at the mention of his father-in-law. "In certain situations, yes," he said. "But it also proves astonishingly effective in the short term. You just have to be smart enough to preempt the long-term consequences."

Or I could bypass it and not have any long-term consequences to begin with.

Before I could respond, my phone's ringtone blared through the sweat-drenched air and sucked the levity out of the room.

Our movements stilled. The air evacuated from my lungs as I zeroed in on the bench where I'd placed my phone.

It could be a telemarketer, my assistant calling with a question, or a dozen other possibilities, but my gut told me it wasn't.

It was eleven in the morning here, which meant it was near

the end of the workday in London. Perfect timing for a CEO announcement.

My heart pounded hard enough to drown out the ringtone. A metallic taste welled on my tongue, flooding me with equal parts anticipation and foreboding.

After everything—the schemes, the scandals, the setbacks—this was it. The moment of truth.

"Kai."

Dante's low voice pulled my attention back to him. His eyes were fixed on something over my shoulder, and I followed his gaze to the exit.

An anchor dragged my stomach straight to the boxing ring's black canvas floor. A low buzz filled my ears.

Isabella stood next to the door, her chest heaving with quick breaths. I didn't know how she got in, but I knew why she was here. It was written all over her face.

I'd lost the vote.

~

ISABELLA

The silence was deafening.

Dante had muttered an excuse about meeting Vivian for lunch and made a quick exit, leaving me and Kai alone in the boxing gym.

He stood still as stone in the middle of the ring. Sweat gleamed on his bare torso and dampened his hair, making him look like a warrior fresh from battle.

I'd caught the tail end of his match with Dante. It was my first time seeing Kai box, and it'd taken my breath away. The precision, the power, the lethal grace—it was like watching a master execute a beautifully choreographed dance.

If I were here for any other reason, I would've savored the experience, but all I felt was an icy ball of dread in the pit of my stomach.

"Who?" Kai's face and voice were wiped clean of emotion.

I swallowed past the tightness in my throat. "Someone named Russell Burton?"

He reacted then. A tiny jerk of his shoulders, followed by a dark, burning realization in his eyes.

The name had surprised him.

I waited for a bigger reaction—a curse, a rant, *something* that would indicate his acknowledgment of what happened. Instead, he stepped down from the ring, wiped his face with a towel, and unscrewed the cap of his water bottle. If it weren't for his tightly controlled movements and the tension cording his neck, I would've thought he hadn't heard me.

I walked toward him with the caution of a hiker approaching a rattlesnake.

When I saw the news about Russell's selection, my stomach had pitched like I was the one who'd lost. I couldn't imagine how Kai must've felt. This was *his* family. His company. His legacy.

A sympathetic Alessandra gave me the day off. She'd gotten ahold of Dominic and somehow convinced him to get me access to Valhalla, where I knew Kai was boxing with Dante.

I didn't know what to do or how I could help, but I just wanted to be here for him.

"Maybe it's a mistake," I ventured. I'd rushed here as soon as I could and hadn't read the article in its entirety. "Maybe they—"

"It's not a mistake." Kai sounded eerily calm. He looked up, his skin stretched tight over his cheekbones. The uneven rise and fall of his chest betrayed his masked emotions.

My heart wrenched. "Kai—"

He crushed the rest of my words between our mouths. The kiss was so sudden, so unexpected, that I stumbled back a step before I caught myself.

We'd kissed before, many times. Sweet, scorching, hungry, languorous...the nature of our embraces ebbed and flowed depending on our moods, but he'd never kissed me like *this*. Hands tangling in my hair, teeth scraping across my lips, muscles vibrating with coiled energy. Desperate and feverish, like he was drowning and I was his only lifeline.

Pieces of his stony mask clattered to the floor around us. Emotions poured through the jagged cracks, dragging my hands to his shoulders, his teeth down my neck, and his fist around the hem of my skirt.

Kai yanked it up and backed me against the boxing ring at the same time. A tear of silk, a rustle of clothing, and then he was inside me, fucking me with an intensity that had me gasping for breath. My body shook with the force of each thrust, and I scrabbled for a hold on something, anything, that could ground me while we worked out his anger together.

A symphony of grunts, cries, and the slap of flesh against flesh echoed in the otherwise empty room. One hand fisted his hair while the other clutched at the ring ropes above me. We'd had rough sex before, but this wasn't sex. It was a catharsis.

Hard. Urgent. Unforgiving.

Still, it didn't take long before pleasure overtook my senses. One more thrust, and my orgasm detonated, rippling through my body in a series of shudders and aftershocks.

Kai came soon after me, biting out a harsh "Fuck" as his cum dripped down my thigh.

We held each other for a moment, our breaths ragged in the silence. Languid warmth flooded my veins, but it was tempered by the knot in my throat.

When Kai lifted his head again, his eyes were filled with remorse. The knot tightened. "Isa..."

I didn't have to ask for the reason behind his guilt.

"It's okay," I reassured him. "I'm on the pill." He wasn't the only one who'd gotten carried away. The thought of condoms hadn't even crossed my mind until now.

"I shouldn't have... I didn't..." He wiped a hand over his face. "Fuck," he repeated. His gaze swept over me, lingering on my neck and chest. I looked down and winced when I saw the hickeys marking my skin. "Are you okay?"

"More than okay, if my orgasm was anything to go by," I quipped, hoping to erase his frown. It didn't work. My mouth softened with fresh worry. Now that my post-sex high was fading, the severity of the situation returned in full force. "I should ask you the same question."

It was a stupid question because *of course* he wasn't okay. He'd just lost control of his family's company. But I had no experience dealing with issues like that, and I would rather he talk about it than pretend everything was fine. I'd learned from experience that bottling things up only led to more problems in the future.

Kai's throat bobbed. "Russell Burton."

My heart split at the numb disbelief in his voice. "Yeah," I said softly.

I didn't know who Russell was, but I hated him more than anything else in the world right now. No, correction: I hated the *voting committee* more than anything else. I hope they all choked on their bad decisions and ugly corporate pens.

Kai didn't cry, shout, or say another word, but when he buried his face in my neck and my arms wrapped around his back, I felt the intensity of his pain like it was my own. It reverberated through my body, strangling my lungs and stinging my eyes. He was always so cool and composed that seeing him break apart, even a little, ignited a raw ache that punched me straight through the heart.

I wished I had the power to turn back time or knock some sense into the voting committee. Since I couldn't and there was nothing I could say that would make things better, I simply held him and let him grieve.

CHAPTER 34

I *lost.*
   The phrase looped in my mind so many times it no longer had shape or meaning. However, its impact didn't change.

Every time it echoed in my head, it triggered the same gut punch. Released the same dark, oily sensation that slithered through my veins and formed a bottomless pit in my stomach.

It was the *feeling* of losing, which was infinitely worse than the word itself.

I tossed back my scotch. It didn't erase the bitterness coating my throat, but it did insulate me from the stares and whispers. To an extent, anyway.

Three days had passed since the CEO election results. In that time, I'd carried out my job per usual. I took meetings, congratulated Russell, and fielded endless calls, emails, and messages. At night, I went to Isabella's house, or she came to mine, because now that the vote was over, I didn't care who saw us together.

We didn't discuss work, but in the hazy hours between late night and early morning, when I buried myself inside her and she came apart in my arms, we found ways of comforting each other without words.

The bartender slid another glass of scotch across the counter. I nodded a curt thanks and glanced around the bar. Valhalla was packed. It always was on a Friday, which was why I deliberately showed up tonight.

People could talk all they wanted, but I refused to give them the satisfaction of hiding away and licking my wounds like a whipped dog.

I was Kai Young, dammit.

I managed to take one sip of my fresh drink before a familiar, oily voice ruined my appetite.

"Well, well. Look who's out and about so soon after their defeat." Victor Black oozed onto the seat next to mine, reeking of smugness and tacky cologne. "You're braver than I thought, Young."

"You're in New York an awful lot these days." I arched a disdainful brow. "Has D.C. finally banned you from its city limits?"

Trading insults with someone like Victor was beneath me, but I needed a distraction with both Isabella and Dante out of town. She'd flown out to California for her mom's birthday the night before, and Dante and Vivian were in Paris for the weekend.

"What can I say? New York has gotten so interesting these days." Victor's breath wafted over in a cloud of vodka. I grimaced. The man was clearly drunk out of his mind, not that he had much of a brain even when he was sober. "It must be humiliating, losing your family's company to an outsider. To Russell Burton, no less." He shook his head in mock disbelief. "If I were you, I'd never show my face in public again."

"One can only hope," I said coolly, fighting the slow creep of anger beneath my skin. "And if *I* were *you*, I'd worry more about your own company. It won't be around much longer."

My lawyers were already tearing the *National Star* apart for libel and defamation, but that was only a distraction while we dug deeper into the parts that could topple the entire Black & Co.

empire. The threads were there. We just had to locate and unravel them.

Victor's mouth twisted. "That silly defamation lawsuit? It's nothing. Do you know how many lawsuits we face and *win* every year?"

"More than there are brain cells rattling around that overly gelled head of yours, I'm sure."

I indulged in another sip of Macallan and took great pleasure in the scarlet flush adorning Victor's cheeks.

"You want to know what your problem is?" He leaned in, his eyes glinting with malice.

"I'm sure you'll enlighten me."

"You think you're so fucking smart. That you're better than everyone because you went to fancy schools and grew up with a silver spoon shoved up your ass. You have no idea what it means to *work* for something the way Burton and I do, and you were so blinded by your superiority complex—your belief that no one could possibly touch you because you're so above them—that you didn't see what was right in front of you. I even slipped you a little hint at the Saxon Gallery." Victor shook his head.

So he's the one who left me that note. He did it to fuck with me, no doubt. I should've connected the dots earlier; besides Isabella, he'd been the only one close enough to reach my pocket.

But that wasn't the part I was stuck on. What he said before that was.

"Your pride is your downfall, Young," he said. "And I'm here to document it every step of the way."

I let him ramble on. He was too bloated on overconfidence and cartoonish gloating to notice his slipup.

You have no idea what it means to work *for something the way Burton and I do.*

Russell was based in London, so I hadn't seen him in person since the election. He'd sounded shocked and overwhelmed when I called him, but something had been off. He'd almost sounded *too* shocked, like someone trying to convince their friends that they hadn't known about the surprise party beforehand. I didn't give it much thought at the time because I'd wanted to get off the phone as quickly as possible, but in hindsight...

Russell Burton, Chief Operations Officer. Handles all internal affairs, oversees the company's day-to-day administrative and operational functions...

Realization struck with sudden, blinding clarity.

I bit back a curse and stood, ignoring Victor's blathering. He'd moved on from the vote results and was currently spouting nonsense about his house in the Hamptons.

Twenty minutes later, I locked the front door of my penthouse behind me and dialed Tobias's number.

It was two a.m. in London, but he picked up as expected. The man never slept.

"What do you want?" Irritation ran hot and bitter beneath his voice. It was the voice of someone who'd been forced to give up something they wanted only to watch a lesser peer take it.

I knew the feeling well.

"About your withdrawal from the CEO vote," I said. "We need to talk."

CHAPTER 35

Isabella

On Friday morning, I arrived in California with one carry-on suitcase, a concrete block in my stomach, and no finished manuscript in hand.

I tried. I really did. But no matter how hard I pushed, I couldn't figure out the last quarter of the book. My creativity had dried up completely, leaving a husk of discarded ideas and incomplete sentences in its wake.

Luckily, Friday was so hectic no one asked about the manuscript. My family celebrated Christmasbirthdaynewyearpalooza in chronological order, which meant I was thrown into Christmas festivities the second I landed. After I dropped my luggage off in my childhood bedroom and took a quick shower, I helped my mom and brothers make our traditional holiday feast—bibingka rice cakes, pancit bihon noodles, lechon manok spit-roasted chicken, buko pandan salad, lumpiang ubod spring rolls stuffed with shrimp, vegetables, coconut, and pork.

By *help*, I meant chop vegetables and wash dishes. Sadly, my talent in the kitchen rivaled only my ability to run a four-minute mile for nonexistence.

Food preparations bled into the actual meal, followed by a gift exchange in which we all had to guess the presents before we opened them. It was a whirlwind of laughter, alcohol, and merriment and the last night we spent together as a family before it all went to hell.

The next morning, we crowded in the living room for my mom's birthday, tired but upbeat. For the most part anyway.

Nerves rattled in my veins as my mother made her way through her pile of gifts. Gabriel sat next to her, handing her a new item whenever she finished oohing and aahing over the previous one.

Romero, Miguel, Felix, and I were squeezed onto the couch opposite them—Felix doodling in his sketchpad, Romero fidgeting with his watch, and Miguel sprawled wide, looking like death warmed over. He'd drank the most last night.

My lola and lolo occupied the corner. Every few minutes, my lolo would nod off and my lola would smack his arm, jerking him awake.

"Oh, this is lovely." My mother held the hand-painted crescent moon necklace from Felix up to the light. "Thank you."

"I'm glad you like it," he said easily. "I thought it would be fitting, considering it's both your and the company's birthday."

Hiraya Hotels' logo was a crescent moon and four stars, one for each Valencia child. Its twenty-fifth anniversary was at the end of the month.

Felix was adopted, but he was the most thoughtful one of us all.

"Oh, *iho*." My mother hugged him, her eyes shimmering with emotion. She'd been best friends with Felix's parents before their deaths, and sometimes, she overcompensated for their absence by lavishing extra care and attention on him.

Neither my brothers nor I resented them for it. We loved Felix as much as she did, and we were equally guilty of giving him special treatment. We knew what it was like to lose one parent; we couldn't imagine losing both.

"Isabella's is the last one," Gabriel said, handing my mother a large, gaily wrapped box. He flicked an unreadable glance at me.

No one had mentioned the *National Star* or Kai since I arrived. As a rule, we didn't discuss negative topics during Christmas or Lunar New Year celebrations, which left today as the exception.

My nerves intensified, scraping my insides raw. I wished Kai were here, but I didn't want my failure to taint his first meeting with my family. He had enough problems of his own to deal with, and I couldn't always use him as a buffer. I needed to face the music on my own.

"Stop jiggling your foot," Miguel moaned from next to me. "You're shaking the couch and giving me a headache."

"Maybe you shouldn't have drunk so much sangria last night," I said. "I think *that's* your problem, not my foot jiggling."

He mumbled something that sounded like a curse mixed with a groan.

"Isa, this is wonderful!" My mother admired the luxe gift box I'd bought from her favorite spa resort in Palawan. It consisted of a full range of toiletries, skincare, and their signature perfume. The resort didn't sell the box online, so I'd had to ask one of my cousins in the Philippines to buy it and ship it to me. "I've been meaning to buy this. I'm almost out of the perfume."

"Perfect timing then." I mustered a smile, praying no one asked about the *other* gift I was supposed to give her today.

Move on. Move on. Move—

"Yes, it's very nice." Gabriel's crisp voice interrupted my silent prayers. "But I believe Isa has another gift."

My mother's brow furrowed. Miguel lifted his head while my lolo cracked one eye open, roused by the prospect of drama. Seven gazes pinned me to the spot like a bug on the wall.

Saliva turned to sawdust in my mouth.

"What other gift?" A line of puzzlement dug between Romero's brows.

"Her book that she's been working on for the past three

years." Gabriel didn't take his eyes off mine. "You said you'd have the complete manuscript for us today, didn't you?"

Thud. Thud. Thud.

Each heartbeat hammered so high in my throat I thought I might choke on it. My fingers curled around the edge of the couch as a bead of sweat trickled down my spine.

Part of me wanted to sink into the ground and never come back out; another part wanted to punch my brother and knock the knowing expression off his face.

"Isabella?" Gabriel prompted.

The taste of pennies flooded my tongue. "I don't have it," I said quietly. "It's not finished."

Silence fell over the room, punctuated by the chirps of birds outside the window.

Heat marched across my face in a relentless crusade. I tried to draw a deep breath, but the oxygen was too thin, my skin too tight. Shame and guilt inflated inside me, testing the seams of my composure and leaking through the cracks like stuffing through a ripped toy animal.

I'd endured the *National Star* firestorm, the breakup with Easton, and the meeting with Kai's mother, but I'd never felt smaller than I had in that moment.

"That's okay," Felix said, ever the peacemaker. "It's almost finished, right?"

I gave a meek nod. I'd been stuck at *almost* for weeks, but they didn't need to know that.

Gabriel crossed his arms. "I thought it was almost finished four months ago."

"C'mon, man." Miguel glared at him. "Don't be an asshole."

"I'm not being an asshole," Gabriel said coolly. "I'm confirming what Isa told me in late September."

Another silence encroached, heavy with apprehension.

"He's right. I did say that. I..." Leather pressed tight against my curled fingers. "I wasn't as close as I thought."

I could blame a number of people and things for my failure—

the tabloids, my day job, my relationship with Kai, my brother for setting the deadline. But at the end of the day, it was my fault. I was the one who didn't have the discipline to get it done. I was the one who'd let myself get distracted by sex and parties. I was the one who'd let myself and others down over and over.

Gabriel was harsh, but he was right.

My eyes felt hot and scorched, and I was suddenly glad Kai wasn't here. I didn't want him to witness my spectacular implosion and realize what a mess he'd been involved with this entire time. I was part of the reason he'd lost the CEO vote, and I wasn't worth it.

"The spa gift is enough," my mother said, giving her eldest son a reproachful stare. "Come. Let's eat. *Tigil muna sa mga bigating usapan.*" *No more heavy talk for the day.*

She reassured me with a pat on the way out. Lines of worry bracketed her mouth, but she didn't mention what just happened. After my father's sudden death, she hated anything that disrupted our family's harmony; I think she was afraid any argument would end up being the last words one of us said to the others.

However, the ghost of her disappointment trailed after me the rest of the afternoon and followed me out onto the patio that night, after the festivities died down and my mother and grandparents retired to their rooms.

I curled up on the bench, taking solace in the familiar give of the seat and the softness of the cushions. Motion-sensor flood lights illuminated the backyard, casting a pale yellow glow over the pool where I'd learned to swim, the treehouse where I'd hidden when I was upset, and the various nooks and crannies where my brothers and I had fought, played, and grown up together.

A wistful sense of nostalgia floated over me. I hadn't lived here in so long, but every time I visited, it was like I'd never left.

The sliding glass door opened. "Hey." Felix stepped out, his tall, lean form backlit by the house lights. "You okay?"

"Yeah." I hugged my knees to my chest, my chest tightening at his concerned voice. "I'm fine."

He took the seat next to mine. He'd changed out of his nice celebration clothes and into a faded T-shirt and shorts. "You don't sound fine."

"It's my allergies."

"You don't have allergies."

"Know-it-all."

Felix's soft laugh pulled a small smile out of me.

"If this is about earlier, don't think too much about it," he said. "You know how Gabe is."

"But he's right." Fresh pressure bloomed behind my eyes. I blinked it away, determined not to cry. I felt pathetic enough without having my nicest brother feel sorry for me. "I should've gotten the book done, and I didn't. I never follow through. I don't know why..." I tucked my knees tighter to my chest. "I don't know why it's so hard for me when it's so easy for you guys."

"Isa." Felix fixed me with a disbelieving stare. "It's not easy for any of us. Do you know how long it took for me to figure out what I wanted? How hard it was for Miguel to choose a specialty? Even Gabe has problems getting people to listen to him because he's so young."

"And Romero?"

"Oh, he's a freak. I'm pretty sure he was born with a computer for a brain."

Laughter melted some of the tension in my shoulders. "He'll take that as a compliment."

"I'm sure he will." Felix smiled. "The point is, you're on the right track. You've started your book, which is more than what a majority of the population has accomplished. It might seem like we're quote, unquote *ahead* of you, but we're also older. We have more life experience." He pinched my cheeks. *"Baby ka pa lang."* *You're just a baby.*

"Stop." I batted him away with another laugh. "Don't act like you're so old and wise. You're only four years older than me."

"You can live several lifetimes in four years." Felix leaned back and stretched out his legs. "The point is, you're not behind. You're still young. You have plenty of time to figure it out."

That was what I thought when I was twenty-two and convinced I would be the next great talk show host. Now I was twenty-nine and no closer to figuring it out, whatever *it* was.

I appreciated Felix's attempts to reassure me, but the more we talked about it, the worse I felt. Reassurances from someone so successful sounded patronizing even when that wasn't his intention.

"I know," I said, more because I wanted to end the conversation than because I agreed with him. My eyes fell on his bare neck. "Where's your necklace?"

His mentor, some woo-woo "be at one with the wave" type, gifted it to him after his first exhibition. I'd never seen Felix without it.

He scratched the back of his neck, his cheeks inexplicably red. "I, uh, lost it."

My sisterly radar went on full alert. He was lying, but before I could probe further, the door opened again. Gabriel appeared, his backlit silhouette an ominous spill of darkness in the doorway.

Felix quickly stood. "It's getting late, and I'm beat. I'll see you guys tomorrow. You got this," he added in a small whisper when he passed by me.

If by *this,* he meant utter and total dread, then he was right.

The third, tensest silence of the day sprouted as Gabriel took Felix's vacated seat and the door shut behind my other brother.

I tucked my hands beneath my thighs.

He tapped his fingers on the bench.

I stared at the pool.

He burned a hole in my cheek and finally spoke. "I'm trying to help you, Isa."

"Help?" Indignation ripped the word from my throat. "How is humiliating me in front everyone going to *help*?"

"I didn't humiliate you. I asked you for something you promised us." Gabriel's mouth thinned. "Everyone always coddled you because you're the youngest, but you're an adult now. Words and actions have consequences. Promises require follow-through. We've been patient for years while you 'figured things' out in New York." He made air quotes with his fingers. "Obviously, that hasn't worked."

Every word hit with the force and accuracy of a guided bullet. The flimsy walls of my indignation collapsed as quickly as they'd been erected, leaving me raw and exposed.

You're an adult now.

Promises require follow-through.

That had always been my problem, hadn't it? I could never keep a promise to myself.

I'd vowed I would finish the book by today and I couldn't. I'd said I would swear off men after my ex and I didn't. I'd pledged to prioritize my job at Valhalla and, well, we all knew how *that* turned out.

I didn't regret getting together with Kai, but the weight of my failures carved hollows in my chest.

"You know what the clause says," Gabriel said. "Find your passion and settle into a career by thirty, as judged by me and mom, or you forfeit your inheritance."

That clause was the biggest hold Gabriel had over me. By the time our mom added it, he was already working for her and serving as the de facto head of the household, so it made sense to add him as judge and arbitrator.

The weight on my chest pressed heavier and heavier, squeezing tears into my eyes.

I didn't care as much about the money. Obviously, I didn't want to lose it, but forfeiting my inheritance meant more than giving up millions. It meant, without a shadow of a doubt, that I'd failed where everyone else had succeed.

"You don't have to remind me," I said quietly. "I know."

"You have a year left. Move home. We'll figure it out together."

"Moving home isn't going to change things, Gabe." I couldn't leave New York. Besides my family, everyone and everything I loved was there. "It'll only make them worse."

His mouth thinned further. "You have no accountability in New York. No one pushing you. If you stay there, you'll never—"

"Stop." A thousand voices crammed inside my head, fighting for attention. Mine. Gabriel's. My parents'. Kai's. Leonora Young and Parker and Felix and every other person I had let down in some way or another.

I didn't humiliate you. I asked you for something you promised us.

Chase your dreams.

You'll finish it. You're too strong not to.

You and my son make a poor match.

The club has a strict non-fraternization rule. It is clearly stated in your contract.

It's almost finished, right?

"Just stop." Emotion cracked the syllables into half. "I'm not moving back. Let me figure this out on my own, okay?"

I didn't know what I was going to do, but I knew I couldn't do it with Gabriel hovering over me. His judgment would crush any freedom of thought out of me.

A long pause ensued.

Then he stood, his shadow shrouding me beneath the patio lights. "It's your choice," he said, his tone cool with disapproval. "But don't say I didn't warn you."

A second later, the door slid shut behind him, leaving me alone in the darkness and misery.

CHAPTER 36

"I want this done cleanly. No blackmail, no skirting the law," I said. "I don't want a single illegal activity traced back to me."

"If you insist." Christian Harper's smooth drawl flowed over the line. "I have to say, it's been a while since I've dealt with someone who has such inflexible morals. It's almost refreshing."

Only Christian would utter the word *morals* with such potent disdain.

I leaned back in my chair and tapped my pen against the desk. I tried to keep my dealings with him to a minimum, but when it came to unearthing digital trails and digging up dirt, he was unmatched. He was the only one who could get me what I need before the CEO transition ceremony next week.

Snippets from my conversation with Tobias on Friday dug into my brain. He was initially reluctant to talk, but bitterness and resentment proved to be an effective tongue loosener. Within half an hour, he'd divulged the real reason behind his withdrawn candidacy—an envelope containing candid photos of his daughter taken over the course of two months and an anonymous note threatening to harm her if he didn't drop out of the CEO race.

Bubbling fury scalded my veins, but I forced it aside so I could focus on the task at hand. I needed to plan my next steps carefully, or it would all fall apart.

"I need the evidence by close of business tomorrow," I said. "Can you get it done?"

"Please. This job is child's play." Christian sounded bored. "I've already found what you need. It turns out your intrepid COO has been engaged in quite a robust program of corporate espionage and sabotage. He'd hired private investigators to follow key board members and senior executives for months. You might recognize some of the names. Tobias Foster, Laura Nguyen, Paxton James...Kai Young."

"All the candidates for CEO," I said flatly. "What a coincidence."

I'd already suspected Russell after Victor's slipup. His unlikely election aside, Victor had mentioned Russell's name with a familiarity that went beyond the professional commiseration of people who'd both clawed their way to the top from modest beginnings. Russell's role as COO also gave him access to virtually every aspect of the company, including classified personnel files, internal emails, and chat logs. Even private investigators couldn't dig up some of that information.

That was a lot of leverage over voting members, a majority of whom wouldn't have voted for him over me, Paxton, or Laura without heavy motivation.

However, I'd needed outside confirmation of my suspicions and the scope of his activities, both of which Christian just gave me.

"He was smart," Christian said. "He included a fake tail on himself so his involvement wouldn't be obvious if anyone discovered the spying, and he buried his payments beneath several shell accounts. It took me about an hour to unmask him. The details are in the vault, next to his communications with Victor and several board members."

I opened the digital vault Christian had shared with me and skimmed through the files.

Blackmail. Coercion. Conspiracy. Russell had been a busy boy.

"I assume I'll see some of these photos in the news soon?" Christian sounded like he couldn't care less.

"Not until after the transition ceremony." I stared at a photo of Victor and Russell meeting under a bridge. It was such a cliché shot I almost laughed. They could pass for actors in a low-rent police drama. "I wouldn't want to preempt the in-person reveal."

"Of course." This time, a note of relish entered Christian's voice. "Much more dramatic that way."

We discussed a few remaining details before I hung up and logged out of the vault. My earlier fury abated, replaced with cool-headed clarity.

Asking Christian to prioritize my request would cost me in the future. His standard fee was exorbitant, but he traded in favors more than money.

I'd cross that bridge when I got there. Last week, I'd wallowed in the shock of my loss. This week, I had a purpose again: expose Russell and force a new CEO vote. According to company bylaws, if an incoming CEO was deemed unfit to serve before their official appointment, the voting committee had fourteen days to select a replacement.

Victor had been right about one thing. My hubris had cost me the leadership role the first time because I'd refused to ask for help; I wouldn't make the same mistake twice.

I picked up the phone again, a thrill of impending victory shooting through me. I had six days to pull my plan together, but the hard part was already done.

Now, it was time to get my family's company back.

CHAPTER 37

Isabella

B y the time Christmasbirthdaynewyearpalooza ended, I was mentally, physically, and emotionally exhausted. Too many forced smiles, sixteen-hour days, and concerned looks from my other brothers when they thought I wasn't looking.

I tried to sleep on my flight back to New York, but my mind was plagued with indecision over my next steps.

I *wanted* to finish my book, but if I hadn't done it by now, I probably wouldn't ever do it. I should just give up instead of wasting my time chasing something I'd never catch.

I enjoyed working with Alessandra, and I was decent at my job. Maybe I'd become a full-time assistant instead. It was easier to follow instructions than to create something from scratch for myself, and I'd rather work for her than Gabriel.

You have no accountability in New York.

It's your choice. But don't say I didn't warn you.

My chest tightened as I unlocked the door to my apartment and flipped on the lights.

I already knew what Gabriel would say. He'd berate me for being a flake, pressure me to work for the hotel, and insist I move home instead of wasting my time in New York, all in that irritatingly calm, I-know-better-than you tone of his.

Sometimes, his unflappable demeanor reminded me of Kai, except Kai was infinitely less annoying and more encouraging.

My heart gave another wrench at the thought of Kai and what I had to do, but I pushed it aside.

Don't worry about that until you have to.

I showered, unpacked, and said hi to Monty. I'd fed him right before I left, so he was good for another week.

"Hey, bud. Did you miss me?" I stroked his cool skin with one hand as he twined around my other arm and flicked his tongue in greeting. Reptiles couldn't feel emotions the way humans did, but I could've sworn his eyes glinted with concern when he looked at me. Or maybe that was my exhaustion talking.

I gave Monty one last pat before I released him back into his tank.

I fished the new Ruby Leigh thriller I bought at the airport out of my bag and was preparing to sink into an evening of sex, murder, and self-soothing when the doorbell rang.

I groaned. "It *always* has to ring after I get comfortable."

I threw off my faux fur blanket and padded, barefoot, to the door. I looked through the peephole, expecting to see the old lady in 4B who was always asking me to fix her Wi-Fi.

Black hair. Glasses. Cheekbones that could cut glass. Kai.

My heart dropped several inches.

"I picked up Juliana's on my way here," he said when I opened the door. "White pie, your favorite."

He stepped inside, looking even more impossibly handsome than usual in a pale-blue button-down and charcoal suit. He must've come straight from work.

"Thank you." I mustered a weak smile, trying to ignore the greasy knots of tension forming in my stomach. "You have perfect timing. I was just about to order delivery."

Kai gave me a quick kiss. We didn't get a chance to talk over the weekend since I was so busy with my family, but his movements were easy and relaxed as we settled at my coffee slash dining table and dug into the pizza. I hadn't seen him so serene since before the CEO vote.

"You look happy," I ventured. "Did something happen at work?"

A grin flashed across his face. "You could say that."

I listened, mouth open, while he relayed what had happened over the past few days. When he finished, my jaw was practically scraping the ground.

"Wait. Russell was *spying* on the candidates and blackmailing board members into voting for him? How does that even work?"

My head spun. I couldn't grasp this level of corporate subterfuge; it sounded like something out of a TV show, not real life.

"He focused on taking Tobias and me down since we were his biggest competition," Kai said. "He couldn't blackmail me into withdrawing since it's my family's company and people would never believe I dropped out willingly, so he attacked in a different way. He left most of the board members alone. The only ones he pressured into voting for him were the ones who were already on the fence."

"Including Richard?"

Kai's features hardened. "No. Richard reportedly voted for Paxton."

So his last-minute outreach to Richard hadn't worked. Knowing Kai, it must gall him to no end, considering how he'd swallowed his pride to ask for the other man's support.

"I thought you said Russell didn't want to be CEO," I said. Russell had worked at the Young Corporation for over a decade. According to Kai, he hated dealing with external affairs, so why would he go to such lengths to be the public face of the company?

Kai's mouth pressed into a thin line. "I misjudged him."

Coming from someone who was used to being right all the time, it was a huge admission.

The knots in my stomach tightened as he described his plan for exposing Russell and forcing a new CEO vote, which he was bound to win if the first part of his plan succeeded.

I didn't doubt for a second that it *would* succeed. This was Kai. When he set his mind on something, he always got it done.

Besides Russell, the only reason he'd lost was because I distracted him. If it weren't for me, he might've caught on to Russell sooner, and he wouldn't have to deal with all this.

"Enough about work. What about you?" Kai asked. "How was Christmasbirthdaynewyearpalooza?"

For some reason, hearing him utter *Christmasbirthdaynewyearpalooza* in that posh voice made my throat close.

He'd done so many ridiculous, reckless things because of me, and I wasn't worth it.

"It was good." I picked at my pizza crust, unable to look him in the eye.

"That's the same way you said good when I asked if you enjoyed James Joyce," he said dryly.

I winced at the reminder. Reading *Ulysses* had cemented my opinion that one, classics weren't for me, and two, stream-of-consciousness writing made me want to gouge my eyes out.

"It was nice seeing my family again." *Except Gabriel.* "But I..." I shredded another piece of crust. "I, um, didn't finish my manuscript on time."

Given the craziness surrounding the CEO vote, we hadn't discussed my book's progress before I left. I felt even shittier admitting my failure to Kai than I had to my family. He'd tried to help so much, with the typewriters and the writer's block suggestions, and I'd still let him down.

"That's okay," he said gently. "You will. It wasn't a hard deadline."

Once upon a time, his unwavering faith had bolstered me. Now, it only made me feel worse because I didn't deserve it.

"Maybe not with a publisher, but it was to my family." I gave him a brief overview of what happened on my mom's birthday.

Anxiety hummed, high-pitched and tight like I was sitting in the living room shriveling beneath my family's scrutiny again.

When I finally looked up, my stomach pitched at the darkness cloaking Kai's face.

"Your brother," he said, "is an asshole."

The sentiment was so blunt and unlike him that it startled a quick burst of laughter out of me.

"Yeah, he prides himself on it." My smile melted as easily as it formed. "But he wasn't wrong. Neither..." I forced oxygen into my lungs. *Just say it.* "Neither was your mom. About us."

Just like that, the air shifted. Levity vanished, giving way to a thick, creeping tension that strangled me like a thorny vine.

Kai fell eerily still. "Meaning?"

My heart wobbled. "Meaning we're not a good match," I said, forcing the words past the hard lump in my throat. "And we should...we should see other people."

I stumbled on the last half of my sentence. It came out jagged and broken, like it'd been dragged through barbed wire on its way up my throat.

I didn't know where the sentiment came from because the last thing I wanted was to see someone else or see *Kai* with someone else, but talking was the only way to keep my emotions at bay.

Kai's eyes were flat, fathomless plains of granite. "See other people."

"You have so much going on with the company and work, and I have a lot of life stuff I need to figure out." I rushed the excuses out before I lost my nerve. "We would be distractions to each other. I mean, it was fun while it lasted, but we never had a future. We're too different. You know that." My words tasted like cyanide— bitter and poisonous enough to stop my heart from beating.

"Is that what we have?" Kai asked quietly. He still hadn't moved. "*Fun?*"

Misery closed my throat. I was drowning again, weighed down by self-loathing and helplessness. If I were someone else watching me do what I was doing, I would scream at me to stop being an idiot. I had this gorgeous, brilliant, *amazing* man—a man who supported and encouraged me, who kissed me like I was his oxygen and made me feel seen for the first time in my life—and I was pushing him away.

Not because I didn't care about him, but because I cared about him too much to hold him back or have him resent me down the road. One day, he would wake up and realize I was so much less than who he thought I was, and it would crush me. I was saving us both from inevitable heartbreak before we got too deep.

You're already in too deep, a voice whispered before I pushed it aside.

"Yes." I forced my response past stiff lips. "The holidays, the secret room, the private island...they were incredible experiences, and I don't regret them. But they're not sustainable. They were—" The sentence broke, flooded with tears. "They were never meant to be forever."

Something hot and wet slipped down my cheek, but I didn't bother brushing it off. My eyes were too full, my chest too tight. I couldn't breathe fast or deep enough, and I was certain I was going to die here, at this table, with my soul empty and my heart in pieces.

A muscle jerked in Kai's cheek, his first visible reaction since I broached the subject. "Don't do this, Isabella."

Steel hands crushed my lungs at the raw, aching sound of name.

"You're better off with someone like Clarissa," I continued, hating myself more with each passing second. My voice was so thick and watery it sounded unrecognizable to my own ears. "She's what you need. Not me."

Another tear dripped off my chin and into my lap. Then another, and another, until there were too many to account and they blended into one ceaseless, unending river of grief.

"Stop." Kai's fingers curled into white-knuckled fists. "If I wanted someone like Clarissa, I would be with Clarissa, but I'm not. *I want you.* Your laugh, your sarcasm, your inappropriate jokes and strange love for dinosaur erotica..."

A tiny laugh bloomed in the desert of my grief. Only Kai could make me laugh at a time like this. *To think I once said he was boring.*

His fleeting smile matched mine before it slipped. "We're so close, Isa. Valhalla, the *National Star*, the CEO vote...there's nothing stopping us from being together. Don't give up on us. Not now. Not like this."

My brief moment of lightness died.

The pain in his voice matched the one consuming me. It was worse than the times I broke my arm or accidentally sliced my hand because it wasn't physical. It was emotional, and it stole so deep into my soul that I was sure I could never dig it out.

Gut-wrenching, soul-stealing, breath-defying pain.

I wanted to believe Kai. I wanted to sink into his confidence and let it carry me away because I did understand the irony of breaking up when the things that'd kept us apart were no longer applicable. But this wasn't about external obstacles. It was about who were as people, and we were fundamentally incompatible.

An invisible band cinched around my torso, crushing my chest.

He was successful and driven; I was flaky and unreliable.

He achieved every goal he set his mind to; I couldn't keep a job for more than a year and change.

Our lives had intertwined for a brief, glorious moment, but we were ultimately on different paths. Eventually, we would stray too far apart to stay together without one or both of us breaking.

I hugged my arms around my waist, trying to hold myself together when I was slowly shattering to pieces. "I'm sorry," I whispered.

My love.

I'm sorry.

Two pairs of words. Two settings. Both devastating in entirely different ways.

I felt more than I heard the latter's impact on Kai. A shockwave rippled through the air and outlined his face with bright, blazing agony. It was gut-wrenching in its silence and all-consuming in its potency, its effects clearly etched in the ragged rise of his chest and the glossy brightness of his eyes.

He reached for me, but I hugged myself tighter and shook my head. "Don't make this any harder than it has to be." Tears scalded my skin. "Please, Kai. Please just leave."

My sobs broke free. Waves of pain unfurled inside me, slamming against my defenses and dragging me beneath their terrible, ferocious fury until I drowned in anguish.

Kai wasn't the type to stay when he wasn't wanted. He was too proud, too well bred. Nevertheless, he lingered, his anguish a tangible mirror of my own, before he finally left and the air grew cold.

I didn't hear the door shut. I didn't feel the hard wood bruising my skin when I sank to the floor or hear the hiccupping gasps of my breaths.

The only thing that existed in Kai's absence was nothing.

CHAPTER 38

Kai

The CEO transition ceremony took place at a hotel ballroom in London. Every Young Corporation executive was in attendance along with a smattering of local employees and VIP "friends of the company."

It was the perfect occasion for a takedown, but I couldn't savor the moment as much as I would've liked.

Please just leave.

The memory of Isabella's anguished voice and face ate at me like acid. I hadn't talked to her since I left her apartment last week, but she haunted me every second of every day.

Everything reminded me of her—books, alcohol, even the color purple. It was particularly unbearable tonight, when the company's purple peacock logo adorned everything from the podium to the gift bags at every seat.

I set my jaw and focused on the stage, trying to ignore the agonizing cramp in my chest.

The evening had progressed smoothly so far. Dinner went off without a hitch, and my mother was finishing her speech with remarkable composure. If Leonora Young was upset about ceding control of her family's company to an outsider, one couldn't tell by looking at her. Her voice sounded genuinely sincere as she thanked the board and employees for their support during her tenure and introduced Russell onstage.

I knew the truth. Inside, she was incandescent with rage.

My ears were still bleeding from our post-vote call. She didn't know about Russell's manipulations and had blamed my loss on Isabella.

I told you she was a distraction...If you had listened to me, you would've never lost...Our family name will never recover...

We hadn't spoken since.

The room greeted her speech with thunderous applause. My mother shook hands with Russell, her face a canvas of carefully constructed professionalism, before walking back to her table.

My hand closed around the stem of my wineglass as Russell took the podium after her to a more muted reception.

Average height, average build, average brown hair and brown eyes. He was the type of person who blended into the background so seamlessly he practically disappeared. I'd dismissed him as a nonthreat, but I finally saw his unmemorable facade for what it was: a masterful disguise, honed and perfected over years of operating under the radar.

My skin prickled.

Russell was the one talking, but all eyes were on me, waiting for a reaction I'd never give.

If people wanted a show, they'd get one soon enough. Just not from me.

Across the table, Vivian's concern—over Isabella, the CEO vote, or both—burned a hole in my cheek. The Russo Group accounted for over fifty percent of our company's print advertising, so Dante received invites to every important function. He normally declined, but he'd showed up tonight for "the entertainment," as he called it.

He and Vivian were the guests of honor at my table. Most of the big advertisers were. My mother reigned over a table of board members while Tobias, Laura, and Paxton occupied seats near the stage. They watched Russell speak with varying expressions of anger, distaste, and contemplation. He hadn't deemed Laura or Paxton threatening enough to blackmail, but I wondered what they would say when they found out he'd been spying on them.

"I want to give a special thank you to the board members who believed in me..." Russell droned on, unaware his fifteen minutes in the spotlight were about to expire.

I ignored Vivian's concern and scanned the room. I appreciated her solicitude, but I had one goal and one goal only tonight.

My anticipation spiked when the ballroom's service door opened and a half dozen servers entered. Each one carried a stack of menu-sized packets, which they quietly distributed to guests while Russell spoke.

Their reaction came swiftly.

Confusion rippled through the crowd when they received the papers, followed by shocked murmurs.

Russell faltered at the swell of noise but forged ahead. "...promise to execute my duties as CEO to the best of my abilities..."

The murmurs grew louder. People were getting agitated; silverware clinked, bodies shifted, and coughs and gasps punctuated the gathering tension.

"That bastard." Dante's soft laugh traveled over the din. "Didn't think he had it in him."

I'd given him an overview about the Russell situation last week, but I hadn't shared the details printed for all the one hundred-odd guests in attendance.

"What's going on?" Vivian whispered. "I thought this was a handover ceremony."

"It is, *mia cara*." Dante was still laughing. He placed an arm around his wife and kissed the top of her head. "Just not the kind you were thinking of."

I sipped my wine and returned my attention to the stage. Satisfaction rattled in my chest at the perspiration coating Russell's face. *It's about to get so much worse for you.*

With Christian's help, I'd put together a special highlight reel of Russell's transgressions—payments to private detectives; instructions for said detectives to follow board members and high-ranking executives; emails conspiring with Victor, a competitor, to damage my reputation.

The clamor reached a point where it drowned out Russell's speech.

He finally stopped, his eyes bouncing around the room. A mix of alarm and anger peeked through the cracks of his affable demeanor. "What is this?" he demanded. "What's going on?"

I typically didn't relish other people's misfortune, but in his case, he deserved it.

I smoothed a hand over my tie. At the agreed on signal, the techs dimmed the lights and turned on the projection screen behind Russell.

The earlier slideshow of my mother's career highlights flipped to photos of Russell and Victor meeting in person. Of the threatening note to Tobias, blown up and sharpened in high resolution. Of similar notes to key board members, coercing them into various votes. He'd had them split their support among himself, Paxton, and Laura so he won by a tiny margin, thereby reducing suspicion.

The room exploded.

Laura jumped up, expression murderous, hands gesticulating wildly at a stunned-looking Paxton. On her other side, Tobias's eyes gleamed, his mouth twisted with grim pleasure. A glass shattered several tables down, and several blackmailed board members tried to sneak away before my mother's cutting glare froze them in their tracks.

Unlike a majority of the guests, she didn't react to the revelations on-screen. Her expression mirrored that of someone waiting in line at the grocery store, but when her eyes found mine, they glinted with surprise and a fierce, unyielding pride.

She didn't have to ask whether I was the one responsible for the mayhem. She already knew.

I stood, and the room fell silent so quickly it was almost comical. Every pair of eyes swung toward me as I walked up to the podium and took the mic from a frozen Russell's hands.

He hadn't moved since the projector switched on. The color had slipped from his cheeks, but otherwise, he seemed to have trouble grasping the abrupt turn in events.

"Apologies for interrupting your speech," I said, deceptively polite. "I realize you're quite excited about your selection as CEO. However, before we officially conclude your transition, I thought you might like to share your extracurricular activities with the company. It seems fitting, given how prominently they feature in said activities."

Since the evidence was there for all to see, I kept my rundown short. Spying, conspiring with a competitor, using employee records for personal and unethical purposes. The list went on.

"That's preposterous." Nerves pitched Russell's laugh into a higher octave. "I understand you're upset about losing the vote, Kai, but to frame me for—"

I tapped the podium. A second later, a video replaced the photos on-screen.

Russell and Victor in Black & Co.'s Virginia satellite office, discussing in detail how and when to publish the articles about me and Isabella. The conversation soon shifted to Victor's payment—a considerable sum of cash plus Russell's promise to give him several future news scoops if he was selected as CEO.

Thank you, Christian.

The photos and documents were damning, but the video was the death blow.

Panic pooled in Russell's eyes. He turned, but he must've realized he had nowhere to go, because he didn't attempt to flee while I closed out the night's show.

"You're right. I *am* upset about losing the vote," I said. Iron underlaid my voice. "I'm upset about losing it to someone who cheated his way into winning. You were a decent COO, Russell.

You could've competed fairly instead of lying and manipulating the very people you promised to serve."

"Fairly?" The word brought a violent tide of crimson to his face. "*Fairly?* There was nothing *fair* about the process, and you know it. I worked my ass off for the company for two decades, ten of them as COO. I'm supposed to be the second-in-command, yet the minute you swan in, fresh out of school with your fancy degrees and family name, people defer to you like you're in charge. Well, I'm sick of it."

Russell's hands fisted. "The CEO selection process was a farce. Everyone knew you were going to win simply because you're a Young. I was included as a pity candidate despite everything I've done for the company. While Leonora was busy traveling and you were busy chasing pie-in-the-sky deals, *I* kept the lights on and the offices running. I deserve recognition, dammit, and I *refuse* to serve under some arrogant, peacocking upstart who thinks he's better than everyone!"

His voice escalated with each word until it boomed like thunder through the stunned room. A vein throbbed in his forehead, and flecks of spittle sprayed from his mouth. The stench of rage and indignation poured off him in thick, rolling waves, making my stomach turn.

This was a man who'd been bottling up his feelings for years, if not decades. A man who believed so firmly in his martyrdom that he saw nothing wrong with what he did. In his mind, he was well within his rights to lie, cheat, and blackmail his way to the top because he "deserved" it.

I wasn't immune to my shortcomings. Looking back, I could admit I felt as entitled to the CEO position as he did. The only difference was, I didn't fuck other people over to try and get it.

I kept my gaze steady on his. "You say that," I said, each syllable sharp enough to cut. "Yet you considered Tobias strong enough competition to threaten him into withdrawing. If it were truly rigged, you could've stopped with me and left him alone.

But you didn't, did you? Because you know that underneath your justifications and excuses, you simply aren't that good."

The low blow landed with unerring accuracy. The remaining color leached from Russell's face. His mouth opened and closed, but nothing came out.

I typically wouldn't resort to ad hominem attacks, but he'd made my and Isabella's lives hell the past few weeks. Even if he hadn't targeted me, I would never forgive him for what he and Victor did to her.

The lull finally prompted a measured reaction from the board. To my surprise, Richard Chu was the first member to speak up and declare Russell's selection invalid. Others fell in line, and things moved quickly after that.

By the time the dazed guests filed out of the ballroom half an hour later, Russell had been stripped of his company titles and responsibilities, his deputy had been appointed his interim placement, and the date for a new CEO vote was set for two weeks from now. There would also be a criminal investigation into Russell's activities plus a reckoning for the board, a quarter of whom had succumbed to his blackmail for various reasons, but those were issues for another day.

"Kai." My mother stopped me after I said goodbye to a wildly entertained Dante and a shell-shocked Vivian. "Quite an evening you directed tonight."

"Thank you. If I lose the vote a second time, perhaps I'll pursue a career in show production," I said dryly. "I seem to have a knack for it."

A smirk touched her lips.

Between Isabella, my mother's surprise visit, and my initial loss, our relationship had been strained to its limits the past month. However, I sensed a tiny thaw as we faced each other in the now empty ballroom, both too proud to back down first but too exhausted to leave our relationship on bad terms.

"You did well," she finally said. Giving the first compliment after an argument was her version of an apology. "I never would've suspected Russell. After so many years..."

"He fooled a lot of people, myself included," I said in my own admission of fallibility.

Another silence descended. Neither of us were used to bending, and our concessions rendered our standard modes of operation obsolete.

"It's been a long night. We'll talk later this week, after things have settled," my mother said.

I nodded, and that was that.

It was a short conversation, but it was all we needed to reset our relationship. That was the Young family way. We didn't indulge in heart-to-hearts or drawn-out apologies; we acknowledged the problem, fixed it, and went on with our lives.

I exited the ballroom after her and returned to my suite, but I didn't make it halfway before my adrenaline flatlined. The high from successfully exposing Russell faded, replaced with a familiar, piercing ache.

Now that I was alone, away from the noise and distraction of other people, Isabella's voice crept back into my head like a ghost I can't escape.

Please just leave.

The ache sharpened into a spike.

I set my jaw and headed straight to my suite's mini-bar, but no matter how many glasses of alcohol I tossed back, I couldn't blunt the impact of her memory.

Six days. Four hours. One eternity.

Tonight should've been one of my greatest victories, but in the quiet, luxurious confines of my room, I found it hard to celebrate anything at all.

CHAPTER 39
Isabella

"Y ou've been working nonstop for the past week." Alessandra regarded me with naked worry. "When was the last time you slept more than three hours a night?"

I rubbed a hand over my bleary eyes. "I don't need sleep. I need to finish the website copy."

The mouthwatering smells of espresso and pastries saturated the air, but every bite of croissant tasted like cardboard. I hadn't enjoyed a single meal since I returned from Christmasbirthdaynewyearpalooza, and the thought of forcing more bread down my throat made my stomach churn.

I pushed my plate aside and took a gulp of coffee instead.

Alessandra, Sloane, and Vivian exchanged glances. We occupied a corner table at a new café in Nolita, which buzzed with Saturday morning activity. Fashionably dressed couples, models, and a minor celebrity from a new hit TV drama crammed around pale wooden tables while servers circulated with lattes and mimosas. Potted plants hung from the glass ceiling and gave the airy space a greenhouse feel.

It was the perfect location for catching up after Vivian's return from London and Sloane's business trip to Bogotá, but everyone was only focused on me.

"No, you need sleep," Sloane said, blunt as always. "If the bags under your eyes get any bigger, you'll have to pay an oversize luggage fee."

Self-consciousness prickled my skin; it took all my willpower not to check my reflection in my phone's camera. "Thanks a lot."

"You're welcome." She sipped her black coffee. "Friends don't let friends walk around with raccoon eyes, even if they're heartbroken."

My meager breakfast surged back up my throat. "I'm not heartbroken."

It wasn't like every breath resembled shards of glass piercing my lungs. I didn't wake up every morning missing his warmth or reach for my phone to text him only to remember we weren't talking. I didn't see him everywhere I turned—in the pages of my books, the soft strains of a distant piano, or the reflection of a passing shop window. And I definitely didn't lie awake, sleepless and restless, replaying every memory we shared like that was my life instead of the tattered reality around me.

I wasn't heartbroken because I did this to myself. I didn't have the *right* to be heartbroken.

But I would be lying if I said I didn't want to hear Kai make his dry little quips one last time. Just so my final memory of him wasn't the anguish on his face and the knowledge that I'd put it there.

It's scientifically proven, my love.

A sob broke halfway in my chest. I turned my head away, eyes wet, until I regained control over my emotions. When I looked up again, my friends were watching me, their expressions soft yet knowing.

I'd skipped over the details of why I ended things with Kai. I simply told them we weren't a good fit anymore and I needed time alone, which was true, but I could tell they didn't believe me.

I didn't blame them. I didn't believe me either.

Fortunately, none of them called me out, and they acted like I didn't almost have a breakdown at the table.

Sloane lifted one perfectly shaped brow. "Is that why you've been working like the hounds of hell are after you for the past week?" she asked, circling back to her concern over my recent habits.

"I have a good work ethic," I said, grateful I didn't have to talk about my feelings this early in the morning. "Is that a crime?"

"No, but you're working yourself to exhaustion," Vivian said gently. "It's not healthy."

That's the point. If I was exhausted, I didn't have energy to dwell on Kai or the shitshow that was my life. I didn't have to spend my waking hours wondering where he was and how he was doing or my sleeping hours dreaming of his face, his voice, and his touch.

Exhausted was good. Exhausted was safe.

"I'm fine," I said. "If I collapse in the middle of work, *then* you can berate me."

"I don't—"

"How was London?" I interrupted Vivian's reply. She flew there with Dante for the Young Corporation's CEO handover ceremony, which didn't make it the best subject change, but I couldn't help myself.

I'd read about Kai's coup in the news. In one week, he'd taken down a top executive and reclaimed his spot as a CEO front-runner. Meanwhile, I'd burned rice, avoided my mom's calls, and set a personal record for how many days I could wear the same sweat-pants in a row. I was proud of him, but it only underscored how incompatible we were.

"London was...interesting," Vivian said. "I can safely say I've never attended a similar event before."

"That's good." I bit back the rest of my questions.

How was Kai? Was he there with anyone? Did he mention me?

It was hypocritical of me to hope the last answer was yes. I was the one who ended things, but it didn't change the fact that I missed him so much I couldn't breathe.

Vivian looked like she was about to say something else. Fortunately, Sloane received a news alert about some big political scandal, and the conversation shifted to speculation over a well-known senator's future.

Relief returned a portion of my appetite. I attempted to eat my croissant again and found it mildly more appetizing the second time around.

My friends meant well, but talking even indirectly about Kai enabled my addiction. The only way to break free was to quit cold turkey, though that was easier said than done. I still hadn't been able to bring myself to turn off the news alerts for his name.

I'll do it tonight.

I'd told myself that the past three nights, but I'd actually do it this time.

While Sloane ranted about the state of modern politics, I scrolled through my inbox for any urgent emails.

LAST DAY! BOGO 50% off our clearance collection

Spring into the new season with these florals!

Re: Floria Designs website

I was about to click on the last email from Alessandra's web designer when the subject line below it caught my eye.

Your book submission to the Atlantic Prose Agency

My heart catapulted into my throat. I'd never queried any literary agency, but I couldn't resist clicking into what was obviously a spam email.

Dear Isabella,

Thank you for your submission. I've read your sample chapters, and I love your voice. I have some notes in the attached feedback letter. Can you resend after you've revised?

-jill s

"What is it?" Alessandra asked.

My friends ended their conversation about the senator and stared at me with varying shades of curiosity.

"An email from someone claiming to be a literary agent." My heartbeat crawled from my throat to my ears. I shouldn't have drunk all that caffeine; I was one palpitation away from flatlining. "She said she read my sample chapters and liked them, which is bullshit, because I never queried an agent."

The universe had the shittiest sense of humor. I was already spiraling about not finishing my book; it didn't need to kick me while I was down.

"What's the agent's name?" Sloane asked. As a high-powered publicist, she knew everyone who was everyone in New York.

"Jill S? Stands for Sherman, according to her email address. I don't...what? Why are you looking at me like that?"

Her eyes had sharpened the second I mentioned Jill's name.

"Isabella," she said slowly. "Jill Sherman is one of the biggest thriller agents working right now. She reps Ruby Leigh." A trace of rare excitement ran through her voice.

Shock knocked the breath from my lungs. Ruby Leigh was my favorite erotic thriller author and my introduction to the genre. I had an entire shelf dedicated to her books. I hadn't researched agents yet because I wanted to finish my manuscript first, but querying Ruby's agent had been at the top of my post-completion to-do list.

"But...I don't..." How the hell did Ruby Leigh's agent get my email? Was this simply someone pretending to be her? If so, I didn't see the point; the email didn't contain any phishing links or requests for payment.

The more I thought about it, the more real it seemed.

Croissant flakes and coffee churned next to a tiny, dangerous seed of hope.

"Let me see the email." Sloane studied the message after I handed it to her. "This is her. Right email, right signature. She always signs off in all lowercase with her last initial, no period. It's not something people outside the industry would know."

"That doesn't make sense." My pulse thundered as the implication of what she was saying sank in. *Not a scam.* "Unless she hacked into my computer, there's no way she could've gotten a hold of those chapters."

"Did you show your manuscript to anyone?" Alessandra asked.

"No, I..." My sentence trailed off, subsumed by an unbidden memory.

I'm not sure whether it counts as a gift since I can't guarantee it's good, but you wanted to read it...

"Kai," I whispered.

A deep, unsettling ache reverberated in my chest.

He hadn't said a word about my book after I gave him the sample chapters. Why would he submit them to an agent without telling me?

"Because he thinks it's good, Isa," Vivian said softly, and I realized with a start I'd voiced my thoughts aloud. "You know Kai. He wouldn't have shown it to anyone if he didn't stand behind it."

Not just anyone, but *the* one. The biggest agent in the genre.

Sloane returned my phone. I took it, my throat aching with unshed tears.

It wasn't just about Kai or Jill. It was about the fact that *someone* believed in me. Enough to send my manuscript out when I didn't have the courage to do it myself; enough to take the time and give detailed notes when her inbox must be flooded with similar queries.

Kai always said he had faith in me, but seeing him act on it was different from simply hearing it. I'd spent so many years internalizing my failures that I didn't trust anyone who didn't confirm my insecurities. There was comfort in the familiar, even if the familiar sucked. Being small was easier than putting myself out there for other people to judge.

"Well, what are you waiting for?" Sloane's voice dragged me back to the café.

I swallowed my tears and blinked, trying to reorient myself to the present. "What?"

"Jill's request for a revise and resubmit." She nodded at my phone. "I skimmed the notes. There aren't many. You could probably knock out the edits in a week."

"What a coincidence," Alessandra said innocently. "You also have the next week off at Floria. I'm...taking a work-free vacation."

A frown bent my brows. "Didn't you just go on vacation over the holidays?"

"Isa!" Sloane, Alessandra, and Vivian's groans formed an exasperated chorus.

"Okay, okay! I get it." A trickle of exhilaration leaked into my blood, erasing some of my melancholy. *Ruby Leigh's* agent wanted *my* revised manuscript. Why the hell was I still sitting here? "Do you guys mind...I have to..."

"If you don't leave right now, I'm pushing you out the door myself," Vivian said. "Go!"

"Good luck!" Alessandra called after me. "Drink lots of caffeine!"

I waved at them over my shoulder as I rushed out the door. I almost knocked over a passing couple in my haste to catch the next train home and rushed out an apology. The guy yelled something at me, unappeased, but I didn't bother stopping.

I had a book to edit—and finish.

∼

For the next week, I camped out at the local coffee shop during the day and guzzled energy drinks at my desk at night.

Was it healthy? No. Was it effective? Yes.

Jill didn't give me a deadline for the resubmission, but I didn't want to risk falling into a creative rut again. I needed to finish the edits and the rest of the book while I was still riding high from her email.

I'd been so in my head about the book that it took the validation of a neutral, professional third party to break my creative dam. The words gushed out like a broken fire hydrant, and exactly six days and eight hours after I opened Jill's email, I replied with my full, revised manuscript. It was risky, considering she hadn't asked for the full book, but I was tired of playing it safe. No risk, no reward.

"Do you want another latte?" Charlie, my favorite barista, picked up the half dozen empty mugs crowding my table. It was almost seven p.m.; I'd been here since eight in the morning. "We're closing in ten minutes, but I can whip you up one last drink."

"No, it's okay." I leaned back, lightheaded with disbelief as I stared at the email chain on my screen. I had to wait for Jill's follow-up, but my book was out there. There was no taking it back. "I'm done for the night."

I'd wanted to finish my manuscript for so long. Now that I was done, I felt an inexplicable twinge of sadness. I'd forgotten how much I *enjoyed* writing. Getting to know the characters, letting them take me on their twists and turns, building an entire freaking world—it was incomparable to anything else I'd ever done.

"You sure? It'll be on me. I owe you." Charlie gave me a bashful smile. "I, um, proposed to my girlfriend. In Tagalog. And she said yes."

"Oh my God!" I shot up straight again. I'd been teaching him random Tagalog phrases every time I came in, but I hadn't thought much about him asking how to say *Will you marry me?* He'd also asked me how to say *I'm a defensive lineman in the NFL*, which he most definitely wasn't. "That's incredible. Congratulations!"

"Thank you." His face resembled a ripe beet. "Anyway, like I said, your next coffee is on me. I would've gotten you one of these"—he gestured at my empty mugs—"if you hadn't ordered before my shift."

"Don't worry about it. Pay me back by showing me photos from the wedding instead. I'm nosy like that."

Charlie laughed and agreed. While he closed up shop, I grabbed my phone and texted the group chat.

Me: *I did it. I sent it. *nervous face emoji**

Vivian: *The manuscript?*

Vivian: *That's amazing. Congrats!*

Sloane: *See? I told you you could do it*

Sloane: *I'm always right*

Alessandra: *We should go out and celebrate:)*

My smile dimmed. I hadn't been in a going out mood since my breakup with Kai. Every time I tried, I would remember our night together at Verve and The Barber, and my heart would feel like it was getting raked over hot coals again.

My manic writing haze had temporarily pushed him out of my mind, but now he came roaring back with a vengeance.

I should call him. To thank him, to tell him what I'd accomplished, to just hear his voice and not feel so alone. But I didn't want to muddle our relationship or lead him on when our fundamental differences remained. Besides, he might not even want to talk to me. I hadn't heard from him since our breakup, probably because I told him I wanted space. Still, I couldn't stop a pinch of disappointment every time my phone rang and it wasn't him.

I forced a deep breath through my nose and squared my shoulders. No wallowing. *Not tonight.* Tonight was a night of celebration.

Me: *We should DEFINITELY go out*

Me: *If you guys aren't opposed to Brooklyn...I know just the place*

No one objected, so I packed up my things, went home, and got ready with record speed.

An hour later, my Uber dropped me off at my favorite cocktail bar in Brooklyn Heights. I preferred Bushwick for nightlife, but getting Sloane to step foot in a non-Manhattan borough of New York was hard enough. If I made her go to Bushwick, she might spontaneously combust.

As expected, she was already waiting for me in a corner booth. The woman was freakishly punctual. Vivian and Alessandra showed up minutes later, and soon, we were warm and tipsy from two rounds of drinks.

"I'm so proud of you." Vivian hugged me with one arm, her face flushed red from tequila. "Don't forget us when you're famous."

"I have a long way to go before I'm famous." I laughed.

"I once had a client who went from posting videos on You-Tube one day to signing a multimillion-dollar contract with a major recording label two months later," Sloane said. "Trust me. *A long way* isn't as long as you think."

"Publishing moves way slower than that, but I appreciate the support," I said with a grin.

Alessandra raised her glass. "To chasing dreams and kicking ass."

Cheers and laughter mingled with the clinks of our glasses. Warmth fizzed in my chest. I might not have a boyfriend or a concrete book deal, but I had my friends, and they were pretty fucking awesome.

I lifted my drink to my lips and scanned the room. People came and went, each one trendier and better-looking than the last, but a creamy laugh drew my eye to the entrance.

My heart plummeted to the ground.

Dark hair. Glasses. Crisp white shirt. Next to him, a familiar woman laughed again, the sound as elegant as her black designer dress and jewelry.

No. It can't be.

But no matter how long I stared or how hard I wished them away, the pair didn't disappear. They were real.

Kai was here. With Clarissa.

CHAPTER 40

Isabella

The noise from the rest of the bar dulled to a muted roar.

Kai and Clarissa. Clarissa and Kai. Here. Together.

The thought replayed in my head as I tried to process the sight before me. They hadn't seen me yet—my booth was tucked in a corner next to the entrance, and they cut straight to the bar without looking around.

Half-digested tequila sloshed in my stomach as Kai bent his head and said something to Clarissa. Their backs were to me so I couldn't see her reaction, but they made a good-looking couple. Same elegance, same refinement, her willowy height a perfect complement to his.

A fierce wound reopened, sending a deep ache through my chest. I was freezing despite the alcohol and the body heat drenching the bar, and shivers snuck through my body in tiny, rattling waves. I tried reaching for my coat, but my limbs were as heavy and unresponsive as concrete blocks.

Alessandra noticed my silence first. Her brows dipped. "What's wrong?"

Nausea trapped my response in the back of my throat, rendering me mute, but my friends were smart enough to follow my gaze to the bar. Kai's hair, build, and clothing were unmistakable even from the back.

A shocked silence wiped our earlier gaiety clean.

"We can leave," Vivian said after a long, tense pause. "There's another bar a few streets over that's supposed to be good, or we can head back to Man—"

"No." I finally regained control over my faculties. "We're staying. We were here first, and there's no...there's no reason why we can't be in the same room at the same time."

Besides the fact that I feel like someone is taking a sledgehammer to my heart. A shift of his body. A turn of his head. Blow after unerring blow.

I forced oxygen past my tight lungs.

Kai and I were broken up. I'd *told* him we should see other people when I ended things and that he was better off with Clarissa. I had no right to get mad.

Still, seeing them together so soon after our breakup hurt. So fucking much.

Sloane motioned for our server. "Another round of margaritas, please," she said. "Extra strong."

Compassion darkened Alessandra's eyes. "Is this the first time you've..."

I nodded, swallowing past the lump in my throat. Of all the bars in all the world, he had to walk into this one.

Once upon a time, I thought it was romantic how the universe kept throwing us together. Now, I wanted to wring its skinny cosmic neck.

Clarissa laughed again at something Kai said, and I couldn't take it anymore. I stood abruptly. "I'll be right back."

My friends didn't stop or follow me as I speed walked to the restroom. Luckily, it was next to our booth, so I didn't have to pass by the happy couple on my way there.

My heart pounded out a deep, painful rhythm.

What were they doing in Brooklyn? Neither of them were

Brooklyn people. Were they on a date or here as friends? Was this their first time going out together or one of many?

It doesn't matter. It's none of your business.

But no matter how many times I told myself that, I couldn't bring myself to believe it.

I took my time using the facilities and washing my hands. I never thought I would find solace in a public bathroom, but I would climb into a windowless metal box if it meant avoiding Kai and Clarissa for another second.

It was a small bar; they were bound to see me eventually. That didn't mean I had to speed up the process.

My reflection stared back at me from the water-spotted mirror above the sink. I was two shades paler than usual, making me look like I was on the verge of a terrible illness.

I reached for a lipstick to add some color to my face when the door swung open and Clarissa walked inside.

We froze at the same time—my hand halfway to my bag, her stride broken next to the Dyson hand dryer.

Then the moment passed and we resumed our activities, but the awkward silence persisted. Part of me wanted to run out before I had to face her again; another, larger part stayed out of sheer morbid curiosity.

The toilet flushed. Clarissa came up beside me as I finished reapplying my lipstick. I looked better with a fresh pop of red, though my cheeks remained pale, and my skin was clammy with nerves.

Instead of alleviating the tension, the rush of the water faucet exacerbated it.

God, I hate awkward silences.

"Small world," I finally said. My attempt at a light tone came out rusty with distress. I cleared my throat. "No offense, but I didn't take you for a Brooklyn type of girl."

"It was Kai's suggestion." Like Kai, Clarissa had a British accent, but hers was creamier, more fluid. "He said there was a great cocktail bar here."

Of course he did. I told him about this bar when we were dating, which made him bringing her here all the more distressing.

"Oh." I fought a sharp pang at the sound of his name. I imagined them discussing date options on the phone, and the pang grew worse. "Well, you two make a cute couple."

I would've been embarrassed about my blatant fishing for information if I didn't feel so sick.

Clarissa dried her hands and opened her clutch. "Thank you. Kai *is* quite handsome, but..." She retrieved a sleek black lipstick tube. "Between you and me, he's a bit boring."

Indignation flushed hot beneath my skin. I'd accused him of the same thing a lifetime ago, before I really knew him, but hearing her say it in her haughty accent made me see red. "He's not boring. He's *introverted.* There's a difference."

"Maybe." Clarissa's lip color went on smooth and muted, its neutral shade a contrast to my brick-red stain. "He only talks about books and work. It gets tiring."

You didn't seem tired when you were laughing with him earlier.

"There's nothing wrong with talking about books." I yanked a paper towel from the dispenser and wiped my already dry hands. I needed something to do or I'd scream. "Reading is his hobby, and he's *busy.* He helps run a multibillion-dollar company. Of *course* he's going to—" I broke off at Clarissa's laugh. "What's so funny?" I demanded.

"You should see how red you're turning." Her eyes twinkled. "I'm sorry. I know it's not funny, but Kai has been so miserable over you that it's nice to see you haven't dismissed him completely."

I hated how my heart skipped a beat at her words. I didn't *want* him to be miserable, but if he was and she was admitting it, then that meant...

"We're not on a date," Clarissa added, accurately reading my silence. "We're here as friends. He wanted to thank me for agreeing to our staged date after the *National Star* photos. In fact…" She dropped her lipstick back in her bag. "We were discussing how much *better* we are as friends."

My anger drained away, replaced by relief and a hint of doubt. "So you're not interested in him at all?"

Clarissa shook her head. "Kai and I grew up next to each other," she said. "Our parents have pushed for us to be together since we were children. To them, it's a business arrangement. An alliance between two old, powerful British Chinese families in a world where there aren't many like us. But we were never close friends, and we didn't talk for years before I moved here."

She drew her bottom lip between her teeth. "I admit I was curious about him at first. He's handsome, successful, and a decent person, which is exceedingly rare for someone with his wealth and status. But I realized that while he may look perfect on paper, the chemistry simply isn't there. Not like…like it should be." A delicate blush colored her cheeks.

"Oh," I said again. For a writer, my ability to find the right words was distressingly low. "Well, that makes sense, but you didn't have to tell me all of that." *I'm so glad you did.* "It doesn't matter." *If I say it enough times, it'll be true.* "Kai and I aren't…we're not together anymore. Obviously." *Because I always fuck up the good things in my life.*

I rummaged through my makeup bag, searching for nothing in particular. The adrenaline of running into Clarissa faded, and a crushing pressure returned to my chest.

She and Kai weren't on a date, but that didn't erase the reasons why we couldn't be together. It just meant I had more time before he started dating someone else for real.

"If it didn't matter, you wouldn't have gotten so upset when I called him boring," Clarissa said gently. She snapped her bag closed and faced me head-on. "You still care about him."

"I never said I didn't. That's not why…" I trailed off, distracted by the flash of white around her wrist. It was a necklace wrapped up to be a bracelet, and it looked wildly out of place with her elegant outfit. It was also made of something suspiciously familiar.

Puka shells.

A memory from Christmasbirthdaynewyearpalooza slammed into me.

Where's your necklace?

I, uh, lost it.

Clarissa was the director of artist relations at the Saxon Gallery—the same gallery that'd hosted Felix's exhibition in December.

My eyes snapped up to hers. Her wide eyes and stricken expression was all the confirmation I needed.

Another thick silence between us.

A minute ago, I'd been worried about Kai and Clarissa. Now I found out she's with my *brother*?

What in the ever-loving hell is going on tonight? Maybe I wasn't actually at the bar. Maybe I passed out at the coffee shop and was having the most vivid dream of my life.

This time, Clarissa was the one who broke the silence. "Please don't tell anyone yet." She twisted the bracelet again, her blush deepening. "My family still thinks I'm interested in Kai, and I don't..."

"I won't tell anyone." I, of all people, knew what it was like to keep a relationship secret.

She gave me a grateful smile. We'd crossed paths a few times before tonight, but she seemed more relaxed compared to our previous encounters. It was probably Felix's influence; he could make even a clam open up.

We didn't talk again until we exited the bathroom. I nearly crashed into Clarissa when she came to an abrupt halt. Her eyes swiveled between me and Kai, who was talking to another customer at the bar.

"You know what? I don't feel well," she said. "Can you tell Kai I had to leave and give him my sincerest apologies?"

"What? No, wait! You can tell him yourself. He's right...there," I finished as she blew out the door like a gust of wind.

There one second, gone the next.

Dammit. I knew Clarissa left to force me to talk to Kai, and it was working. I couldn't leave him sitting there, wondering what'd happened to her.

I walked toward him, my limbs slow and heavy like I was moving underwater. Nerves cramped my stomach, and the curious, concerned stares of my friends weighed heavy on my skin as I mentally rehearsed what I was going to say.

I ran into Clarissa in the bathroom. She doesn't feel well. She left.

She doesn't feel well, so she left and told me to tell you.

She said to tell you…

She said I still cared about you, and she's right.

Kai must've felt the heat of my stare because he looked up right as I approached. Our eyes locked, and time decelerated into a long, endless beat of yearning.

Skin flushed. Pulse pounding. Heart in my mouth.

Just like that, whatever chance I had of avoiding him slammed shut with bone-rattling finality.

Kai's face didn't betray any emotions when I stopped next to him and took Clarissa's vacated seat. I would stand—easier and faster to escape that way—but I feared my knees would crumple and I'd collapse against him like one of those swooning maidens in vintage romance novels.

"I ran into Clarissa in the bathroom." *Stick to the script.* "She's not feeling well, and she told me to tell you she had to leave."

Fortunately, I didn't mess up my lines. *Un*fortunately, they came out hoarse and scratchy, like I was on the verge of tears.

"I see." Kai's expression was an impenetrable fortress. "Thank you for letting me know."

The sound of his voice was so beautiful and familiar it evacuated the air from my lungs. It took every ounce of willpower not to dwell on how much I wanted to fall into his arms. To kiss him and pretend our breakup never happened and that we were still living in our happy bubble on Jade Cay.

K + I.

It's scientifically proven, my love.

The pressure in my chest doubled, and I was saved only by the bartender, who showed up a millisecond before I did something stupid like cry in the middle of a crowded room.

I shoved my emotions down and ordered a strawberry gin and tonic. I didn't know what possessed me to order *that* particular drink, but it was too late to change it.

Kai's shoulders visibly stiffened. A fissure cracked his stony mask, and memories leaked into the air between us like ink spilling on a blank canvas.

What can I get for you?

Gin and tonic. Strawberry flavored.

You think translating a five-hundred-page novel into Latin by hand is relaxing?

You'll finish it...you're too strong not to.

We're so close, Isa.

Don't give up on us. Not now. Not like this.

I drew a shaky breath against the rise of tears and accepted my drink from the bartender. "I received an interesting email last week from a literary agent. Jill Sherman. I don't suppose you know anything about that."

I should've returned to my table, but I didn't want to leave him yet. Being near him again was like coming home during a rainstorm. Warm. Safe. *Right.*

Kai relaxed a smidge. "It depends," he said, his tone measured. "What did she want?"

"She asked for a revise and resubmit." I took a fortifying sip. "I made her edits and sent her the full manuscript tonight. That's why we're here." I gestured at my friends, who quickly looked away and pretended they hadn't been staring. "To celebrate."

A flicker of pride softened Kai's face. "You finished the book."

"Yeah." I mustered a weak smile. "Thanks to a handy digital typewriter." It forced me to keep writing instead of going back and deleting every other sentence.

"It wasn't the typewriter that wrote the story, Isabella," he said, his voice low. "It was you."

My heart twisted itself into knots. The last time we talked, I broke up with him and kicked him out of my apartment, yet he was still encouraging me like I hadn't dragged us both into hell.

"Why did you do it?" I asked. "I thought you didn't even read the manuscript. You never said anything..."

"If I'd said anything, you would've tried to stop me." Kai gave a small shake of his head. "Perhaps I overstepped by sending it to Jill without consulting you, but I didn't want you agonizing over it. Your story is *good*, whether she accepted it or not." His face softened further. "Although I'm glad she did."

"Me too," I whispered. I wasn't upset with him for sending her the chapters; I was more upset at myself for not having the courage to send them earlier.

I used to think I was the one who pushed Kai out of his comfort zone, and maybe I did. But he did the exact same for me, only in a different way.

There was no growth without risk, no progress without change.

I'd broken up with him *because* I was afraid of change. I'd prided myself on being bold and adventurous when really, I was a fucking coward who ran from rejection before rejection could find me.

Kai had never once expressed doubts about me. In fact, he believed in me so much he'd sent my manuscript to one of the top agents in the country. I was the one who'd projected my insecurities onto him, and those insecurities were based on what? Gabriel's words? Leonora Young's disapproval? My history of never seeing anything through?

At the end of the day, only the latter mattered because that was the only thing I had control over. I couldn't change the way other people perceived me, but I could change the way I lived my life.

I was capable. The past week proved that. I'd finally finished something that was important to me, and if I could do it once, I could do it again.

The realization filled me with a burst of confidence that almost erased the ache in my chest.

Almost.

"I heard about what happened in London," I said softly. "Congratulations. I hope you celebrated." If anyone deserved everything good in the world, it was him.

"I'm not CEO yet." His smile contained such aching sadness it made every cell in body hurt. "And I haven't been in the mood to celebrate."

I dropped my eyes, unable to look at him any longer without feeling like someone was tearing my insides into shreds.

This time, the silence between us burst not with memories but with unspoken words. Thousands of them, swirling and hovering with nowhere to go.

Meanwhile, the bar was filling up. The manageable crowd from earlier had swelled to deafening proportions, and the music had switched from mellow jazz to up-tempo funk.

The noise. The people. The raw, blooming pressure beneath my skin.

They pressed against me until something snapped and I made a split-second decision.

I looked up, my gaze catching Kai's again. "Let's go somewhere quieter," I said, hoping against hope I was doing the right thing. "We need to talk."

CHAPTER 41

Kai

Instead of going to another bar, Isabella and I walked the nearby Brooklyn Bridge. The chill of winter thinned its foot traffic considerably, but there were still a handful of couples, photographers, and tourists keeping us company as we strolled toward Manhattan.

The temperature hovered in the mid-thirties, so low our breaths formed small white puffs in the air. Nevertheless, warmth spread through my veins, insulating me from the cold.

Being near Isabella again was worth braving any brutal weather.

I would have to thank Clarissa later. I'd told her what happened with Isabella on our way to the bar, mainly because she was the only unbiased party I could talk to about the situation, and I didn't believe for a second that she'd left because she was sick.

Running into Isabella tonight was a stroke of luck, and I had no intention of wasting it.

"So when exactly is the new vote?" Isabella asked with a sideways glance.

"Tomorrow." I shoved my hands deeper into my pockets to keep from touching her. Her cheeks were red and her hair was tangled from the wind. Her eyeliner had smudged somewhere between the bar and the bridge, lending her an adorably raccoon-esque appearance.

And she looked so damn beautiful it made my heart stop for a second, just long enough to confirm she owned every beat.

Isabella halted dead in her tracks. "Tomorrow? *Tomorrow* tomorrow?"

"Yes." A smile ghosted my mouth at her wide eyes. "Tomorrow tomorrow. As in Friday. D-day. Whatever you want to call it."

The past two weeks had been a whirlwind. Russell was officially fired and under criminal investigation for his activities. A majority of the blackmailed board members had resigned, triggering an emergency shareholder meeting to elect their replacements. The Young Corporation and Black & Co. were embroiled in a nasty legal fight across half a dozen fronts. It was a mess, but the sooner we dealt with it, the sooner we could move on.

Chaos only made for good business when it involved other people, not our own.

"What are you doing here? Shouldn't you be securing votes and doing other...pre-selection things?" A blast of wind tossed Isabella's question through the air.

"There's nothing else I can do at this point." I was remarkably calm about the vote this time around. It was down to the original candidates minus Russell—Tobias (who'd reentered the race), Laura, Paxton, and myself. I was confident about my chances, but a quarter of the board members were new, and I didn't know which way they leaned.

However, I'd discovered over the past two weeks that losing the CEO position wasn't the worst thing that could happen to me.

Losing Isabella was, and that had already come to pass.

A familiar ache surged through my chest. It was torture being this close to her without touching her, but at least she was *here*, in the flesh, instead of haunting my thoughts.

"We can continue discussing the vote, but I'm guessing you didn't ask me here to talk about work," I said.

Her throat worked with a visible swallow.

Our last conversation swirled around us, carrying away our small talk and leaving fresh wounds and shattered hearts behind.

We're not a good match.

It was fun while it lasted...

Please just leave.

Even now, weeks later, the memory of her words punched me through the chest with unrestrained brutality.

"I don't know why I asked you here." Isabella's eyes dipped. "But I...when I saw you, I..."

The ache expanded into my throat. "I know," I said quietly. "I miss you too, love."

A tiny sob rent the air, and when she lifted her head, my heart cracked ever so slightly at tears staining her cheeks.

"I'm sorry," Isabella whispered. "That night, I didn't mean to... I—" Her sentence cut off with another hiccupping sob.

The sound ripped through me like a bullet, and I would've given up anything—my title, my company, my entire legacy—if it meant I could soothe her hurt for just one minute.

"Shh. It's okay." I gathered her in my arms while she buried her face in my chest, her shoulders shaking. She'd always seemed larger than life, with her uninhibited laugh and vibrant personality, but she felt so small and vulnerable in that moment that a sharp pain twisted my gut.

I hoped to God no one ever found out about the power this woman had over me, or I would be done for.

The night I walked out of her apartment, I'd drowned my sorrows in scotch and cursed every single person who had a hand in us meeting. Parker at Valhalla for hiring her, Dante and Vivian for always forcing me into the same room as her, her damn parents for giving birth to her. If it weren't for them, I wouldn't have met Isabella, and I wouldn't have a hole the size of Jupiter in my chest.

I'd played, replayed, and dissected every second of our relationship until the memories bled out of me and I was empty. And when it was all gone—the anger, the hurt, the pain—the only thing left was a dark, gaping numbness.

I didn't blame Isabella for what she did. Not anymore. The past month had taken a toll on both of us, and she'd been reeling from her visit home. The only thing I hated more than being apart from her was the knowledge of how poorly she viewed herself. She had no idea how incredible she was, and it killed me.

I tucked my head against the top of her head and tightened my hold around her when another icy gust slammed into us. The bridge had emptied; we were the only people brave or stupid enough to stay here while the temperatures dipped.

Surrounded by water, with the far-off lights of Manhattan on one side and Brooklyn on the other, the air silent save for Isabella's soft sobs and the wind's whistling howls, I had the eerie sense that we were the only people left in the world.

"You never asked me your question," I said when her cries died down to sniffles.

She lifted her head, her eyes swollen and her brow etched with confusion. "What?"

"From our balloon night in Bushwick." I rubbed a stray tear off her cheek with my thumb. "You never asked me your question."

Isabella let out a half-laugh, half-sob. "I can't believe you remember that."

"I remember everything when it comes to you."

Her smile faded, disappearing into the billows of tension around us. Bone-deep cold stole through me, both from the weather and the agonizing anticipation of what she would say next.

"Be honest," she said softly. "Do you really see a future for us?"

I opened my mouth, but she shook her head.

"Don't give me a packaged answer. I want you to think about

it. Our families, our goals, our personalities. They're completely different. It's easy to say we can overcome the differences now, when everything is new and exciting, but what happens five, ten years down the road? I don't..." Her breath trembled on an inhale. "I never want us to resent each other."

Her words pricked at my chest.

She wasn't wrong. We were opposites in almost every way, from our habits and hobbies to our temperaments and taste in books. There was a time not too long ago when her eccentricities had repelled me as much as they'd attracted me. She was everything I shouldn't want, but it didn't matter.

I wanted her anyway. So much so, I couldn't breathe.

But Isabella didn't want emotion right now. She wanted logic, a concrete reason for why we would work, so I took a page out of my old Oxford debate playbook and refuted her arguments one by one.

"I understand what you're saying, but your premise is flawed," I said. "Our families aren't that different. We have similar cultures, upbringings, and wealth." The Valencias weren't billionaires, but their hotels pulled in several hundred million dollars last year alone. They were more than comfortable. "Perhaps yours is less formal than mine, but that isn't a dealbreaker by any means."

"Your mom also hates me," Isabella pointed out. "It's bound to cause more friction sooner or later."

"She doesn't hate you. Her concerns have nothing to do with you as a person. She was simply worried about the effect our relationship would have on the CEO vote and my future." A wry smile twisted my mouth. "The vote isn't an issue anymore, and she'll come around. Even if she doesn't, I'm an adult. I don't need my mother's approval to be with who I want." My voice softened. "And I want you."

Isabella's eyes glistened with emotion. Moonlight kissed her cheekbones, tracing the delicate lines of her face and lips the way I so desperately craved to do with my mouth.

I almost laughed when the thought crossed my mind. I never imagined I'd be jealous of nature, but here we were.

"There are other women who would fit into your world better," she said. "Women without tattoos and purple hair and...and pet snakes. Who never get caught talking about sex at the worst times."

This time, I did laugh. Quietly, but it was there. Only Isabella could make me laugh in the middle of the most important conversation of my life. It was one of the many reasons why I'd brave the Brooklyn Bridge in the dead of winter for her.

A small smile touched her lips before it faded. "I'm never going to stop being me, Kai, and I don't want you to stop being you. So how can we be together when we belong to separate worlds?"

"By building one of our own," I said simply.

"That's unreasonable."

"I don't care. This isn't about *reason*. It's about love, and there's nothing reasonable about love."

The wind whisked the words away as soon as they left my mouth, but their impact lingered—in the audible hitch of Isabella's breath, in the cascade of nerves rattling through my body. They left me feeling exposed and vulnerable, like my skin was no longer a barrier between me and the outside world, but I forged on.

"I love you, Isabella Valencia." Simple and raw, stripped of all pretense except for the naked truth that had been staring me in the face all this time. "Every single part of you, from your laugh to your humor to the way you can't stop talking about condoms."

One of those laughs I loved so much slipped out, thick with emotion.

A smile flashed across my face before I sobered again. "You think you're broken, but I wish you could see yourself the way I see you. Smart. Strong. Beautiful. Imperfect by your own standards but so wonderfully perfect for me."

A fresh tear streaked down Isabella's cheek. Unlike her earlier sobs, this one was silent, but it seared through me all the same.

I'd never fallen in love before her. Once I did, I did it the way I did everything else. Completely. Totally. Irrevocably.

"I've always prided myself on being the best. I had to be

number one. I had to win. I collected prizes and awards because I saw them as a reflection of my self-worth, and I thought nothing tasted better than victory. Then I met you." I swallowed the emotion burning in my throat. "And everything else...faded. We've been through some dark times, but you were *always* the brightest part of my life. Even when we broke up. Even when I walked out. Just knowing you existed somewhere in this world was enough."

Isabella pressed a fist to her mouth, her eyes glossy in the silver light.

"I never really lived before you," I said. "And I don't want to imagine living after you." I dropped my forehead to hers, my chest aching with need and want and a thousand other emotions only she could make me feel. "Stay with me, love. Please."

A small sob bled through and soaked the night.

"You idiot," she said, her cheeks wet with tears. "You had me at *condoms*."

Relief had the weight sliding off my shoulders. My body sagged, and the hands strangling my lungs loosened enough for a laugh to break free.

"I'm not surprised," I murmured. "You do have a special fondness for condoms, especially of the—"

"Kai."

"Hmm?"

"Shut up and kiss me."

Isabella.

Yes?

Shut up and let me kiss you.

So I did, deeply and tenderly, while the memories of us drifted back into my chest and settled where they belonged.

CHAPTER 42
Kai

The next morning, I took a day off work for the first time in my history at the Young Corporation.

My team could survive without me for the day. I had more important things to do.

"*Syzygy* is not a word!" Isabella slapped a hand against her thigh. "You totally made that up."

The corners of my mouth twitched. "I'm afraid Merriam-Webster disagrees."

"Yes, well, Merriam-Webster is a bitch," she muttered. "Fine. You win. *Again*." Her mouth formed an adorable pout.

We were on our third round of the game. Half-eaten pastries and two giant mugs of hot chocolate littered the coffee table, and flames crackled in the marble fireplace. Snow flurries danced outside the windows, carpeting the city in white.

After last night's frigid stroll down the Brooklyn Bridge, neither Isabella nor I were in the mood to go outside, so we'd holed up in my apartment with food, drinks, and board games.

"If it makes you feel better, you almost had me," I said, leaning over and giving her a kiss. "Qi was inspired."

"*Almost* isn't the same as winning," Isabella grumbled, but

331

her pout melted into a sigh when I deepened the kiss. She tasted like warmth, chocolate, and something wonderfully, uniquely *her*.

My hand slid up her thigh until it reached the soft cotton hem of one of my old button-ups. Seeing her wear my clothes kindled something primal and possessive in me; she looked so beautiful, so perfect, and so damn mine.

Isabella wound her arms around my neck. Our board game would've escalated into an entirely different type of play had my phone not rung, jolting us out of our embrace.

I paused at the caller ID, but I answered without betraying a visible reaction.

"Congratulations." Richard Chu skipped the niceties and cut straight to the chase. "The company stays with a Young after all."

And that was that.

After months of schemes, strategizing, and buildup, I officially became the next CEO of the Young Corporation not with a bang but with a short, simple conversation.

"Well?" Anxiety sculpted Isabella's expression. I'd told her the vote was today; she must've guessed the purpose of the call. "What happened? What did he say?"

I finally allowed a smile to sneak onto my face. "I won."

The words barely made it out of my mouth before she squealed and tackled me to the ground with surprising strength for someone so small.

"I knew it!" Her face glowed with pride. "CEO Young. How does it feel?"

"Good." My blood heated as I framed her hips with my hands. It was hard to form a detailed answer when she was straddling me wearing nothing but a shirt and underwear. "But you feel better."

Isabella rolled her eyes, though her cheeks pinked at my response. "Seriously? You're thinking about sex right now? You just became *CEO*. This is what you've always wanted! Why aren't you, I don't know, popping champagne and jumping up and down with excitement?"

"Because you're sitting on top of me, love." I laughed again when she scowled down at me. God, I adored her. "In all seriousness, I'm happy, but I made my peace with the outcome before Richard's call."

When a vote got dragged out as long as this one had, the anticipation fizzled. Besides, I already had what I wanted right in this room with me.

"So are you two on good terms now?" Isabella asked. "He didn't get caught up in the Russell thing, right?"

"*Good terms* is too optimistic of a term," I said dryly. "But we've developed a mutual understanding."

Richard and I would never see eye to eye on most things, but he was one of the few board members whom Russell couldn't find dirt on, and he'd steered the board admirably through its recent storm. Meanwhile, I'd proved that I was willing to fight for the company and work with him, if only on logistics and making sure Russell and Victor got their comeuppance.

Victor's membership at Valhalla had been terminated. The club frowned on member-on-member sabotage, and with Christian's help, I hit pay dirt on the *National Star*. The tabloid had allegedly engaged in police bribery and phone hacking in pursuit of its stories, and it was under both legal and public fire. Chances were it would fold and take Victor Black down with it. I'd confront him in person, but he wasn't worth a single second more of my time or energy.

When I told Richard, he'd laughed and offered me a congratulatory cigar. We didn't like each other, but we respected each other.

"On that note..." I lifted Isabella and gently set her aside. "I have one more call to make before we continue our rousing game of Scrabble."

She flinched. "Kai, I love you, but please don't utter the phrase *rousing game of Scrabble* ever again."

I was still wearing a grin when I FaceTimed my mother. She must've heard the news by now, but I wanted to confirm and see her reaction.

It was lunchtime in London, so I expected her to answer in

her office. Instead, she picked up after half a dozen rings—a record long time for her—in what looked like a...bedroom? A bay window spanned the wall behind her, reflecting the night lights of a city that was very much not London.

"Kai." My mother sounded flustered. "I thought you were taking the day off. What is it?"

"The results are in. I won." I skipped to the more important issue at hand. "Where are you?" *And who are you with?*

The suite, the redness of her cheeks, the late hour...

Dear God, my mother had a lover.

My stomach lurched, threatening to expel my breakfast. I hadn't felt this horrified since a visiting Abigail snuck into my closet a few years ago and rearranged my ties by length instead of color as a prank.

"Yes, I received the call earlier from Richard. Congratulations." My mother's face softened. "The company will be in good hands."

For a split second, shock edged out my horror. Leonora Young was not the type of parent who coddled her children when it came to business. I couldn't remember the last time she'd been this unabashedly supportive; no matter how much Abigail or I accomplished, there was always more. More accolades, more awards, more power.

This was the first time I felt like what I did was enough.

An uncomfortable warmth crept into my chest, only to vanish seconds later when a deep male voice joined the conversation.

"Nono, it's eleven at night." A flash of salt-and-pepper hair entered the frame. "Tell whoever's calling—ah."

The man next to my mother stared back at me with equal parts guilt, astonishment, and embarrassment.

My earlier horror returned, sprouting fangs and teeth. "*Father*?"

Edwin Young's face flushed a vivid shade of scarlet. "Hello, Kai. This is, uh, unexpected."

Across from me, Isabella's jaw unhinged. *Your parents?* she mouthed. She looked like she didn't know whether to laugh or cringe.

I couldn't bring myself to respond.

My parents. Together. In what was obviously a hotel room doing...

My stomach rebelled again.

"I realize this must come as a shock." My father cleared his throat. At sixty-two, he was still trim and fit thanks to regular tennis games and a red-meat-free diet. "But your mother and I are, uh...we're..."

"Oh, for God's sake, Edwin," my mother said impatiently. "I hope you're more eloquent when you're pitching to clients?" She faced me again. "Your father and I have resumed a romantic relationship. This doesn't necessarily mean we're getting back together, since sexual—"

"Stop right there." I held up my free hand. The word *sexual* leaving my mother's lips was enough to make me want to bleach out my ears. "I don't need the details." I focused on the city behind her. I hadn't paid attention earlier, but the skyline was unmistakable. "Are you in *Shanghai*?"

Her cheeks colored. "Yes. I flew here earlier this week for a last-minute trip."

I didn't have to ask whether the trip was for business or pleasure. I hadn't seen my mother look so relaxed and at ease since... ever.

An idea suddenly struck me. "Is this why you're stepping down?" My gaze roved between her and my father, who was studying the ceiling with apparent fascination.

I couldn't imagine my mother giving up her career for a man, but stranger things had happened. A month ago, I couldn't imagine meek, mousy Russell Burton blackmailing half the board either.

"No. Not necessarily." My mother fell silent for a moment, like she was debating whether to continue. "I had a health scare last year," she finally said, her voice quiet. "Doctors found what they thought was a tumor in my throat. It turned out to be an imaging error, but the scare put a lot of things into perspective."

A vise squeezed my chest. "You never told me or Abigail that."

"It's a good thing I didn't, considering the doctor's utter lack of competency." My mother pursed her lips. "Obviously, I've switched medical teams since then, but I didn't want to burden you or your sister before I had full confirmation. Your father happened to be in London the week after my misdiagnosis, and since I needed to talk about it but didn't trust anyone outside the family..."

"We rekindled our relationship," my father finished. "I still cared about your mother, even though we've been estranged. I didn't want her to go through something like that alone."

"It started platonically, but it was obvious there were quite a few unresolved feelings between us." My mother blew out a sigh. "Long story short, we separated when we were young and stubborn. My priorities have shifted since then, especially with my health scare. I want to spend more time outside the office and with family. Besides..." A rueful smile crossed her lips. "I've been at the helm for a long time. Companies that don't change risk stagnation, and it's time for a CEO with fresh perspectives."

I ran a hand over my face, trying to make sense of everything that had happened over the past twenty-four hours. Between my reconciliation with Isabella, the CEO news, and my mother's double bombshell, my life had tilted so far off its axis I couldn't think straight. However, it didn't bother me as much as it would've a few months ago.

Companies that didn't change risked stagnation, but the same could be said for people. My life had followed ruler-straight lines for over three decades, and a little chaos was good for the soul.

"Since it's confession time, there's one more thing I have to tell you." I angled my screen so my parents could see Isabella, who greeted them with a weak smile and a wave. "I'm back with Isabella. And this time, we're staying together."

My mother didn't look surprised. "I figured as much," she said dryly. "Clarissa called her parents yesterday and told them a Teo-Young wedding isn't in the cards."

"I've never met you nor do I know when and why you broke up," my father told Isabella. "But I'm glad you're back together."

Her smile carved dimples in her cheeks. "Thank you."

Since it was so late in Shanghai, I didn't drag out the conversation. I promised not to tell Abigail about my parents until my mother spoke with her and hung up.

Relief loosened the fist around my heart. Perhaps it was her vacation, my victory, or a combination of both, but my mother's reaction to our relationship was surprisingly muted. Other than a few sighs and disapproving frowns, she'd refrained from her usual barbs. She must've realized her objections would fall on deaf ears, and Leonora Young was smart enough not to waste her time fighting a losing battle.

"That went way better than expected," Isabella said as we started a new round of Scrabble. "It's amazing how much sex can loosen someone up."

I nearly spat out my drink. "Are you trying to traumatize me?" I asked, appalled. "That's my mother you're talking about."

"Sorry, I thought you were already traumatized from seeing your parents in bed—" She broke off with a squeal of laughter when I pulled her toward me and pinned her to the ground.

"Finish that sentence, and I'll hide all your thrillers until you read every word of *The Divine Comedy*," I threatened. "The Latin translated version."

Her laughter vanished. "You wouldn't dare."

"Try me."

"If you do that..." She hooked her legs around my waist, her eyes glinting with challenge. Heat raced straight to my groin. "I'll withhold sex until you put the books back."

"Darling, we both know you would cave before I did."

Isabella arched one brow. "Wanna bet?"

We never resumed our board game that day.

I was normally a stickler for finishing what I started, but hours later, when we lay sweaty and satiated in my bed, I didn't care that we'd left dirty plates and a half-finished game of Scrabble in the living room.

After all, we had the rest of our lives to finish it.

Epilogue

I SABELLA
Two years later

"Oh my God. It's here." I stared at the shelf. "*It's here*."

"Of course it is. That's why we came." Vivian nudged me toward the bookcase. "Go! This is your moment."

I didn't move. I couldn't quite process the sight in front of me.

The red spine. The name printed in white. The years of work and editing, all bound up in one paperback.

My debut novel *Mistress in Waiting*, sitting right there in the middle of my favorite bookstore's thriller section.

A warm hand touched my back. "Congratulations," Kai said. "You're officially a published author."

"I'm a published author," I repeated. The words tasted ephemeral at first, but then they solidified, taking on the earthy flavor of reality. "That's my book. Oh my God." My heart rate accelerated. "I did it. *I did it!*"

My stupor snapped, and I threw my arms around him as the weight of my accomplishment sank in. He laughed, his face wreathed with pride as I squealed and did a little happy dance.

I didn't care how stupid I looked because after all the agonizing, the failures, and the setbacks, I was finally a *published author*.

Jill Sherman had loved the revised manuscript and officially offered me representation two years ago. She shopped the book around, and after a couple of nibbles but no bites from the big houses, I signed with a small but well-respected publisher who was building out their thriller imprint. Now, after endless edits and revisions, it was out in the world.

I wasn't going to turn into Nora Roberts or Dan Brown overnight, but I didn't care. I finished my story, I loved it, and that was all that mattered.

I was already in the middle of drafting the sequel. Kai read it in chunks as I wrote it, which made the process much smoother than the original. It was hard to get lost in my own head when he was always there to pull me out.

But even if he *weren't* there, I'd have an easier time. I'd developed a routine that worked for me, and I put less pressure on myself to write a perfect first draft. Everything got edited and revised to hell before it went to the printers anyway.

Once I released my need for perfection, the words flowed. There were still days when I wanted to tear my hair out over sentences that wouldn't form or a scene that wouldn't crystallize, but for the most part, I was really fucking excited to work on the story.

After years of drifting, I'd finally found my purpose—to create, both for myself and others.

"Let's take a picture," Alessandra suggested. "We need to commemorate the moment." She, Vivian, and Sloane had accompanied me for moral support.

I was no longer working at Floria Designs, but it was always supposed to be a temporary job. Alessandra had built a great team since I left, and the small business was thriving. The same couldn't be said of her relationship with Dominic, but that was a whole other story.

I plucked one of the copies off the shelf and posed with it. It was probably the cheesiest picture I'd ever taken; I couldn't wait to print and frame it.

"Turn two inches to your left," Sloane ordered. "Now lift your chin, smile...smile some more...perfect."

She was such a perfectionist that her photos took forever, but they came out so good that no one complained.

I held onto the book after the picture, reveling in its weight and texture. I'd received advance copies from my publisher, but until that moment, it didn't feel *real*.

This was mine, from concept to execution. I'd taken an idea and created a whole world, one that other people could enter and get lost in. Every book was a footprint in history, and I'd made my mark.

A lump formed in my throat as my tiny seed of pride blossomed into a full-grown tree, roots and all.

My phone buzzed with an incoming FaceTime call. Felix's face filled half the screen when I answered. Behind him, Miguel and Romero poked their heads above his so they could see too.

"Well?" he said, skipping his usual greeting. "Is it there? Show us!"

"It is." I grinned, swinging the camera around to show the paperbacks of *Mistress in Waiting* sitting pretty on the shelf. "If you're nice to me, I'll autograph one for you."

"We don't get a family exception? That's cold." Miguel shook his head. "Just published and you're already forgetting about us."

"It's a natural progression," Romero said. "The cost of celebrity."

"Oh, be quiet, you two. Stop teasing your sister." My mother's voice appeared before she did. Felix stepped to the side, and her gentle features replaced his chiseled ones onscreen. "Oh, look at that," she breathed. "Your name on the cover! I'm so proud of you. Now, make sure to send copies to your relatives in the Philippines, or I'll never hear the end of it when I go back—"

"Isa!" My lola shoved my mother aside and peered at me. Her wrinkles seemed to have doubled since the last time I saw her, but her eyes were as sharp as ever. "Let me see. Hmm. Are those cuff-links on the cover? I can't tell. Eyesight's not so good these days. Arturo!" she yelled, calling my grandfather. "Get over here. Do those look like cufflinks to you?"

I laughed, warmth fizzing in my chest as my family shoved and argued on the other side of the screen. They were a mess some-times, but they were my mess, and they'd been incredibly supportive of my publishing journey. Most of them anyway.

My smile faded when Gabriel showed up. He was the last to get on the call, and his stern, solemn demeanor was a marked contrast to my other brothers' teasing.

"Congratulations," he said. "Publishing a book is a big accomplishment."

"Thanks." I hugged it tighter to my body with my free arm. "Proved you wrong, didn't I?" I said it lightly, but we both knew I wasn't joking.

"You did." To my shock, a tiny curve of his mouth softened the severity of his expression. "And I've never been happier to be wrong."

My voice stuck in my throat. I was so thrown off by Gabriel's answer I couldn't summon a proper response.

He *hated* being wrong. I thought he wanted to see me fail just to prove he was right about my flakiness, but he looked genuinely happy for me. Well, as happy as Gabriel could look, which was still dour by normal standards.

Maybe I wasn't the only one in the family who'd underesti-mated a sibling.

"Oh." I coughed, heat coating my skin. "Um, thank you."

Perhaps I should've seen his reaction coming. I came into my inheritance last year after he and my mother agreed that my fin-ished manuscript and book deal met the clause's terms. My mother had done most of the talking during our call, but Gabriel had voted yes on giving me the money. That counted for something, right?

"You're welcome," he said. "I'll see you in a few months for Mom's birthday. Hopefully, you'll have started your second book by then. You can't make a career off of one."

I rolled my eyes as our moment of sibling bonding evaporated. It was nice to see Gabriel hadn't changed *that* much.

When I hung up, my friends had drifted over to a non-fiction display featuring Leo Agnelli's new travel memoir and a former Black & Co. executive's tell-all detailing the company's demise. Alessandra kept checking and pocketing her phone. It was probably Dominic calling—and getting ignored—for the hundredth time. Good. The man deserved to suffer a little. Kai, on the other hand, was flipping through the latest Ruby Leigh.

"No," I said. "Absolutely not. You're not allowed to ruin her by translating her into Latin."

"I hardly understand how that would ruin her," he said, sounding offended. "I can translate Wilma Pebbles, but I can't translate Ruby Leigh? You love both of them."

He hadn't done many Latin translations lately because he was so busy at the office. The work of a CEO never ended, especially not after the DigiStream acquisition, and its integration with the Young Corporation had taken over his life for months. Fortunately, it'd gone as smoothly as he'd hoped.

I guess he had time to indulge in his hobbies again, but I refused to let him touch my favorite author.

"I do love both of them, but I only let you translate Wilma so I can watch you struggle to find the right phrase for *dinosaur dick* in Latin."

Another laugh bubbled in my throat when he placed the book back on the shelf and pulled me toward him with a mock threatening scowl.

"You should be glad it's your big day, or I wouldn't let that slide." Kai stroked the back of my neck with his thumb. "How does it feel to be a published author?"

"Pretty damn amazing." My face softened. I'd moved in with Kai last year, but no matter how many mornings I woke up next to him or how many nights we fell asleep together, I couldn't quite get over the fact that this amazing man was mine. "I couldn't have done it without you."

"Yes, you could have." His mouth skimmed mine in a gentle kiss. "But I'm glad we were able to do it together."

He'd been there through the late nights, the caffeine crashes, and the mid-edit breakdowns. Yes, I could've survived them on my own, but he made the journey so much better. He always did.

I smiled and returned his kiss. "Me too."

~

KAI

"Are you cheating?" Miguel demanded. "There's *no way* you can win this many times in a row. It's statistically impossible."

"I don't cheat." I cleared the Scrabble board of tiles. "I simply have a large vocabulary."

"Don't bother arguing," Isabella said over her family's groans and protests. "He's insufferable when it comes to board games."

"To *any* game," Romero muttered, obviously still smarting over his tennis loss earlier that day.

Isabella's family and I were gathered at her mother's house in Los Angeles for Christmasbirthdaynewyearpalooza, which they'd finally shortened to CBNYP. When I suggested the solution at last year's celebration, they'd stared at me like I'd sprouted an extra head. Apparently, shortening the ridiculously long name into an acronym had never crossed their mind.

It was my second year celebrating with them, and I was comfortable enough that I no longer held back when it came to our games and activities.

We'd started the day with piano performances in honor of Isabella's father. She'd played a Chopin piece while I followed it up with the "Hammerklavier." My rendition had come a long way since the stunning realization that Isabella could outplay me years ago. After much practice, I'd perfected it to the point where even her lolo greeted its conclusion with tears in his eyes.

Isabella insisted I owed my improvement not to practice but to finding the thing I'd been "lacking."

Heart.

Which was ridiculous. Practice made perfect, not heart. But I kept her close to me anyway.

"What's next? I don't think I can stand losing another round to Mr. Vocabularian here," Clarissa quipped.

In her jeans, tank top, and sandals, she looked wildly different from the pearls and tweed-wearing socialite who'd moved to Manhattan two years ago.

Clarissa and Felix officially started dating not long after Isabella and I got back together. She'd moved to L.A. last year and currently worked at the local museum where he was the artist in residence. Her parents had pitched a fit, but there wasn't much they could do about it, and California suited her. She seemed happier and more relaxed here than she ever had in New York.

"Darts," I said, exchanging a quick glance with Felix. "Last game of the day."

This time, Isabella was the one who groaned. "I'm convinced you're doing this on purpose," she said as we walked out to the backyard. "You keep choosing the activities I'm not—oh my God."

Her steps came to an abrupt halt. She stared, open mouthed, at the sight before her.

With her brothers' help, I'd replicated the balloon wall from our first unofficial date in Bushwick. We woke up at the crack of dawn that morning to set it up, but it was worth it for the shock on her face.

"How did you do this?" Isabella breathed.

"With an overabundance of caffeine and assistance from your brothers," I said. "I figured everyone should experience this at least once in their lives. Also, Gabriel is a big *Princess Diaries 2* fan."

He glared at me from his spot next to the darts. "I'm not a *fan*," he said. "I enjoy the storyline. That's all."

Our rocky relationship had smoothed since he confronted me in the hotel bar two years ago, but we were too similar in too many ways to ever be best friends.

"Sure." Romero smirked. "That's why you make us rewatch it every Christmas."

"I don't *make* you do anything," Gabriel snapped. "I don't have time for this foolishness. Lola needs my help." He spun on his heel and marched stiffly to where Isabella's grandmother was trying to open a jar of salsa.

"It's not CBNYP if Gabe doesn't get pissy over something," Isabella said with a laugh. She went on her tiptoes and pressed a quick kiss on my mouth. "Thank you for putting up with my family. I know they can be a lot sometimes."

"I like them. They're entertaining." I looped an arm around her waist and grinned down at her. "Besides, you put up with my parents' vow renewal, so I owe you."

We both shuddered at the memory.

My parents officially renewed their vows seven months ago in a lavish ceremony on Jade Cay. The ceremony itself had been beautiful; the preparations leading up to it had not. My mother had roped Isabella into helping her and Abigail plan the event, which meant *I'd* been roped into helping with the event. I still had nightmares about tulle and floral designs.

"Quit the PDA. It's sickening." Miguel shoved a dart in each of our hands. "C'mon. Let's get this show going. The sun is about to set."

Isabella had gotten better at darts, but her aim was still fifty-fifty. I was counting on her skills to fall on the worse end of the spectrum today.

Nerves played beneath my skin as she shifted her stance and drew her arm up. The late afternoon sunlight found her, spinning purple-black silk with gold and etching shadows across her bronzed skin. Her brows furrowed, and despite my anxiety, I couldn't help but smile at her concentration.

We'd been together for two years, but I would never get over the fact that she was mine.

The dart whizzed through the air and bounced harmlessly off the wall.

Relief wisped through me, followed by a second barrage of nerves.

346

"*Dammit.*" Isabella huffed, seemingly oblivious to my inner turmoil and the way her family slipped back inside the house. "I appreciate you taking the time to set this up. I really do. But next year, you *have* to choose something I'm good at, like a timed shopping spree or reading marathon."

"I'll keep that in mind." I fished a folded scrap of paper from the jar and handed it to her. A tiny blue dot marked the corner. "In the meantime, here's your question."

She sighed and unfolded the slip. "I swear, if I have to talk about my biggest fear again..." Her sentence trailed off.

I'd written what I wanted to say before I said it, and when she looked up from the note, her eyes glossy and mouth trembling, I was already on one knee. A dazzling diamond glittered in the open ring box in my hand.

We'd had to face plenty of tough questions to get to where we were today, but my next question was the hardest and easiest one of all.

"Isabella Valencia, will you marry me?"

Thank you for reading *King of Pride!* If you enjoyed this book, I would be grateful if you could leave a review on the platform(s) of your choice.

Reviews are like tips for author, and every one helps!

Much love,
Ana

~

For bonus Kai & Isabella content, visit anahuang.com/bonus-scenes

~

He had her, he lost her... and he'll do anything to win her back.

Order *King of Greed* now for Dominic and Alessandra's story.

Keep in touch with Ana Huang

Want to discuss my books and other fun shenanigans with like-minded readers? Join my exclusive reader group, Ana's Twisted Squad!

facebook.com/groups/anastwistedsquad

You can also find Ana at these places:

Website:
anahuang.com

Bookbub:
bookbub.com/profile/ana-huang

Instagram:
@authoranahuang

TikTok:
@authoranahuang

Goodreads:
goodreads.com/anahuang

Acknowledgments

Becca—My brainstorm buddy, cheerleader, and fellow sushi lover. You go above and beyond and I am so grateful to have you in my life. One day, I'll finish clearing the coffee cups from my desk, and we can celebrate with more hand rolls :)

Brittney, Salma, Rebecca, Sarah, and Aishah—We've been through so many books together, and I couldn't have asked for better alpha/beta readers. Thank you so much for your constant support and feedback!

Cait—Your enthusiasm for my couples always makes me smile. Seeing you react to Kai and Isa was one of my favorite parts of the process, and I can't thank you enough for sharing your knowledge and insights into Filipino culture. The Valencias wouldn't be the same without you.

Theresa—Your ability to provide thoughtful notes with such a tight turnaround is incredible, so thank you!

Amy and Britt—Working with you is a joy. Thank you for your attention to detail and for making my stories shine.

Cat—You're a genius. That's all.

Kimberly—My agent extraordinaire. Thank you for all you do.

To Christa, Pam, and the Bloom Books team—Thank you for the love and attention you show my books. It's truly a dream come true seeing them in bookstores across the US & Canada.

To Ellie and the Piatkus team—Thank you for sharing my stories with the world. Seeing my books in so many countries is an incredible experience, and I can't wait to meet and celebrate with some of you in person soon.

Nina and the Valentine PR family—You make my book releases such a breeze, and I appreciate you to the moon and back.

Finally, to my wonderful readers—You are the best part of being an author. I couldn't do this without you, so thank you for always making my day brighter.

xo, Ana

Don't miss Dante & Vivian's story in . . .

Available now from